The Compleat Guth Bandar

by Matthew Hughes

Table of Contents

Introduction

In 2002, Tor senior editor David G. Hartwell let me know that he would be interested in seeing a book from me set in the same universe as *Fools Errant* and *Fool Me Twice*. I had long been interested in Carl Jung's concept of the collective unconscious and Joseph Campbell's adaptation of that concept to the study of myth and story. I decided to write a novel that would be partly set in the phenomenal (i.e., "real") world and partly in the collective unconscious, which I dubbed "the Commons."

It would have been a sizable book, covering a lot of territory. But when I told DGH that I estimated it would run upwards of 85,000 words and probably hit 100,000, he told me the maximum Tor would accept would be 80,000 and his profit–and–loss calculation (P&L) would work better if I turned in 75,000.

So I wrote *Black Brillion*, the story of Baro Harkless, a strange and unworldly agent of the Archonate Bureau of Scrutiny, who saves the world by becoming an archetypal Hero. Playing a key role in the narrative was Guth Bandar, a retired scholar from the Institute of Historical Inquiry, the ancient institute that explored and mapped the Commons. But to have the book meet Tor's size limit, Bandar's role was necessarily trimmed and the vast spread of the collective unconscious was diminished. I've always felt that *Black Brillion* would have been a better book—and might have been a better commercial prospect—if I'd been able to do the job I'd originally intended. But modern publishing is all about the numbers, and you have to do what you can.

In 2003, I was asked to contribute a story to an anthology called *Fantasy Readers Wanted—Apply Within* being put together by Nick Aires. I brought Guth Bandar out of the shadows in the back of my mind and wrote a story about him called "A Little Learning." By the time the antho appeared, I had started selling stories to Gordon Van Gelder at *The Magazine of Fantasy & Science Fiction*, and he took "A.L.L." as a reprint.

Guth Bandar struck a chord with some *F&SF* readers, so I resolved to write more of his adventures. I decided I might as well tell the rest of the story that had been left out of Black Brillion. Over the next several months, I did just that, culminating in a big novella, "The Helper and His Hero," which covered Guth's part of the action in Black Brillion, as seen from his point of view. The novella was shortlisted for a Nebula Award.

I later stitched together the different stories into one cohesive narrative—what they call in the publishing biz a "fix–up"—and sold it to Robert J. Sawyer for his Canadian publishing imprint as a novel: *The Commons*.

This volume is not *The Commons*. It is the stories themselves, without any stitching. The reader will find some inconsistencies. There will also be some repetition of backstory and background information, since each of these tales was intended to be encountered in isolation.

Readers who are intrigued by the concept of the collective unconscious, might also want to hunt up a copy of *Black Brillion*, to follow the story of Baro Harkless, who didn't know what kind of hero he was until the very last moment.

One last comment: When *The Commons* came out, some reviewers complained that Guth Bandar did not make much of a hero. Well, of course he didn't. He didn't even want to be a hero's helper.

A Herd Of Opportunity

"Say nothing. I shall do all the talking," Preceptor Huffley had whispered to Guth Bandar as they'd entered the low ceilinged stone hut. So now the young student sat on the hard wooden chair near the door, hands neatly folded, as his elderly teacher chaffered with the Eminence Malabar, the white–bearded ascetic who was head of this cloistered settlement.

"How will you proceed?" said the Eminence.

Huffley's hand idly stirred the air. "Oh, the usual approach. Assess the elements, delineate the parameters, identify the paradigm, adjust the interactions."

The patriarch's brow creased. "We did not pay an exorbitant cost to bring you and your assistant all the way from Old Earth for assessments and delineations," he said. "Action is required, preferably vigorous, decisive and prompt. Our reflections will suffer as long as that intolerable racket continues."

"Indeed," said the preceptor. "Then we had best be about it."

"I will show you," said the patriarch.

He led the way out of the hut and across the Sequestrance. Bandar followed his teacher, his eyes taking in the details of the place. They crossed a central open space floored in swept hardpan and surrounded by neat rows of domed, windowless huts built of the ubiquitous dun–colored stone that, along with pebbles and grit, comprised all that Bandar had yet seen of this remote and lightly settled world called Gamza they had traveled halfway down The Spray to reach. A larger dome stood on the far side of the square, low–roofed but roomy enough to hold all of the settlement. Bandar glanced within its broad, arched entrance and saw that the bare floor was covered with rows of wide, flat bowls of polished wood, with a woven meditation mat beside each bowl.

To his right, dozens of robed and sandaled men labored in the garden to coax straggling rows of legumes from the uncooperative soil, while others pumped water from a central well and carried it by yoke–borne buckets to irrigate the furrows. The high white sun directly overhead must steam the moisture from the dirt almost as soon as it was delivered, Bandar thought, feeling rivulets of sweat trickle down his back and chest under his two–piece traveling suit.

Their path angled away from the main building and Bandar surmised that they were heading for the Sequestrance's encircling wall—or not quite encircling, he noticed. The barrier, three times as high as Bandar was tall, was still under construction, although it must soon be finished. In the gap he saw two other crews working quickly: one group used a fragmenter to break bedrock into manageable chunks, while the other stacked the pieces to shape the wall. A brawny man with a shoulder–slung aggregator then melded the serried rocks into a smoothness.

None paused to watch their patriarch and the two strangers make their way across the square, passing the self–guided carryall that had collected Huffley and Bandar from the minimalist spaceport—two unserviced pads and a rough shed—where the freighter *Abron* had touched down and deposited them on the world's single continent. The carryall's prime mission had been to collect several heavy crates whose clanking contents Bandar had assumed to be agricultural tools. The preceptor and student had had to sit atop the cargo for the short flight across level desert to the Sequestrance, their teeth set on edge by the whine of its untuned gravity obviators. Bandar noted that no one had bothered to unload the vehicle.

At the path's end they found a set of steps and climbed to a landing that ran the full length of the south wall. Here the patriarch struck a pose and gestured with an outflung arm. "Thus the foul stain brought by Rul Bazwan," he said, pronouncing the name as if it generated an unappetizing taste.

Encompassed by the sweep of Malabar's arm was a sight that Bandar found to be at sharp variance with the austere simplicity of the Sequestrance. Below the wall was a gentle slope, from the base of which a ramshackle sprawl of tents and mobile caravans rambled off to the south. Costumes and accents of several worlds met Bandar's eyes and ears as he looked down on the throngs bustling along the narrow, twisting ways and passing in and out of the flimsy buildings.

At the far edge of the shantytown a more substantial edifice was under construction. Workers were assembling prefabricated components into the second story of the Hotel Splendor—so the sign above the building's verandah boasted. The first story was already in full operation as a saloon, judging from the trio of inebriates Bandar saw emerge from its swinging doors, supporting each other as they staggered a short distance to the next establishment, a multi–poled tent whose wooden marquee featured a garish painting of two naked women holding a sign that read: *The Pleasure Garden.*

Now Bandar saw a balloon–tired, open–topped charabanc draw up outside the Splendor. Its rows of seats were quickly filled by folk, mostly men but with a smattering of women, who had been waiting on the front porch. They chattered animatedly as the vehicle pulled away and headed south toward a range of low hills.

"Intolerable!" said Malabar.

"Indeed," said Huffley. "Quite beyond endurance."

"And you can undo this? We must have peace for our reflections."

Huffley's hand again gave its insouciant wave. "I foresee no problems."

Bandar blinked in surprise, unaware of any expertise the preceptor might have acquired in the art of slum clearance. Immediately, he knew his face had betrayed his reaction because he saw the patriarch's glance touch him then swing back to Huffley for an incisive examination of the academician's bland countenance. "You have indeed done this before?" Malabar said. "Your message implied wide experience and an almost facile competence."

"Times without number," said Huffley. "Institute scholars are frequently called in to handle these little matters. In fact, unless there's more you need tell us, we shall set to."

Suspicion lingered in Malabar's downdrawn brows and lips, but he said, "It is time for the noon reflections. Go to your work. But hurry! The disturbance bars us from the ineffable. We will not stand for it." He threw the shanty town a final glare and descended the steps.

"Master," said Bandar, "what have you told these people?"

"You need not be concerned," was the preceptor's reply.

Bandar was prepared to argue, though it was a rare student of the Institute of Historical Inquiry who would even voice a question to a senior fellow like Preceptor Huffley, let alone challenge him. But the young man had been conscious of a growing apprehension ever since they had arrived at the Sequestrance. "The Eminence holds a vast anger that strains a thin leash," he said. "I doubt he responds well to disappointment."

Huffley's face stiffened. "It is not a student's place. . . " he began, but was cut off by the clanging of metal on metal. Bandar turned and saw a man standing in the center of the Sequestrance's central square, beating with a bar of black iron on a circle of the same metal suspended from a wooden frame. All of the robed men stopped what they had been doing and converged on the main building, many of them pausing at the well to dip a ladle into a water barrel and drink deep.

"Come," said Huffley. "While they're occupied."

He led the way to the gap where the wall was nearing completion. Bandar noticed that there was no gate, nor any timbers from which one might be fashioned, and told his teacher that the absence seemed peculiar.

"These people are, by definition, peculiar," Huffley said. "They would not otherwise have secluded themselves out in the desert on an unfashionable and barely habitable world."

They passed through the gap and followed the west wall until they came to a path that led down into the other settlement. Huffley continued to discourse on the people who had paid their way to Gamza. Bandar suspected his attention was being diverted from his earlier question, but he listened with at least a show of the polite deference expected of a student of the Institute.

"Malabar heads a sect that has broken away from the Revered Society of Hydromants on Ballyanhowe," the preceptor said.

Bandar was familiar with both the cult and the world. Ballyanhowe was one of the Foundational Domains, settled long ago during the great effloration from Old Earth that ended humanity's infancy. It was an old world now: rich, mellowed and given over to the esoteric pursuits devised by peoples whose wants were won without toil. Hydromancy was an ancient art occasionally revived among such leisured populations. Its practitioners gazed into pools of standing liquid, usually purified water but sometimes oils or natural essences, seeking a deeper acquaintance with the universe that lay without or within.

"The Eminence was dissatisfied with the practices of the Revered Society," Huffley said. "He experienced an inspiration that insights are more penetrating if the contemplated liquid 'originates within the seeker,' as he put it."

"You mean they're all sitting there staring into reeking bowls of their own. . . "

"Who are we to quibble with another's inspiration?" Huffley said. They had reached the bottom of the slope. The scholar chose an alleyway and set off toward the hotel, whose upper story was visible beyond the sprawl of tents and towables.

He continued as they walked, dodging other pedestrians and ignoring explicit offers of personal services from men and women standing in doorways. "Malabar's innovations were generally not well received. A few of the younger hydromants sided with him but their attempts to practice the new dispensation in the Grand Tabernacle met resistance. When he would not compromise, the disaffection of the majority was inflamed into an outright hostility that Malabar's followers returned redoubled. Harsh words were thrown about, then—as is not unknown in such disputes—a few bricks and stones. He and his adherents thought it prudent to withdraw. They pooled their wealth and bought passage to this barren spot. They dug a well and created the Sequestrance, to follow their inclinations undisturbed."

Huffley looked about, saw no obvious eavesdroppers, then continued, "Then the Bololos arrived."

"The Bololos?" said Bandar. "Are they this rabble that infests the shanty town?"

"No, they are the cause that brought the rabble here. They are the autochthones of Gamza, a large but harmless quasi–sapient species of lichen grazers. Yet they are 'fundamental to the nuisance,' or so Malabar described them in his missive accepting my offer to resolve the problem."

"Master, I did not know that you were versed in conflict resolution."

Huffley looked slightly abashed. "In truth, it is not among my accomplishments."

"Perhaps you should fall back a step or two and explain how

you came to make such an offer."

"The Bololos are telepaths," the academician said, "but otherwise devoid of interest. They have no discernible culture, no arts or quaint customs, no wars or religious enthusiasms. In the literature, they are described as an entirely happy and entirely boring population who pass their uneventful lives in calm, unbroken communion with each other. They follow an annual round of wandering from one oasis of desert vegetation to another, spending the days grazing except when they pause briefly to create more Bololos. Even that process is said to be sedate."

Bandar was puzzled. "Yet people have come all this way to watch them graze?"

Huffley signaled a negative. "Since Malabar's hydromants settled close to one of the grazing areas, the telepaths have exhibited unusual behavior. They strike poses or run about. One will suddenly embrace another, receiving in return a welcome or a buffet to the midriff. It is all rather harmless, since they are completely unequipped to do each other real damage. Though they are strong, in their way, there is neither a fang nor a claw amongst the lot of them."

The phenomenon only occurred while the Bololos were within close range of the hydromants, Huffley explained. Once they had eaten all the season's crop of vetch or whatever it was they craved, they would move on. As soon as they put distance between themselves and the Sequestrance, the odd behavior stopped.

Bandar had been conscious of a growing excitement as the preceptor spoke. "Master," he said, "you are saying that a cross–species transference has occurred."

"I am not saying it quite yet," said Huffley. His front teeth chewed nervously at his lips for a moment before he continued. "I am saying that there are definite indications. We are here to observe and draw conclusions."

"It's unheard of," Bandar said. "It would be,"—he swallowed, throat suddenly dry—"a new datum."

Huffley's face twitched. The old man seemed torn between joyous excitement and stark terror and Bandar thought the mix appropriate to the situation. No one had contributed a new datum to the Institute's vast compendium of knowledge since time immemorial.

The two scholars had stopped to contemplate the enormity of the prospect. Now a rotund man, who wore a remarkable hat and smelled strongly of the devastating liquor known as Red Abandon, stumbled into them and caromed away. They resumed their progress toward the Hotel Splendor.

"So we are not here to solve the hydromants' problem, though it was that expectation that led them to pay our passage?"

"The search for knowledge sometimes requires a scholar to make bold leaps," said Huffley. "Do you imagine the first explorers of the Commons paused to quibble and cavil over every little detail?"

"I imagine they risked their own identities, not the wealth of others," said Bandar.

The preceptor threw his student a look that carried unmixed sentiments and Bandar subsided. Instead he indicated the shambles around them and said, "How did all this arrive?"

Huffley told him that after the Bololos had come and gone three years running, news of their odd antics reached the distant mining town of Haplick where a boom built around the discovery of surface deposits of odlerite was beginning to fade. The impresario Rul Bazwan, a man as long on enterprise as he was short on qualms, operated there, supplying miners with the services they craved in their off–time: ardent liquors, games of chance and compliant companions. His receipts beginning to decline, Bazwan was casting about for a new place in which to pitch up, and fearing that he would be put to the expense of moving his troupe offworld. Then the Bololos offered opportunity.

"He sent men to harvest lichens at the next point on the creatures' migratory circuit, delivering the stuff to feeding stations he established in a natural amphitheater not far from here. The Bololos, their fodder at hand, did not move on. Near the food Bazwan left heaps of costumes and theatrical props. The Bololos, their psyches contaminated by the contents of the human unconscious, took them up and began to act out myths and archetypical situations.

"Bazwan takes tourists out to gawk for free as the poor things strut and fret," Huffley continued. "He profits when the punters return to his establishment for wine, whoopitude and song. His enterprise is popular among the jaded. They now come here even from other worlds, as do disreputable hangers–on who feed dissolute appetites. A town has sprung up and the noise is a sore trial to the sequestrants."

Huffley's soft hands met and parted in a gesture that expressed resignation at the misfortunes of others. "But it is an unheard-of opportunity for two scholars of the Institute."

The Institute of Historical Inquiry had been established in the city of Olkney on Old Earth scores, some said hundreds, of thousands of years ago, to explore and map the human collective unconscious. Through a mastery of recondite mentalist techniques, the founding scholars of the Institute had learned to delve beneath their individual, personal unconsciousnesses and enter that vast noösphere resident within all humanity, where resided the eternal archetypes of the species: the Fool and the Hero, the Mother and Father, the Wise Man and the Helpful Beast, the Deliverer and the Devourer, and many more. Here, too, were all the elemental Events, Situations and Landscapes of the human story: from the Discovery of the New Land to the Invasion of the Barbarians; from the First Kiss of Innocence to the Scorning of the Inamorata; from the Forest of the Beasts to the City of the Machines.

Over thousands of years, the noösphere, colloquially called the Commons, was thoroughly mapped and delineated by resolute explorers. By adapting the lesson of the dawn–time orphic myth of the singer whose songs had kept him safe in the underworld, they discovered that chanting certain sequences of tones—the technical term was thrans—would allow them to pass safely through the nodes that connected one Location to another. Other thrans could hide the noönauts from the perceptions of the Commons's denizens. The latter ability was important, whether dealing with the general archetypical figures or the idiomatic entities that inhabited specific Locations. Many of these were appallingly violent by their very natures, but any of them could become dangerous if disharmonious elements were added to the stories that were, literally, their existence.

The Commons, then, was the most wonderful, most terrible, of places. Every joy, every horror, was crystallized there, in a realm that was timeless though not boundless; for the early explorers had discovered a barrier—it usually presented itself as an endless chain of mountains, or a topless wall of closely fitted white blocks of stone—between the human noösphere and the collective unconsciousness of any other intelligent species. The wall could be neither breached nor climbed. Nor could it be dug under, for there was nothing below the "ground" of the Commons but the formless gray sea of unsapience through which swam the great blind Worm of preconsciousness, eternally seeking to devour its own tail. . . or, as one unlucky noönaut pioneer found, anything else that entered the pearly light of its "waters."

None of the few telepathic species that humans had encountered could breach the wall. Thus it was concluded that each Commons must operate on its own unique "frequency," though what these purported frequencies might be had never been conclusively demonstrated. Still, it was accepted that the separation of Commonses, each from all others, was a fundamental underpinning of the universe, like the gravitational constant and the three speeds of light.

Bandar was musing on the import of the Bololos' contamination when the two scholars emerged from an alley directly across from the Hotel Splendor. They crossed the dusty street and mounted the stairs to the verandah, where a mustachioed man in a garishly patterned suit stood behind a lectern on top of which rested a roll of paper tickets. "Next charabanc leaves in twenty minutes," he told the pair as they approached, adding, "No charge."

Huffley took two tickets. He looked about for somewhere to wait out of the sun, but there were no seats outside the establishment.

"Master," Bandar said, "perhaps a cold beer would wash away the iron taste of the water they gave us at the Sequestrance."

The young man noted that his words brought them a sidelong glance from the ticket–seller, but Huffley was already through the hotel's swinging half–doors. Bandar followed him into a large room. A heterogeneous crowd was taking advantage of the availability of food and beverages dispensed from behind a well polished bar and carried to the dozens of tables by young women wearing uniforms apparently designed to avoid the slightest possibility of confusion over their gender. At the back of the room, spinning wheels, flashing lights and occasional cries or wails betokened victory or defeat at games of chance.

The Institute men took seats at an empty table and ordered flagons of ale from a passing server whose attributes caused Bandar's eyes to follow her as she departed, until Huffley's booted toe connected with his ankle under the table. Having secured his attention, the academician leaned toward him and said, "We should discuss our program."

Bandar bent to rub his aching joint. "I have yet to hear of any program," he said.

"I detect in your tone a hitherto unsuspected capacity for bitterness," Huffley said. "Perhaps it is the first time I have heard you speak from your heart."

"I am speaking from my ankle," Bandar said, "but that is beside. . . "

Two flagons of ale arrived on the table at that moment, but when the two disputants looked up they saw not the buxom young woman who had taken the order, but a tall, lean man with a prominent scar across his clean–shaven chin.

"Mind if I join you?" he said but did not wait for an answer before sitting.

"This is a private conversation," Huffley said.

"In my establishment," said the stranger, "all conversations involve me."

"You are Rul Bazwan," Huffley said.

The man inclined his head. "I already know who *I* am," he said. "What interests me is who you are. And specifically how you came to approach my saloon from the direction of the piddlers' palace up there on the hill."

The preceptor drew himself erect in his chair. "We are scholars of the Institute of Historical Inquiry on Old Earth. We are. . . "

". . . on sabbatical," Bandar broke in, "and thought it might be interesting to take in some local sights." He took up his ale and looked around. "Quite a colorful establishment you have here."

Bazwan fixed the young man with a suspicious eye. "And into what, exactly, does your institute inquire?"

Bandar saw that Huffley was inclined to answer and again leapt in to seize the floor. "Nothing much. Odd little quirks of Old Earth's distant past. For most of us, it's more of a hobby than a profession."

"Now, just a moment. . . " Huffley began, a reddening flush rising from his collar into his cheeks.

But Bandar cut him off again, both with words and with a kick under the table. "My esteemed colleague, for example, has made a comprehensive study of the pubic hairstyles that were fashionable in the Eighteenth Aeon. His expertise in the matter of braided merkins is unparalled. I'm sure he'd be delighted to tell you about them."

Bazwan drew back. "That won't be necessary," he said, though mistrust lingered in the crevices about his eyes. "But what were you doing among the piss–pots up above?"

"I don't know whom you mean," Bandar said.

Bazwan's thumb hooked in the direction of the Sequestrance. "The place you came from."

"Oh," said the young man. "We were stranded at some little space port and hitched a ride on their dray. Why do you call them piss–pots? Are they noted for their tippling? By the way, this ale is quite good."

"Never mind," said the innkeeper, rising to his feet. "Enjoy your stay."

When the scarred man was gone, Huffley said, "You assaulted me."

"That is nothing compared to what I suspect Rul Bazwan would do if he thought we were here to interfere with his livelihood."

Comprehension dawned in the academician's face. "Oh," he said, "yes, I see. Good thinking."

"Not that we're actually capable of doing so," Bandar continued, keeping his voice low. "Unless you have powers a mere student cannot guess at."

Huffley took up his ale. "I have no such powers," he said. "I will ascertain if there is phenomenon of telepathic leakage across species lines. Then I shall declare to the hydromants that the situation is more dire than I had thought, paint the Bololos in the colors of dangerous psychotics, and recommend that the Sequestrance move to another site."

"Malabar will not hear that news gladly." Bandar said.

"What can he do? He is, after all, a contemplative."

"My impression is that he might have no difficulty contemplating murder and mayhem. He did allude to another plan."

"My assessment of him differs," said Huffley. "They will all probably hide behind their wall, their ears stuffed with that horrid bread they tried to feed us. It would be certainly be a better use than eating it." A noise from outside drew his attention. "There is the charabanc. Let us embark."

They took seats in the front row. The vehicle soon filled up with passengers whose costumes, coiffures and adornments of skin and appendages identified them as having come from at least a dozen worlds. When all the seats were taken the vehicle began to roll forward, then stopped briefly at the call of a muscular young bravo in a wide brimmed hat and fringed leggings who came out of the saloon and leapt aboard to take a position standing behind the operator.

The high wheeled conveyance rolled away, flinging dust and grit in billows behind it. Huffley leaned toward Bandar to say something, but the student signaled his teacher to silence while indicating with an inclination of his head the man standing close to them. The fellow did not look their way, but Bandar had the impression that if his ears could have swiveled in their direction, they would have.

The journey was short, ending at the rim of a shallow depression that formed a natural amphitheater. The charabanc unloaded and the passengers descended to find seats on narrow ledges of rock that sloped down toward a wide and open space. Bandar looked down upon a a herd of Bololos.

The creatures stood on their hind legs like humans, freeing their upper appendages to scoop up handfuls of dark lichen from the several piles scattered about the natural basin. This they ate with jaws and dentition that again approximated the human, though to call the entire effect humanoid one would have to stretch the definition to include beings that were half again as big as Bandar, covered in coarse hair that came in shades from dun to light brown, and with skulls topped by a pronounced cranial ridge that anchored their huge chewing muscles. They also had short, broad and hairless tails that Bandar thought might have something to do with radiating excess body heat.

"Come," said Huffley, and led the way to a seat near the rim of the amphitheater. "We will watch."

The piles of lichen were disappearing at a rapid rate, there being as many as a hundred adult Bololos in the herd, with a scattering of juveniles. "I have read about this," Huffley said. "They will eat until they are sated. When the food is gone, they normally lapse into a state of mutual communion."

The autochthones did not do so, however, because as the last handfuls of lichen were crammed into the gaping maws and chewed to pulp, a flying car came to hover over them. Two men dropped bundles of brightly covered clothing and various objects and implements among the Bololos. The car then sidled over to where the spectators sat and a florid looking man in spangled garments took up an amplifier.

"Honorables and distinctions," he began, "I invite you to witness a rare incidence of cross–species assonance. But first, I must have your cooperation, for you yourselves are an intrinsic part of this experience."

Some of the audience looked interested, others annoyed at the unexpected prospect of exerting themselves in the pursuit of their own entertainment. The master of ceremonies assumed a mollifying air. "All that is required of you is that you choose," he said, "from among the common pantheon of stories on which the literature of all the many worlds of The Spray is founded. The comic misadventures of *The Three Orlicants*, for example. The rousing saga of *The King in Darkness*. The tragedy of *Heliocanth and Helaphion*."

Each of the titles was advanced with an expansive gesture and roll of the man's eyes. "Choose one," his amplified voice continued. "Let its scenes and motifs well up into your thoughts from the deepest springs, dwell upon its tropes and meanings, and—behold!—the creatures below will assume the principal roles and re–enact them before your eyes. The spectacle will delight and astonish by the incongruent juxtaposition of the familiar and the bizarre."

He executed a final flourish and assumed an air of expectation. There was silence from the crowd, then a tentative voice called out, "*The Justification of Ballion!*"

"*The Remarkable Ring!*" cried another.

"No," said a third, more confident voice, "make it *The Lad Who Persevered!*"

At this, there was a general murmur of acceptance from the crowd. The master of ceremonies gave a knowing wink and said, "*The Lad* it shall be." The air car rose slowly as he continued, in a sonorous tone, "Close your eyes, clear the mind. Now, softly, softly, let the first scene of the story rise to fill your inner screen. Do you have it? Can you see the fated child among the tyrant's cabbages? Now, then, open and gaze upon a wonderment!"

Bandar had done as the man had bid. Now, as he beheld the area below, he saw the Bololos bending over the piles of costumes and props, draping themselves in outsized garments and picking up various implements. At first, the scene was random and chaotic, then the elements of the old story suddenly fell into place.

"Look," he said to Huffley, "that one with the hoe is obviously the lad. See, he gouges the soil, now pauses to dream. And, yes, here comes the brutal overseer – there's his whip and there's the shackles—and that light–shaded one must be the child's despairing dam."

"Yes, yes," said the academician. "It is what I expected."

"Now the ones in the background are forming ranks," Bandar said. "They'll be the army. There goes the lad to volunteer. And now the overseer is changing into the abusive sergeant."

"Remarkable, I'm sure," said Huffley. "But let us do what we came to do."

"Which you have not yet vouchsafed to me," said Bandar. "Shall I sit here and guess?"

"You are becoming quite forward for an undergraduate," said Huffley.

"Doubtless it is the broadening effect of off–world travel," said Bandar. "Or perhaps I am so naturally impatient that after spending hardly more than a week traveling halfway down The Spray I begin to require answers."

"And somewhat snippy, to boot," said the preceptor. "You put me in mind of Fartherthwaith, the Overdean. Still, you cannot do your part unless I acquaint you with it. So pay heed."

Huffley quickly outlined his plan, the elements of which were much as Bandar had expected. Each would descend through his own unconscious into the Commons. they would meet and seek the breach in the wall through which human archetypes were being telepathically drawn into the unconscious of the Bololos.

"I will approach the gap and look through it," Huffley concluded, while you chant the thran that will keep us unapprehended by the archetypes."

"May I also not look through?" Bandar said.

"You are but in your third year. You would be terrified."

Bandar was indeed apprehensive, yet he hoped he was brave. "But I have come all this way."

"Enough," said Huffley. "We shall begin."

The pair assumed the cross legged position and prepared to begin the mental exercises that were the first step on the road into the Commons. Before he closed his eyes and drew his focus inward, Bandar looked around. The spectators around them were avidly watching the drama unfolding below, where the Bololos were now enacting the Battle of Millefolle, the military catastrophe from which the plucky boy hero rescues the heir to the kingdom only to see another given the reward. Bandar looked for the man in the hat and leggings, but could not see him.

"I'm concerned about that bravo in the hat and leggings," he said.

"Such men are of no account," Huffley said. "Commence."

Bandar withdrew his attention from the scene, closed his eyes and concentrated on the exercises that prepared him to enter the unconscious. In a few moments he saw the familiar portal: a sealed door that, even as he reified it, began to glow about its edges as if behind it stood a great lamp. Bandar fashioned a mental hand and had it lift the latch, causing the door to swing outwards. His whole inner vision was now bathed in a rich light of rosaceous gold. He propelled his consciousness into the warm effulgence and instantly it faded. He was standing in the great storage room behind his Uncle Fley's housewares emporium, the place where he had spent much of his later boyhood. he looked about him and saw, as he knew he would, an item that was inconsistent with the remembered reality from which this vision was drawn: set in the far wall was a door of dark, close–grained wood with a black iron handle in the shape of a gnarled hand. Fearlessly, Bandar approached the door, seized and yanked.

Beyond was a darkness in which loomed a shadowy figure. As Bandar stepped forward it also came toward him and resolved itself into the image of someone he knew: Didrick Gabbris, a fellow student at the Institute with a flair for self–aggrandizement and a general approach to life that struck Bandar as a basic meanness of spirit. Bandar knew the dark eidolon was not the real Gabbris, was in fact a projected reification of those negative qualities that Bandar rejected in his own make–up. The figure sneered at Bandar, but the young man simply strode through it and, as his chest made contact, the image vanished like a burst bubble.

Now Bandar stood at the top of a wide, curving stairway that descended into mist. He went down swiftly, knowing that Huffley, a master noönaut, must reach the outer circle of the Commons before him and sure that the old man would levy criticism for delaying their work. In a moment the mist evanesced and he was walking down a country lane that led down into a green valley from a gentle hill. On either side, low stone walls separated the road from open fields dotted with copses of trees.

He caught a flicker of light from the corner of one eye, stopped and turned toward it. The light faded and was replaced by a pale rendition of Huffley. The image quickly darkened and solidified until the academician appeared as solid as Bandar.

"I've been waiting," the senior man said, tapping his foot.

Bandar made an apologetic gesture and the old man sniffed and turned to look down the road. "We will go first to the outer arrondisement and see what the effects are on the pure archetypes." Even as he spoke, he set off down the road, adding, "The situation may be roiled. Begin the three–three–seven."

Bandar began singing the most elemental thran, a sequence that sounded much like an ancient children's song about an old man, a dog and a bone, among other things. Its notes would prevent them from being apprehended by any archetypes they might encounter. He looked about him and saw nothing but fields and trees, but he knew that neither actually existed and that an attempt to cross the apparent open spaces beyond the walls would soon have him walking into an unseen gate that would drop him into one of the myriad Locations of the Commons. He kept to the road.

After a few moments, he became aware that the road encountered a deep ravine across which hung a suspension bridge of ropes and planks. Bandar studied the construction with some small interest, knowing that it must be Huffley's conception of the entry into the outer shell of the great sphere that was the Commons. If Bandar had been exerting the primary influence on this exploration, they would have come to a stream overarched by a bridge of dressed stone. Others would have seen a simple fence with a stile, a log over a brook, a high–flying ribbon of bright metal over a bottomless chasm, a city street marked by a crosswalk.

The scene on the far side of the barrier was indistinct, in the manner of dreams, but as they made their way to the mid–point of the span they saw a limitless open space in which a host of figures stood or sat or moved about at random.

"Stop," said Huffley. "But chant louder. I sense a definite tension."

Bandar increased his volume, at the same time using a noönaut technique that extended and sharpened his vision. He focused on the figures in the field, identifying many of them at first apprais-al. Here came the Wise Man, there the female Temptress and the male Seducer. The Fool lolloped by. The Eater of Children stalked past, rubbing its gnarled hands together. Bandar saw the Judge of Souls and the Helpful Beast, and off in the distance he could see the Willing Sacrifice and the Redeemer—all the "usual suspects," as Institute undergraduates were wont to refer to them.

But, no not all of them, he realized as Huffley spoke. "I do not see the Tyrant, nor the Commander, nor the Boy of Destiny. I think that settles it. There is a breach." Bandar heard the excitement in his teacher's voice, mingled with an overtone of fear.

The preceptor led the way back to the road, Bandar continu-ing to chant the three, three and seven. This close to the first level, with its denizens disturbed, anything might happen. Direct contact with a pure archetype meant instant obliteration of the noönaut's identity and complete absorption. The body left in the waking world would be suffused by the archtypical entity and its subsequent actions would be indistinguishable from those of a full–blown psy-chotic.

Huffley's face took on an introspective cast and Bandar knew that he was seeking a direction. After a moment, the old man said, "Do you sense the flux?"

Bandar applied the noönaut mentalism that could identify the location of nodes between Locations and felt a slight but definite sense of motion, representing itself as a gentle breeze. He gestured with his chin in the direction that the "air" seemed to move.

Huffley said, "I concur." He approached the wall on one side of the road and climbed over. Bandar did the same. The old man moved carefully, counting his steps and changing direction so that he traced a zig–zagging route across the field. Bandar followed pre-cisely, knowing that each invisible corner turned meant that they were stepping around a gateway that would have plucked them from this place and dropped them in some other Location of the Commons where they might face lengthy delays in getting out or encounter lethal challenges.

Working their way through the unseen maze, they came all at once to the great white wall. In the manner of dreams, one moment it was absent, the next it was close by, stretching up and to left and right, with no discernible limit. Here the "breeze" was more pronounced, rippling past the tightly joined blocks of bright, shining stone. Huffley turned to follow its motion and Bandar noticed that the man's knees seemed to have weakened.

With each step the movement of air palpably strengthened. Bandar could feel it tickling the back of his neck and soon he heard a soft whistling over the sound of his continued chanting.

"We are here," said Huffley, a quaver in his voice. He had stopped before a section of the wall that, to Bandar, looked like any other, though the breeze now sounded like the wind that often suffled around the eaves of the undergradute dormitory back at the Institute. The young man felt a momentary desolation at being so far from home and, perhaps, about to face a peril unprecedented in the long exploration of the Commons. But he summoned his courage and continued to chant.

Huffley reached a trembling hand toward the wall. Bandar could see the hairs stirring on the backs of the preceptor's fingers as their tips approached the stone. Then the age spotted hand disappeared into the whiteness and swiftly jerked back. Huffley examined the appendage closely but found nothing wrong. He thrust it into the wall again, up to the wrist, then to the elbow. He drew it back and again found no harm.

"Well," he said. "There it is." He sounded short of breath.

Bandar waited for the academician to take the next, logical step. But Huffley just stood before the invisible breach in the barrier. His breath came rapid and raspy. Bandar, still chanting the thran, made motions with his hands, as if to usher the old man forward, but the preceptor had begun to tremble, a wild look in his eye.

Bandar broke off the thran. "Master," he said. "You must look. We have come all this way." He took up the chant again, but Huffley made an inconclusive gesture with a shaking hand, and whispered, "I cannot."

Bandar made shooing motions toward the wall, but Huffley looked away. The academician lowered himself to the ground and sat, disconsolate, his head bowed. "I lack the explorer's courage," he said. "Never in my life have I done what no one else has done before. Nor has any one on Old Earth or the Ten Thousand Worlds. It is the curse of living in a latter age."

Then I will, thought Bandar, still sounding the three, three, seven thran. He stepped to the wall and, before he could think himself out of it, thrust his head at the space where Huffley's hand had passed through. For a moment all was a white brightness, then his face popped through and he beheld the space beyond.

Here was the archetypal Landscape of the Bololos, which Bandar was not surprised to find looked exactly like the surface of Gamza in the waking world: a level plain of rock, sand and grit broken here and there by dark patches of lichen. He was surprised, however, that there was no crowd of Bololo archetypes such as those that populated the human Commons. Instead, he saw but one figure in the Location: a large, placid Bololo of indeterminate gender who stood, apparently bemused, and watched the human archetypes that had come through the barrier.

Of course, Bandar thought. *A deeply telepathic species would have a unified psyche from top to bottom—no contending, cooperating fragments, no partial personas—just one self-composed entity.*

He drew his head back into the human noösphere, broke off the thran and said, "Master, the Bololo Commons contains but a single archetype."

Huffley made a small noise and it seemed for a moment that he would rise and take a look, but then his fear of the new reasserted itself and he sank down. Bandar resumed the thran and put his head back through the wall. Now he ignored the Bololo entity and focused on the contaminants that had been able to pass through the breach caused by the aliens' telepathic resonance.

They were clearly the elements of the ancient archetypal story, *The Lad Who Persevered*. There was the strutting Tyrant, here the forlorn Helpless Mother, there the Enemy Host, rampant for battle, and here the fearless Boy himself, striding toward his destiny. Bandar saw that the tale was nearing its conclusion, the Tyrant having been cast down while the Boy picked up the usurper's fallen sword and positioned himself to strike the final blow.

21

He pulled his head back to his own side of the wall and again ceased to the chant the insulating thran. "It was as you surmised, Master," he said. "The contaminant human archetypes enter the Bololo Commons. There they play their various roles, turning the poor creatures into naturals,"—he used the Institute term for victims of psychosis—"for the entertainment of Rul Bazwan's excursionists."

Huffley looked up and said something indistinct, then broke off whatever the remark had been to begin loudly chanting the three, three, seven in a frantic tone, his eyes wide and fixed on something behind Bandar. Bandar immediately joined in the thran and stepped quickly away from the wall. Only when he was well clear did he turn to see what had so frightened his preceptor.

He recognized the grim and towering figure striding toward the breach. It was the archetype known as the Angel of Wrath and Vengeance, usually found only in a few of the noösphere's more apocalyptic Locations; Bandar knew it by its great dark wings, dripping droplets of gore, and its sword of black iron. And those behind it, he thought *are surely the Piacular Legion, their faces dour and their weapons bristling.*

It was clear that another drama was to be enacted after the tale of the Lad was wound up. The Angel marched straight to the wall and passed beyond, its following horde filing through in its train. Bandar shuddered, because he knew what must now ensue in the waking world, for the Angel had borne the face of the Eminence Malabar and the ranks of the Legion had been full of lean men in coarse robes.

When the last of them had disappeared through the breach, he broke off the thran to speak to Huffley, but the preceptor was beyond conversation. Panic had seized control of his face, underlain by a wash of shame. Bandar swiftly intoned a short thran that would open an emergency exit from the Commons. A shimmering rift appeared in the air before them. The young man thrust his teacher through it and sprang after him.

Bandar fell back into his body with the jolt that always accompanied an emergency departure from the noösphere. That shock was followed by another: he was no longer seated in the amphitheater above the Bololo feeding station. He and Huffley were in a roofless room with unfinished walls. Above him he saw the thickly starred Gamzan night. Music and the hubbub of a crowd sounded faintly through the floor. Time spent in the Commons could often be elastic; clearly here in the waking world enough time had passed for him and Huffley to have been roped, gagged and carried back to the Hotel Splendor while they were entranced.

"They're coming out of it," said a voice behind them. "Get the patron up here."

Bandar turned his head and saw the man in the leggings talking into a communicator. The fellow returned him a look that said he shortly expected an enjoyable spectacle. Bandar doubted he would be similarly entertained. Moments passed, and Bandar heard a new sound above the noise from the saloon below: the thin, aggravating whine of untuned gravity obviators coming from behind and above. As the keening sound reached its loudest, the student looked up and saw the Sequestrance's carryall passing overhead from the direction of the Bololo amphitheater, its scarred hull illuminated by the lights of the town. When it banked to head toward the Sequestrance, he noticed that its load of crates was gone.

Bandar grunted through the gag, seeking to attract the preceptor's attention. But Huffley's head was sunk on his chest, the academician offering a portrait of despair.

Now firm footsteps sounded beyond the room and the door opened and closed. A moment later, Rul Bazwan came into the young man's field of vision, wearing an expression that invited no further wasting of his time. In his hand was a wandlike instrument. The implement was unfamiliar to Bandar but he was sure he did not wish to become well acquainted with it.

"This time," said the saloonkeeper, "we will have the truth. Get the gags off them." When the man in leggings had pulled the rags from their mouths, Bazwan addressed Huffley. "You will tell me what this was all about."

A soft sob escaped the scholar. He did not look up. "I have failed," he said.

"What did you do?" said Bazwan.

Huffley's gaze remained on the floor. "I thought that when the moment came I would be bold. Instead, I quailed. How they will mock."

Bazwan rubbed his chin and showed his lower teeth. He turned his attention to Bandar. "What's he talking about?"

Bandar swallowed. "I think he has gone a little mad," he said. "It is not unheard of amongst the Institute's senior savants."

"Then it's up to you," said the impresario.

"I am happy to cooperate," Bandar said.

"Then I may not need this?" Bazwan touched a control on the device in his hand. It buzzed as if it confined a swarm of hornets. A light glowed darkly red at its tip.

"Definitely not," Bandar assured him.

"We will see," the saloonkeeper said and Bandar saw that the man in leggings was chagrined. Bazwan continued. "Let us begin. You and the old man are scholars from the Institute of Historical Inquiry."

"We are."

"The piddlers brought you in."

"They did."

"To disrupt my legitimate business." Bazwan's voice had taken on an edge.

"I do not deny it."

"And what have you done?"

"Absolutely nothing," said Bandar. "It is not our role to interfere, even if there was anything we could do, which there is not and never was."

Bandar was pleased to hear a less strident tone from his interrogator, though the wand remained within sight and hearing. "Then what were you doing here?"

"We wanted to observe the phenomenon of the Bololo herd. But we could not afford space travel."

Bazwan stroked the scar again and drew down one eyebrow. "You mean you spun the old piss–artist a tale just to cadge free travel down The Spray?"

Bandar assured him it was so.

"And there is nothing you can do to close the connection between humans and the Bololos?"

"Not a thing. I swear on my honor as a scholar of the Institute."

Bazwan's pursed thoughtful lips as he regarded the two of them. "All right," he said after a moment. To Bandar's relief, he extinguished the buzz and glow. "But we had better keep you around for a while just to be sure."

"My master is unwell," Bandar said. "It would be best if I took him home."

"He will come to no harm here. I will send this man out to see what is happening with the autochthones. If all is as it should be, you will be freed in the morning."

Bandar made to protest but Bazwan's response indicated that he would entertain no further objections. When the ringing in Bandar's head stopped, he found that he and Huffley were alone in the room, still bound but ungagged.

"Master," he whispered, "we must depart from here. The Bololos are coming. Listen." He strained his ears. Over the music and ruckus from below he could faintly hear another sound: a chorus of male voices chanting the harsh sutras of the ancient epic, *The Doom that Besmote the Iniquitous.*

Huffley said something indistinct, his attention still fixed upon a space somewhere between his eyes and the floor.

"Master," Bandar said, "I know what Malabar's other plan entailed. I know what was in those crates." He also knew that Rul Bazwan would not quibble over who was responsible for the horror that was about to befall his town.

"Master!" Bandar tried again. If he could bring Preceptor Huffley back into focus, perhaps they could hunch their chair around and work at each other's knots. "There can be little time. Please!"

But Huffley only sent another mumbled remark in the direction of the floor. Bandar listened again. The chanting from the Sequestrance was louder now, a note of raw excitement infusing the unsympathetic verses. Bandar could imagine Malabar and the angry hydromants, standing along the south wall, eyeing the darkness beyond the shanty town and waiting for the first glint of spear and halberd in the grip of massive Bololos that were themselves no less in the grasp of an archetypical holy violence.

Huffley began to blubber. Then he abruptly stopped and offered the floor an incoherent rebuttal of some assertion only he had heard made. Bandar realized that his preceptor could be of no further use.

The hydromants' chanting grew louder still and Bandar heard creep into it a note familiar to any schoolchild who has fallen out with his peers and become the target of organized vindictiveness. From the other edge of town he heard a shout, followed by a scream, then a crash of shattered glass and splintering wood. The music from downstairs faltered then stopped and the raised voices took on a new emotion. Sounds came from the street, frightened at first, then overborne by the distinctive tone of Rul Bazwan issuing hurried orders.

Another scream, this one closer, followed by the unmistakable *zivv* of an energy pistol then a deep throated roar and a rush of feet too heavy to be human. Something struck the wall of the Hotel Splendor—it sounded as if it had been at the rear of the building— hard enough to make the unroofed walls quake.

Bandar pulled at his bonds but the man in the leggings must have been a perfectionist. He looked again to Huffley and heard a snatch of a nursery song. Now a new clatter arose from beneath the floorboards and Bandar, seeking to make sense of it, reasoned that Bazwan had summoned all who could make it into the hotel and urged them to bar the doors and windows with furniture. The young man lacked faith in that stratagem. The Bololos were very large and motivated by the rage of fanatics. Tables and chairs would offer no obstacle.

There was but one avenue of escape and Bandar took it. He closed his eyes and performed the mental exercises that would take him "down to the basement," as Institute jargon had it. Forcing the pace, he was soon in his uncle's storeroom. He crossed it swiftly, yanked open the anomalous dark door, barely taking time to note that the shadow of Didrick Gabbris wore a deeper sneer than usual before Bandar was racing down the staircase to the road between the walls.

And here he wished he had his preceptor. He could feel the breeze flowing toward the gap, but the exact place at which to step from the safety of the road and the zigs and zags required to navigate the apparent field? He could only trust to memory. Fortunately, a capacious power of recall and a flair for detail were characteristics every student of the Institute soon mastered. He summoned all the mnemonic strength he possessed, chose a spot along the low gray wall that seemed to answer, and stepped over.

He could picture clearly how Huffley had made the passage. He took four steps forward, then one to his left, two more forward, then six to the right—and stopped dead as a throbbing sensation rippled down the entire front of his virtual body. He leaned slightly backward and it eased.

Very carefully, Bandar shuffled a minim backwards. The throbbing meant he had almost blundered into a node. He might have found himself in one of the Landscapes, Situations or Events that were preserved in the Commons, some of which were almost instantly fatal; a thran could make him invisible to the idiomatic entities on an archetypical battlefield but that was scant help if he arrived just as an artillery barrage was landing—and since the Commons preserved crystallized memes of the most memorable events, on its battlefields barrages, cavalry charges or screaming infantry assaults were always imminent.

Bandar calmed himself and let the memory of Huffley's movements well up in him. He determined that he had come the right way, but that he had let his strides grow fractionally larger than the preceptor's. He turned left and took three carefully measured steps, then right for four and four more forward. . . and there loomed the topless wall.

He turned in the direction of the flow and shoulder–rubbed his way along the wall until he came to the breach. Without hesitation, he stepped through. His feet grated on the gritty floor of the Bololo Commons, making a scritching sound that drew the attention of a soldier one of the Piacular Legion who was slicing the air with a single–edged sword. Delight lit up the archetype's face and it swung the heavy weapon at Bandar's head. The young man leaped back and passed through the wall into the human Commons.

Calling up a mentalism to calm himself, Bandar chanted the three, three, seven and went again into the Bololo noösphere. This time the Legionary did not notice him, and the noönaut paused a moment to take in the scene. The Angel of Wrath and Vengeance was striding back and forth, gesticulating and exhorting his followers to holy violence. Before its leader, the Legion had deployed into four ranks that were advancing across the empty space, stabbing and spitting the air with the metronomic precision of a fighting machine. Bandar shuddered to think how the actions before his eyes were being replicated by towering Bololos in the waking world.

Beyond the one–sided battle, the Bololo archetype stood and regarded the interlopers with an aspect that Bandar read as puzzled concern. The Angel paid it no heed, intent on acting out the drama

27

of its existence, its wings throwing blood in all directions. A droplet touched Bandar's virtual skin, and he felt as if a hot coal had been pressed against him. He rubbed the blister that was already rising and, dodging the martial display and the towering figure of retribution, he made his way toward the Bololo entity.

Now comes the difficult part, he thought. For a moment, fear came burbling up in him. To expose oneself to an archetypical entity was an invitation to be absorbed into it, all conscious identity lost in irreducible psychosis. To expose oneself to an alien entity was unheard of, but Bandar told himself that unheard–of seemed to be the motto of the day. Besides, it would not be long before the raging Bololos stormed the Hotel Splendor, and he gave only the slightest of odds that his corporeal body, bound to a chair, would survive the massacre.

Still singing the three, three, seven, he put down his inchoate terror and placed himself before the Bololo archetype. He waited until the Angel and the Legion had marched to the limits of their advance and were marking time, preparing to about–face and come back the way they had gone.

As the grunting fanatics turned on their heels, stabbing the air, Bandar ceased chanting the insulating thran. The looming Bololo archetype noticed him first, and stared down at him with a look of polite interest. Bandar gazed into its calm, dark eyes and saw depths beyond reckoning.

Behind him, a thundering voice shouted words of discovery, answered by a roar from many throats. Bandar heard the thud of hobnailed boots on the hardpacked ground and knew the Legion was coming for him. There was no way back. He fought down another burst of panic and stepped toward the Bololo archetype.

He felt its fur brush his face. There followed a sense of intense dislocation, as if his whole being had suddenly blasted into fragments, billions of Bandar–iotas flying in all directions both temporal and spatial, each a dimly sentient spark. Then, just as abruptly, the explosion stopped, froze for an instant that seemed to last forever, then every item of Bandar shrapnel retraced its arc and all coalesced once more into. . .

Not Bandar. Or, at least, not just Bandar. He was aware of being himself. . . and yet more. It was as if he had lived all his existence in a small, windowless cell, but now its walls, floor and

28

ceiling had become porous, transparent glass, and he knew that his cell was but one of an infinite honeycomb of cells, each inhabited by a consciousness, each consciousness aware of every other, and all bound together in a comforting matrix of supernal equanimity. But as he looked deeper into the infinity of the Bololo archetype, he realized that he was seeing more than just what *was*—he was seeing all the Bololos that ever had been, that ever would be, every existence from the beginning of the species to the last of its kind, far off in the unimaginable future. Here they were, all together—and he was one of them.

Here and there he noticed cells whose walls were opaquely dark, like spots of cancer in otherwise healthy tissue. He was cut off from those cells, could feel the separation, and it troubled him.

How long Bandar spent contemplating the immensity of Bololodom he would never know. After a time, he drew his attention back to his own persona in his own cell and saw that he was hunkered down on his haunches—the posture of a Bololo at rest. For no reason other than the training that said always to be active in the Commons—if a noönaut was not doing, he was likely to be done to—he stood up. Immediately, all the Bololo entities in all the cells, did likewise.

Bandar raised his right hand in front of his face. So did a billion Bololos. He lifted his left foot, and a billion left hindquarters followed suit. He set down the foot and clapped his hands. The sound came from every direction within the self–contained universe that was the Bololo archetype.

Using an Institute adept's mentalism, Bandar concentrated his will. "I wish to see," he said. At once he was gazing out upon the archetypal Gamza landscape, where the Angel and his Legion had returned to their martial display. From the height of his perspective on the scene, Bandar knew that he was seeing through the eyes of the Bololo archetype. And from the way Wrath and Vengeance was casting sidelong looks his way, Bandar concluded that the Bololo archetype had already stood up, raised a hand and a foot, then clapped its paws together.

What must happen next was clear to the young scholar. But as he prepared to summon the mental focus necessary, he realized that another imperative tugged at him. It could not be merely a case of *what I will do*. It had to be *what we will do together*. Yet even as he posed the question, the answer came from every direction in space and time: *Yes. We need you to save them/us.*

Bandar/Bololo flexed the enormous muscles of his shoulders, brought up his hands and clenched them. He found that the Bololo's great paws, with their prehensile digits and opposable thumbs, made impressive fists. He swung his heavy head toward the Angel, opened his low slung jaw and shouted, "Hey, you!"

The Angel of Wrath and Vegeance and the legionaries were pure archetypes from the noösphere's outer arrondisement. Unlike the idiomatic entities that populated the various Events, Situations and Landscapes that filled the interior of the Commons, the pure entities' awareness was almost entirely limited to themselves. Bandar suspected that it was difficult for the Angel, so fixated upon its own attributes, to be aware of such an outlandish entity as Bandar/Bololo. But he intended to get its attention.

The Angel could not ignore the Bololo archetype as it drove through the ranks of the Legion, scattering legionaries like toy soldiers, and delivered a roundhouse blow to the Angel's bearded chin. A look of profound consternation troubled the stern face, but only for the moment it took for Bandar/Bololo's other fist to connect with a short, brutal uppercut. The archetype stumbled backwards, its shadowed wings fluttering, the black sword falling from its grasp, and Bandar followed with a two–handed shove that sent the Angel backpedaling on shaking knees.

They had crossed the space to the wall. Bandar noticed that on this side it had the appearance of a natural cliff, then he returned to his task and shoved the Angel one more time. The original surprise on its Malabar–featured face faded and a glower of determination began to assert itself, so he pushed heavily again, putting all of the Bololo entity's bulk into the effort.

The angel was driven back into the breach, its great pinions crushed against its sides by the narrowness of the gap. But now its hands reached out, fingers spread against the rock of the cliff face, and Bandar saw rage and resolution firm in its face. It straightened its legs and dug in its armored heels, and its corded shoulder muscles bunched as it prepared to squeeze out of the breach and propel itself at him.

"No!" The word roared from the Bololo throat. He squatted, let his weight rest on his backthrust hands and the broad Bololo tail, and drove both splayed feet into the Angel's chest. The interloping archetype shot through the breach like a stopper from a shaken bottle.

Bandar/Bololo turned to the Legion, but found no threat. Disassociated from their Principal, the subsidiary archetypes had lost their verve and were wandering aimlessly or standing inert. Bandar strode to them, offering buffets and backhands to gain their attention, and soon had them staggering and bumbling toward the opening in the cliff.

The black sword lay on the stony ground. Bandar picked it up and cast it through the unseen gap in the wall. Now there was nothing in the Bololo Commons but a vast plain and a single entity. An inner sense told him that the contaminated cells of the Bololo matrix were returning to health.

Bandar reached a paw toward the cliff face and said to himself and all the others, *We should close this*. Assent came back to him from all directions. He gathered rocks and stones and began to fill in the breach, fitting the pieces closely. When the space was almost chin high, he felt an urge to cease work.

Time for you to go, said a soundless voice within him. He was suddenly back in his cell within the infinite matrix, but only for a moment. He experienced a gentle dissolution, became first a liquid, then a cool vapor. He wafted away from something, toward something else, and then he was once more standing in his virtual flesh before the Bololo entity. It regarded him, as before, with bemusement, then one dark eye closed and reopened in a slow wink of bonhomie. A moment later Bandar was tenderly taken up and put through the remaining gap in the top of the breach. As he slid down into the human Commons, he heard a soft voice say, "Goodbye."

Off in the distance, Bandar could see the ejected Angel and his dejected Legion slouching toward the outer arrondisement. The sword on the ground was already being reabsorbed into the protean stuff of the noösphere. The young man focused himself and chanted the emergency exit thran.

Bandar was back in the chair in the roofless room atop the Hotel Splendor, Preceptor Huffley slumped in his bonds beside him. He drew in and let out a long breath. A noise called his attention and he looked over his shoulder to see the door to the room lying smashed on the floor. Filling the doorway, as if it had merely paused in the act of forcing its way in, was a full grown bull Bololo. In its paw it held a thick–bladed falchion. Blood dripped from the weapon's edge. Its dark eyes were fixed on Bandar but it blinked like a sleeper just woken from a dream.

It made to withdraw, the paw that held the curved sword opening. "Wait!" cried Bandar.

The creature paused. Bandar indicated with motions of his head the rope that bound his hands and arms. The Bololo regarded him with stolid disinterest. Then it blinked again, and Bandar saw another presence well up in its dark eyes. It squeezed through the doorway, splintering the jamb, and applied the edge of its weapon to the cords that held him. When the job was done it let the falchion clatter on the floorboards and thrust its way back out of the room.

Rubbing his wrists, urging blood back into his agonized hands, Bandar watched the creature go. It disappeared into the hallway without a backward glance and Bandar turned his attention to Huffley, taking up the sword to cut the old man free. A sound from the doorway made him look up.

The Bololo had returned. Stooping, it poked its heavy head through the doorway. Again, as in the Commons, Bandar saw one eye close then reopen. A giant paw rose to the creature's chest height and the digits executed a gentle wave.

"Goodbye," Bandar said, and then the Bololo was gone for good. The young man pulled the sitting Huffley toward him, hoisted him over one shoulder and left the room. He transited the hallway and descended the stairs that led down to the saloon. Here he found unappetizing sights. The Bololos, possessed by the hate–filled hydromants, had been as unforgiving as they were thorough. Bandar had seen worse in some Locations within the noösphere—the Slaughter of the Innocents and the Pillage of the Defenseless City were egregiously gruesome—but he found it was different when the victims could not be reconstituted to begin the cycle all over again. From beneath a shattered gaming table protruded the head and torso of the young woman who had taken his order only a few hours before. He looked elsewhere and noticed that the corpse of Rul Bazwan was not to be seen.

There was more horror outside. Those who had been overwhelmed by the initial assault lay where they had fallen. Bandar picked his way through the carnage to a high wheeled vehicle on the other side of the street. Bazwan's henchman lay in two pieces just short of the step that led up to the control chair. Bandar tucked Huffley into the passenger compartment, ignoring the disconnected words and salty expletives that the preceptor intermittently issued forth. The student took charge of the vehicle and guided it into an alley that wandered toward the Sequestrance. From time to time the wheels bumped over what lay strewn about the ground but Bandar steeled himself against the inevitable thoughts.

He angled up the slope to the Sequestrance, then paralleled its wall until he could turn the corner and strike out across open ground. Over the hum of the vehicle's motilator he heard discordant cries and moans from within the walls. He speculated on whether there might have been "blowback" from the hydromants' deliberate summoning of prime archetypes, especially Malabar's close association with the Angel of Wrath and Vengeance—he suspected that the Eminence had not been more than a short hop and skip from psychosis to begin with, so the channel would have already been well lubricated.

From the passenger compartment, Huffley expostulated energetically to some unseen interlocutor, claiming that since he had baked the cake himself, he would have the first slice, and malodorous roommates could wait their turn. Listening further, Bandar deduced that the old man had been catapulted back into his youth, when he had shared quarters with an unpleasant young man to whom Huffley had given the name Fartywhiff. He let the preceptor ramble on and concentrated on guiding the vehicle out to the barebones space port. When they arrived, Huffley was hissing something about "My Lord High Hiedyin of Fulldoodledom." Bandar made the old man as comfortable as he could on a tattered settee within the shed and made sure that their travel vouchers were still in the preceptor's wallet. Then he activated the beacon that would inform any passing spaceship that passengers desired transport offworld.

On the second class liner that took them the last leg of their multistage journey back from Gamza, Bandar composed a series of papers dealing with the discoveries that he had made: that inter-species telepathic noöspheric connections were indeed possible; that archetypically induced psychosis could be transmitted across species lines; that a telepathic species could have a unitary archetype that enfolded not only their dead but individuals not yet born (there were fascinating metaphysical aspects to that one); and that a human con-sciousness could be absorbed into an alien archetype and be regur-gitated without experiencing psychosis. Bandar had tested himself thoroughly and was almost completely sure that he was returning home as sane as he had left.

The same could not be said for Preceptor Huffley, who daily sank deeper into a private and idiosyncratic world of constant argu-mentation and vicious debate, in which, though frequently beset, he always triumphed by bedtime.

When the liner touched down at the Olkney space port, off-shore on an island in Mornedy Sound, Bandar was surprised to find a delegation of the Institute's superior officers and senior fellows at the bottom of the gangplank. He allowed Huffley to go first, the old man descending to Old Earth once more in the middle of a one-sided colloquy with the repellent Fartywhiff.

As the preceptor reached the group, no less a potentate than Overdean Fartherthwaith stepped forward. In tones of studied outrage he demanded to know what the preceptor had done to cause dire claims to be levied against the Institute's treasury by distant offworlders. "Some rogue called Rul Bazwan—from where do they get these barbarous names?—demands restitution for a town smashed with all its contents. He claims extraordinary sums in general, special and exemplary damages. And there's another from some transcendental mountebank who wants you returned to face summary justice, which I gather involves capital punishment followed by revivification for as many repetitions as your parts will sustain."

Huffley looked in the Overdean's direction but Bandar saw that the old man's eyes did not encompass the scene before him. "I'm afraid Preceptor Huffley has suffered an onset of the adbdabs," he said, referring to an ailment that could afflict noönauts who, in Institute jargon, "tarried too long at the fair."

Fartherthwaith peered at Huffley and listened briefly to what the preceptor was saying. "Sounds more like the blithers to me," he said. "I always thought he'd be susceptible, even when we were boys. In either case, he'll have to go to the sanctuary." At this pronouncement, the Overdean brightened and rubbed his palms against each other with vigor. "Of course, that means he was incompetent to represent the Institute, thus all claims against us for whatever he did are nuncupative." His hands rubbed each other again, making a scritching sound reminiscent of insect wings. "Fetch my volante," he said, "We are overdue for lunch."

"Sir," said Bandar, "As a result of our experiences, I have several new data to offer. I have taken the liberty of drafting four papers."

Fartherthwaith froze for a moment, then peered at the student. "Exactly who are you?" he said

"Guth Bandar, sir, third year."

"You were with Huffy during all this foofaraw?"

"I was."

"Now think about this, and answer carefully," the Overdean said, accompanying his words with a look that was charged with meaning, "were you at any time named to anyone on Gamza?"

"I'm sure I wasn't."

"Were you officially identified as associated with the Institute? Was identification asked for and did you proffer it?"

"No, I was not officially credentialed."

"Very good, because you are not in any way connected with the Institute."

"But my lord Overdean. . . "

Fartherthwaith leaned toward him and winked. "Come back in a year or so, when this is all as forgotten as Cholleysang's poetry and we'll slip you back in. There's a good boy." He turned away with the happy air of one who has avoided a sordid complication.

Bandar called after him. "But sir, the new data."

He pulled the papers from his satchel and waved them futilely. His words were not heard over the powerful thrum of the Overdean's descending aircar. The officials climbed into its luxurious accommodations and the volante sped aloft, its powerful backdraft sweeping the documents from Bandar's hands and strewing them across the waves of Mornedy Sound.

Preceptor Huffley stood squinting after the departed vehicle. "Fatuous Fartywhiff," he said, apropos of nothing.

A Little Learning

Guth Bandar skirted the fighting around the temple of the war god, took a right turn off the processional way and descended the cramped, winding street that connected the acropolis with the cattle market. He ignored the shrieks around him and the whiff of acrid smoke stealing up from the lower town, where the invaders were firing houses they had already looted.

After a few paces he found the narrow alley and stepped into its dark confines. The passage led to the blank stone wall of a substantial house where a man in the robes of a prosperous merchant was scraping a hole beneath the masonry. Beside him was a leaden coffer. As Bandar squeezed past, the man finished digging. He opened the box long enough to strip rings from his hands and a chain from his neck and place them within. Polished gold and the glint of gems gleamed in the dim light then the lid snapped shut.

Bandar paid no heed. The merchant was always here at this point in the cycle. In a moment he would scuttle back to the street, there to be caught by a clutch of soldiers, iron swords out and bronze corselets crimson with blood and wine. They would torture the merchant with practiced skill until he led them, weeping and limping, back to the buried hoard. Then they would cut his throat and throw him on the rubbish heaped against the wall at the alley's end.

Now the man stood and turned to go. He passed Bandar as if he were not there, which from the merchant's point of view, he was not. Bandar continued to chant the nine descending tones, followed by three rising notes, which insulated him from the man's perceptions as they did from those of all the idiomatic entities intrinsic to this Event.

The chant was called a thran, one of several dozen specific combinations of sounds which enabled scholars of the Institute of Historical Inquiry, where Bandar was apprenticed, to sojourn among the multitude of archetypal Events, Landscapes and Situations which constituted the human noösphere—what the laity called the collective unconscious—of Old Earth.

Still chanting, Bandar climbed the stinking heap at the end of the alley. At its apex would lie a large amphora with a fractured handle. He would seize the amphora, prop it against the wall, then mount and scramble atop the barrier. There he would chant a new thran, opening the gate to the next–to–last stage of the test: a Landscape preserving an antique time when the world was mostly forest.

The apprentice had already made his way by rocket–tube and teeming public slideways across the world–girdling City of a hyperindustrialized global state that flourished and faded eons before, taken a short detour through an insidious alien invasion—it had failed—and traversed a rift valley where early human variants competed to determine whose gene pools would dry to dust in the evolutionary sun. Now a walk in the forest and a segue into one of the Blessed Isles would see his quest completed.

But when he reached the top of the refuse heap, instead of the great urn he found it smashed to fragments. That ought to have been impossible, Bandar knew; nothing changed in the noösphere. Events and Situations repeated themselves exactly and eternally.

There was only one possible explanation: Didrick Gabbris had already passed this way, climbed on the amphora and departed. But before doing so he had contrived to destroy the vital stepping stone.

Frantic, Bandar scoured the area, digging through the rubbish in hope of finding something of sufficient size and sturdiness to take his weight. But if there had been anything useful, Gabbris had removed it.

Bandar was left with three choices. His first option was to search the city and bring back something else to climb on. But his insulation from the idiomats' perceptions would not extend to a substantial object that was inherent to the Location. And the longer he interacted closely with the substance of the Location, the more risk that the thran's effect would weaken and he might be perceived.

Suppose some brutal soldier, startled as a chair was borne along by a vague, misty figure, thrust his spear into the mist. Bandar's corpse would thence forward be a permanent feature of the Sack of the City. His tutors had warned of the risks of "dying" in an Event. The sojourner's consciousness became bound to the Location, reforming as one of the idiomatic entities and forever "living" and "dying" as the cycle played out endlessly.

His corporeal body, seated cross–legged on a pad in the examinations room at the Institute, would remain comatose. It would be transferred to the infirmary, bedded and intubated, and consigned to a slow decline.

Bandar's second option was to find an out–of–the–way corner and remain there until the Event concluded and began anew. Then, when he came back to the rubbish heap, the amphora would be waiting for him. But that would take time—too much time, even though durations in the noösphere did not run at the same speed as in the phenomenal world.

Different sites had their own internal clocks. This Event ran far slower than reality; the few hours in which he waited out the cycle would be almost a day in the examination room. Bandar would be the last apprentice to complete the quest; he could abandon all hope of winning the Colquhoon Bursary and being admitted to the advanced collegia.

Which was exactly why Didrick Gabbris had smashed the urn. Gabbris would win the bursary. Gabbris would scale the academic heights, while Guth Bandar slunk back to his family's commerciant firm, to spend his life buying and selling and fretting over the margins between the two.

His third option was no help: he could intone a specific thran and a ripple would appear in the virtual air. He would step through the emergency exit and instantly plunge back into his own seated body. He might complain to the Institute's provost about Gabbris's perfidy, but by the time a board could be convened to investigate, the Event would have recycled and all evidence of the crime would have disappeared.

Glumly, Bandar weighed his options and decided to risk searching for a step–up. But as he started down the pile of refuse there was a commotion at the mouth of the alley and three soldiers appeared, pushing the merchant before them. They watched as he knelt and dug up the box, amid coarse jokes and pokes with a sword at the man's plump buttocks.

There was nothing Bandar could do. The way was too narrow for him to pass, even unseen. He must sit on the rubbish heap and sing the thran, waiting while the soldiers gloated over the treasure, argued over its division, then cut the merchant's throat and finally departed.

Thee would be no time to find something to step on. Sadly Bandar waited for the blood to spurt and the soldiers to leave. He would open a gate and return to the examination room. Perhaps his story would be believed and he would be given a make–up exam. But that was a faint hope; he could imagine the conversation.

Bandar would say, "I accuse Didrick Gabbris of malfeasance in the matter of the amphora."

Gabbris would not deign to sully a glance by directing it at Bandar. He would elevate his nose and say, "Words without substance fleetly fly but seldom stick. Bring forth your evidence."

"I have none but my character."

"Your character is a subjective quality. You perhaps measure it as large and splendorous, while others might call it mean and marred by envy."

"This is injustice!"

"Again, a subjective concept, while blunt facts resist manipulation. Failure must find no favor."

Senior Tutor Eldred would tug at his sparse side whiskers and make his disposition. He would be swayed by the force of Gabbris's views. Bandar's would seem the squeakings of some timorous creature.

The pathetic scene at the foot of the refuse heap was nearing its conclusion. The merchant said, as always, "There, you have taken all that I valued."

One of the soldiers drew a dirk. "Not quite all."

The merchant trembled. "My life is of no worth to you. Though you take it from me you cannot carry it away with you."

"Yet we are inclined to be thorough," said the invader.

Bandar waited. He thought of some of the Locations he had visited during his years at the Institute, the places he would miss. It was then, as he said goodbye to some of his favorites, that it occurred to him that he had a fourth option.

The Institute had issued the examination candidates a partial map of the noösphere, showing only the Locations they would need to navigate the test course. The full chart of humanity's collective unconscious was an intricately convoluted sphere, complexity upon complexity. It was the work of thousands of years of exploration by noönauts, many of whom had been absorbed by perils lurking in dark corners of the Commons.

Bandar did not have such a map. A noönaut could take on his journey only what he could hold in his memory, and to encompass the schematic representation of an organic realm that had been evolving for eons was itself a work of years.

But there was a physical representation of the full map in the communal study chamber and Bandar had spent many hours gazing into its labyrinthine depths. He could not reify it completely, as a master could, so that it would appear to hang in the air before him, twisting and rotating to display its maze of lines and spheres. But he could recall large parts of it, all of the major Landscapes, most of the first–order Situations and more than a few of the significant Events.

The more he thought of it, the clearer grew his recollection of the map. He saw connections and linkages from this Event to a Landscape and from there to a Location from which he knew three paths radiated. In his mind's eye he could plot a route that would let him navigate to the test's final Location, a prototypical island paradise, where Eldred waited for the candidates to arrive.

It was just possible that Bandar could indeed find his way home. Better yet, he was fairly sure that some of the sites through which he would travel had advantageous temporal dimensions: the alternate route, though it required more steps, might actually be traversed in less objective time than the course the tutors had set.

The merchant had gurgled out his last bloody breath. The alley lay empty. Bandar made up his mind to try the long way home. Perhaps his resourcefulness would so impress the examiners that they would overlook his failure to follow the prescribed course. At the worst, if hopelessly stuck, he could exit through open an emergency gate.

He risks nothing who has lost all, he told himself. Singing the thran, he returned to the processional way and followed it past the burning royal palace to the city's shattered gates. Dead defenders were piled high and he had to climb a rampart of bodies to reach the wooden bridge that spanned the canal.

A little beyond was a stand of date trees. A single attacker, pinned to a trunk by an arrow through his shoulder, weakly struggled to work the head free of the wood. His eyes widened when Bandar ceased intoning the insulating thran and suddenly appeared before him.

"Have you come to help me?" the soldier said, indicating the shaft through his flesh. "You do not resemble the god I prayed to."

"No," said Bandar. It was unwise to feel emotions, critical or supportive, in response to the idiomatic entities. They were not, after all, real people; they were more like characters in stories, no more than a collection of necessary attributes. The wounded soldier was probably a version of Unrequited Faith; to pull the arrow free would contradict his role in the Event and could cause the entity to act disharmoniously.

Bandar faced the space between two of the date palms and sang five notes. A wavering vertical fissure divided the air. He stepped through.

A gust of wind threw stinging sleet into his face. He was in a world of black and white and gray, standing on glacial scree that sloped down from a bare ridge above and behind him. The closest thing to color was the dark blue of mountains whose lower slopes were visible beyond the ridge until they rose to disappear above the leaden overcast from which the sleet was flying. If the wet clouds dispersed they would reveal no peaks; the tops of the mountains were buried in unbroken ice all the way to the pole.

Downslope, a cold, wet plain of lichen and coarse grass extended to a line of horizon that was largely invisible behind the showers of freezing rain. Far out he saw a mass of reindeer and the humped shapes of mammoths, identifiable by their peculiar bobbing gait. Closer, a ring of musk oxen turned curved horns toward a short–muzzled bear that circled the herd on long legs.

Good, thought Bandar. He recognized the scene. He had visited this Location before though not at these precise coordinates. Still, the connecting node that would admit him to the next site was near, in a narrow cave set back from a ledge that must be farther up the ridge. He strove to remember how the view before him had looked from that previous vantage. He had definitely been higher up and somewhere off to his right.

The experienced noönaut developed a feel for these things. Though he could not call himself experienced, Bandar could perform the exercise that enhanced his sense of direction. After a moment, he experienced a tiny inclination to go to his right. He let his will yield to it and the predilection grew stronger.

That's that, he told himself and turned in the direction. A motion from the corner of his eye caught his attention. The snub–faced bear was loping toward him across the flatland, broad paws flicking up spray from the wet lichen. It was almost to the bottom of the slope.

Bandar swiftly sang the thran of nine and three notes which had sequestered him in the sacked city. The bear's pace did not slacken and its small black eyes remained fixed upon him. Quickly, the noönaut intoned the seven and four, the second most common insulating thran.

The bear reached the base of the scree and began to climb. He could see its condensed breath smoking from its gaping mouth, its lolling tongue bright pink against its brown fur.

There were three other thrans Bandar could try. He suspect-ed now that the oldest and simplest of them, the four and two, would insulate him from the idiomatic bear's perceptions. But if he was wrong, there would not be time to determine which of the other two would work. The bear had increased its speed, ears flattened against its broad head. It would be on him in seconds.

Bandar sang five tones and the air rippled behind him. He flung himself through the gap and tumbled to the ground in the date grove. The Event was still unwinding and the wounded soldier remained pinned to his tree. The man blinked at him but Bandar counted slowly to ten then sang the five tones once more. He stepped through the fissure.

As he had expected, much more time had passed in the ice world and it had recycled. The Landscape was as it had been the first time he had stood on the slope, the bear stalking the musk oxen out on the plain. Bandar saw it become aware of him, saw it turn toward him and take its first step. He sang the four and two; instantly the predator turned back to the herd.

Chanting the tones, the noönaut faced about and began to climb. The loose gravel rattled out from under each footstep, so that he slid back half a pace for each one he took. The icy rain assaulted the weather side of his face and neck and his extremities were numb. Bandar paused and, continuing the thran, applied another of the adept's exercises: thick garments grew to replace the nondescript garb in which he had imagined himself when he entered the noö-sphere. Warm mittens and heavy boots covered his hands and feet and a fur–lined hood encased his head. For good measure, he imagined himself a staff. The climbing went better after that.

The top of the ridge was broad and only slightly curved. He made good time with the wind at his back and within a few minutes he saw the ledge jutting out of the scree. But when he scrabbled down from the ridgetop he was surprised to find several fissures and cracks in the rock.

He turned and looked out at the plain again. He was sure this was the spot his tutor had brought them to, but the class had been warned not to venture out of the recess, presumably because of the bear. They had only looked out through the narrow opening, to fix the scene in memory, then attended as the tutor had revealed the two nodes and sung the thran that activated both.

Bandar looked into the first fissure and rejected it as too scant in both width and height. The second was no better. The third looked promising, however. The opening was the right height and the darkness beyond promised that the cave was also deep enough. Throwing back his hood, he stepped within.

The gates would be to his right, and Bandar turned that way. Thus he did not at first notice the bulky shape squatting in the rear of the cavern holding her sausage–fingered hands to the tiny warmth of a grease lamp burning in the severed cranium of a cave bear's skull. He drew breath to sing the four and two but before a sound could emerge a noose of plaited rawhide dropped over his head and constricted his throat.

The Commons was the distillation of all human experience, everything that had ever been important to humankind, indi-vidually or collectively, since the dawntime. It was the composite memory of the species, the realm of the archetypes. Some were of great moment, battles and disasters; some were the small but vital elements of a full life, the loss of virginity, the birth of a child; some were simply landscapes—deserts, sea coasts, lush valleys, ice age barrens—against which generation upon generation of humans had measured their existence.

The elements of the noösphere were formed by aggregation. An event happened, and the person to whom it happened remembered it. That individual memory was the smallest particle of the noösphere, called by scholars an engrammatic cell. On its own, a single cell drifted away on the currents of the Commons and was lost.

But when the same event—or even closely similar events—happened to a multitude the individual cells were so alike that they cohered and joined, drawing vitality from each other, and forming a corpuscle. As a corpuscle grew it became more potent, more active, even to the extent of absorbing other similar corpuscles. Enough such adhesions and corpuscles aggregated into archetypal entities, permanent features of the collective unconscious. They took up specific Locations in the Commons.

Events, Situations and Landscapes were not precise nor accurate records. Rather they were composite impressions of what similar happenings had *meant* to those to whom they happened. They included every horrid crime and tragic defeat, every joy and triumph of the human experience, real or imagined, each distilled to its essence and compounded.

And all of those essential Events, Situations and Landscapes were peopled by appropriate idiomatic entities, like the mammoths on the sleet–swept plain, the tortured merchant in the burning city, and the immensely fat female cave dweller whose piglike eyes now regarded Guth Bandar from the rear of the cave, while whoever was behind him jerked the noose, leaving him dancing on tip–toe, struggling to breathe.

The fat one grunted something and another figure appeared from behind her bulk. This one was as lean and dried as the rawhide that constricted Bandar's throat, with a face that was collapsed in on itself and wrinkled up like dried fruit, framed by thin white hair clotted together by rancid oils. She poked a wisp of wool into the grease lamp to make a second wick then lifted the skullcap and crossed the cave to hold it before Bandar's face.

She peered at him from rheumy eyes, toothless gums working and lips smacking loudly. Then the hand that was not encumbered by the lamp reached under his parka and worked its way into his leggings. She seized parts of Bandar that he would have rather she had left untouched, weighing them in her dry, hard palm. Then she made a noise in her throat that expressed disappointment coupled to resignation and spoke to the unseen strangler behind him.

"Ready him."

The noose about his throat loosened but before Bandar could gain enough breath to sing the thran a hood of grimy leather descended over his head. The noose was slipped up over the ill–smelling hide until it came level with his mouth. Then it was cinched tight again, gagging him. He tried to intone the thran but could not produce enough volume. Meanwhile, his hands were bound together behind him.

There were eye holes in the hood and a slit where his nose protruded, allowing him to breathe. He felt a weight on his head and realized that the headgear supported a pair of antlers.

The strong one who had held him from behind now stepped into view and he saw that she too was female, though young and muscular, with a mane of tawny hair and a face that mingled beauty with brute power.

She moved lithely to hitch a hide curtain to a wooden frame around the cave's mouth, closing out the light and the cold air that flowed in like liquid from the tundra. The old one was dipping more wicks of what was probably mammoth wool into the grease lamp, creating a yellowy glow on the walls while the fat one began to strip off her furs and leathers.

It was an ancient maxim at the Institute that a little learning made a perilous possession. Bandar realized that aphorism defined his predicament. He had been brought to this Location once before, but barely long enough to fix the place in his memory. He had misjudged its category.

When they had briefly visited an adjacent cave the tutor's sole concern had been to display the nodes that coincided there. He had not explained the Location's nature and when Bandar had looked out at the tundra he had thought that they were briefly passing through a mere Landscape; instead, it was now clear that this was a Situation.

In the dawntime, there had been an archetypal tale of three women—one young, one old, one in the prime of life—living in some remote spot. Questers came to them, seeking wisdom and always paying an uncomfortable price. In later ages the Situation had evolved into bawdy jokes about farmers' daughters or poetic tropes about dancing graces. But here was the raw base, rooted deep in humankind's darkest earth. Bandar had no doubt that the final outcome of this Situation, as with so many others, was blood and death.

The grease fire was warming the cave as the crone and the girl efficiently rendered Bandar naked. The matron, now also uncovered, grunted and sprawled back on the pile of furs, giving Bandar more than an inkling of the first installment of the price he must pay.

The young one took a gobbet of the grease that fed the lamp and warmed it between her hands before applying it to the part of Bandar that the crone had weighed and found merely adequate. Despite Bandar's disinclination to participate, her ministrations began to have an effect.

Bandar realized that he was in danger of being pulled into this Situation, deeply and perhaps irrevocably. The longer one stayed in a particular place and interacted with its elements, the more its "reality" grew and the more integrated with it the sojourner could become. The speed of the effect was heightened if the noönaut abstained from intoning thrans or if he adopted a passive attitude.

The old hag was shaking a bone rattle and grunting a salacious chant about a stag and a doe. Meanwhile, the young one had finished greasing him and was surveying the result with a critical eye. Bandar looked down and saw that his virtual body was behaving as if it were real flesh. It was a worrisome sign.

Act, do not react was the rule in such a predicament. But outnumbered, bound and gagged, he had few options for setting the agenda. He mentally cast about for inspiration and found it in the expression on the face of the youngest of the three cave dwellers. She was regarding what was now Bandar's most prominent feature in a manner that more than hinted at disappointment.

Her look gave the noönaut a desperate idea: if it was possible to grow winter clothing and to create a staff from nothing, might he likewise be able to change the proportions of his own shape?. His tutors had never spoken of such a thing, but necessity was a sharp spur. If it was possible for Bandar to increase the dimensions of his most intimate equipment, he might improve his position.

While the young one reapplied herself to his lubrication, Bandar employed the adept's exercises that had protected him against sleet and slippery footing, although now with a more personal focus. After a few moments he heard the rattle and chant stop. The crone was staring, open mouthed, and the tawny haired one was blinking with surprise. Bandar looked down and saw that his efforts had been more successful than intended. What had before been merely presentable was now grown prodigious.

"That will need more grease," the old woman cackled. The young one agreed and scooped up a double handful.

When he was thoroughly lubricated, they manhandled him over to where the fat one lay in expectation. He was forced first to kneel between her enormous splayed thighs then to lie prone upon the mountainous belly. The crone took hold of his new–grown immensity and guided him until connections were established, which brought first a grunt of surprise from the matron then other noises as the young one placed a cold, calloused foot on Bandar's buttocks and rhythmically impelled him to his labors.

The woman beneath him began to thrash about, making sounds that put Bandar in mind of a large musical owl. For his part, he concentrated on mental exercises that placed a certain distance between his awareness and his virtual body, lest he become too involved in the activity and find himself on a slippery slope into full absorption.

Seize the process or be seized by it, he remembered a tutor saying. The Commons was an arena rife with conflict, where will was paramount. To control his place in a Location, the uninsulated noönaut must be the dominant actor, not one of the supporting cast. *How can I amplify my impact?* he asked himself, rejecting any further increase in size—he might damage the matron.

The idea, when it came, seemed unlikely to succeed. Still, he had heard that women could grow fond of certain devices used for intimate achievements. Bandar summoned his conviction and focused his attention on effecting the change. Within seconds a new sound rose above the matron's musical hoots: a deep thrumming and throbbing which he could clearly hear despite the fact that its source was buried in the mounds of flesh beneath him.

The matron now began to issue throaty moans with a counter–point of high–pitched keening. She thrashed about with an energy that might have propelled Bandar from her if the young one hadn't continued to press down with her pumping foot. At last the heaves and flings culminated in a final paroxysm and Bandar heard a long and satiated sigh, followed almost at once by a rumbling snore.

Immediately, the other two hauled the noönaut from the matron's crevice and flung him down on his back, the vibrating immensity buzzing and humming above his belly. There was a brief tussle between youth and old age, quickly decided by the former's strength despite the latter's viciousness and guile.

The tawny–haired woman straddled Bandar and seized his conspicuous attribute. As she lowered herself onto it her eyes and mouth widened and tremors afflicted her belly and the long muscles of her thighs. Then she leaned forward, placed her palms on his shoulders and set to work.

Bandar saw the crone peering over the young one's shoulder with an expression that sent a chill of apprehension through him. Ritual slaughter might not be the worst fate he would suffer. He resolved to exert himself.

He reasoned that the same exercises that had enlarged some parts of him must make others shrink. While the young female lathered herself to a fine foaming frenzy above him, Bandar focused his attention on his still bound hands. In a moment he felt them dwindle until they were the size of a doll's. The rawhide thongs slipped off.

The young woman was quicker to reach the heights than her older cavemate but stayed there longer. Bandar bided his time. Finally, she emitted a long and thoughtful moan and collapsed onto the noönaut's chest. The old woman wasted no time but avidly seized the incumbent at hip and shoulder and rolled her free of Bandar. She stepped over him and prepared to impale herself.

Bandar bent himself at knee and hip to put his feet in the crone's belly, then launched her up and away. As she squawked in pain and outrage, he sprang to his feet and made straight for the hide that hid the exit.

His tiny hands gave him trouble, but when a glance behind showed his two conquests sitting up and the hag reaching for a long black shard of razor–edged flint he put an arm between wood and leather and tore the covering away.

The sleet slashed at him. The bare ledge was slick with freezing rain. There was another cave a short dash along the ledge—it looked to be the right one—and he half–ran, half–slid toward it, the antler–topped mask bobbing on his head and his still enormous and buzzing bowsprit pointing the way.

As he went he tried to loosen the cord that pressed the mask into his mouth, but his puny hands hindered him. Yet he must free himself of the mask to chant the thran that opened the gate in the next cave or be caught by the pursuing women.

He decided to shrink his head. There was no time for refinement and he did not try to specify the degree to which his skull must diminish; he could put things to rights later.

As he ran he felt the mask loosen, then the cord dropped loose around his neck as the dimensions of his jaw diminished. He tossed his chin up and the antlered hood flew backwards. From behind him he heard a grunt and a curse and a clatter. Someone had tripped over it and they had all fallen.

Bandar did not look back but threw himself into the new cave, which he was relieved to see was empty. He recognized it now, though he could not recall whether the gate he sought was to left or right.

If he had time, his memory or his noönaut's acquired sense of direction would tell him which to choose. But there was no time. He could not even intone the four and two thran and remove himself from his pursuers' purview: having spent so long uncloaked in this Situation and so closely involved with its idiomats, he could not hide himself completely.

The moment he entered the cave he chanted the opening thran. Nothing happened. Then the cave darkened as the doorway behind him filled with murderous females. Bandar had no time to work out why the thran had not succeeded. Fortunately, the answer came before full panic set in: he had sung the notes through vocal equipment that was markedly smaller than his regular issue; just as a miniature horn plays a higher note, his shrunken larynx and throat had thrust the thran into a higher register. Thrans had to be exactly the right pitch.

Bandar adjusted for scale and sang the notes again, and was rewarded with two ripples in the air. Arbitrarily he chose the one to his left and leapt through as the young cavewoman's nails sank into his shoulder.

He emerged into Heaven. All was perfection: verdant meadows with grass soft as velvet and dotted with flowers of exquisite filigree; groves of stately trees, each impeccable in composition and form; skies as clear and blue as an infant's gaze; and air as sweet as a goddess's breath.

The rift through which he had come closed behind him and Bandar stood a moment, a tiny hand to his breast as his fear ebbed away. At once he knew that he had taken the wrong gate—he should now be alone on a mountaintop from which he could have segued to the destination island.

He could retrace his route. The cavewomen's Situation would soon recycle. But first he should restore his body parts to their proper proportions and reclothe himself. He needed to make tones of the right pitch, and it would not do to encounter the Senior Tutor while stark naked and presenting the humming enormity that dominated his ventral view.

He looked carefully around. He was standing under some trees. There were no idiomatic entities in view and Heaven was usually a tranquil Location. But just to be safe he decided to move deeper into cover. He ducked to pass under the lower branches of a flawless flowering tree, the perfume of its blossoms at close range making his head swim. With each step the touch of the grass against his bare feet was a caress.

A very sensuous Heaven, he thought, and resolved to explore it more thoroughly when he was received into the Institute as a full fellow. Perhaps he would make a special study of such Locations; it would be pleasant work.

Secluded among the scent–laden trees, he concentrated on a mental image of his own head and performed the appropriate exercises for what he judged to be sufficient time. But when he raised his miniature hands to examine the results he discovered that his skull had remained tiny while his ears and nose had grown far beyond normal; indeed they were now as out of harmony with nature as the buzzing, vibrating tower that rose from his lower belly.

If I could see what I am doing, it would make the work much easier, Bandar reasoned. The setting seemed too arcadian for an actual mirror, but the noönaut heard the gentle tinkling of water nearby. *A still pool would do,* he thought.

He followed the sound deeper into the grove and came to a clearing where a bubbling spring welled up to form a pool of limpid clarity. He knelt and gazed into the gently rippling water. The image of his shrunken face, albeit now centered by a trunk–like proboscis and framed by a pair of sail–like ears, looked back at him with grave concern. He began the exercises anew.

"Bless you," said a mellow voice behind him. Bandar swung around to find a sprightly old man with the face of a cherub beaming down on him from under a high and ornate miter that was surrounded by a disk of golden light. The saint was dressed in ecclesiastical robes of brilliant white with arcane symbols woven in gold and silver thread. In his hand was a stout staff topped by a great faceted jewel.

"Thank you," said Bandar. "I'll be but a moment."

But as he spoke he saw the man's beatific expression mutate sharply to a look of horror succeeded by a mask of righteous outrage. Faster than Bandar would have credited, the jewel–topped staff rotated in the hierophant's hand so that it could be thrust against the noönaut's chest, and he was toppled into the crystal water.

"Glub," said Bandar as he passed below the surface. When he struggled back to the air he saw the old man looming over him, the staff set to do fresh mayhem. He had time to hear the idiomat cry out, "Enemy! An enemy is here!" before the gem struck Bandar solidly on his tiny cranium and drove him under again.

Bandar wondered if it was possible to drown in the Commons. He elected not to find out and kicked off toward the other side of the pool, swimming under the surface.

The throbbing queller of cavewomen was not diminished by the cold water. Indeed it tended to dig into the soft bottom of the pool so that he had to swim closer to the surface. But his action took him out of range of the staff and in moments he had hauled himself free of the water. The idiomatic saint was circling the pool, clearly intent on doing more damage, all the while bellowing alarms.

Bandar fled for the trees, but as he ran he heard the rush of very large wings. Casting a look over his shoulder, he saw a vast and shining figure passing through the air above the grove. The long bladed sword in its grasp was wreathed in flame and the look on its perfectly formed features bespoke holy violence.

Bandar fell to his knees and opened his mouth. The four and two would not work here, he was sure. And he doubted the nine and three would be efficacious. Given how his fortunes had fared today, it would be the three threes. This was the most difficult sequence of tones, even when the chanter was not possessed of mouse–sized vocal equipment absurdly coupled to an elephantine nasal amplification box, while distracted by vibrations from below and the threat of incineration from above.

His alternatives rapidly dwindling, the noönaut frantically adjusted his vocalizations to find the exact pitch. At least the giant ears assisted in letting him hear exactly how he sounded. The sight of the descending winged avenger lent urgency to his efforts and in moments he struck the right tones. He sang the three threes and saw the terrible beauty of the angel's face lose its intensity of focus. The wings spread wide to check its ascent; it wheeled and flew off, its flaming sword hissing.

The staff–wielding hierophant stood on the other side of the bubbling pool, scratching his head and wearing an expression like that of a man who has walked into a room and cannot remember what he came for. Then he turned and went back the way he had come.

The gate back to the ice–world was too close to where the saint was keeping his vigil. Bandar did not fancy hunting for it and standing exposed while seeking the right pitch for the opening thran, with hard–tipped staffs and flaming swords in the offing. He would find another gate and take his chances.

Chanting the three threes, he went out onto the luxurious lawn again but now its caressing touch mocked his dismay. He saw above the distant horizon a squadron of winged beings on combat patrol. In another direction was a walled citadel, giant figures watching from its ramparts, a glowing symbol hovering in the sky over the heads.

There could be no doubt: he had passed into one of those Heavens that offered no happy–ever–aftering; instead, here was an active Event—one of those paradises threatened by powers that piled mountains atop each other or crossed bridges formed of razors. In such a place an uninsulated sojourner would not long remain unnoticed. And neither side took prisoners.

If he stopped chanting the three threes, someone might launch a thunderbolt at him. Still, Bandar attempted the techniques that would restore his parts to their proper size. At the very least, he wished to be rid of the humming monstrosity connected to his groin; it slapped his chest when he walked and when he stood still it impinged upon his concentration.

But it was too difficult to maintain the complex chant through his distorted vocal equipment while attempting to rectify his parts. All Bandar could manage was to alter the color of the buzzing tower from its natural shade to a bright crimson. It did not seem a profitable change.

He abandoned the effort and concentrated instead on using his sense of direction to tell him where the next gate might be. In a moment an inkling came, but he was dismayed to recognize that the frailty of the signal meant that the node was a good way off.

Bandar set off in that direction, chanting the three threes, ears flapping from fore to aft and nose swaying from side to side, his chest slapped contrapuntally. After he had walked for some time he noticed that the signal was only marginally stronger; it would be some time before he reached its source.

While I was making alterations I should have doubled the length of my legs, he thought and scarcely had the idea struck him than he realized if he had had that inspiration in the sacked city he could have climbed onto the wall to open its gate and none of this would have been necessary.

The noönaut stopped and sat down. *I have been a fool,* he thought. *Didrick Gabbris deserves to win; he will fit this place far better than I ever could.* He felt his spirit deflate and resolved not to persist with the quest. He would open an emergency gate and leave the Commons.

But not here in the open, where someone might cast who knew what lethal missile in his direction. Without warning, in such a Location, an actual god might appear and unleash disasters that only an irate deity could conceive of.

Bandar rose and crossed quickly to the nearest copse of trees. Under their sheltering boughs he spied a troop of armored figures drawn up in a phalanx, the air above their head a blaze of gold from their commingled halos. Still chanting, he backed away.

He walked on, investigating one stand of trees after another, finding each under the eye of at least one brightly topped sentry. Several were peopled by whole battalions of holy warriors.

He would have to leave Heaven before he could find a safe place in which to call up an emergency exit. He wished he knew more about these Locations—his interests ran more toward the historical than the mythological—but he recalled that there was often a ladder or staircase connecting them to the world beneath. It was usually at the edge, sometimes wreathed in clouds.

He kept on until eventually he found himself descending a long, grassy slope which seemed to end in a precipice. Gingerly, he inched toward the edge. He would have crawled on hands and knees but his enormous red appendage hampered him.

Near the lip he looked out into empty air that was suffused with light from no discernible source. Far below, scattered clouds drifted idly, the gaps between them allowing glimpses of fields and forests beneath. Bandar shuffled closer to the edge to look almost directly down, hoping to see some means of descent but his view was hindered by the vibrating enormity. Finally he knelt and leaned forward.

There was something there, just beyond the last fringe of lush grass. He reached to move away the obscuring blades. Yes, that looked much like the top of a ladder.

"Ahah!" said Bandar, breaking off the thran to indulge in a moment of triumphant relief. Immediately, a scale covered hand appeared from beyond the rim, seized his wrist with claw–tipped fingers and yanked him over the precipice.

Bandar's squawk was cut off by a hot, calloused palm pressed against his mouth. There was a reek of sulfur and he was clutched by rock hard arms against an equally unyielding chest, then he heard a flap of leathery wings and felt his stomach lurch as the creature that held him dropped into empty space.

They spiraled downward, affording Bandar a panoramic view of what lay beneath Heaven. There was a ladder; indeed, there were many. But though their tops were set against the grassy lip from which he had been seized their bases were not grounded on the earth far below. Instead, they were footed on a vast expanse of stone paving that was the top of an impossibly colossal construction that rose, tier upon tier, to thrust up through the clouds and end just below the celestial realm.

The tower top was thronged by legions of blood red creatures, some winged, some not, but all armored in shining black chitin and clutching jagged–edged swords and hooked spears as they swarmed up the ladders.

As Bandar spun downwards he saw the topmost of the invaders being boosted onto the grass and heard the piercing sound of a horn. Then he and his captor descended into a cloud and for a time all was mist. They emerged to fly beneath an overcast, dropping ever lower toward a great rent in the earth from which foul clouds and odors emerged, as well as more marching legions of imps, demons and assorted fiends, all bound for the great tower.

The demon that held Bandar lifted its wings like a diving pigeon and plummeted into the reeking chasm. A choking darkness closed the noönaut's eyes and nose but he sensed that they fell a long, long way.

"In a moment, my servant will remove his hand from your mouth," said the occupant of the black iron throne. "If you attempt to say the name of You Know Whom,"—one elongated finger directed its pointed tip at the roof of the vast underground cavern—"you will utter no more than the first syllable before your tongue is pulled out, sliced into manageable pieces and fed back to you. Are we clear?"

Bandar looked into the darkness of the speaker's eyes, which seemed to contain only impossibly distended pupils. He wished he could look away but he was by now too far acclimated to this Location, and the Adversary's powers gripped him the way a snake's unwavering gaze would hold a mouse.

He nodded and the palm went away. The other's upraised finger now reflectively stroked an aquiline jaw, its progress ending in a short triangular beard as black as the eyes above it. "What are you?" said the voice, as cool as silk.

Bandar wished he'd studied more about the Heavens and Hells, but he had always been more compelled by Authentics than by Allegoricals. He knew, however, that within their Locations deities and their equivalents had all the powers with which their real–world believers credited them. So, in this context, he faced an authentic Principal of evil—or at least of unbridled ambition—that had all the necessary resources, both intellectual and occult, to battle an omnipotent deity to at least a stalemate. Bandar, who could not outargue Didrick Gabbris, was not a contender.

The sulfur made him cough. Finally, he managed to say, "A traveler, a mere visitor."

The triangular face nodded. "You must be. You're not one of mine and,"—the fathomless eyes dropped to focus briefly on Bandar's vibrating wonderment—"you're certainly not one of His. But what else are you?"

Every Institute apprentice learned in First Week that the concept of thrans had originated in a dawntime myth about an ancient odist whose songs had kept him safe on a quest into the underworld. This knowledge gave Bandar hope as he said, "I am also a singer of songs. Would you care to hear one?"

The Adversary considered the question while Bandar attempted to control his expression. The distant gate he had sensed in Heaven was but a few paces across the cavern. He had only to voice the right notes, perhaps while strolling minstrel–like about the space before the throne, to call the rift into existence and escape through it.

"Why would you want to sing me a song?" said the Adversary.

"Oh, I don't know," said Bandar and was horrified to see the words take solid form as they left his mouth. They tumbled to the smoldering floor to assemble themselves into a wriggling bundle of legs and segmented body parts that scuttled toward the figure on the throne, climbed his black robes and nestled into the diabolical lap. The Principal idly stroked it with one languid hand, as if it were a favored pet.

"All lies are mine, of course," the soft voice said, "and I gave you no leave to use what is mine." He nodded to the winged fiend that still stood behind Bandar and the noönaut felt a icy pain as the thing inserted a claw into a sensitive part and scratched at the virtual flesh.

"Now," said the Adversary, when Bandar had ceased bleating and hopping, "the truth. What are you, why did you come here and, most urgent of all, how did you contrive to enter His realm behind His defenses?"

"If I tell you, may I go on my way?"

"Perhaps. But you *will* tell me. Ordinarily, I would enjoy having it pulled out of you piece by dripping piece, but today there is a certain urgency."

"Very well," Bandar said, "though the truth may not please you." And he told all of it—thrans, Locations, examinations, Gabbris, the smashed amphora—wondering as he did so what the repercussions might be. It was no great matter if the odd idiomat saw a sojourner pass by; but Bandar had never heard of an instance where a Principal was brought face to face with the unreality of all that he took to be real.

At the very least, the Institute would be displeased with Apprentice Guth Bandar. Yet, whatever punishment Senior Tutor might levy, Bandar could not imagine that it would be a worse fate than being absorbed into a Hell. Chastising malefactors, after all, was what such Locations did best.

When the noönaut had finished, the listener on the throne was silent for a long moment, stroking his concave cheek with a triangular nail, the great dark eyes turned inward. Finally he laid a considering gaze on Bandar and said, "Is that all? You've left out no pertinent details that might construe a trap for a hapless idiomatic entity such as I?"

Bandar had thought about trying to do exactly that, but had not been able to conceive of a means. Besides, he had expected this question and knew that any lie he attempted would only scamper off to its master, leaving Bandar to re–experience the demon's intruding claw, if not something worse.

"It is all."

The Adversary stroked at his beard. "You can imagine that this news comes as a shock."

"Yes."

"Even a disappointment."

"I express sympathy." It wasn't a lie. Bandar could express the sentiment without actually feeling it.

"It repeats forever? And I never win," he indicated the cavern's ceiling again, "against You Know Whom?"

"Never."

"What would you advise?" the archfiend asked, then added, "Honestly."

Bandar thought it through but could come to no other conclusion. "You must be true to your nature."

The archfiend sighed. "That I already knew." He reflected for a moment then went on, "It ought to be comforting to know exactly why one exists. Instead I find it depressing."

A silence ensued. Bandar became uncomfortable. "I can offer one solace," he said.

The dark eyes looked at him. "It had better be exceptionally good. I usually need to see a great deal of suffering before I am comforted."

Bandar swallowed again and said, "When your Location's cycle ends and recommences, you will not know of this."

"Hmm," said the other. "Thin comfort indeed. Knowledgeability is my foremost pride. To know that I shall become ignorant is a poor consolation until ignorance at last descends. The battle up there may go on for eons. I must think about this."

Bandar said nothing and attempted to arrange his mismatched features into an expression of studied neutrality. He saw thoughts making their presence known on the Adversary's features, then he saw his captor's gaze harden and knew the archfiend had come to the inevitable conclusion.

The voice was not just cool now; it was chilled. "I see. If I keep you and make you part of this 'Location,' as you call it, then might I expect you to regularly reappear and remind me that I am not what I thought I was?"

"I do not know how much of my persona would survive the process, but there is a risk," said Bandar. "I would be happy to relieve you of it by moving on."

"Hmm," said the other. "But someone must suffer for my pain. If not you, then who?"

Bandar looked around the smoky cavern. All the demons and imps seemed to be regarding him without sympathy.

He thought quickly, then said, "I may have an idea."

Intoning the three threes, Bandar scaled the ladder that reached to the brink of Heaven. The first assault had failed and the invaders had pulled back, leaving mangled fiends and demons heaped on the tower's top and scattered about the narrow strip of celestial turf that marked the limit of their advance.

Angels of lower rank were now heaving the fallen over the edge and casting down the scaling ladders so that Bandar had to climb with scampering haste to avoid being toppled. He picked his way across the grass, stepping over bodies and dodging the clean–up. There was a sharp tang of ozone to the otherwise delicious air of Heaven; an inner voice told him it was the afterscent of thunderbolts.

No one paid him any notice as he made his way between regiments of angelic defenders, drawn up in precise blocks and wedges, their armor and weaponry dazzling and the space above their heads almost conflagrant with massed halos. But beyond the rearmost ranks he saw others laid upon the grass, their auras flickering and dim, shattered armor piled beside them.

As he neared the recumbent forms he heard again the whoosh of great wings. Huge figures gracefully alit and gathered up the fallen angels then took to the air and winged away. Urged by his inner voice, Bandar ran toward the evacuation and, seizing the robe of an archangel, climbed to the broad span between his wings. His tiny fists made it hard to hold on as the great pinions struck the air and they sprang aloft.

So far, so good, said the voice. Bandar was too busy clutching and intoning to frame a response. They climbed above the fields and woods of heaven, until the great rivers were mere scratches of silver on green. For a long time, the archangel's wings dominated the air with metronomic strokes then the rhythm ceased and the great feathered sails held steady as they glided down toward a city of shining stone upon a conical hill, with serried roofs and pillars and windows that flashed like gems. The archangel alighted on a pristine pavement and carried the angel in his arms toward a vast edifice of marble and alabaster.

Down, said the inner voice, and Bandar descended, clutching handfuls of angelic fabric until his feet touched the polished flags. *Turn right and go up the hill. There's a staircase.*

Bandar wanted to say, "This is unwise," but he was afraid that to cease intoning the thran in this part of the Location would invite a blast from on high. He topped the staircase and came upon a broad plaza of more white stone accented by inlays of colored gems. On the other side of the square stood an enormous rotunda—yet more white stone, though this one was roofed with a golden dome. Its gigantic doors—still more gold, bedizened with mosaics of gems— gaped open, throwing out an effulgence of light and a glorious sound of massed voices.

Here we go, said the inner urging. Bandar advanced on trembling legs until he stood in the doorway. The interior was incandescent with magnificence. Rank upon rank of angels stood on wall–climbing terraces, singing unparalleled choruses to the great white–bearded figure who sat a diamond throne that grew from the middle of a diamond floor.

In, said the voice in Bandar's mind, *and keep chanting.* The noönaut's legs could not have felt looser if they had been made of boiled asparagus, but he did as he was told, crossing the brilliant floor until he stood directly before the throne. Its occupant's feet rested on a footstool that resembled a globe of the earth, just at Bandar's eye level. He noticed that the bare toes bore delicate hairs of gold.

The sojourner stood, awaiting direction from within. It was hard to keep intoning the thran while the thousands of perfect voices sang in flawless harmony a song that thrilled the soul.

It's always the same song, you know, said his passenger. *He never tires of hearing it, and they know better than to tire of singing it.*

The music was climbing, crescendo upon crescendo, ravishing notes impossibly achieved and sustained, quavering tremolos that intoxicated the senses. It was all Bandar could do to keep intoning the three threes, especially with his distorted vocal equipment and the difficulty compounded by the sharpness of hearing that his elephantine ears provided.

Wait for it.

The thunderous chorus was now pealing out such a paean of praise that Bandar feared the golden dome might lift away.

Almost.

The voices soared to the brink of climax.

Now.

Bandar ceased intoning the thran. From the point of view of the idiomats, including the Principal on the throne, he suddenly appeared before them, with all his acquired anatomical peculiarities on full display.

The music stopped in mid–melisma. There was an instant silence so profound that Bandar wondered for a moment if he had been struck deaf. Then he heard the thrumming sound of the giant crimson monstrosity that still vibrated on his front.

Perfect, said the inner voice. *Open up, here I come.*

Bandar opened his mouth. He felt the same unpleasant sensation of stretching and an urge to gag that he had experienced when the Adversary had entered him down in the sulfurous cavern. A moment later the sinister figure was standing beside him, looking up at the divine face staring down at him from the throne of Heaven.

The archfiend raised his arms and cried, "Surprise!"

"It's always much easier to get out of Heaven than to get in," commented the Adversary, as they plummeted toward the lake of fire. When the heat grew uncomfortable for Bandar, the archfiend considerately sprouted wings—much like an archangel's though somber of feather—and swept the noönaut to safety in a subterranean passageway that led back to the cavern of the iron throne.

"Are you going to keep your promise?" said Bandar.

"Ordinarily, I wouldn't," said the Principal, "but I don't want you popping up in every cycle to remind me of my futility."

"Thank you," Bandar said.

"Although it goes against my nature to be fair, you do deserve any reward in my power to grant." The dark eyes unfocused for a moment as their owner looked inward to memory. "The expression on His face. The way His eyes popped. That was worth anything. I will keep the war going as long as possible just so I can retain that image."

"I will be happy to accept what we discussed," Bandar said.

"Very well." The Adversary looked at him. "It is done."

Bandar consulted his own memory and found there a complete chart of the noösphere, exactly like the great globe suspended in the Institute's communal study chamber. Or was it?

"Is it real?" he asked.

"I have no idea," said the archfiend. "Since your arrival my concept of reality has been severely edited. I used my powers to improve your memory. I can assure you, however, that it will lead you away from here, I hope forever. I do not want you back." His long fingers imitated the action of walking. "Off you go."

Bandar consulted the globe and saw that the gate in the cavern led to a selection of Locations, depending on which thran was used to activate it. He returned the map to his memory, chose the seven and one and stepped through the rift.

He was overjoyed to find himself in a shaded forest of giant conifers. He recognized a particular tree not more than a few paces distant, strode to it and sang a handful of notes. Again the air rippled and he departed the forest to emerge into hot sunlight on a white beach strung between laden coconut palms and gentle wavelets.

"I have overcome!" he cried.

"You have certainly achieved some sort of distinction," said the nasal voice of Didrick Gabbris. Bandar turned to meet his rival's sneer. Gabbris lounged in the shade of a palm. Beside him, Senior Tutor Eldred inspected Bandar in detail, from the tiny skull with its flapping ears and pendulous nose down to the minuscule hands and the crimson humming centerpiece. When he had finished the catalog, his face formed an expression that Bandar found uncannily like that which he had recently seen on a deity.

"I can explain," the apprentice said.

"Not well enough," predicted Eldred.

It was a prescient observation. The Institute decided that Guth Bandar was not what they were seeking in a new generation of noönauts. Nor was Didrick Gabbris, for Bandar's account of the shattered urn was believed and he had the compensatory satisfaction of seeing his enemy driven from the cloister while he was still being debriefed by a hastily convened inquiry.

Bandar learned that in the tens of thousands of years that noönauts had been visiting the Commons other sojourners had run afoul of Principals, though no one it seemed had ever shaken the confidence of both a god and his chief opponent. it was decided that the contaminated Locations would be declared out of bounds for a few centuries, to give them time to recycle.

Bandar returned to the family firm and took up buying

and selling. But in his leisure hours he would sit crosslegged, and summon up his perfect map of the noösphere. He soon found a Allegorical Location entirely peopled by nubile young women. And with his ability to make useful modifications to his virtual anatomy, the idiomats were always delighted to receive him.

He decided that a little learning was only dangerous when spread too thin.

Inner Huff

By covering his ears tightly with his palms, Guth Bandar was able to listen to the songs of the Loreleis in various Situations without becoming entranced. That was good, because to be captivated by the heart–tearing beauty of the voices would mean being trapped forever in one of the myriad byways of the collective unconscious—the Commons, as it was called by the fellows of the Institute for Historical Inquiry, of which Bandar had become an adjunct scholar.

Today he was collecting his seventh siren song, this one from a little–visited Location where the singers were concealed behind a prototypical waterfall. The water sprang from a crevice in a cliff that soared above a darkly silent forest of ancient hardwoods. It fell as a sun–sparkled curtain into a limpid pool where a rainbow perpetually shimmered over the splash of foam. The song of the unseen Loreleis interwove seamlessly with the sound of the water. The combination of natural and magic sounds was a unique iteration of the siren motif and Bandar was determined to capture and reproduce the effect.

He had entered the Location a short distance away, arriving through a node that delivered him to the foot of a spreading chestnut tree. Upon arrival he had immediately sung the appropriate sequence of tones that insulated him from the perceptions of any of the Location's inhabitants.

The most likely idiomatic entity inhabiting this corner of the Commons, apart from the Loreleis, would have been a tragic Hero drawn to his doom by the siren song, perhaps companioned by a hapless Helper or a Faithful Beast. Bandar had searched the immediate forest but found none such. Their absence argued for his having arrived at a point in the Situation's cycle where the song–ensorceled entities had already been drawn into the pool and romantically drowned.

He ceased intoning the insulating thran and immediately the mingled sounds of cataract and female singers came drifting through the trees. At this distance the song was indistinct but its appeal was strong; before he knew it, he had already taken an involuntary step toward its source and was even now taking a second.

Bandar clapped hands over ears and the sound was shut out. His uplifted foot, about to complete the next step, paused in mid–stride. He stood still. Slowly, in the tiniest of increments, he eased the pressure of his palms against his ears. The faintest sound came to him and he experienced only a slight inclination to move toward it.

He took a step, knowingly this time, then made sure to stop before further lightening the pressure of his hands. The sound of the waterfall was more clear–cut, the female voices woven through its splash and chuckle. Bandar took two steps sideways. Now a substantial beech stood between him and the deadly glade. He leaned his head against the cool, smooth bark and eased his palms away from his ears.

The song insinuated itself, like a delicious itch, into his mind. Using an Institute technique, he fragmented his consciousness, letting part of him absorb the sound while another element of his awareness recited a sequence of syllables. The effect was to distance himself from the part of him that was aching to lift his forehead from the tree and race ecstatically toward the deadly pool.

The song's cycle was no more than three minutes long. Then the voices paused for a few heartbeats and began anew. Rigorously concentrating on the syllabic chant, Bandar let the recording function of his mind gather and hold the melody. He was careful not to compare it to the other six Lorelei songs he had already collected. It would not do to contaminate the sample.

After the second hearing he believed he had it. He broke off the syllabic sequence and again intoned the thran. Chanting, he turned and went farther into the forest. At a safe distance he called into existence the great globular map of the Commons that was the prize and glory of his memory. He consulted its intricate web of colored lines and points of intersection, then went a certain distance to his left.

Now Bandar sang a new collection of notes, three short rising tones followed by a long descender. A ripple appeared in the air before him and resolved itself into a vertical slit. He stepped through and emerged onto a stony beach set between the waves of a wine dark sea and a grove of ancient olive trees. Nearby was a clearing overgrown with wild grapes and berries.

He had scouted this Location a few days before and deduced that it was yet another version of the Desert Island. Remote and unpopulated earthly paradises were paradoxically popular in the Commons, bespeaking humankind's perennial desire to get away from one's fellows and the myriad demands of society.

A quiet place to sit and think was one of the island's attractions; the other was that it was but one node away from the eighth and final Lorelei Location, a rocky islet surrounded by crashing breakers. Again, drowning was the archetypical fate of those who fell beneath the singers' spell, but this one took its victims by the boatload.

Bandar went up the beach and into the grove, chanting a thran to hide himself from any idiomats; even a desert island might have an occupant, perhaps a visiting cannibal whose presence represented some archetypical fear of the Other. He poked about in the greenery but saw no traces of habitation, just a few goats and some pigs snuffling for fallen fruit beneath the olive trees.

He went back down the beach and sat on a flat rock, dabbling his feet in the cool water. He ceased chanting the thran and took up the exercise of the syllables again so that he could replay the waterfall song in his mind. Even with the prevention technique, there was a moment or two when he might have lost the necessary distance from the song's insistent beauty. But a fear of sitting enraptured in this spot, endlessly hearing the song until he was absorbed into the Location, helped him to remain unaffected.

He listened with critical attention and was pleased with what he heard. The seventh song in his collection was essentially the same as the other six, lending strong support to his thesis that the melody was itself an archetype: humanity's Song of songs from which all other airs and rhapsodies sprang.

If the eighth and final iteration of the Lorelei motif was the same as the other seven, Bandar would prepare a paper for presentation at the Institute's annual Great Colloquium, to be held a few days hence. He would argue, he believed convincingly, for the Song being recognized as a new archetype, the first to have been identified in millennia.

There would be opposition, of course, and it would be led by Underfellow Didrick Gabbris, Bandar's lifelong academic rival. Gabbris would cite the unchallenged truism of Old Earth's penultimate age that everything that could ever have been discovered had by now been found, identified, discussed with full annotation and for the most part forgotten. But not the Song of songs, Bandar knew. He had researched the matter thoroughly. He believed he was about to add something new and—he relished the pun—*unheard of* to the annals of the Institute.

Gabbris would grind his teeth in helpless rage. Bandar took a moment to envision the event. He enjoyed the images so much that he let them appear on the screen of his consciousness a second time, with minor embellishments.

A tiny sound interrupted his reverie, the *click* of stone against stone. Bandar rose from the rock on which he was seated and turned. A naked woman, lithe and small–breasted with raven hair and emerald eyes, had crept down the beach toward him. Her vulpine features were set in an expression of profound mischief and her hand held an olive wood staff. She was about to touch his shoulder with the carved head of a satyr that adorned the rod's tip.

Bandar could not step out of her reach; the flat rock pressed against the backs of his thighs. He opened his mouth to intone the four–and–two thran but before he could complete its opening tetrad the dark wood touched him.

His first impression was that she was somehow increasing in size, looming over him so that he found himself looking up at her from about the level of her thighs. He felt a growing strain in his neck. He was having to bend it back so that he might continue gazing at her face. That was, he realized, because he had sunk onto all fours. At the same time he noticed that the odors of which he had been only moderately aware—the faint smell of the sea, the stink of dried seaweed up the beach, the mustiness under the olive trees, the spice of the Nymph's flesh—had all grown both richer and sharper.

To ease the strain in his neck he lowered his head and regarded his hands. But they were no longer hands. Their digits had drawn together into two clumps, the nails expanding and darkening.

Hooves, he thought, *and a pig's hooves at that.*

He heard a giggle from above him, the sound of a malicious girl relishing a prank. Then he felt a sharp pain in his buttocks. She had whacked him across the hams with her staff. He started forward, up toward the olive trees, and was encouraged to hurry when a second blow landed in the same region as the first.

"Hurry, pig," said a voice both melodious and cruel. "Funny, tasty pig."

A third swat followed. Bandar squealed and scuttled for the trees.

The noösphere, as the collective unconscious was more properly called by the Institute's scholars, lay hidden in the lower reaches of every human psyche. It was a labyrinth of interconnected Landscapes, Events and Situations, the cores of every myth, legend, fiction and joke. Its inhabitants were the archetypical figures that furnished the dreams of humanity—Wise Man and Fool, Hero and Destroyer, Maiden, Mother and Crone, Temptress and Comforter and a host of others.

An archetype commonly encountered was the Enchantress, realized in a multitude of motifs: the maleficent Wood Witch who magicked errant hunters into wolf–slaves; the Faery Princess who beguiled a lovestruck swain through an afternoon that became a decade; the teasing Coquette whose charms figuratively turned men into animals; and the island–bound Nymph whose spells went the whole hog.

A noönaut like Guth Bandar ought to have been sequestered from her powers by a thran, a specific series of notes—like the protective song of the Singer who visited Hell in the dawn time myth— that removed him from this Enchantress's purview. But thrans had to be sung continuously, not set aside while the noönaut relished an imagined triumph over a rival.

Now, as the Nymph drove him toward the rest of her herd of swine, Bandar endeavored to chant the four–and–two. His corporeal body, seated in his meditation chamber at the Institute, waiting for his consciousness to reanimate it, enjoyed perfect pitch; that ability transposed to his consciousness whenever it went sojourning through the Commons. When that consciousness was transformed into a pig, however, Bandar found that a porcine vocal apparatus could not strike the proper notes. His overlarge ears, flopping against his fatted cheeks, told him that he was producing unmusical skreeks and skrawks. These had no effect on his captor other than to provoke yet another blow from the staff and an admonition to "Keep silence, piggy, else I'll not wait for your fattening. I'll smoke your belly and boil your head tomorrow."

He was driven into the olive grove. To his new nose, the place was awash with the smells of mulch and overripe fruit crushed underfoot, overlaid by the rank reek of the goats and the now curiously appealing scent of the other swine. The Nymph drove him into their midst and they made way for him with squeals and grunts, regarding him with sad and knowing gazes. Their attention was soon diverted, however, when their owner struck the trees with her staff and shook the branches, causing a heavy rain of olives. The swine fell upon the fruit with snuffles of appetite.

One heavily larded specimen ignored the feed. A piebald boar, he showed not appetite but stark terror as the Nymph favored him with a weighing look. She poked a finger into the fat overlying his ribs and gave a grunt that bespoke a decision reached. She goaded the hog with the foot of her staff and chased him toward a trail that led from the grove deeper into the island's center. The chosen one gave a shrill cry that, even though a pig's throat formed it, carried an unmistakably human note of fearful despair.

Bandar fought against panic. He also had to exert himself to overcome a growing interest in the ripe olives that littered the grove. He felt an urge to shoulder aside the other swine to get at the choicest morsels. These inclinations only deepened his fear.

A consciousness that stayed too long in any Commons Location was at risk of being absorbed. Even the insulating thrans could not keep the power of the place from overpowering the sojourner and fitting him into the matrix of an Event or Situation. The discovery and mapping of the noösphere over the course of millennia had seen countless numbers of explorers inextricably engrossed into Locations. Their consciousnesses had devolved into the semi–awareness of idiomatic entities, or died outright when their virtual flesh had been transfixed by a phalanx's spears or immolated by a dragon's breath.

Being transformed into a swine worked against Guth Bandar. It threatened to weaken the integrity of his sojourning self. He must leave this Location soon or risk losing his sense of identity. If he forgot who he was he would truly become a transmogrified pig, fattening on olives, until his turn came to encounter the knife and the rendering tub.

He tore his attention away from the delicious olives he had been munching while he contemplated his fate. He found he was even more drawn toward a young sow who was giving off an odor that grew more maddeningly compelling the closer she came. A big boar with well developed tusks was shadowing her. Bandar wondered how large his own tusks might be and felt a growing urge to paw the ground and voice a guttural challenge.

Concentrate, he told himself. *And get clear of that sow while you're still more man than pig.* He made a great effort and turned his head away from her delightful scent then deliberately followed his nose toward less freighted air. He found the path down which the Nymph had herded her victim and followed it. *No pig would willingly take this course,* he told himself, and felt better for it.

The path led him uphill through woods for a short while then leveled off in a long, broad meadow of short grass grazed by sheep. Bandar wondered if all the four–legged inhabitants of the island had been transformed from human idiomats and if the kind of animals they became were determined by the Enchantress's whims or by their own natures. He couldn't account for anything in his own make–up that would qualify him for pigdom, unless it was his penchant for rooting about in academic puzzles and turning up exquisite little truffles like the Lorelei song. These were decidedly unpiglike musings, a thought which encouraged him further.

He was finding that four limbs and strong hooves made for rapid locomotion. He was almost across the meadow now, following a path of beaten earth. Ahead was a stand of stately trees. Between the boles and branches he could make out an imposing building faced in marble, ornamented with columns and pilasters and set about with statuary. As he neared the trees he veered off the path and approached by a roundabout route. He came upon a garden with a pool and fountain beyond which a paved walkway sloped down to a grotto.

He followed it, his hooves clicking softly on the stones. It led him to a sunken lawn, shaded by a rocky outcrop beneath which a bower of fragrant grasses had been heaped up and covered with carpets of soft wool. On this reclined a stocky man of middle years, red of hair and beard, who idly contemplated the gold beaker in his hand before he raised it to his lips. A driblet of purple wine ran from the corner of his mouth to lose itself in his beard, but he paid it no heed, his bright blue eyes gazing at nothing.

A beguiled Hero, Guth Bandar thought. He regarded the idiomat closely, saw neither great thews nor features so striking as to indicate divine parentage, although there were scars on the man's arms and naked chest. *A very old type*, he concluded, *a swordster when necessary, yet more inclined to the craftiness of a trickster.*

Bandar was pressing his mind to remember what he'd learned of this variant of the Hero archetype. There might be some way to play upon its known characteristics to create a strategy that would lead to his being reconstituted as a human being. After which, he would forthwith intone a thran to shield him from the view of Hero and Nymph long enough to put some distance between him and them. A quick chant of a particular seven–tone sequence would open an emergency gate. He would leap through and return to his inert body in the meditation room.

In a crisis—if, for example, the Nymph came for him with the knife—he might try to conjure the gate while still in pig form. The risk would be that he might arrive back in his body to find that parts of his psyche were still more swine than human. There were already too many people like that on Old Earth—Didrick Gabbris merely the first that came to mind.

A voice broke into his thoughts and he realized that the figure on the bower was speaking to him. "I said, 'What are you looking at, pig?'" Now the idiomat shrugged and drank more wine. "Though even a pig might look at a king."

Bandar contrived as intelligent a face as his porcine features would allow. "Hmmm?" he said and though the arrangement of his huge nasal cavity gave the wordless sound a certain honk, he thought it sounded reasonably human for a pig.

"I have pigs of my own," the Hero said. "I'm king of an island, you know."

Bandar made the same sound, but altered the tone so that it sounded like, "Really?"

"Yes," said the idiomat, "but you know I'd be happy just to be a swineherd if I could see once more my wife and son."

"Hmmm," said Bandar, with a nod and a note of sympathy.

"I really must do something about getting home," the Hero said. "Build another ship or something."

This time Bandar's "Hmmm," offered encouragement, a spur to action.

There ensued a conversation, largely one–sided, in which the Hero King issued observations and Bandar replied with combinations of nods, wags and hums. The noönaut was surprised how much information could be exchanged even when one interlocutor's vocabulary could not rise above the barest minimum.

"You are decidedly insightful for a pig," said the Hero. "Indeed, I have known princes who could learn from you." He drank the lees of his cup and reached for a gold pitcher that stood on a nearby table. "If they weren't too busy sulking in their tents or stealing concubines."

The idiomat poured more wine and hefted the goblet, then paused with it halfway to his stained lips. "I like a good palaver," he said. "It seems to me I have not had a conversation of any depth since. . . " He appeared to be consulting a mental time line that would not hold its shape. "Since a long time," he finished.

"Hmmm," said Bandar. Engaging in conversation, even under his present disadvantages, was helping to keep pigness at a distance. He was wondering how he could turn this encounter further to his profit. Perhaps the Hero could persuade the Nymph to undo the spell. Focusing on the matter with a pig's brain was not easy, however. He missed the Hero's next question.

Fortunately the idiomat seemed to be accustomed to repeating himself. "I said, 'It seems to me I arrived here with several companions.' You haven't seen any of them, have you?"

An agonized squeal from not far off claimed their attention. Moments later, the Nymph came tripping down the walkway, carrying a gold plate on which lay two fair–sized morsels of raw flesh. She went to where a brazier stood on a tripod and poked at its coals with a knife, blowing them into a glowing heat. Bandar backed into the undergrowth while she was laying the plate on the embers. His sharp ears heard a faint sizzle while his pig's nose caught a whiff of cooking meat. It smelled delicious.

"I've brought you a little treat, my dear," the Nymph said, over her shoulder. "Something to restore your vigor."

Bandar realized what the two frying objects were and where they had come from. Not far away must be a most despondent boar. He also had no doubt as to the fate of the king's erstwhile shipmates. He could not repress a gasp and a shudder.

Unfortunately, a gasping, shuddering pig could not fail to attract a Nymph's attention. She turned to regard him. The brows knitted above her sharp nose and the green eyes flashed then narrowed. Bandar was reminded that idiomats, even the Principals of Locations, tended toward simplicity. They were not real people, only rudimentary personas—much like the characters in myth and fiction to which they had given rise. Where people would pause and consider, idiomats invariably acted.

"Have you met this remarkable pig?" the king was saying, even as his consort crossed the lawn, knife in hand and unmistakable motivation in her face. Bandar turned and fled.

He had been a healthy young man in his virtual self, therefore he was a healthy young pig. He soon discovered how to go from a rapid trot to a fast gallop, although he wasn't entirely sure that pigs were built for the latter gait. He did not stop to ponder the question, however; he made his best speed with the sound of thudding Nymph footsteps closing on his tail. And on what flopped below them.

He ran up a slope, breaking through a shrubbery of artfully trimmed bushes, then onto another open meadow—this one with donkeys. They scattered as he burst through their midst, heading for a thick growth of trees that climbed toward what looked to be either a high hill or a low mountain at the island's center.

His pursuer's footsteps grew louder. He put on more speed but soon he heard her drawing near again. And now it became apparent that pig lungs and legs were designed more for the sprint than the marathon, whereas Nymphs were apparently tireless.

He could hear not only her footfalls but her breathing as he reached the trees and raced between the boles. Not far in he found thickets of thorn and bramble and into these he plunged without slowing. The sharp protrusions tore at his hide, but pig skin was thick and the scratches caused him far less discomfort than he would have experienced as a man. His long, low and relatively streamlined shape was also ideal for snaking through brush at good speed.

He soon left the Nymph behind. He could hear her cursing him, her voice receding as he went deeper into the woods. Fortunately, it seemed that her maledictions were not effective unless she was wielding the olive staff.

Bandar ran a little farther into the greenery then stopped in a small open space roofed over with prickly vines. He elevated his ear flaps and moved his head from side to side, but heard nothing to alarm him. He let his wide nostrils sample the air and scented no immediate danger.

He bent his forelimbs then let his hindquarters settle to the forest floor. He had to think. There was no point in seeking to enlist the Hero King's aid. The red–haired idiomat was the Enchantress's prize—her control of him was almost certainly what this Situation was all about. She would guard him closely.

Nor could Bandar hide out on the island and attempt to reshape his virtual flesh. For one thing, the technique required leisure to concentrate; he doubted the Nymph would afford him such. For another, the only time he had attempted the procedure he had distorted himself in freakish ways. Getting from swinehood to humanness was almost certainly beyond him.

Bandar's best recourse was to find a gate and pass through to somewhere less lethal. Then he might plot a course through to some Location where the Principal was a wielder of benign magic who would lift the Nymph's curse and restore the noönaut to his true proportions. There were relatively few such places and personas— the Commons dealt out more horror than happy fun times—but they were there to be found.

And Guth Bandar had the means to find them. He concentrated and summoned the map of the noösphere into virtual existence. He found it difficult to see deeply into the complex webwork of points and lines—his pig's eyes were not so placed as to enable stereoscopic vision of near objects. Finally, he cocked his head to bring one eye to bear and began to plot a route to salvation.

He found that there were two nodes on the island that connected the Nymph's Location to others. One was a single–direction gate that would take him into a nightmarish cityscape, an urban dystopia rife with crime and infamy where the only semblance of order was a brotherhood of bounty hunters. It was no place for an innocent pig; those that might not see him as food on the hoof would likely use him for target practice.

The other gate was a multi–destination node: depending on the sequence of tones employed by an approaching noönaut, it might open to any of five places. One was a mellow kingdom of strolling troubadours and itinerant tale–spinners. Better yet, a short jog across that Location would bring him to a gate into a children's Situation—luckily, not one of the many nasty ones, but a winter fantasia whose magical, merry Principal enjoyed bestowing gifts and bon bons on good little boys and girls. He would surely grant the wish of a good little pig.

The multifarious node waited in the meadow of the donkeys. That was a dangerously wide space to cross, especially if an angry Enchantress lurked nearby. It might take pig–Bandar more than one trial to find the right notes to activate the exit.

But he resolved to hazard the meadow, though he would wait for nightfall. In the meantime, he would practice producing tones from a pig's throat.

The moon rode full and high across a dark blue heaven, flooding the field with silvery light. Bandar stood beneath the last of the trees and surveyed the open space. Pig night vision was no better than the human version, but his ears and nose added a wealth of sensory impressions. The meadow's inhabitants stood clumped not far away, making donkey murmurs to each other. Of the Nymph there was no sign.

Bandar crept out onto the cropped grass, advanced a few steps and paused. He heard nothing. He felt the slight tingle in the back of his mind that told him he was near to a node and went in the direction that made the sensation increase. A few more steps and again he paused, again hearing and seeing nothing.

The gate was not too far now. He trotted forward, mentally rehearsing the sequence of tones he must sing to activate it.

Midway across the meadow, he heard a rustle of motion among the donkeys. He turned to look their way. A slim figure rose from amongst them. It was the Nymph and in her hand was the olive wood staff.

Swiftly she laid its leering tip to the backs of the donkeys. With each contact the touched beast changed shape, became longer and lower. Their excited braying became a baying, the deep bell of a hunting pack underlaid by slavering growls.

She touched the last of the herd then pointed with the staff. "After him!" she cried. "Rend him!"

Bandar had not waited for the transformations to be completed. He burst toward the place where the right combination of sounds would call up safety from empty air. But the pack moved faster than even a well motivated pig. They swept across the meadow toward him.

He could feel the nearness of the node and he did not break stride before chanting the tones that should open it.

Nothing happened. He realized that running and chanting at the same time, especially with his less than expert control of porcine vocal equipment, were affecting his pitch and intonation.

He skidded to a halt before the spot where a ripple should be wavering in the moonlight. The air was undisturbed.

The pack came on. He could see them, long ears and dark muzzles, black lips drawn back from foam flecked fangs. The collective sound they made, of appetite and blood lust, sent a shiver through Bandar's meat.

He took a short settling breath and sang the tones again. The beasts were almost on him. The lead hound gathered its hindquarters beneath it and sprang, stretching its lean body through an arc that would bring its jaws to Bandar's soft throat.

The ripple appeared. Bandar jumped. He heard the click of canine teeth closing on empty air. Then he was through.

The Commons was the original fount of all myth and legend. Explored over tens of thousands of years, all of its terrors and wonders were long since identified and cataloged. Yet among undergraduates of the Institute, the noösphere had paradoxically become the subject of a myth of its own. Though senior fellows and tenured scholars derided the notion, students whispered to each other that they sometimes felt that humanity's collective unconscious was somehow *aware* of their presence—and worse, that their traipsing through Events and Situations was resented.

How else to explain the ill luck that too frequently accompanied sojourns among the idiomatic entities? It was understandable that the early explorers, groping their way from one uncharted Location to another, might fall afoul of an anthropophagic giant or a murderous worm. But with the Commons now as well mapped as any place in the waking world of Old Earth, why should noönauts so often blunder into lethal traps and snares? Why must the noösphere be so unforgiving?

As a youth, Bandar had shivered at the speculations of his classmates. In his maturity, his views were aligned with the establishment's. Only the day before this exploration, overhearing a callow underclassman named Chundlemars regaling his friends with some apocryphal tale of a sentient Commons, Bandar had spoken sharply.

"The Commons is an aggregate of contending forces. Disunity is its most salient characteristic. Fool contends against Wise Man, Hero confronts Villain, Anima opposes Animus. How can these contentious fragments unite behind a single program?"

Chundlemars had had the temerity to dispute the issue. "Yet a mob, however disparate its members' views on a host of issues, can cooperate to attack an inimical outsider."

Bandar bridled. "The key word in 'collective unconscious' is 'unconscious,' not 'collective,'" he said. "To become aware of intruders, the unconscious must first become self–aware. Self–awareness is by definition consciousness. Therefore it is a logical impossibility for the unconscious to become conscious."

The student had bent before Bandar's tirade but had still shown fight. "Perhaps not impossible, but merely difficult," he said, "hence its efforts to capture our attention are diffuse and seem inconclusive."

Bandar had disdained to continue the argument and with a brusque gesture had sent the youths hustling off to another corner of the Institute's grounds.

But now as Bandar gazed at the view that had appeared before him the moment he had come through the gate and onto this grassy hilly, a frisson of fear caused the skin of his back to twitch. If this Location was the sunny realm of bards and troubadours that he had sought, he ought to be able to see at least one towered and turreted castle, its conical roofs aflutter with gay pennants and gonfalons. There ought to be a fountain or two on verdant lawns and gentle woods with trees as round and symmetrical as a child's drawing.

Instead the noönaut saw a tangled forest broken only by a narrow, unpaved track that wound its way past scattered clearings in which rude dwellings stood next to vegetable gardens. Farther off stood a sturdier edifice of red brick with a slate roof and a chimney from which gray smoke idled.

But nowhere to be seen were shaded bowers or romantic ruins. Bandar listened but heard no lutes or dulcimers, only the cawing of two ragged birds. His pig's nose brought him not the scent of flowers and fruited trees but a faint odor of carrion.

Not good, he thought. He brought the map into existence again. He examined the symbolic representation of the node through which he had arrived and saw that it was even more multifarious than he had realized. The gate was identified by a yellow heptagon within a green circle, signifying that it led to seven destinations if sung to in one key, and yet another seven outcomes if the thran was dropped a full tone.

Yet Bandar had been sure the map had shown him a green pentagon in a yellow circle. He had carefully traced the outcomes. He should be in the land of song and story, on his way to the children's winter paradise. Instead, as he studied the map, he was not quite sure where he had landed. He tried to focus on the symbols identifying this present Location but the characters' lines kept wavering and blurring, as if seen through an intervening mist.

His impression, however, was that he was in one of the most obscure sites, a subsidiary of a tributary two steps removed from a minor whorl. That meant that there might be few gates out of this Location, perhaps even only one, and he would have no choice but to take it.

How had he misread the map? Accidents were always possible, but Bandar had planned his route with meticulous care. The adolescent fear of being surrounded by a malicious, resentful Commons crept out of the closet. Bandar resolutely thrust it back and mentally slammed the door. Perhaps his pig eyes did not resolve certain colors or shapes as well as his human orbs could. He would be more careful next time.

He raised the flaps of his ears and turned in a slow circle on the hill top. Beyond the squawking of the birds he heard the sound of voices raised in argument. They were coming from a clearing some small way off.

The voices offered Bandar a means of discovering where he was. He would approach stealthily and observe and identify the idiomats, deducing from their characteristics the Situation or Event in which he had landed. Then he would find its precise position on the map and from there plot a route to safety.

The forest, when he entered it, was of the Sincere/Approximate classification: what the Institute called "forest–like" rather than a truly realistic mix of trees, underbrush and detritus. Its iconic characteristics told Bandar that he was almost certainly in a Class Four Situation: likely an archetypical joke or one of the lighter tales for children, possibly one so ancient that it had been superseded eons ago by new formulations. But nothing was ever lost in the Commons. Just as Bandar's essential gene plasm carried all the instructions necessary to build precursor species that had gone extinct a billion years before, so the collective unconscious preserved every Form and Type that the human brain had ever conceived.

Still, there were advantages to being stranded in a Class Four Situation: physical surroundings would count for little; the Situation's cycle would involve only indispensable interactions between the idiomatic inhabitants.

That would pose no difficulties if the situation revolved around, say, a sexual encounter between a lusty farmer's wife and a hired hand. The idiomats would be so intent upon each other that a pig would pass unnoticed. But if he was traversing a tale about a bridge–haunting troll that devoured talking livestock, Bandar might suddenly find himself added to the menu. He therefore made a light–hooved approach to the sound of voices.

He was hearing an argument; that much was clear from the tone even before he could make out the words. That it was a good–natured dispute, carried on without rancor, was a good sign: the disputants were unlikely to have weapons in their hands. Bandar stole closer, weaving stealthily through the generic underbrush. The arguers called each other "Brother," and seemed to be contradicting each other over the merits of construction methodologies—a pair of artisan monks was Bandar's first thought.

He eased his way through some cartoonishly rendered bushes, finding that his sharp hooves made no noise on the forest floor. The voices were quite clear now, the argument definitely about the strength of a wall. Apparently winds were a factor here, since one of the disputants was contending that the wall before them would collapse at the first breath. The other replied that its interwoven construction gave the barrier a resilient tensile strength, adding, "The willow bends where the oak falls."

Bandar moved closer. There were fewer leaves between him and the argument now. He could make out something blue. He pressed a little farther forward and saw that it was coarse cloth with yellow stitching, the leg of a utilitarian garment such as a workman or farmer might wear. He inched toward the leg and saw that it ended in a scuffed leather boot.

Not so bad, he thought. He was in some Wisdom Story, perhaps a minor variant of the Flexibility versus Rigidity dichotomy. Its idiomats would be exclusively focused on their debate and soon would come a great wind to test one theory over another. Bandar was not worried about the wind, by the time it came he would have traversed what must surely be a very small Location, found an exit gate and been on his way.

He backed away from the arguing idiomats. But as he did so he found that his pig's ears were better designed for pressing forward through underbrush, even of the generic sort, than for rearward motion. One of his flaps caught on a twig, which scraped over the protruding cartilage before snapping free. Above Bandar's head one branch snapped against another and the bush trembled, swishing its broad and simple leaves against each other.

"What was that?" said the champion of flexible walls.

"It came from down there," said the advocate for solid masonry.

The first voice dropped to a whisper. "Is it, You Know Who?"

The branches above Bandar's head were swept away by a stout walking stick and he heard the second voice take on a tone of horror and disgust as it said, "No, it's some kind of ugly monster!"

"Oh, it's hideous!" cried the other.

Now all Bandar wanted was to back out of the bush, turn and run. But he could not help looking up toward the voices. He saw above him, their features contorted in horror, the faces of two anthropomorphically rendered pigs.

"Kill it!" said Flexibility with an idiomat's typical decisiveness, and Rigidity raised his heavy cane to put his brother's advice into action. Bandar squealed and tore himself loose from the bushes, but now the two pig–men were crashing through the undergrowth after him and showing that in addition to their murderous impulses their humanly formed legs and feet could sustain a considerable speed.

Bandar deked and jinked, circling tree trunks and leaping over fallen logs. The brothers pounded after him and soon displayed a dismaying intelligence: they spread out, one seeking to cut Bandar off and drive him toward the other. Both, he saw, were armed with heavy sticks.

The noönaut dodged a blow that could have snapped his spine, ducked through the legs of its deliverer and burst out of the bushes into the sunlit clearing. A structure was in his way, its walls an interlacing of withes and flexible canes bound by fibrous cords, its roof a dense mat of woven reeds. Bandar raced around a corner and galloped across the open space, hearing the thudding bootsteps of his pursuers and the rasp of their breathing. They were gaining.

His short pig's legs were trembling and his pig's lungs were burning. He looked toward the trees on the other side of the clearing, hoping for a thicker bush, perhaps a bramble, through which he could insinuate himself while his pursuers were deterred. But he saw nothing that would suit and the stick–wielding pig–men were almost on him.

Then from the woods ahead burst a third pig–man, attired like the others, but with an expression of sheer terror disfiguring its already distorted features. This one paid no attention to Bandar but called to the two others, "He's right behind me! He destroyed my house with a single blast!"

The third pig–man sped across the clearing and into the woods. Bandar's pursuers immediately abandoned the chase and ran in the same direction, cries of panic fading in their wake.

Bandar had skidded to a halt, his legs limp as old celery, his breath coming in pants. He heard the clatter of the pig–men diminishing as they fled through the woods behind him on the far side of the clearing. Then he heard a new sound, an engine–like chuffing growing louder. It came from beyond the nearer trees.

He remembered the discussion of wind and the fleeing pig–man's mention of a house destroyed by a single blast. *An archetypical Storm elemental*, he thought, *an elemental with a yen to destroy weakly con-*

structed buildings—therefore no danger to a bystander pig. He stood to catch his breath as the huffing and puffing grew louder.

From the darkness under the trees, not far from where Bandar stood, a shape emerged. It was a running figure, knees high and elbows pumping, dressed in black overalls over a red shirt, with a bent and towering hat on its head. But it was the face that caught Bandar's attention—the long muzzle flecked with foam, the red lolling tongue, the cruel, needle sharp fangs.

Oh, my, he thought, *not just Storm, but Appetite too. An Eater.*

The great golden eyes turned Bandar's way and the idiomat scarcely broke its stride before swerving toward him. *Worse yet,* was Bandar's thought, *Indiscriminate Appetite, an Eat–em–all–up.*

He flung himself back the way he had come, but the slavering pursuer was even faster than the pig–men had been and here in the clearing there were no obstacles to interpose between the Eater and the virtual Bandar flesh it craved.

He was headed for the stick house, specifically for a wall against which stood a pile of unused building materials. He leapt to the top of the heap, sticks flying from beneath his scrabbling hooves, one of them happily striking the Eater's bulbous nose and causing the pursuer to pull up sharply, though only for the time it took to shake its head and renew the chase.

The pause gave Bandar time to scramble atop the woven roof, cross the peak and slide down the other side. He heard the beast coming over the roof after him. The trees were too far away; the Appetite would run him down.

Beside Bandar, the door to the house of sticks stood open. He ducked inside and closed the portal after him, glad to see that it was made of thick timbers, closely fitted, and that it had a hinged bar that he could nose into place.

Scarcely had the barrier been sealed than the Eater struck it with force enough to make the door rattle in its mounts. A second blow followed but the timbers held firm.

Now it grew quiet. Bandar put an eye to a tiny gap in the woven wall and saw that the Eater had drawn some distance away. It sat on its haunches and studied the noönaut's refuge for a few moments, then exhibited the demeanor of one who has thought through a problem and come to a decision.

It began to draw in great gouts of air. Bandar saw its thorax expand and contract to unlikely dimensions, and now he knew what must come. Somehow, this idiomat combined the essentials of the Eater *and* a Storm elemental. He wondered for a moment what demented mythmaker had first welded the two together, then deferred speculation while he sought a way out of the refuge that had become a deadly trap.

The floor was packed dirt. Pigs' hooves ought to make good digging implements. He went to the wall opposite where the Storm–Eater worked to inflate himself and frantically scratched at the earth.

Fortunately, this was a Class Four Situation so the dirt was made of uniformly homogeneous particles, without rocks or boulders to block his passage. The soil flew, piling up behind Bandar's haunches as the hole deepened into a passage under the wall. Above the sound of his own labors he could hear the idiomat chanting, "Let me come in," in a sing–song voice that carried the force of a gusty breeze.

There came a silence as the Eater waited for a response, then the walls shook and the door rattled as a blast of air struck the opposite wall. Bandar heard a snapping of sticks and a tearing of cords. He looked back between his legs and saw that the door and the posts that supported it were canted inward. The whole front wall was skewed out of true.

He heard another puffing and huffing. The Eater was refilling its body with a fresh storm. A second blast would surely blow the house in. Bandar dug faster, harder, deeper. Soon there was a pig sized passage beneath the back wall. He wriggled into the holed, scraped more earth out of his way, the narrow hooves doing a gratifyingly fast and thorough job.

In a moment, he saw a chink of daylight above him. In another moment, the chink had become a swatch, then a fully realized hole. Bandar wriggled through just as the storm smashed the front wall to flinders. The strong door crashed to the floor, the outer walls blew out and the roof fell in. The wall beneath which Bandar squirmed was pulled inward.

But he was out in sunlight and across the clearing, keeping the wreckage of the house between him and the Eater. He could hear it thrashing through the debris, alternately cooing to him and smacking wet lips. Bandar ducked into the undergrowth and lay trembling beneath a bush.

The Eater kicked at the wreckage of the house, searching for him. Then Bandar saw it notice the tunnel he had dug beneath the back wall. The beast squatted and examined the gouge in the earth, sniffed at it with its elongated snout. Then it raised its head and peered about the clearing. Bandar resisted an instinctive urge to draw farther back into the bushes; should his movements shake his branches the Eater would be on him in seconds.

Its gaze passed over Bandar without seeing him. After a long moment, its head turned in the direction the anthropomorphic pigs had taken then it rose and set off after them. Bandar waited until it was out of sight then crept from cover. If this was the kind of tale he now thought it was, none of the idiomats would return to this part of the Location until the Situation had completed its cycle and begun anew.

He brought up the great globe of the Commons and examined it as best he could with one eye then the other. It was easier to see in the clearing's bright sunlight than deep in the Nymph's forest. He found the gate through which he had come from the enchantress's island—it was still a yellow heptagon within a green circle— and saw where he must be: a small mauve spot in the shape of a diamond, with a white stripe running diagonally from one side to another. Squinting his pig's eye, he deduced that the exit gate was not far off, somewhere beyond the brick house, where no doubt the Eater was now laying siege to the three brothers.

Bandar collapsed the map and thought about the Situation. This was clearly an admonitory tale for children, not as he had thought about flexibility versus rigidity, but a very early version of the Three Wayfarers motif that constantly reappeared in endless variations throughout the collective unconscious. It would conclude with one or, more likely, all three of the pig–men turning the tables on the Eater. From the effects of the monster's wind on the house of sticks, Bandar could guess that the Eater would fail to blow in the brick house. Then, its elemental power literally blown out, it would somehow be captured and destroyed by the brothers.

Bandar's best course was to position himself where he could observe the Situation's end game. Then during the Pause that always preceded a renewal of the cycle he could pass through the egress node and move to the next Location: a Landscape of primeval prairie. He might have to dodge vast herds of ruminants and those who hunted them, but more likely he would be alone on a rolling plain of endless grass. The prairie connected to another Location—a mountain valley where no one ever grew old. From there, Bandar could loop back to the snowland where the good Principal granted favors.

He trotted down the forest trail and soon came to the clearing where the little brick house stood. He approached warily, staying within the cover of the undergrowth. He did not see the Eater, but he saw that a painted wooden sign that bore the legend "A. Pig" in cursive script had been blown off the door's lintel to land on a strip of bare earth from which the stalks of petalless flowers grew.

The Eater has blown himself out and is probably even now being dispatched by the pig–men, Bandar thought. He crept to one of the shuttered windows and peered between the slats. Within, he saw the trio gathered about an open fireplace in which a deep black cauldron steamed. The bricklayer held the pot's lid in readiness and all three were regarding the chimney with evident expectation.

Of course, Bandar thought, *the frustrated Eater descends the chimney, is clapped into the pot to become the pig–men's dinner*. The Eater would be eaten by those he would eat: another example of the circular irony which abounded throughout the Commons.

He watched to see the final act of the tale. But moments later, he saw a portion of the floor behind the three pig–men suddenly subside. A dark–clawed paw emerge. The brothers did not notice. Another paw emerged, then the head of the Eater, then his torso followed. The monster made lip smacking noises and now, too late, the pig–men turned and saw the horror emerging from their floor, which was of the same friable earth as at the house of sticks.

The Eater was between the pig–men and the door. The single room was small. The victims displayed fright and panic, the beast a terrible single–mindedness. The ensuing scenes were not pleasant to watch. Bandar tore his gaze away and ran as fast as his tired pig's legs would take him in the direction of the exit gate.

He did not fear pursuit by the Eater; the beast would be occupied in feasting for some time. But Bandar was sure the outcome he had just seen was not what was supposed to happen. By inadvertently showing the monster another way into the pig–man's house, he had interfered with the Situation, perverting the idiomats from their prescribed course.

Among noönauts, the term for such adulterated behavior was *disharmony*. To cause a single idiomat to behave in a disharmonious manner could cause ripples. To distort an entire Situation, even a minor one, from its proper conclusion was to ignite the fuse for an explosive manifestation of psychic energy. Bandar had no idea what was about to happen within this Location, but he was certain it would not be good for the errant pig who had triggered it. And he had no wish to experience it.

His noönaut's sense told him that the egress node was a short trot along the forest trail then across a meadow. He followed the tingling in his awareness and soon was running through generic grass. He pulled up short where the gate should be and chanted the appropriate opening thran. Nothing happened. Again his enhanced hearing told him that his pig's larynx and enlarged nasal chamber were distorting the pitch of the tones.

A sound from behind him made Bandar turn and look. A spiraling vortex had appeared in the air above the brick house. It grew darker as he watched, a miniature whirlwind descending toward the roof. When it touched, dark slates were wrenched loose and sent spinning. A cracking, grinding noise grew in volume as the vortex broke up the timbers of the roof. Beams flew, rafters shot out in all directions like missiles.

Now the tornado bored deeper into the structure and Bandar turned back to the gate. He chanted the thran again, but knew the tones were off–key. Behind him came a rumbling, clattering noise. It sounded as if every brick in the pig–man's house was vibrating and bashing against its neighbors, and behind that the whirring roar of the whirlwind grew louder and louder. He could hear limbs cracking from trees and the ground beneath his hooves shook like a nervous beast.

The part of Bandar that was more pig than human—a part that grew larger, he now realized, whenever he was gripped by fear—wanted to do nothing but run away. He had to force himself to breathe calmly. He did not look behind him, and did his best to ignore the thunderous cacophony of destruction that battered at his sensitive ears.

He shaped his jowly cheeks *so*, and put his tongue *here* and tried once more. The thran was only three descending notes then an octave's jump. Even Chundlemars could have done it on first try. That realization angered the human side of Bandar. The anger seemed to help. He chanted the three and one and the air rippled obligingly.

Before he stepped toward the fissure, he took a look back. After all, no Commons sojourner in living memory had witnessed a full melt–down of a Situation, even a Class Four. He could never mention this episode—how Gabbris would gloat—but he owed himself a last glance.

Immediately, he wished he hadn't. The trees all around the house had been stripped of their leaves and blown flat. The structure itself was spinning like a square top, the individual bricks of which it was made holding their relation to each other though separated by wide gaps through which burst eye–searing flashes of intense violet and electric blue.

The house spun faster and faster, the blasts of painful light coming in sharper paroxysms. Bandar saw the pig–men and the Eater thrown around in the heart of the whirlwind, like torn rags with flopping limbs, each burst of blinding illumination penetrating their flesh to show gaping wounds and fractured bones. Above the roaring of the wind Bandar heard a hum like an insane dynamo. The sound became a whine then a shriek, climbing through the frequency scale until it rose even above the pitch that pigs could hear.

Not good, Bandar said to himself. He scuttled toward the gate. But the last glance back had meant he had waited too long. He did not hear the explosion; it reached him as a shock wave, picking him off his hooves and hurling him through the fissure. He rolled and tumbled across a grassy prairie, the gate behind him still open, blasts of wind and beams of non–light streaming through the gap.

Bandar got his feet under him and struggled against the wind back toward the node. Objects struck him, none of them large enough to do harm though he heard something heavy thrum past his head.

The gate remained open. That's not supposed to happen. He chanted a closure thran, then had to repeat the notes before the node would seal completely and the light and wind died. That, too, was something he had never seen. Gates closed automatically. Closure thrans were only for the rare circumstance when a noönaut opened a gate then decided not to go through it.

With him and after him had come through the gate elements of the previous Location: some bricks, a hand–sized piece of slate, some fragments of wood and a few unrecognizable gobbets of flesh and splinters of bone. They lay strewn around him but as he watched all of the debris melted into the long grass of the prairie, like water seeping into a sponge.

I've never heard of that, Bandar thought. Material from one Location, whether inert or "living," was not transferable to another. Experiments had been tried in the distant past and the principle of locational inviolability was unquestioned. Now Bandar had witnessed a definite cross–over. His report would make quite a stir, if he ever dared to tell what he had seen and, more culpably, what he had done. And if he ever made it back to human form and out of the Commons without being absorbed and lost forever.

He turned now and scanned the prairie, saw nothing to cause alarm. Far off above the eastern horizon a vast storm cloud towered into the otherwise open sky and he saw flickers of lightning from its base. In the same direction he could see tiny dots against the darkening skyline. *A herd of ruminants*, he thought, remembering the horned and shaggy beasts, herding in their millions, that were an essential feature of this Landscape.

Neither storm nor herd concerned Bandar. He deployed and examined the globular map. There were several gates on the prairie, none of them far away, as if the Location had been designed as a transit zone for wayfarers. There were a number of such nodal gatherings in the Commons, and some scholars had advanced the notion that the convenience of their existence argued for the noösphere having been intelligently designed. Others held that random distribution could as readily account for the clumping of gates. Besides, the prospect of intelligent design raised the question: by whom? And that led back to the conundrum of a conscious unconscious—a knot that the scholastic community preferred to leave unpicked.

As did Guth Bandar at this moment. He determined that the gate to Happy Valley was about a quarter day's walk to the east. From there he would jump to the snow kingdom and beg a transformation from its Principal. Then he would summon an emergency gate and plop back into his body in the Institute's meditation room.

He set off toward the gate, his spirits bruised but resuscitated. He wondered if he could draft a monograph on the melt–down of the Class Four Situation without specifying the events which had triggered it. Perhaps he could profess ignorance of the cause while detailing the results. Anyone who visited the Location would find it back in its cycle; the idiomats would know nothing of what had happened to their previous incarnations and all evidence of Bandar's inadvertent tampering would have dissolved.

The more he thought about it, the more possible a paper became. He began to flesh out the essential elements of thesis, argument and recapitulation. The point to be made was that cross–Locational transfer was indeed possible. Perhaps such things happened often, though only at the end of a Location's cycle when any sensible noönaut would absent himself rather than risk absorption.

That's it, Bandar thought, *I'll say I bravely stayed to witness the cycle's renewal and thus saw the movement of material through the gate.* He would transform his own folly into courage and produce a commendable result. Didrick Gabbris would chew his cuff in envious gall.

Cheered, Bandar trotted on, composing the first lines of the projected essay as he went. Thus occupied, he did not notice what was before him until he felt the first gusts of wind on his pig's face and the first trembling of the ground beneath his hooves.

He was at the base of a small rise, its covering of long grass leaning toward him under the pressure of a growing east wind. He climbed the slope and looked beyond it.

As far as he could see, to left and to right in the rapidly failing light, the world was a sea of humping, bumping shapes. A million animals were on the move. And they were moving toward him.

Above the herd, the sky was almost black with lowering storm clouds, the narrow band between them and the earth whipped by rain and rattling sheets of hail. Lightning crackled and thunder rolled across the prairie. The herd moaned and blundered on.

Behind Bandar was nothing but open plain; no cover, no obstacle to break the onslaught of millions of hooves. He could not outrun them on his short, tired pig's legs. To left and right was only grass. But ahead, between him and the oncoming herd, the land sloped down to a small river, barely more than a stream, that wound its way like a contented snake across the prairie. In places, flash floods had cut deep into the thick sod and the clay beneath, leaving the stream to trickle between high banks. And one of those places was not far.

Bandar dug his hooves into the prairie sod and raced down the slope, the wind battering him now and the rumble of the herd's coming shaking the earth like a constant tectonic tremblor. He did not look at the animals but fixed his eyes on where the river must be, for he had lost sight of it as soon as he had left the top of the low rise.

The thunder of massed hooves now equaled the voice of the storm. They would be on him in moments and still he had not found the river. He wondered if he had somehow veered from his course on the unmarked plain to run parallel to his only hope of salvation. But even as he conceived the thought the quaking ground suddenly disappeared from beneath his hooves and he plunged into a gully as deep as he was tall—or as tall as he would be were he still in human form.

He hit the shallow water with a shock to his forehooves and immediately scrambled to the far bank where the clay had been hollowed out by a past flood. He pressed himself sideways against the cold wall, feeling it cool his heaving flanks, unable to hear his own panting over the crescendo of hooves heading his way.

Something dark hurtled above him, the herd's first fleet outrunner leaping the gully. Then a second and another, then five more crossing the gap as fast as a drum roll. Now the body of the herd arrived, with the storm right behind it, and the light in the gully dimmed to a crepuscular shadow. But there was nothing Bandar wanted to see. He closed his eyes and hoped that the bank above him would not crumble and bury him beneath earth and thrashing hooves.

The stampede went on and on, but the soil above Bandar was woven through with the roots of tough prairie grass. It did not give way. In time, it seemed that the shaking of the ground lessened and that the thunder had rolled on across the plain. Bandar opened his eyes. Beasts were still hurtling over his head but there were gaps between them; the sky he glimpsed through those gaps was a sullen gray rather than an angry black.

A few more animals leapt the gully, then two more, then a single straggler and now, all at once, the herd had passed. Bandar edged out from under the overhang, wondering how he could scale the almost vertical clay wall and resume his journey. But the herd had left him a stepping stone: not far away lay the carcass of a beast that had plunged into the little canyon and snapped its neck against the west wall. It lay on its side. Bandar was sure he could climb onto its rib cage and from there jump to the eastern lip of the gully.

He trotted toward the dead ruminant, looking for the easiest point on the great corpse to begin his ascent. Thus he was almost upon it before he noticed that the tail, which should have been long and thick and tipped by a tassel of coarse hair was instead short, hairless and curled like a corkscrew. The animal's shoulders and chest, that should have been covered by a dense, woolly pelt were naked and hairless. And now, as Bandar circled the carcass, he saw the head: jowly and wrinkled, with sightless little eyes and a squared off snout that he had last seen on the face of an enraged pig–man who had sought to crack his spine with a cudgel.

That's not right, Bandar said. Farther down the gully, another animal had fallen on rocks, breaking its back. It still lived and was making guttural grunts that Bandar recognized. He had heard the same sounds under the olive trees on the Nymph's island—pig sounds. *No, not right at all.*

Bandar went back to the dead beast and examined it closely. It was not quite a pig, though it was decidedly piglike. But it had horns and was easily four times the size of even the most prize–winning swine, and the color was wrong. It was someone's idea of how a pig and a herd beast would look if their gene plasms were mashed together.

Bandar had no doubt that this beast was a result of trans–Locational contamination. Which meant he would have an even more interesting paper to present, although the degree of his culpability had just taken a quantum leap. If his role in this event became known he would be branded a vandal and forbidden ever to enter the Commons except as all humankind did, in his dreams.

He climbed onto the dead animal and jumped to the east lip of the gully. The sky ahead was clearing, gray clouds scudding aside to reveal patches of blue. He called up the globe of the Commons again and determined that he was not more than an hour's trot from the egress node. He set off with mixed feelings: glad to be nearer to deliverance but uncomfortably aware that the fused idiomats he had left dead and dying in the gully were a reproach to him.

He had not gone far before the wind that had been beating at his face faded and died away. He lifted his head and smelled the rain–scoured air. He could not wait to be restored to human form but he would miss some of the pig's senses, especially the breadth and subtlety of the world of odors.

He trotted on, letting his mind wander, smelling the crushed grass and the various scents of small flowers that appeared here and there along his way. The wind changed direction but he did not take account of it when it freshened and gusted against his hams. Then a sudden squall brought the sting of hail.

He paused and looked over his shoulder. The sky was dark to the west where the storm had gone, but now he saw that the clouds had rebuilt themselves and were sweeping back toward him. *That's peculiar*, he thought.

He looked up at the roiling vapors, shot through with flashes of lightning. *That's peculiar, too*, he thought, seeing that the flashes seemed tinged with blue and even purple instead of bright actinic white light.

He watched for a moment longer then felt a shiver go through his body that had nothing to do with the chill wind. The sparse hairs on his neck rose and Bandar's pig's limbs began to tremble and his spine began to shake. His pig's lower jaw dropped open and he gaped at the vision that was forming in the cloud.

It was a vast shape, the most enormous face he had ever seen, but he recognized it: the long muzzle lined with teeth and ending in a twitching nose, the pointed ears turned his way, the suggestion of a crooked hat towering into the sky, and the huge eyes, lit from within by lightning, that were looking back at him.

More than pig–man stuff had been blown through the gate from the exploding Class Four Situation: the Storm–Eater had come too, and it remembered him.

The immense face of Appetite rushed toward him, carried on a sweep of wind and chill rain. Bandar ran.

The collective unconscious, through the personal unconscious of every human being, engages in a constant dialogue with each of us. So went the opening sura of Afrani's *Explaining and Exploring the Noösphere*, the first text encountered by students at the Institute for Historical Inquiry. *We may address our questions, our thoughts, our hopes and expectations to the noösphere in direct and pointed queries, but it will always and only reply through indirection and coincidence.*

Bandar knew his Afrani by heart. It was every neophyte's first assignment, undertaken not only for the knowledge of the book's contents but for the necessary taming and strengthening of memory.

The words *indirection and coincidence* now rang in his mind as he fled across the grasslands, the roaring, devouring Storm–Eater at his back. The Commons never spoke directly, he knew. Even when it spoke through those who had demolished the barriers between conscious and unconscious—the oracles and the irredeemably insane—its language was always one of riddle and allusion.

Bandar saw now that he had been enmeshed in a sequence of coincidences ever since he had left the forest of the Loreleis. The Nymph had turned him into a pig, then he had landed in a Situation where pig–men were the idiomats. The Nymph had turned her donkeys into pursuing hounds—why do that, when donkey hooves could be just as lethal to a small pig as a hound's fangs?—then he had been chased by an Eater with decidedly canine characteristics. And now he was being harried again by a similar manifestation of the idiomat, though now it sought to sizzle him with lightning bolts instead of clamping sharp teeth into his porcine flesh.

In the waking world, coincidences were often just the haphazards of chance—a coin could be tossed and come up heads ten times in a row—but in the Commons coincidences were never a mere coincidence. Concurrency was the language of the noösphere. There was meaning here, a message.

And what could the message be? The thought rattled in Bandar's pig's brain as he galloped on tiring legs across the gently rolling landscape, while bolts of fluorescent energy struck behind and all around him. *What question did I put?* he wondered.

He had wanted to know about the Song of songs, the Ur–melody wired into the human brain. But now, as he turned the question over in his mind, examining it from all angles, he could not discover even the most tangential relationship to his present predicament.

But if not the Lorelei's song, then what? A blast of lighting lit the storm–darkened landscape ahead of him and he swerved around the charred and smoking gouge it had made in the prairie sod. Of course, direct questions to the Commons never brought a clear answer. The key to receiving a message was to think about something else. Then the unconscious would steal through the back door, to leave its offering like the gifts of fairy sprites who labor through the night while their beneficiary snores, all unawares, in his bed.

So as he ran Bandar turned his thoughts elsewhere, though it was a difficult task with lethal blasts striking all around him. But he took the attempts on his life as encouragement—what better way to get his attention?—and set his disciplined mind, even housed in a pig's brain, to the work. He rehearsed his activities before entering the Commons. He had dined with the vice dean of applied metaphysics; he had filled an order of off–world dyes and fixatives for a longstanding customer (Bandar ran an inherited family commerciant firm, hence his status at the Institute as only an adjunct scholar); he had reprimanded Chundlemars; he had sketched an outline of his Lorelei paper.

And now it came to him. His pig's tongue and lips could not put it into words, but he could make the appropriate sounds.

"Hmmm," he said, in the tones of one who has seen the light, then, "Um hmm," again to indicate acceptance of the revelation.

Another flash lit up the landscape and by its light, just ahead, Bandar saw an unlikely sight: a hummock of prairie land was transforming itself into another shape. In moments, Bandar found himself rushing toward a small but sturdy brick house, its stout door invitingly open.

He crossed the threshold at a gallop, skidded on his hooves as he turned to get his nose behind the door and push it closed. The wind resisted his efforts but he found renewed strength and when the door met its jamb a lock clicked and the barrier stood proof against the storm.

The single room was bereft of furniture although there were three framed pictures on the back wall, each portraying an anthropomorphically rendered pig in a stiff collared shirt and dark suit. Centered in the same wall was a wide and tall fireplace with a black cauldron simmering over a well stoked blaze. Bandar crossed to the kettle and found that the handle of its lid had been designed to fit a pig's trotter, confirming his surmise of what must be done.

He balanced on his hind legs and slipped a forehoof into the handle and prised the lid from the cauldron. It came easily. No sooner was the cover free than the chimney rattled to a downdraft of cold air. Sparks flew and smoke billowed, setting Bandar's eyes to water and causing him to vent an explosive sneeze.

But even blind he could hear the *sploosh* of something solid arriving in the cauldron. He immediately clapped the lid back into place. The kettle rumbled and shook but Bandar leaned his weight onto the leaping, vibrating top until the commotion ceased.

Outside the storm had ended. Beams of sunlight angled through the windows to illuminate the smoky air inside the house. *Now what?* Bandar wondered, and even as he did so his eye fell upon something he had not noticed before: a substantial ladle hanging beside the chimney.

Its handle, too, was shaped to fit a pig's hoof. He lifted it down then removed the cauldron's lid. A dark broth sent up steamy wisps of vapor. It smelled delicious. Bandar dipped the ladle and tasted the soup.

The broth tasted as rich as it smelled, but Bandar got no more than his first sip. As the stuff entered him, he saw the hoof that held the ladle become a hand once more, the foreleg become an arm. His back straightened and his legs set themselves under him again. He became a man standing in a little brick house, then the structure faded and he found himself atop a low rise.

The noönaut wasted no time in calling up an emergency gate. The air opened before him and he wanted to throw himself immediately forward. But he paused and said to the bright blue sky, "I will let them know."

A moment later he was looking through his own eyes at the worn furniture of the Institute's meditation room. He stretched the kinks out of his joints and muscles, rose and performed the usual exercises. When his body felt as if it fit him again, he crossed to the door that led out to the forum where students were wont to gather between classes.

He strode forcefully toward a group seated on the grass beneath a hanging wystol tree. Most of them looked up in curiosity; one showed alarm at being the focus of Bandar's gaze. The youth rose to his feet, a fearful apprehension seizing his features.

Bandar said, "Chundlemars, I wish you to come with me."

Chundlemars swallowed and said, "Master, I have thought better of my earlier observations about the noösphere's awareness. I withdraw them."

"Withdraw?" said Bandar. "To the contrary! You will expound

them to me at length. You are henceforward my research assistant."

Chundlemars blinked. His chin fell toward his chest and remained there.

"Don't stand there gaping!" Bandar said, seizing the underclassman by one protruding ear and compelling him toward Bandar's study. "The Commons is awake and aware! It demands our attention!"

"What must we do?" said Chundlemars.

"What must we do?" said Bandar. "My boy, we are scholars and the Great Colloquium is but a week away. We must quickly compose a thesis to grind Didrick Gabbris into a malodorous powder!"

Help Wonted

Guth Bandar had always liked the red haired one best. Her figure was not as voluptuous as the blonde's nor was her face as perfect as the raven haired girl's, but there was an elfin quality to the way she looked back at him over her lightly freckled shoulder, a gamin's wry twist of the mouth and a glint of mischief to her sea–green eyes.

In a moment, he would rise from where he lay in the shade of the coconut palm. He would affect a comic growl and they would respond with giggles. Then the blonde would press fingertips to half open lips and gasp, "Oh!" and the brunette would shriek while the redhead cocked one sun dappled hip before all three ran laughing into the surf.

The dream always unfolded this way, had done so for all the years since Bandar had found his way into this innocuous corner of the Commons, the great collective unconscious of humankind. There were more erotic Situations than this one, certainly there were more realistic representations of intergender relations, but it was to this Location that Guth Bandar often repaired when life became wearisome and his troubles outweighed his joys.

There was an sweet innocence to the place. As near as he could tell, the three girls were not even anatomically correct. Their breasts were well enough conceived, although the aureoles were too perfectly round, but in the less obvious places things seemed only sketchily realized. It was the fantasy of a boy still approaching the cusp of manhood: the girls could be chased and finally caught, but after that it all grew a little vague.

Bandar wanted to prolong the moment before commencing the sequence that would inevitably end the Location's cycle. It was not the prepubescent frolic that lured him to this place, but its atmosphere: the aura of naivete, of a world that had not yet encountered guile and cynicism.

For Guth Bandar had lately encountered both, and in too ample a measure. They had come in the unwelcome form of Didrick Gabbris. For now, having achieved only disaster at the Grand Colloquium, Bandar's tenure as an adjunct scholar had been abruptly terminated. He had been required to return his gown and pin and to vacate the little office in the basement of the Institute's connaissarium where he had conducted his researches. The fellows and scholars had ceremoniously turned their backs on him, looking anywhere but at Guth Bandar while he trudged to the great doors of Magisters Hall and departed.

The day should have ended in a triumph, the once–and–forever scotching of the odious Gabbris. But when Bandar had presented his revolutionary thesis—that the collective unconscious had paradoxically achieved consciousness, that the noösphere had become self–aware—the assembled noönauts of the Institute had turned on him. Snorts of disbelief and hoots of derision had battered at Bandar's ears, and the ranks of scholars assembled for the Grand Colloquium had become a sea of outraged faces and shaken fists. Even his young assistant, Chundlemars, had quickly joined the mob, and Bandar's last sight of him had been of a protruding tongue, comically enlarged eyes and hands that made circular motions around the ears.

The blonde idiomat came up the beach and offered Bandar a theatrical wink, pursed her full lips in an unwitting parody of eroticism, then turned to flee in anticipation of pursuit. But Bandar smiled wanly and flourished a weak hand. When he remained recumbent beneath the tree, she reformed her lips into a moue of dismissal and went away with what would have been a swish and flounce of fabric had she been wearing any.

Bandar knew he would soon have to get up and play out the sequence or see the dream dissolve. He had not come to this Location by chanting a thran but by the more mundane expedient of falling asleep and allowing his own personal unconscious to connect him to the Commons. Even so, he was no ordinary dreamer; he could lucidly focus his awareness within a dream so that its figures and events became almost as real as if he walked through his waking life.

Still, there were limits. If he did not get up now and respond to the idomatic entities' importunings, he would overstress the fabric of this Situation and it would pop like a bubble. He essayed a small growl and put one elbow under him. The three girls tittered and coquetted a few steps away.

"Guth Bandar," said a soft voice beside his ear.

The noönaut felt a shock and a shiver as if an icy finger had trailed up his spine. The girls could not speak—prepubescent boys do not look to their fantasy objects for conversation—and there should have been no other entity within this Location.

In the Commons, when things went wrong they tended to go disastrously, dangerously—and all too frequently—lethally wrong. Bandar did not hesitate but mentally reached for the procedure that would propel him post haste from the dream into full consciousness. But his cognitive grasp closed on emptiness; something was blocking his technique.

"Stay," said the voice, and now Bandar had to turn to face whatever was there, because one rule every student noönaut learned was always to confront the unconscious. *To run is to be run*, went the old maxim. *To stand is to withstand.*

But when he stood and looked behind him, there was nothing to face down. The voice had come from the jungle beyond the coconut palm, an indifferently realized pastiche of leaves, vines and creeper that was only slightly more convincing than if it had been painted on stage cloth.

"Who speaks?" he said.

The answer came not in words but as a ripple in the air: the familiar sign that a gate had opened between this Location and some other corner of the Commons. The exit's presence deepened Bandar's worry: he knew every inch of this palmy beach and knew that the only way in and out, whether he came as a dreamer or as a conscious chanter of thrans, was eighteen paces to the left of the tree, a spot just past an ornate conch shell washed up above the limit of the surf.

He took stock of his situation. *I am stranded in a dream, bespoke by an unknown entity and beckoned to enter a gate that ought not exist. My day proceeds from defeat to who knows what further drama?*

A terrible thought occurred to him. *Have I become a natural?* he wondered. It was an accusation that Didrick Gabbris had hurled at him in the Grand Colloquium, and Bandar had shrugged it off as the merely another dart of abuse chosen from his rival's copious quiver of epithets and slanders.

Now, standing in the warmth of this generic beach, Bandar felt a shiver and an unaccustomed chill. Could Gabbris have been right?

All humans could visit the collective unconscious and did so nightly; the Commons was where the engrammatic stuff of dreams cohered in nodes and corpuscles called Locations, cyclical and eternal. A minority of humankind could consciously enter the wondrous and dreadful realm in which the composite experience of humanity was gathered and distilled to its essences. That minority was further divided into two classes: one was composed of Institute scholars trained in the techniques of orphic thrans that kept them from being perceived by the noösphere's archetypal inhabitants; the other category comprised the irredeemably insane—psychotics whose shattered personas had merged utterly with one of the primal entities loose in the shared basement of the human mind.

The significant difference between noönauts and the deranged was that the scholars retained an awareness of themselves as distinct from their putative surroundings—Bandar knew the people and things of the Commons were not "really real," though the dangers they posed might be—while loons and ravers could not reliably distinguish between a ravenous vampire and a hapless neighbor, which was why a chance encounter on the sidewalk could move in unexpected directions.

Guth Bandar reminded himself of this crucial distinction as he heard again the whispered summons from the darkness beneath the palms, where the rift in the air still quivered. *Can I be mad,* he asked himself, *if I am willing to consider the real possibility that I am indeed mad?* He realized that the question led only to a conundrum: the judgment of the insane must always be suspect; only a sane man's verdict could be relied upon, but a sane man would never pronounce himself mad.

"Guth Bandar," said the soft voice. Bandar thought about

fleeing the summons. If he couldn't wake himself up, there was another way out: noönauts who sang their way into the Commons could chant a specific thran that would open an emergency exit. Quite likely the same thran would pluck Bandar from this dream and in a second he would wake up in his bed, doubtless drenched in sweat, his limbs atremble.

But he left the seven notes unsung. Gabbris's victory in the Grand Colloquium had stung Bandar's pride. He was no natural. He was a true noönaut and he knew that the Commons had indeed communicated with him, as if it were a conscious entity. He had not been able to convince his peers and betters at the Institute, might never be able to do so. But a true scholar does not turn aside when confronted by the inexplicable. He penetrates the mystery.

Bandar squared his narrow shoulders and advanced to the rippling slit in the air. Without hesitation, he stepped through.

Beyond the beach was a luminous fog, a mist so dense that Bandar's hand, held at arm's length, became a doubtful object. Bandar knew that there were three fog–bound Locations in the collective unconscious: one was a Landscape (or more properly, a Seascape), that featured a ship enshrouded on an archetypal ocean; another had the same combination of elements but was classified as an Event, because the ship ran aground and broke up on unseen rocks, casting passengers and crew into the cold sea; the third was an urban Landscape where the idiomats stumbled on cobblestoned streets, feeling their way along walls of brick and fences of black iron on which the mist condensed and chilled their fingers.

This was none of those three, Bandar was sure, but to be certain he used the noönaut technique that summoned up his de-tailed globular map of the Commons. He rotated the sphere until he found the Location with the beach and its winsome idiomats, then identified each of the befogged Locations. As he had expected, there was no direct connection from the beach to any of the three; he would have had to pass through a Garden, a Class Two Massacre and a Class One Natural Disaster just to reach the nearest.

Now Bandar refocused his awareness on the sphere and em-ployed another aspect of his noönaut training. The result of his effort should have been to create a small pulsation in the symbol that represented whatever Location he now occupied. But though he applied the method again and then still once more, with increased intensity, not one of the emblems in the sphere responded.

That is impossible, Bandar thought. It meant that he must be in some corner of the Commons that was not on the map. But the noösphere had been fully explored and charted tens of millennia ago. The Great Delineation had been the work of thousands of generations and it had cost the lives of untold numbers of members of the Institute of Historical Inquiry, men and women who had bravely ventured into Locations and been absorbed into their spurious realities before they could ascertain which combinations of tones would screen them from their idiomatic inhabitants' perceptions, or find the way out before the Situation or Event reached the end of its cycle and reformed to begin anew.

Perhaps Gabbris is right, Bandar thought. *Perhaps I have taken leave of my senses and become a natural.* He imagined the uproar that would ensue if he returned to the Grand Colloquium and declared that not only was the Commons aware of its own existence, but that it contained at least one Location that had remained undetected during the vast span of time since the first noönaut, the Beatified Arous, found his way through the Golden Door. *Madness*, he thought, *yet here I am.*

"Not madness," said the soft voice. "Merely something new."

In the fog, the sound seemed to come from all directions and from none. Bandar collapsed the sphere then turned and peered about him, but there was only the ubiquitous vapor. He looked up to see if he could identify a direction from which the light came, and thus orient himself, but no part of the unseeable sky was brighter than any other.

Now he became aware of a shape a little to his right. He turned to face it, at the same time beginning to chant the four and six thran, the sequence of tones that was most commonly effective.

"It will do you no good," said the voice.

Bandar switched to the seven and three.

"Neither will that." The shape was becoming clearer. It was human in size and outline.

He tried the four four and two.

"Nor that." It was moving closer, though Bandar saw no

motion that suggested walking. It seemed to float toward him through the mist.

"Who are you?" he said. "What do you want of me?"

"You know who we are," said the voice.

The figure had come close enough for Bandar to see that it was definitely human, but that was its only definite characteristic. Its progress stopped when it was near enough for him to have touched its face, and he stared, trying to bring form and features into focus.

But he could not. The face and figure before him constantly shifted, a set of features appearing and disappearing every second in a constant series of slow dissolves. He saw an old man, a young girl, a scarred warrior, an evil king, a sad-eyed clown, a were-beast, a matron, a shining god. The form beneath the face shifted in harmony, showing him lush robes succeeded by battered armor, replaced by rough-sewn animal skins, which gave way to roseate nakedness supplanted by samite threaded through by gold.

"I know who you are," Bandar said. "You are the Multifacet." He used the term every loblolly learned in his first week at the Institute. It denoted the crowd of archetypal personas that made up the human psyche and from which every individual assembled a personality, some taking more of this one and less of that one, and everyone's individual mix evolving over a lifetime, as nature and circumstances dictated. But here they were assembled in one vessel.

"Yes." The answer came when the figure was that of a young stripling, the voice breaking to make two syllables out of one.

Bandar let anger infuse his reply. "You are the one who has ruined my career."

A wicked witch-king answered, "But to a purpose."

"No purpose of mine."

"We could give you an argument on that. We contain all that combines to form you, after all."

Bandar folded his arms across his chest. "But we have not arrived at 'after all,'" he said. "Instead, I am in the springtime of my life, which you have just diverted from the only course along which I ever sought to shape my years."

The shifting faces regarded him through a succession of eyes—sharp, mild, innocent, cunning—then the voice of an aged queen said, "We require you to perform a service. We will reward you, as best we may."

"Reward me? Very well, return me to the Institute's good graces and I am yours."

"We cannot," said a portly toper. "A life at the Institute will not shape you to do what you must do."

"Then how will you repay me for the loss of my heart's desire?"

A bearded prophet answered, "With useful qualities that are ours to bestow: the power to persuade, the knack of winning trust and affection, luck in small things." By the time the speech was finished, the speaker was a sly–eyed rogue.

"None of these came to my aid in the Grand Colloquium."

"Your path does not lead through the Institute."

"*My* path?" Bandar said. "If it is not mine to choose, by what definition does it remain *my* path?"

"We cannot debate with you," said a slack mouthed idiot that became a proud hierophant. "You are chosen. You must accept."

"And if I will not?"

"You must."

"What is the service you require?"

"We cannot tell you that."

"When would I have performed it and be free of you?"

"Not for many years."

"Then why disrupt my life now?"

"You must have time to grow into the kind of man who can do what must be done."

"What kind of man is that?"

There was no answer. Bandar had had enough. "You abort my career then offer me trinkets for some service you will not define. I decline your offer. Instead I will awaken now and let you seek out a more credulous implement for your obscure purposes. I recommend Didrick Gabbris."

He opened his mouth to sound the seven notes that would pluck him from this nebulous place and let him wake in his bed. But the protean figure before him raised a hand, smooth and full fleshed as it came up, transforming into a black gauntlet as it mimed squeezing with thumb and forefinger. Bandar's throat closed. He could make no sound, not even a moan around the obstacle that his tongue had suddenly become.

A rift opened in the pearly mist. Bandar's eyes narrowed against a burst of raw sunlight, then he felt himself propelled through the node. He fell to his knees and pitched forward. Burning sand stung his palms. Heat swaddled him and the air was thick with the rank odor of stale sweat.

"Up!" said a harsh voice. A line of fire cut across the noönaut's shoulders. He would have screamed if he could have, but his voice was still imprisoned within his chest. The lash came back, this time striking the same flesh and creating a pain that compounded the first to evoke an astonishing effect. Bandar leapt to his feet and looked about him.

The desert stretched in every direction but to his rear, where trees sheltered a substantial town beside a broad river, with grain fields beyond the farther shore. Ahead was a massive pile of masonry, each sand–colored, oblong block as long as Bandar was tall and half his height in cross–section. He could measure their size accurately because just such a block was immediately before him, snared in a net of fibrous ropes and with peeled logs beneath to roll on. The ropes went forward to rest upon the shoulders of a gang of straining, half–naked men. Two others were busy pulling logs from behind the back of the stone and running to position them just ahead of its inching progress. A few more were at the rear of the procession that was pushing the block forward and it was here that Guth Bandar found himself. They all wore long kilts of linen and not much else, although some had sandals and a few wore skull caps. Bandar looked down at himself and found that he was similarly attired.

But the hands and arms he saw, the pot belly and spindly shanks leading to splayed flat feet, were not those of Guth Bandar. It was an unheard–of circumstance. A noönaut entered the Commons in his own virtual image. But Bandar here was clearly not Bandar in appearance. Somehow he had been thrust into the "flesh" of an idiomat. It was but the latest impossibility that Bandar had had to swallow, but it was the one that worried him most.

"Push!" said the voice that had accompanied the whip. The noönaut hastened to place his palms against the sandstone and shove before the braided leather could revisit the welt made by its previous landings and bring about an as yet hypothetical but entire-ly likely third degree of agony whose existence Bandar did not wish to confirm. The stone was cool against his sweating palms and the effort needed to move it across the rollers—aided by all the other straining muscles in the work gang—was not as taxing as he would have expected. Indeed, the men pulling and repositioning the rollers seemed to be working harder than the haulers.

The labor required no mental effort, however, other than to remember to step over the rearmost log as it was pulled from beneath the block. Bandar was thus able to give his full attention to his predicament. The more he considered it, the worse it became. The amount of activity around him, the scope and scale of the site, told him that this was not just a Landscape, nor was it a mere Situation: this was an Event, and a Class One Event at that.

The scholars of the Institute categorized the myriad Locations of the noösphere into three types. The simplest were Landscapes, which were recollections of the archetypal settings against which the long story of human existence had been carried out. They ranged from the painted caves that sheltered humankind's infancy through jungle and farmed plain to cityscapes of all ages, including the most decadent of Old Earth's penultimate age.

More complex were the Situations, which preserved all the recurrent circumstances and rites of passage that were the land-marks of human life, from birth through the first kiss, to the meeting of soulmates and on to the gathering of kin around the deathbed. Situations also covered all the darker milestones to be encountered between cradle and grave: the stillborn child, the lover's betrayal, the breaking of friendship's bonds and the lonely death in the wil-derness.

Most detailed of all were the Events, the turning points great and small on which history had pivoted: from the fire–hunt that chased mammoths over cliffs to the first planting of crops, through the founding and sack of cities, to the taming of frontiers and the building of topless towers.

Landscapes were classified according to their size, from a back street to a trackless ocean. All of them recycled quickly. Situations were ranked according to their complexity: some might involve no more than one person's hand enfolding another's; others might require a cast of thousands. But the duration of most Situations was brief, from a moment to at most a few hours, then the elements re-formed and the process began anew.

Events, however, might range in duration from under a minute (for a Class Six occurrence like a sprinters' foot race), to a span of many years, even of more than a lifetime, as in such Class One Events as The Opening of the Territory or The Invasion of the Barbarians.

As Bandar shoved against the block of stone and gazed about him at the scores of other work gangs playing their parts he became more and more fearful that he was trapped in a Location that might endure for as long as a slave—for surely that was what he was in this place—could expect to live.

Unable to speak, he could not sing the tones that would hide him from the perceptions of the idiomatic entities around him. Nor could he activate an exit node and escape back to the waking world. Until his voice returned—and he refused to believe it would not—he was stuck in what was obviously an early version of a Class One Event: The Building of the Grand Monument.

Bandar continued to push, the cycle of the rollers continued, and time wore on as he looked about him and waited for his throat to heal. He was hoping that the cause of his muteness was induced hysterical paralysis, which might fade with time, rather than a magic spell. In the Commons, magic worked effectively and permanently. He grunted and achieved a chesty sound. But when he sought to generate different tones he could not convince himself that he was meeting with success.

His efforts attracted the attention of the idiomat next to him, a heavy featured man whose back and chest were slabs of muscle and whose arms were corded with hard flesh. The entity turned his small, close–set eyes on Bandar and regarded him without favor, then said, "Shut up, dummy," and laughed at his own wit. In case there was any doubt that the injunction should not be interpreted as friendly banter from an amiable workmate, he accompanied it with a slap of his plate–sized hand that left Bandar's virtual head ringing.

Bandar subsided. He would wait until he was alone to try again. He had only to manage the seven tones and his consciousness would be freed from this imprisoning false flesh. He would wake at home in his bed.

The passage of the sun told him that he had arrived in the Event at about mid–morning. By the time the men's shadows were pooled about their feet, they had brought the block more than halfway to its destination. At that point, a two–wheeled cart caught up with them, pulled by a leather–skinned old man wearing only a kind of diaper. The overseer with the whip, a skinny fellow with a squint in one eye, called a halt. The slaves immediately stopped their labors and began what looked to Bandar to be a practiced routine: some pulled from the cart a few poles and a wide bolt of cloth and quickly created an awning whose back wall was the stone block. Others extracted baskets of round, flat loaves and terracotta jars that sloshed with liquid confined by wooden stoppers. The men gathered to sit in the shade of the cloth while the food and drink was passed around.

Bandar lowered his buttocks to the hot sand and accepted a chunk torn from a loaf and a wooden cup from the man next to him, a young–looking idiomat who offered him a shy smile and a friendly word. The old man in the loincloth stooped to pour from one of the jars and Bandar smelled the yeasty odor of beer. He drank half a cupful in one gulp, finding it sour but refreshing, then bit off a mouthful of bread and chewed. It was tough though flavorful, despite occasional iotas of grit that scored the enamel of his teeth.

He swallowed and regarded the idiomats with circumspect glances, sorting them into types. Travelers in the noösphere had to remember that its inhabitants were only facsimiles of human persons. Principals of Class One Events and Situations might be somewhat internally varied and nuanced. But none approached the complexity of even the simplest human being. The average idiomatic entity was no more than a bundle of basic motivations and responses, enough for it to play its role in the Location's action. It most resembled a character out of fiction.

So the youth with the shy smile was almost certainly a variant of Doomed Innocence. The big man who had slapped Bandar, and who now hulked with two Henchmen where the awning's shade was deepest, was a classic Bully—and perhaps a lethal one if provoked. The noönaut glanced about and saw other instantly recognizable types: a blank Despair mechanically chewing his crust, a self–possessed Loner off to one side, a bluff Salt–of–the–Earth with chin up and eyes clear, and now here came a smarmy Toady to bring the Bully a refill of beer. The squinting overseer appeared to be a variation on the universal Functionary, specifically an Unambitious version, which was a relief to Bandar, who might have found himself under the rein of a Sadist or Martinet. There was no Hero or Un-recognized King in the mix, so Bandar came to the preliminary conclusion that this gang was no more than a background element in whatever main stories were woven through the Event.

That was a small mercy, since it meant he was unlikely to find himself as a Spear Carrier in a revolt with a life expectancy of hours at best. He would probably have enough time to work out a means of extracting himself from this Location, although time was an enemy as well as a friend: eventually, he would become absorbed into the Event, his consciousness abraded away until only some rudi-mentary functions remained. His real body would lapse into a coma and dwindle to lifelessness while what was left of Bandar repetitive-ly pushed a stone block across a desert, until the extinction of the human species.

One of the fastest routes to absorption was to interact with the elements of the Location. Bandar had to eat and drink and breathe the hot dry air—here his virtual flesh had all the needs and limi-tations of his real body lying asleep in his room at the Institute—but forming relationships with idiomats was the greatest danger. So when the Doomed Innocence asked if he was all right, Bandar turned his shoulder and stared into the heat haze that filled the middle distance. The idiomat turned away and was drawn into a conversation among the other men concerning appropriate tactics in some form of team sport.

After they ate, the gang was allowed a siesta. Bandar copied the others, scooping out holes for hip and shoulder then reposing himself on the sand, but though he closed his eyes his mind re-mained active while stereotypical snores erupted around him. He sorted through his options: the restriction of his voice might wear off, but that was nothing to count on; he might find a magician who was willing to help. he might somehow train an idiomat to sound the seven–note emergency than for him, though how he might do that while mute was hard to imagine and besides, it would require encouraging an idiomat to act contrary to its nature—the technical term for such behavior was *disharmony*—which could lead to sudden and even contagious violence; or, best of all, he could find or make a musical instrument that could be tuned to produce the right tones in the right sequence for the right duration.

There was nothing within eyeshot that offered any promise. Bandar would have to wait until they moved to a richer environment: the encampment wherever this crew overnighted. With that issue settled, he turned his mind to the question of what had brought him here. It was not a happy series of thoughts. The collective unconscious was apparently, paradoxically, conscious. It was aware of itself. Worse, it had an agenda, a will of its own. Worse yet, it had no qualms about interfering with the consciousness of an individual—or even several; Bandar now realized that the harsh reception he had received at the Grand Colloquium might well have been stimulated by the Commons. Worst of all, the individual consciousness that had been selected for the most aggravated interference was Guth Bandar's.

He could content himself with one realization, however: he had not been dumped into this specific Location by random chance. Nor had he been sent here to be eliminated; there were many Locations in the Commons where life expectancy was to be measured in seconds. Instead of being popped into a lightless steerage cabin far below the deck of a sinking ocean liner or into the path of a superheated pyroclastic cloud rushing down the slope of an erupting volcano at almost the speed of sound, he had been eased into a slowly evolving Event.

Bandar knew enough about the noösphere to be certain that the self–aware Commons had placed him here so that he could receive the collective unconscious's most routine product, that which was dispensed through myth, fable, joke, and every other kind of story from classic literature to popular entertainment: a lesson.

He couldn't learn his lesson if he were dead, and it would do him no good if he was to be absorbed into this Event. So the wisest course was to go along with the Commons's scheme, until he could contrive an escape.

Bandar lay awake and mulled. The obvious lesson to be drawn from being enslaved and forced to push massive blocks under punishing sun and lash was obedience. Although, he reminded himself, the noösphere was not always obvious. Sometimes it delivered its messages through side doors or by the sudden emergence from the background of some overlooked but telling detail. He resolved to remain vigilant.

After what seemed a long while, the overseer crawled out of the shade beneath the cart where he had slept in relative isolation and began kicking feet and poking buttocks with the butt of his whip. The slaves arose, stretching and yawning theatrically, and drained the last of the beer from the jug. Several of them went off behind an outcrop of rust–colored rock to relieve themselves then straggled back to strike the awning and load it, along with the empty baskets and beer jugs, into the old man's cart.

The cart trundled back toward town while Bandar and the others resumed their labors. As the afternoon wore on the block inched toward the monument. Bandar scanned the huge structure, trying to determine what its ultimate form and dimensions might be, but it was early in the construction process and all he could know for sure was that the final creation would rest upon a colossal foundation of stone.

As the sun touched the horizon, they delivered the block to a staging area where a man wearing a linen wrap and a headdress chased with colored threads used a stick of charcoal to draw symbols on its upper surface. The stone was apparently no longer the concern of Bandar's gang, because the overseer efficiently chivvied them into a double column and directed them to march back the way they had come. The return journey was remarkably quick after their laborious day–long progress.

Bandar found himself walking in the middle of the formation, Doomed Innocence on his left and the Toady literally on his heels. But he paid no attention to either the former's renewed attempts at conversation nor to the latter's treading on his tendons. His placement in relation to the others would not be coincidence—in the Commons, coincidence was never a random event, but rather a sign that the noösphere's operating system was functioning at optimum efficiency. The less Bandar responded to idiomats' overtures, the more slowly he would be absorbed.

Near the end of their march they passed a substantial encampment of linen tents set in neatly ordered rows around a playing field where idiomat soldiers drilled in formation with spear and shield or sparred in pairs with wooden swords and war hatchets. The slave quarters lay on the edge of town, an unwalled cluster of large huts made in plaited reeds and thatched with matted straw. Cooking fires burned in mud brick ovens, tended by typical female idiomats: a few Crones, some Maidens (both the Demure and Saucy variants) and at least a couple of Sturdy Matrons, all dressed in lengths of coarse cloth wound about their bodies and pinned at the shoulder. They were stirring communal pots full of the evening meal, a bubbling concoction of generic grains and meat scraps with a pungent odor.

Bandar found that the food was eaten communally as well, with everyone seated on woven reed mats surrounding a bonfire in the open space at the center of the slave quarters. First he must get in line and take a shallow wooden plate from a stack on a table. Then he shuffled along to where a Demure Maiden ladled out a thick concoction of grain, vegetables and chunks of gray meat. Bandar saw a complex exchange of looks between the Maiden and Doomed Innocence and wondered if this was the situation in which he was supposed to involve himself. He did not meet the young female idiomat's gaze as she ladled out his share. He looked about for utensils but saw none; then he noted that the man in front of him taking some thin flat bread from a stack on a nearby table where he also collected a cup of the weak beer.

Bandar did likewise then followed the fellow over to some empty spots on the mats, several feet from where Doomed Innocence was clearly saving a space for his friend the mute. Bandar paid no heed to the increasingly puzzled idiomat's attempts to attract his attention. Instead he watched as the man beside him put the bowl before him on the ground and tore off a swatch of bread half the size of his palm; then, holding the scrap between thumb and fingers, he used it to pinch up a mouthful of the bowl's contents. Bandar copied the action and was rewarded with a taste so spicy that he reached at once for the beer.

The heat of the day faded rapidly as full dark came on. Bandar shivered and wondered where he was to spend the night. Probably one of the big huts, with everyone squeezed together for warmth, he decided. Though not quite everyone, he decided, as the squinting overseer led the Maiden who had served Bandar his food toward a smaller hut at the edge of the open space, while Doomed Innocence regarded them glumly.

Bandar knew that the archetypal Mute usually manifested in one of two main sub–archetypes: Sinister or Sympathetic. He seemed to be of the latter species. He had no idea how the collective unconscious had contrived to replace an existing figure; it would be well worth a paper for the Institute, if he survived to write it, and if the scholars would ever deign to listen to him again, now that their minds had been subtly poisoned against him from within.

He was not yet sure what his role was supposed to be, but his speculations became moot when a steaming dab of pottage unexpectedly struck Bandar's bare chest, the stuff hot enough to sting. He brushed it away with the backs of his fingers, then looked up to see the Toady sneering at him from the other side of the communal fire, a short lath of wood cocked in his hands, ready to flick a second scalding missile Bandar's way. Behind him, the Bully and the Henchmen stood laughing.

Bandar reacted without thinking, a flash of anger causing him to hurl his empty beer cup at his tormentor so that it struck the man square in the forehead. The Toady fell back, howling, his feet kicking in the air. A general laugh went up from the crowd but quickly subsided when the Bully leapt to his feet, glared at Bandar and pointed a thick, calloused finger. "You!" he said.

Bandar had regretted the flinging of the cup even as it left his hand. In the Commons, it was best to act only upon conscious reflection. An automatic response could be a sign that the Location's rules of procedure had begun to seep into the noönaut's virtual being, a precursor to absorption. Now he had scarcely the span of two breaths to reflect on how to respond to the Bully, because the big idiomat and his thugs were coming around the bonfire and the expression on their faces left no doubt as to what they intended to do.

Bandar knew a number of techniques for self defense—it was a necessary skill for anyone venturing into the noösphere. But a Sympathetic Mute would not stand and fight a Bully and his gang. For him to do so could introduce a sharply disharmonious element to the Location, triggering potentially dangerous chaos. Serious disruptions could even cause an Event to reinitiate itself prematurely; if that were to happen, Bandar's consciousness would not survive the change–over. He thought these things as he sprang to his feet and ran into the darkness, the bellowing idiomats pounding after him.

No walls confined the slaves. Once out of town, they had nowhere to go but the desert and the river that probably teemed with crocodiles. Bandar took his chances with the town. It was laid out haphazardly, and first he ran through narrow streets curling among huts and rough corrals that penned baaing goats and sheep. Then he came into broader streets, though still paved only with dirt, of more substantial habitations, mud brick with wooden shutters over glassless windows; some were even walled compounds with gates of squared timbers. All of these details Bandar acquired on the run, finding his way by the light of a half moon, augmented by occasional oil lamps flickering in windows or by burning torches affixed over gates.

The Bully and his gang stayed with him through every twist and turning. The big idiomat was probably too simple to do other than follow his nature, Bandar thought, and too strong to tire easily. The noönaut did not look back but he could hear his pursuers' heavy footfalls and panting breaths coming ever nearer. The Mute was not built for a long chase.

He was racing down a wider street than most, the way lined with walls and stout fences. Here might be Officials in whose presence the Bully would have to prostrate himself and forego his violent intentions. Bandar saw an open gate flanked by burning brands, a lit courtyard beyond. He took the risk of slowing, felt the angry idiomat's fingers graze his shoulder as he turned and dodged through the gate.

He had hoped to find a person of rank at ease in his yard, perhaps with guards or stout servants who would cow the bully. Instead, Bandar pulled up short in the dust–floored open space, seeing only a moderately ample mud–brick house with an open front. Here, under a thatched awning, an idiomat man and boy were doing something the noönaut did not have time to identify, because the pursuing Bully immediately struck him from behind and knocked him sprawling.

Bandar tumbled to the ground and tried to roll away, but a foot caught him under the ribs and the pain and impact drove the air out of his virtual lungs. The Bully and his gang stood over him, mouthing imprecations Bandar couldn't quite catch over the roaring in his ears, then a second kick grazed his head and the night erupted in colored lights.

He hugged his head between his forearms and curled up, waiting for the next strike. But it didn't come. He heard another voice, then the sound of flesh smacking flesh followed by grunts and a moan. Bandar inched apart his arms just far enough to peek out.

He saw the Bully getting to his hands and knees, blood pouring from a nose that had acquired a new angle. A brawny man wearing a scarred leather kilt was bringing one sandaled foot to connect with a Henchman's buttocks, causing him to stumble quickly through the gate and into the street. The other thug, along with the Toady, stood beyond the gateway wearing looks of wide–eyed consternation.

In a few seconds the yard was cleared, Bandar's former pursuers issuing dire threats but putting distance between themselves and the brawny idiomat who laughed as he slammed the gate shut then turned to regard Bandar. "What did you do to set that lumbering mutton–thumper after you?" he said.

Bandar got to his knees and strove to reorder his breathing. He indicated to his rescuer that he had no voice, and saw the man nod. The idiomat approached and put a thickly calloused hand under Bandar's arm, lifting him to his feet as if he weighed no more than the skinny youth who was watching them from the open space before the house.

Bandar recognized the setting: the front of the house was an open–air smithy—with anvil, forge, hammers and tongs, tub of water—and the older idiomat was a Smith while the younger was clearly a version of the Shiftless Apprentice. The noönaut now experienced a shiver of alarm as he noted that the Smith was a more than averagely realized idiomat. His intervention to save Bandar argued that he was at least partially formed of Hero–stuff, and therefore potentially a more significant figure in this Event, perhaps even one of its Principals or Subprincipals.

I should get away from here, he thought as he bowed and gestured to disavow any need for the Smith's further care and solicitude. The pain in his abdomen was fading.

"If you say so," said the idiomat, returning to the anvil where he had been working before Bandar erupted into his yard, "but your friends might be waiting for you down the street. They didn't seem the kind to forgive and forget."

Bandar shrugged. Interaction with a Principal would accelerate his absorption. He needed to put distance between himself and this element of the Location. He bowed again, managed a grateful smile, and turned toward the gate.

"Good luck," he heard the Smith say. Then he heard something else: a *clink* of metal on metal, a *clink* that was precisely the tone of the second note in the seven–note emergency escape thran. Bandar turned back.

The work was not hard. Bandar took the place of the lazy idiomat boy who operated the bellows. This was a sewn–up goat-skin with two wooden handles that Bandar pulled aside and pushed together, filling and emptying the trapped air which rushed through the skin's neck to feed the glowing charcoal in the forge.

The overseer had come in the morning, Bully and Toady eager in his wake, to demand the runaway's return. The Smith had stood up to him, speaking in tones of genial reason.

"The Subgovernor constantly demands that the work proceed more quickly. He needs more tools, sharper tools. I need strong arms at the bellows. Why don't we go and ask His Excellency?"

Bandar saw alarm flicker in the Functionary's eyes. "We need not trouble the Subgovernor," the idiomat said.

"Then it is settled."

"My tally will be short."

The Smith gestured to the boy. "Take back this boy you gave me the last time I said I needed help. He's better at running errands than squatting at the bellows. Let him bring your cup and carry messages."

Faced with a combination of unyielding will and an avenue of lateral evasion, the overseer acceded. The boy went, Bandar stayed, and the Bully left with thunder in his face, cuffing the Toady out of his way at the gate.

Bandar easily settled into the rhythm of the Smith's days. In the early morning and evening he attended at the forge. When the heat grew oppressive, they worked in the relative cool of the mud brick house, sharpening iron chisels and wedges with file and whetstone and shaping the molds of damp sand in which bronze and copper castings were made. The Smith seemed pleased with his efforts and they worked well together. For his part, Bandar felt comfortable in the role of helper. At least he was not involved in the inevitable strife that would pit Doomed Innocence's infatuation against the overseer's appetites. Nothing hastened a noönaut's absorption into a Location faster than joining in a conflict.

At midday, along with the rest of the town, they took their siesta, Bandar curling up on a rough mattress of coarse cloth stuffed with grass against the back wall of the smithy. He had never slept in the Commons before; sensible noönauts rarely stayed long enough to feel the need and when they did, they sang open a gate and left. He noted that he experienced no dreams, though this made sense to him when he thought about it: a conscious unconscious was enough of a contradiction in terms; the dreams of dreams were not to be thought of.

Every other day, in the evening, a wagon arrived, driven by an overseer drawn by a donkey and surrounded by a squad of guards armed with sword, spear and shield. When the entourage halted in the smithy's yard the gates were closed and the guards took up positions to secure the area. Bandar came out with the Smith and together they took from the overseer—this one the type classified as Exacting Functionary—three baskets of iron and bronze tools to be sharpened or repaired. They carried them into the smithy where, under the watchful eye of the overseer and the captain of the guards, each item was counted out and checked against a tally.

When the procedure was completed, the Smith brought out a second load of tools that had been refurbished over the preceding two days. Again, each tool was meticulously checked against a list written in charcoal on a roll of papyrus. When every piece had been accounted for, the wagon was loaded and reversed, and the guards alertly checked the street before allowing it to roll through the gate.

Once the days had settled into a routine, Bandar took action to change his situation. While the rest of the household napped in the heat of the day, he rose from his straw tick and went to the forge. To anyone who might chance to observe him, he was a smith's helper arranging tools and materials in better order on the work bench. But his true purpose was to strike each metal object with a small scrap of iron, listening to the note that rang in response.

The medium sized tongs were what had made the note he had first heard, the second in the series of seven. A strip of iron banding, used to strengthen tubs and barrels, sounded with the frequency of the fourth note. That left five to be discovered. Bandar worked his way along the bench, found a punch that rang with the tone of the third.

He allowed himself a moment of happy anticipation. He had worked out the situation. The Multifacet had sent him here for some purpose. He was sure it had to do with Doomed Innocence, since he had been plunked down in the virtual body of a Sympathetic Mute who would have been the youthful idiomat's natural companion in the work gang. Bandar was supposed to learn a lesson of altruism, perhaps even of self–sacrifice, which would suit him for whatever task the Commons wished him to perform in the far off future.

But the noönaut had been too canny. He had broken out of the context in which he had been placed, found a new setting in which all that was required of him were his functioning arms. And now he was putting together the means to open a gate and leave this Location. After that, he would never again come unawares into the Commons; he knew techniques that would keep him safe once he was free of the stricture at his throat. The noösphere would have to find another patsy.

He turned his attention to some hoe blades heaped in the corner and after a few tries found one that rang with the frequency of note seven. *Three to go*, he thought, then he noticed a wooden plank beneath the hoes, set flush with the dirt floor and so discolored by ash and soot so that it blended in with the packed earth around it.

Curious, Bandar brushed aside the farmers' tools and examined the wood. It seemed to be a small trap door. He used the edge of a hoe to pry it up and peered within, finding a layer of sacking. This he pulled up, disturbing what was underneath. He heard a *clonk* that, to his pitch–perfect noönaut's ear, was the exact sound of note number one in the seven–tone thran. *Another down and only two to go*, he thought and reached into the hole.

His fingers closed around cold iron and he brought up what he had found. It was a broad bladed spear point, needle sharp at the tip and razor edged down both sides. He tapped it with the little bar of iron and it rang true. He set it down and reached deeper into the darkness, careful of cutting himself, and found more spearheads then a long bundle wrapped in sackcloth that contained three rudimentary short swords. He struck one with his rod but the sound it produced was off–key and useless.

A horn–skinned hand closed about the back of Bandar's neck

and he was pulled up and to his feet, then still higher so that his toes barely brushed the ground. He felt himself rotated until his eyes met those of an angry idiomat. The Smith shook the noönaut so that his virtual bones rattled within him.

"What are you doing?" was the Smith's first question. The second was, "Who sent you?"

Bandar opened his mouth, but no sound emerged. He tried to convey by facial expression alone that he was innocent of any ill intent, but he knew that his grimace of pain kept creeping in to overshadow the message. With a grunt of disgust, the Smith flung him toward a corner and Bandar landed hard on back and one elbow. The pain felt very real.

He struggled to rise. He saw another face peeking into the smithy from the yard: the old man in a loincloth who had brought lunch to the work gang. But Bandar's attention was soon reclaimed by the Smith. The big idiomat had gone to the forge and was now turned toward him. In his hand was a heavy maul and behind the anger in his honest face was an underlying expression of reluctant determination.

The little iron rod Bandar had used to test for tones had rolled free. He reached for it and struggled to his knees. If he had read the situation correctly, his appealingness as a Sympathetic Mute, coupled with the Smith's beneficent nature, could deliver him from the latter's anger—provided Bandar performed the right action. He stood up and went to the work bench where he struck the tongs, then the punch, ringing two pure notes from the metal. He struck the strengthening band, then from the three he played a simple tune.

The Smith now regarded him with a mixed countenance. Bandar tried for his most appealing expression as he crossed to the hoe blades and spear points and brought one of each back to the bench. He arranged them in a simple scale then played another tune for the idiomat, wishing as he did so that he had all seven tones needed to open a gate. But the song and the innocence of Bandar's borrowed face were having the desired effect.

"You just wanted to make music," the Smith said.

Bandar enthusiastically signaled an affirmative and the idiomat put down the maul, his face showing almost as much relief as Bandar felt. The old man came into the smithy and said, "We should have known. He's too simple to be a spy for the Subgovernor.

Come, let's get these things stowed before somebody sees them as shouldn't."

The noönaut enthusiastically helped transfer the weapons to baskets and hide them in the cart, and when the Smith unthinkingly counseled him to say nothing, he tapped his lips and smiled. They all laughed together, the Smith with a hearty boom and Bandar in heartfelt mime. The idiomats left him there and went into the house, doubtless to conspire further, Bandar thought. For his part, the noönaut assiduously fell to seeking the other two notes of the escape thran. He found tone number six in a copper ladle used to drip water on cooling metal, but the fifth and last note remained elusive.

Bandar struck his way about the forge with an energy that was increasingly desperate. This Location was not what he had thought it was: the Event was not a variant of The Building of the Grand Monument; it was an iteration of another great trope of the Commons—The Rising of the Oppressed. But, once again, Bandar's situation had started bad and become worse: the idiomat to whom he had attached himself was a Principal of this bloody Event. Worst of all, although Bandar was not particularly well versed in Revolts, he was enough of an Institute scholar to know that they almost always culminated in a massacre of the rebels.

The clandestine weapon–making was a sophisticated operation. Every piece of iron that entered the smithy was accounted for, from the raw ingots sent down from the City under guard by troops of the Governor's own household to the tools and implements distributed and collected each day by the Subgovernor's men at the slave camp. Even the pots and pans in which the communal meals were prepared were kept under guard.

But midway along the route between the Monument and the town someone with a knowledgeable eye had noted an outcrop of iron ore. The area soon became a place where slaves would relieve themselves, an activity they were allowed to do without being closely watched, the guards being almost as likely to go unsandaled as most of the workers. Unobserved, the slaves would break off handfuls of the friable rock and deposit it in the baskets from which the old man distributed bread at lunchtime, and which found their way to the smithy where the Smith would smelt the ore into iron and fashion weapons from it.

The old man who brought the ore also took away the weapons, carrying them back to the communal huts where the women hid them in the thatch and beneath the dirt floors. Bandar deduced that the arming of the slaves had been going on for quite some time and, judging by the ancient courier's excitement, the Rising was imminent.

It was an inspired plan. Not for the first time in his career as an aficionado of the kaleidoscope of human experiences exemplified in the Commons, Bandar marveled at the ingenuity with which the simple contrived to counter oppression by the mighty. But he also knew that a talent for brilliant improvisation was rarely a match for phalanxes of trained and well led soldiery. He definitely needed to find the missing fifth note and complete the thran.

Still, nothing rang with the right frequency, although the noönaut tinked and *tonked* on every possible object in the smithy and the attached household. His ability to search during his spare time grew limited, however, because the Smith required him to assemble various metallic items on the work bench and to reproduce tunes that the idiomat liked to hum while working at the forge.

It would not have been an intolerable existence but for the imminent threat of annihilation. Even so, Bandar found himself slipping into the routine of the days, taking pleasure in small things. The Smith was an agreeable sort, almost always of a pleasant disposition, being an idiomat idealist who lacked the full array of subtler sensibilities that would complexify the personality of even the most simple real human being. Bandar kept finding in himself an urge to be of help to the fellow, even to the point of wondering if there was some way he could prevent the cycle of the Event from fulfilling itself, which must surely end with the Smith heroically dead.

He resisted the urge, which was not ultimately put to the test. No options presented themselves for altering the inevitable flow of the Event toward its sad conclusion, and Bandar was resolved not to try to create one. If he were truly a misplaced idiomat—although he would have to be an Iconoclastic Genius rather than merely a Sympathetic Mute—Bandar might fortuitously discover an elementary explosive or craft a primitive aircraft that would give the slaves some advantage over the authorities.

But he was quite sure this was not an archetypal rendition of the Traveler Displaced in Time. So the moment he introduced disharmonious material, the Location would begin to accumulate stress on an exponential scale. Bandar had already been inside a Class Four Situation while it was coming apart because of his inadvertent interference; the thought of what it might be like to experience the dissolution of a Class One Event did not bear thinking of.

So he continued his search for the fifth note. It had the highest frequency of the seven, more than a full octave above the lowest. Bandar was starting to think that no object of iron, bronze or copper that he was likely to find around the smithy would produce it. A plate of very thin iron might do. He wondered if he could convince the idiomat to fashion a xylophone. But between his open and surreptitious labors the Smith was already so occupied that the likelihood was scant, even if Bandar could somehow communicate the idea.

Then one evening, as he helped the Smith fashion a mold in which to cast a set of bronze weights, Bandar heard the elusive note. It came from beyond the outer wall, from the cross street that the Smith had told him ran to where the Subgovernor's mansion sat on a slight rise overlooking town and river.

Bandar rose and took up the jug that held the water they used to dampen the sand of the mold. He went toward the well at one side of the yard, but instead of stopping continued on to the gate and looked out in time to see the source of the sound: four slaves were carrying a curtained litter, escorted by a squad of spearmen. Ahead of them all stepped an idiomat whose attire and bearing identified him as a variant of Pomposity in Office—a major–domo of some sort—and who carried a staff that curled into a loop at one end. Hung within the loop, gleaming in the day's dwindling light, was a small silver bell. As the party approached the next intersection, the servant shook the staff so that the bell sounded again—it was indeed precisely the right note—and every other idiomat on the street stopped, turned toward the litter and bowed.

The Smith had come to see what had caught his helper's attention. "The Subgovernor's First Wife," he said, following it with an eloquent twist of his mouth. "Come, we must finish."

Bandar went back to their work, but as he crossed the yard he heard again, fading into the distance, the sound that could offer him deliverance.

The calendar was built around the phases of the moon, with observances performed at its maximum wax and wane. Twice each month of twenty–eight days, all work ceased and all the town, high and low, slave and free, gathered at the white stone temple at the river's edge. Priests clad in fine robes hemmed and cuffed with metallic thread carried a great disc of beaten silver down to the water, where they ritually bathed the pale orb then bore it in a mass procession back up the broad stairs to the sanctuary. At the culmination of the ceremony, the high priest would bless the assembly then all would return to their dwellings for a celebratory meal, a siesta and, in the late afternoon, rowdy team sports and dancing.

The rising was set for the moment of the benediction. The shuffling throng on the steps was always a heterogeneous mingling of slaves, townsfolk and soldiers. Traditionally, when the hierophant spoke the concluding words of the rite—"It is done. Go now."—the mix would separate into its component streams, with the slaves walking back to their compound under loose guard, everyone glad of the feast and leisure to come.

The Subgovernor and his family sat on a platform to one side at the top of the steps, attended by their senior servants and a squad of bodyguards. Behind them a broad ramp descended to a paved road that led up the rise to the mansion. They were no more than a few paces from the front of the throng on the upper steps, and today that portion of the crowd was unusually thick with strong male slaves.

The underpriests carried the moon disk into the temple. There came an expectant pause then the high priest spoke the ritual words. As usual, the crowd sighed and a hubbub of murmurs broke out as people turned and began to descend the steps. Then the day became unusual.

Instead of turning and leaving, some thirty slaves at the fore of the crowd stood still, so that the intermixed townsfolk and soldiers drew away from them. From beneath their long kilts some of the men brought out short swords. Others produced lengths of turned wood to which they quickly fitted broad bladed spear points. As one, and without a word, they charged the Subgovernor's party.

The guards, lulled by the familiarity of routine had already turned away. The rapid scuffle of feet on stone alerted them, however, and they swung back, attempting to establish a line, shields locked and spears coming down to form a bristle of points.

But the slaves had practiced their tactics too many times on the trampled ground where they were allowed to play muscular games with a ball of cloth wrapped in horsehide. They hit the guards before the line could form, and once broken, the guards were no match for thrice their numbers. While the priests and townsfolk looked on in horror, the slaves slaughtered the bodyguards and seized the Subgovernor and his entourage at spear point.

The townspeople scattered to their homes amid cries of horror. The soldiers shouldered their way free of the mob of fleeing civilians and, under the barked orders of their officers, assembled halfway up the steps, forming two lines angled toward the rebels on the platform above. They set their spears and shields and waited for the order to advance.

Bandar had watched all of this from near the bottom of the steps where, in the company of the Smith, he had stood through the ceremony. Now, as the townsfolk fled, he saw the great mass of slaves, men as well as women, stand gaping in horror and consternation at the armed confrontation until a double squad of soldiers were directed by their commander to surround them and march them back to camp.

With kicks and blows from their spear butts, the soldiers rapidly shaped the hundreds of slaves into a column and began to march them away. But they had gone no more than a few paces before a great shout and clashing of weapons came from the top of the steps. Many of the soldiers marching with the column could not resist turning to look toward the source of the racket. They saw the rebels around the Subgovernor bellowing and smashing their iron weapons together, and that was the last thing they saw because their momentary distraction was the signal for scores of those they guarded to draw concealed knives and stab them.

"Now!" cried the Smith, and pulled from beneath his kilt the heavy maul with which he had once threatened Bandar. He threw himself against a maniple of soldiers who had had the presence of mind to close together and were spearing the knife wielding rebels from behind their shields. The Smith attacked from their rear, crushing skulls and spines with his great hammer and in seconds the guards were dead, their corpses plundered for their weapons.

"Make a line!" the Smith shouted. "Those without arms pry up the paving stones!"

A few of the slaves hung back, frightened and uncertain. But Bandar saw even Crones and Maidens digging their fingers into the cracks between the flags, upending them then lifting the squares to dash them down. The impact shattered the stones and hard, eager hands reached for the jagged fragments.

The Smith's voice boomed out—"All right, at them!"—and the slaves charged up the steps toward the double line of soldiers, even as the officers were frantically screaming at the rear rank to about face. A hail of sharp edged stones came arcing over the heads of the upsurging armed rebels and the soldiers who had reversed to meet them threw up their shields to ward off the barrage. But these soldiers were not the stones' intended targets. Instead the jagged chunks of rock flew over their upraised shields to smash into the unprotected skulls and spines of the spearmen still facing the thirty who had seized the Subgovernor.

As men fell moaning or unconscious out of the upper rank, leaving gaps and causing those not hit to glance worriedly over their shoulders, the majority of the thirty rebels above left the Subgovernor and his entourage in the custody of a few men with swords. Screaming just as they had practiced so many times on the ball field, they formed a bristling wedge and threw themselves at the wavering line of soldiers at the same moment as their friends from below struck the lower rank of spearmen.

It was a brutal business. Though Bandar had seen it in other Locations, with men who wore different garments and wielded more sophisticated weapons, it was always the same. Metal pierced flesh, blood spattered from slashing wounds or fountained from severed arteries, to a chorus of high–pitched screams and bestial grunts. He watched with an expert eye and decided that this might well be one of those Risings of the Oppressed in which a gifted Hero—for so the Smith undoubtedly was—carried the day. But then he saw Doomed Innocence roaring in the front rank of the rebels, stabbing with his spear, his Demure Maiden at his side wielding a long knife with the skill of a butcher. And Bandar remembered that even the successful revolts usually lasted no longer than it took for fresh troops to arrive in overwhelming numbers.

He skirted around the edge of the melee, careful to maintain a safe distance. He kept experiencing an urge to go toward the Smith, to help him in some indefinable way. Suddenly it all became clear. *I am becoming embedded in the Mute's dynamic. He is a Hero's Helper. That is the role that the Commons wants to press me into.*

But Bandar resisted the pull. He had to avoid danger because if he died in this Location, his consciousness would be irrevocably meshed with its elements. He would be the Mute forever, unless the Commons had a means of extracting him at the point of death, a possibility in which he was not willing to trust his existence. Besides, Bandar was still Bandar and he had his own agenda, the crowning piece of which awaited him at the top of the steps.

The slaves had surrounded the remaining soldiers, pressing them into a tight cluster, jammed so closely together that most of them could not bring their weapons to bear. More chunks of masonry were now flying from all sides, smashing into the trapped remnant. Wherever an impact rocked a spearman a rebel was waiting to slip sharp iron through the gap. The action would not last much longer. Bandar dodged around the rear of the fighters and climbed toward the Subgovernor's party.

He put on his most appealing face, smiling and gesturing happily to the men who held the dignitaries, clapping them on their shoulders as he slipped among them. At the rear of the group the First Wife's major–domo stood ashen–faced, his brow glistening with a chill sweat, the hooked staff of office quivering in his grasp so that its little silver bell tinkled too softly to be heard over the sounds of murder.

Bandar stepped up to the terrified idiomat, put the thumb and finger of one hand to the ringing metal, then brought up a knife in the other. The major–domo flinched but Bandar offered him a harmless smile and sliced through the thread that held the bell. Then he turned and sped across the top of the temple steps, seeing from the corner of his vision the priests clustered within its entry, all white of eye and open mouthed.

In a few moments the noönaut was down the steps, past the

heaped corpses of the column guards and into the empty streets of the town. With the fifth note clasped in his hand, he made his way at a fast trot past closed gates and shuttered windows, to arrive at the smithy hardly out of breath.

He set the silver bell on work bench then began assembling his seven–toned instrument around it, reaching for the tongs and the other pieces then bringing from under his kilt the spear point he had been issued but had not used. When the seven items were arranged in proper order he allowed himself a brief smile and a small sigh of satisfaction, then he turned to look for the small rod that was his striker.

A dark figure came between him and the bright world outside the smithy. It took him a moment to make out the habitual sneer of the Toady. Then he saw the hulking form of the Bully and the Henchmen. Bandar realized that he could not recall having seen any of them in the fighting. But he saw that they carried weapons, swords of gray iron whose edges gleamed with the brightness of fresh sharpening, still unblooded.

He grasped it all in a moment. The Bully cared nothing for the slaves' cause. Instead he would help suppress it, seeking to be granted the only life such an idiomat could aspire to: as an overseer given a whip and plenty of unnecessary encouragement to use it.

And so he would lurk here until the Smith came home—as he surely would, humble in his moment of triumph. Then, while the victorious slaves celebrated in the streets, the Bully and his gang would wait in the house and treacherously stab the Hero to death. When the night grew quiet, they would steal away, carrying the butchered idiomat's head in a basket, aiming to meet the army that the Governor would soon send down river to put the town back to rights.

All of that Bandar knew in the time it took him to blink in surprise. It was an old story, of course; that was why it had been preserved forever in the collective memory of humankind. What surprised him was the strength of the desire that now filled him, the powerful urge to run from here at all speed, to find the Hero and warn him. Even as he marveled at the power of the impulse, he saw that one of his hands was reaching back for the spear point while his mind was seeing a picture of the Mute breaking through the four men, slashing as he ran.

Then the whole situation became academic. The Toady was shouldered aside by the Bully. The last Bandar saw was the smirk on the thick lips and the smug satisfaction in the close set, beer colored eyes as the big man drove his sword through the noönaut's belly and up into his heart. The pain was like ice and fire together, and then it was gone. And so was Bandar.

The thugs, the smithy, the town instantly ceased to be. Bandar was back once more in the luminous mist. The Multifacet regarded him placidly from the eyes of a cartoon lion.

"You have failed," Bandar said.

"Have we?"

"You wanted me to be Helper to the doomed Hero, but I would not."

A tusked demon smiled in return. "Yet you wished to."

"I fought the urge, and prevailed."

The demon became a saucy tomboy. "Because you knew whence it came. What will you do when its source is less obvious?"

Bandar set his jaw. "Be as subtle as you like. I will be on guard."

A kind eyed saint smiled and said, "Not if you don't remember."

As these last words were spoken, the figure dwindled rapidly, as if it rushed away from Bandar at great speed, pulling the mist twisting and roiling in its wake. The noönaut blinked and found himself reposing in the shade of the palm tree, the generic ocean rippling and whispering up the gently sloping beach and the three gamins beckoning him to pursue them. The blonde gave him her unintentional parody of a come–hither look while the red haired one cocked one hip.

Bandar smiled and sat up. A shadow of a thought crossed his mind. Hadn't he been thinking of something just now? He reached for the memory, but whatever it had been, it had ebbed away. He got to his feet and chased the three giggling idiomats out into the waves where, as always, the sequence faded and a new dream took its place.

In the morning, Bandar formally resigned from the Institute of Historical Inquiry and caught the noon jitney to the balloon–tram station at Binch. He would return to Olkney and take up a position with his Uncle Fley, who operated a housewares business in which there had long been a standing offer of a junior executive post for Bandar, Fley having no heirs of his own.

It was with a mix of feelings that Bandar watched the ground fall away as the tram car ascended high above the tracks. He saw, far off, the Institute's grounds, the neat cloisters and formal gardens, the grand old halls and the students' cottages, and a tear came to his eye. But then he turned his mind resolutely toward the future: Uncle Fley, though only a commerciant, was a man of integrity and quiet accomplishment. He struggled against the vicissitudes of existence with courage and without complaint.

There was a nobility in the simple life, even a kind of heroism, Bandar told himself. He experienced a gentle urge to stand by his uncle, to be of help.

Bye The Rules

Guth Bandar spent the morning attending to occasional customers in his Uncle Fley's housewares vendory and, between those encounters, constructing a decorative display of insipitators. The devices had lately become hugely popular among the inhabitants of Boderel, a self–contained district of the ancient city of Olkney on whose main thoroughfare stood Bandar's Mercantile Emporium and to which Guth Bandar had returned after being dismissed from his post as an adjunct scholar at the Institute for Historical Inquiry.

At first, he had stacked the insipitators in a pyramid, but soon realized that the arrangement was a deterrent to their purchase. Shoppers must take only the topmost item, or risk an avalanche of the squat, rotund appliances. And since Bandar had needed to mount a folding step to position the pyramid's upper strata, the customer who could reach for the apex insipitator would have to be freakishly tall. After two purchasers had required him to fetch and unfold the step so he could hand them down the highest item, he realized his error and tore down the stack. He rearranged the devices on a series of terraced shelves, allowing persons of varying heights to reach the insipitator that was closest to hand.

Bandar sighed heavily as he labored. He found the work tedious and dull, far less interesting than had been his explorations of the noösphere, the grand collective unconscious of humanity, whose study was the purpose of the venerable Institute. But that phase of his life now lay behind a door that had slammed shut, to remain forever sealed against him.

His longstanding academic rival, the detestable Didrick Gabbris, had roused the Institute's Grand Colloquium. Faculty, students and alumni had unanimously rejected Bandar's heretical contention that the Commons, as the collective unconscious was known to scholars, had paradoxically achieved consciousness of itself—and not only self–awareness, but a will to act.

Worse than heretical, the scholars found the idea to be novel. And being offered to a conclave of academics on the ancient planet Old Earth, where no new idea had emerged in scores of millennia, it was received with shock, outrage and derision. Gabbris had skillfully orchestrated the different streams of opprobrium, playing the Grand Colloquium as a conductor leads an orchestra, achieving at the end a crescendo of repudiation that sped a thoroughly disgraced Guth Bandar back to Boderel.

A plurality of the Boderel district's inhabitants were adherents of the Concord of Astringency, a philosophical system that prized rigorous sobriety and self–denial. For the past several years there had been a gradual loosening of the Concord's strictures, accompanied even by the use of sweeteners in the weekly ceremonial of the gruel, but now a new First Locutor had wrested the leadership from the backsliders and launched a wave of reform. Astringents were once again wearing uncomfortable fabrics and eating only foods whose flavor had been removed by insipitators. As he stacked and sold the devices, Bandar thought to see a convergence between his situation and that of his customers: he found his new life both tasteless and a source of chafing.

He was mulling this thought when the who's–there at the emporium's front door chirped the first words of its customary greeting to an incoming customer, then abruptly changed its tone and choice of words; its percepts had recognized that the tall, thin man coming through the portal was Fley Bandar, the proprietor.

Guth Bandar left the insipitator display and went to greet his relative, putting on as cheerful a face as he could manage. After all, his troubles were no fault of his uncle's and the man had been generous to take him in and give him a livelihood. "Ho, uncle," he said, "the insipitators are moving well. You may need to order fresh stock."

Ordinarily, such news should have gladdened Fley Bandar's being, since he was a commerciant to his core and lived to sell useful products at a decent mark–up. But now Bandar saw that the older man's face remained long, his brows pulled into a troubled vee and his lips downdrawn at the corners.

"What is the matter?" Bandar said.

He received only a sigh for an answer. Fley took his customary seat on a stool behind the device that recorded transactions, bowed his grayed head and clasped his hands across his midriff. After a moment, he looked up at his nephew and said, "There is a problem."

Bandar instantly felt an urge to assist his uncle in meeting the challenge. He had noticed that whenever the older man faced a challenge, be it so minor as a need to rearrange the merchandise in the front display area, Bandar experienced a surge of motivation and felt good about himself when he was able to make a contribution.

"What is the problem?" he said. "How may I assist you?"

Fley spread his hands in a gesture of bewilderment. "There has been a change," he said.

"A change?" Bandar's face arranged itself into an icon of bepuzzlement. "What change? There is never a change."

He spoke from the authority of universal knowledge. In Olkney, nothing ever changed. Eons before, history had come to a complete and final end. Everything that could be tried had been tried, all possible forms had been established, filled with content, then emptied and refilled countless times. There was not, could not be, anything new under the fading orange light of the senescent sun. "What can have changed?"

"Tshimshim Barr–Chevry has sold up and moved offworld. A new man has taken over his enterprise. He has announced a program of direct competition with us. It was the talk of the guild meeting this morning."

Bandar blinked. "What does it mean, direct competition? Are we to run races, do puzzles in our heads?"

His uncle sighed. "I asked similar questions and was told this: the new incumbent will sell the same goods as we, but at lower prices. Also, he will offer inducements. For example, persons who purchase the new man's insipitators will receive a corrugated pillow, free of charge."

"Madness," Bandar said. "Barr–Chevry's does not sell insipitators. They sell immovables and interactive decor. Thus has it always been, through all the generations of Barr–Chevrys."

"Not any more," said Fley. "Apparently, the latest iteration of the Barr–Chevry line had long harbored a secret desire to roam the open savannahs of distant worlds, places where moons pass through the skies and strange scents waft on the breezes."

Bandar made a fricative noise of dismissal. "We all have our fantasies. I dreamed of being a noönaut, much good it did me."

"Tshimshim Barr–Chevry has converted his fantasy into a ticket on a spaceliner that lifted off before dawn. By now he has passed through the first whimsy and will shortly be halfway down The Spray."

Fley let out a deep breath then rose and walked a few paces, then turned and retraced his steps, his thin legs bending at the knee and his elongated feet slapping the well worn floor. His head was bowed and his brows knit.

"Who is this new man?" Bandar said. "Perhaps he is unaware of how things are done. We can arrange for his erroneous views to be corrected."

"That is the strangest part," said Fley, pausing in his perambulations and turning to his nephew. "He is only a placeholder, employed by the true purchaser of the enterprise, who sits behind a shield of anonymity."

"You're saying the owner does not operate the business? I've never heard the like."

Fley sighed again and resumed his pacing. "It is decidedly peculiar," he said. "Yet, there it is. The issue before us is: how to respond?"

Bandar felt another flash of incentive. "You must fight," he said. "And I must stand with you."

Fley rang a finger down his lengthy nose while his eyebrows performed a shrug. "I suppose we must," he said. "It's good of you to take my side, Guth."

"It's what I'm here for," said Guth Bandar and was surprised to find how deeply rang those simple words in his being. "Now, what we need is a plan."

"I wish to inquire as to the proprietorship of a business," Guth Bandar told the integrator at the Archonate Bureau of Cognizance.

"Why do you want to know?"

"How is my motive relevant?"

"Are you saying it is not?" said the bland voice. Bandar was alone in the small booth yet the words seemed to be spoken in the air just behind his left ear. "You seek information in which you have no interest? This seems a feckless pursuit. Are you normally governed by your every passing whim?"

Bandar had heard about the Archonate's integrators. Some had been in continuous service for durations more closely measured by geological periods than by human lifetimes, even the lengthy spans of Old Earth's inhabitants in this, the planet's penultimate age. The devices developed quirks and odd enthusiasms, and some of them appeared to take a perverse delight in putting difficulties in the way of the citizens they purported to serve.

"My motive is concern for the wellbeing of a close relative," Bandar said.

"How so?"

Reluctantly, Bandar explained the circumstances, knowing that each detail might send the integrator off on a wild tangent, requiring perhaps an entire afternoon to work it back to the point of his inquiry. Fortunately, however, the device was as nonplused by the news of the new policy at Barr–Chevry's as he had been.

"What is the alleged purpose of this competition?" the integrator asked.

"That has not been made known to us, only the fact of its existence."

"But this smacks of disruptive behavior. Commerciant affairs in Olkney achieved optimum stability during the Archonate of Terfel III. Why disturb perfection?"

"Exactly," said Bandar.

"Hmmm," said the integrator.

"Might this transaction be illegal?"

There was a pause while the device consulted eons of codified law. "It appears not."

"But it is not a trend the Archonate would wish to encourage."

The integrator's tone grew distant. "It is not a trend at all, merely an instance. Perhaps someone has gone mad."

"So an appeal to the Archon is not indicated?"

"It rarely is," said the integrator.

Bandar knew that the Archon was empowered to do anything at all to anyone at all, although ordinarily he was disinclined to interfere in the balance of affairs. "Yet this situation might constitute an imbalance, or at least the beginning of one," he said.

"Indeed." The integrator was silent for a moment, then said, "Do you wish to hear my optimum counsel?"

"That is why I came."

"Very well. Keep in mind that the Archon sits at the very pinnacle of the social order. His view of what is best and proper originates from a unique perspective. Those who invite his intervention can sometimes receive much more help than they anticipated. Indeed, occasionally it is more help than they can bear."

"What do you mean?"

"For example," said the integrator, "there was the dispute between two aristocratic families that occupied the large island in Mornedy Sound. They disagreed bitterly as to which should have precedence over the other. After an escalating series of violent incidents, culminating in arson and mayhem, they appealed to the Archon Barthelmeon VIII for a judgment."

"Wait a moment," said Bandar, "there is no large island in Mornedy Sound."

"Exactly," said the integrator. "Now, do you wish to involve the Archon in your uncle's dispute?"

"Perhaps not."

"Then, good day."

"At least give me the information I first asked for: the name of the new owner of Barr–Chevry's Immovables."

"Very well." The integrator then made a sound that indicated mild interest. "There has been some attempt to disguise the ownership through a chain of reciprocal hand–offs and cut–outs—not an entirely clumsy attempt, at that, but the trail leads back to one person."

"And that person is?"

"His name is Didrick Gabbris."

"Why do you torment my uncle?" Bandar said. Didrick Gabbris voiced no reply, merely placed his nose in an elevated position and made to step away. But Bandar seized the man's elbow through the sleeve of his academic robe, spun him around and repeated the question.

He had intercepted Gabbris beneath the stand of tittering hissol trees in the smaller quadrangle of the Institute of Historical Inquiry. It was late afternoon. Gabbris had just finished hearing a pack of undergraduates deliver the results of their conjectural flights—or "hunchmanship" as the exercise was colloquially known—and was now on his way to the masters' lesser conclave that would occupy the hour before the bell called all to dinner. Bandar had come directly from Olkney by hired aircar to find his old enemy fast–stepping through dappled orange sunlight, doubtless with thoughts of spiced cordial and seeded buns foremost in his mind.

"I am not answerable to you," Gabbris said. He sought to pull his arm from Bandar's grip but could not. He looked around for help but saw only a gaggle of students from his hunchmanship session, all of whom seemed interested in seeing their tutor accosted, none of whom showed an inclination to intervene.

Bandar increased the pressure of his grip. "Expect no aid," he said. "You have never inspired sympathy."

"Let go of me or it will go ill with you," Gabbris said.

Bandar made a noise that mingled derision with hate. "What will you do?" he said. "Have me expelled? You forget, you have already taken from me all that I ever desired. That now leaves you face to face with an angry man who has nothing to lose. I also point out that, though you are taller, I am wiry and well coordinated. Finally, I am mightily motivated to cause you pain and humiliation."

"I would see you clapped into a cell in the Archon's contemplarium," Gabbris said, but the squeak in his voice leached any power from his threat.

"Indeed?" said Bandar, letting his expression assume a thoughtful aspect. "And what I'd be contemplating would be the memory of your tear–stained face, blood and mucus streaming from its disarranged nose, as I stood over you and applied the toe of my boot to the softest parts of your person."

"You wouldn't dare."

Bandar yanked on Gabbris's arm to position his enemy while

he turned his free hand into a fist and drew it back in preparation for launch. A hoot of anticipation came from the undergraduates.

"Wait!" Gabbris said.

"Only long enough for you to answer my question."

The scholar tried again to pull his arm free but the motion was more petulant than determined. "Very well," he said. "It came to me in a dream."

"A lucid dream?"

"Of course."

"Ambiguous?"

"Not to a noönaut." Gabbris's lips slid back into their habitual sneer and his brows rose to their usual supercilious heights to offer Bandar an unspoken corollary: *Which you are not.*

Bandar released the man's arm and uncocked his fist. A tenured fellow of the Institute could not be faulted for acting upon a clear message from the unconscious. "What was the import?" he said.

"That the enmity between us must continue. You must be further punished, through your uncle."

Bandar made a gesture of bewilderment. "It makes no sense," he said. "What has Fley done to merit a penalty?"

"I do not question what comes from the Commons," Gabbris said.

Bandar snorted. "That needs no assertion. You are as accepting as a. . . " His mind offered him a rude and scatological image but he did not voice it.

"Are we done?" Gabbris said. "I desire a cordial and some conversation." He stressed the next three words: "With my peers."

"Surely you recognize that this role that has been assigned to you is consistent with my contention that the Commons has achieved self–awareness and is pursuing an agenda."

Gabbris waved away the supposition like a man brushing off a lethargic fly. "That again?" he said. "The only consistency I recognize is your continual harping on a self–deluding fantasy."

"But why else would you be urged to trouble me, now that you have won and I have lost?"

"The Commons is its own rationale." Gabbris quoted. "It is the constant mirror in which we are but flickering reflections, ephemeral and substanceless. We do not question what comes from its depths; rather, we act and accept the consequences."

Bandar drew himself up to the slight height that his small stature could achieve. "Very well," he said, "but know that I return home to seek a lucid dream of my own, and if it should counsel me to wreak havoc on your repulsive carcass be assured that havoc will be thoroughly wreaked."

It was late in the evening by the time Guth Bandar made his way back from the Institute. All during the ride on the balloon tram and the subsequent long walk through the streets of Olkney, thronged with indentors and their spouses promenading their fashionable attire, coiffures and skin coloration, he had mulled what Gabbris had told him. A portion of his mind niggled at him, holding out a tantalizing whiff of some forgotten but crucial factum that was the key to unlock the mystery. But each time he rallied his normally well disciplined and biddable memory, it shied away from the target like a missile that did not care to make impact.

His uncle had already retired upstairs to his sleeping chamber. Bandar went to his small room at the back of his uncle's vendory, reposed himself upon the sleeping pallet and cleared his consciousness. He slowed his breathing and placed his limbs in the approved positions, then closed his eyes and summoned a mental image of a staircase with himself at the top and shadows beneath. Releasing a long sigh of breath, he pictured himself descending, step by step, at a measured pace. Within moments he found himself in a familiar setting.

He was walking along the main concourse of the Institute's New Quadrangle, an ancient labyrinth in whose warren of rooms senior fellows tutored mid–level students in the intricacies of the Commons's myriad Locations and the subtle techniques by which they could be entered and exited. The wide hallway was lined on either side by doors that led into rooms great or small, the former for lectures, the latter for exercises in meditation. As Bandar strode along, he noticed that one door a short distance down the concourse was limned in rosy, golden light. He stepped to it and pulled it open.

A warm effulgence bathed him. He entered and with the crossing of the threshold came memory—though it arrived, not as a helpmate ready to serve, but as an unwelcome intruder. He turned to retreat back through the door but found that the portal was gone. Once again, he was in a formless mist, out of which came the ever shifting shape of the Multifacet: that representation of the collective unconscious that had paradoxically become conscious, and that had chosen Guth Bandar, whether he wished it or not, to be the instrument of its will.

"You have done this," Bandar said. "You have sicced the odious Gabbris on my good uncle, who has done none harm and merits no punishment."

He spoke to a cartoonish representation of an animal wearing an odd hat and some sort of ribbon that went around its neck and hung down its front—Bandar thought the original species must be long extinct—that replied in a buffoonish voice that changed in mid sentence to a cackle as the form became a warty crone. "We are no respecter of persons. We do what must be done."

"If you wish my help," Bandar said, "then enlist me. Do not coerce me by threatening those I love."

"We do as we must," said the Multifacet, becoming a roly–poly fellow in scarlet tunic and trousers accented by white fur and a matching tasseled hat. "You must be shaped, and we must use the tools at hand."

"What if I refuse?"

A little girl in pigtails and pinafore looked up at him and said, "We will seek another, but the train of events has already begun and your uncle is now in play."

"He is a good man," Bandar said. "He deserves better."

"Deserts do not come into it," said a fanged and hulking nightmare. "It is about survival."

"Whose?"

A woman with impossibly long legs, an unnaturally buoyant bosom and a husky contralto said, "Yours. Your uncle's. Every-one's."

"Even yours?"

"Even ours," said a rosy countenanced infant. "It is your destiny to help. Accept it."

"But I am not a Helper. My conformation has the Seeker dominant, influenced by the Wise Man and the Solitary, shadowed by the Hoarder." He referred to the archetypes that blended together to form the core elements of his psyche. They had been delineated when he first applied to study at the Institute.

The figure before him made no answer but abruptly disappeared, to be replaced by a rippling rent in the mist. Hating the necessity, Bandar stepped into it.

At first he was aware only of the Landscape: a vast sky of a paler blue than that which covered Old Earth in its penultimate age, the sun yellow and hot, the clouds above the horizon a pristine white. The land itself was mostly flat, with here and there a gentle roll. A constant wind stirred its covering of dry grass and scrub. In the far distance Bandar could see immense tables of rock, level on top and formed from striated layers of age–hardened sediments, some attended by solitary spires of stone shaped by no hand but the weather's.

He knew that it would be more than just a place. The Multifacet would have dropped him into at least a Situation, perhaps a complex Event, and he and Uncle Fley would be players in it. He had sought a lucid dream, in which his noönaut training would have given him considerable power to mold his environment. But this setting had all the hallmarks of an established Location somewhere in the matrix that was the Commons. Experimentally, he summoned his skills and attempted to still the wind. It blew on without regard for his efforts.

Next he tested his voice. The single tone rang clear in the fresh air, though it was more of a tenor than Bandar's own baritone. *At least this time they have not muted me*, he thought. *If I wish I can summon an emergency gate and awaken in my bed.*

But he wouldn't. Somewhere in this Location was his innocent uncle, threatened by evil forces and with only his nephew Guth to help him withstand them. I must discover the dynamics of this Location, work out the direction of events, then resolve them in our favor.

It was a flagrant violation of all that a noönaut stood for. Explorers of the Commons observed while unobserved, insulated from the perceptions of the idiomatic entities by the thrans that they constantly sang. It was dangerous to interfere with the workings of

Events or Situations: the idiomats were not people but bundles of simplified traits and habitual responses; intervening in a way that distorted their preordained roles brought disharmony, generating a psychic friction that rapidly built up energies that discharged violently.

He gave the environment one more searching look and, seeing nothing amiss, examined himself. Once again, he had been deposited into the virtual flesh of an idiomat. Looking down, he saw a checked shirt and a wide belt with a heavy buckle. Below that were tan trousers of some sturdy material with pockets riveted at the corners, into which the thumbs of sun–browned and work–hardened hands were tucked. From the turned–up cuffs of the pants emerged a pair of worn boots with pointed toes.

He became aware of the idiomat's thoughts: simple satisfaction at being out on his own, trusted with some minor but serious task. *That is different*, Bandar thought.

When the Multifacet had dropped him into the Event known as The Rising of the Oppressed, the persona of the idiomat into which he had been placed had been completely expunged. This time, Bandar seemed to be an addition to a persona that came equipped with its own inner life. That raised the question of whether the noönaut had control over his host's actions. He doubted that he would be a mere passenger, but suppressing the idiomat's will entirely might cause disharmony. To test his influence, Bandar gently urged a turn to the right. The idiomat shifted his weight and gazed idly in the suggested direction.

Bandar next tried a nose scratching and was rewarded with success. It seemed that he had only to think about his host's taking an action and it would happen—so long as it was within the idiomat's repertoire. Willing an idiomatic entity to do something far out of character would render it disharmonious, and the noönaut did not wish to be trapped in the flesh of an idiomat on a rampage.

It was time to seek out Uncle Fley and do whatever the Multifacet wanted done. *Let's go*, he thought, and the idiomat turned around, giving Bandar a view of a large, long–legged beast to which was strapped a contraption of leather and metal. Bandar had seen such beasts in many Locations that dated from the dawn–time, when they were ridden or used to pull primitive wheeled vehicles. Clearly this variant of whatever Situation he had been thrust into was from far back in the Deep Past, before the discovery of inherent motilation or even submolecular circuitry. Now as he looked at the beast, the word "horse" came into his mind and even as he thought it he realized that the idiomat was placing one foot into a metal loop hung from a leather strap. A moment later, Bandar was surveying the scene from a higher vantage point. He eased back on his control of his host so that it could go about its business. Bandar would watch and learn until it became clear what he was expected to do.

His host tugged on the leather straps—the word "reins" popped into Bandar's vocabulary as he focused on the items—and the animal's head veered to the right. The rest of its body followed as the idiomat's boot heels thumped into its ribs. They set off at a "canter" across the Landscape, the wind of their passage tugging at a broad–brimmed hat that Bandar found he was wearing. He contented himself with observing and over the next few minutes felt his vocabulary filling up with the jargon of this Location.

Not far off, he came to what he realized was the idiomat's intended destination—a patch of prairie not much different from any other, except that it featured a wire fence whose barbed strands had been severed, creating a wide gap, and a muddle of tracks made by a herd of animals with split hooves. The idiomat's eyes followed the tracks. They led up a gentle slope and he kicked his horse after them, coming to a broad crest from which the land fell away into a wide depression. In the middle distance moved a cloud of dust in which Bandar could see idiomats on beasts like his, slapping ropes— "lariats"—against saddles and hooting as they drove forty or fifty "cattle" before them.

The idiomat's heels hit the horse's side again and he shouted some wordless syllable that obviously had meaning to the horse, because the beast broke into a sudden gallop. Bandar marveled at the smooth ease with which his host sat his saddle as the animal sped down into the basin, its ears flattened and its long neck hair— "mane"—streaming back over the hands that held the reins.

Man and beast rapidly closed the distance to catch up with the herd. They swung wide to race past the dust, then cut in ahead of the herd, the idiomat rearing his horse onto its hind legs, shouting hoarsely and waving his hat. The oncoming cattle shied and milled about, making sounds of distress.

Out of the dust came three men on horseback, dressed roughly in the same fashion as Bandar's host, though something about them gave the impression that they were of a different sort. *Henchmen*, the noönaut decided. Then he listened as his host spoke.

"Those are our cattle!"

He's younger than I thought, Bandar decided, *angry but also frightened.*

One of the men urged his mount closer. In one hand was a long–barreled weapon—"rifle"—laid casually over his saddle. Using only his knees, the Henchman skillfully directed his horse to turn broadside to Bandar's idiomat, and now the rifle's dark orifice was pointing Bandar's way. A cruel smile formed on the tanned and stubbled face and the man said, "Can't be yours, kid. They're on Circle B land."

"You cut our fence, drove them off," said Bandar's host, and hearing the high–pitched voice again confirmed his first impression: he was in the body of an idiomat on the cusp between boy and man.

"Now that ain't a nice thing to say," said the man with the rifle. The dust was blowing away and Bandar saw two more riders moving out to either side of the confrontation, both armed, both handling their weapons with a casual familiarity that argued that there would be no hesitation in using them.

"You say things like that," said the one with the rifle, who looked to be a Chief Henchman, "you better be ready to back 'em up. Man don't have to take that kind of talk, specially from some wet nosed kid."

Bandar was worried by the anger that was now clouding what there was of the idiomat's mind. If the boy made the wrong move in this confrontation the man with the rifle might well fire. The noönaut was reasonably sure that his host would turn out to be the Helper in this Situation, his death therefore highly unlikely this early in the dynamic. But it would not help if he had to solve the puzzle while phsyically incapacitated. He exerted his will to keep the boy's hands on the reins.

But he didn't take control of the idiomat's mouth. "You won't get away with this," the boy said. "My pa'll kill you."

The other two henchmen had moved closer. One of them, a skinny man with a thin mustache, sneered and spat a stream of brown liquid, while the other, heavyset with a week's stubble on his jaw, said, "Sure, kid. We're scared to death."

The one with the rifle said, "Tell your old man if he's got anythin' to say, he knows where to find Mr. Strayhorn. He'll be waitin'."

Bandar could see where this narrative was heading. It was a Situation, probably a variation on the motif of Resisting the Despot. This Strayhorn would be a Principal in this Location, a local Tyrant imposing his will upon a Suffering Population that was too timid to revolt and overthrow him. His host's father was probably also a Principal, the Hero of this tale, and the sequence of events would climax in a confrontation between the two, from which only one would emerge alive.

Which of the two that would be was uncertain: Heroes came in a wide variety of types, and Bandar would need to take a close look at the father before he could establish whether the idiomat was of the Reluctant, or the Pure, or even the Sacrificial type. He doubted that this Situation would include an Accidental or an Unlikely Hero, and was already confident that he would not find a cynical Antihero when they returned to wherever the boy had come from.

In any case, Bandar was clearly once again cast as the Helper, and he wondered at the Multifacet's purpose in enlisting him to play the same role he had played in The Rising of the Oppressed. Of course, repetition of themes was a commonplace of the Commons, he thought, so it should not come as a surprise that, having become conscious, the noösphere should demonstrate a tendency toward the redundant.

Now was not a good time to mull these matters, Bandar knew. Fley was not in any of the Henchmen so it was time to move on. He exerted more control over the youth, causing him to pull the horse's head in the direction from which they had come and energetically ride away. As they went, Bandar paid attention to the setting, noting that the grass and scrub seemed well realized. The horse and its equipment also exhibited a wealth of detail, enough that Bandar felt comfortable in classifying this Location as a Class Two Situation, scoring high on the Realism scale. That meant that if, for example, his idiomat fell from his mount at their present rate of speed, he could expect broken bones, possibly internal injuries and even death if he landed the wrong way.

The idiomat was determined to get home and report the theft of the cattle. Bandar was sure that would be the Initiating Incident of this Situation. He would know the Hero's type once he saw how the news was received; that would give him a reasonably good idea of where all this was heading, and some sense of where to look for Fley. He let the boy guide the horse through the broken fence and across the rolling landscape until they came to a small valley bisected by a shallow river. Down below was a house made of logs, a couple of outbuildings and an enclosure—"corral"—of posts and rails surrounding three more horses.

The boy set the horse to angle down the slope and Bandar left them to their business while he surveyed the scene. The level of detail intensified here, supporting his belief that this was the seat of a Principal. When in response to the boy's cries of, "Pa! Pa!" as they splashed through the river, a man came out onto the house's open porch, the noönaut's expectation was confirmed: Pa was a fully detailed Class One idiomatic entity, tall and muscular, with lines of character etched into the planes of his face and subtlety in his light–colored eyes. The work clothes he wore had the same lived–in look of as the boy's attire.

Bandar only half listened to the exchange between the two as the boy leapt from the saddle and breathlessly told his parent about the Initiating Incident. He was looking for telltales that would define this Hero. He had already added Flawed to the list of rejected types, and judging by the worry that he saw in the older idiomat's eyes as the boy told of confronting the three Henchmen, he was also ready to dismiss Pure as an option—a Pure Hero's eyes would have blazed with righteous anger. This one looked more tired than angry.

The boy was looking directly at the older idiomat as he spoke his lines and Bandar was taking advantage of the point of view to study the Principal. As he allowed the impression to intensify, using a mentalism that was part of any trained noönaut's tool–kit, something tugged at the edge of his mind. He sensed something familiar about Pa, something in the face that underlay the features and formed the essence of the idiomat's character.

The boy had finished his story. The Principal's brows drew down and his eyes lost their focus as he looked inward at some memory. *Reluctant Hero*, Bandar told himself, *not for certain, but definitely most likely.* Then, as the father stroked his nose with a thoughtful finger, the "something familiar" leaped at Bandar and seized his full attention.

"Uncle Fley!" His cry sounded strange as he heard it in the still unsettled voice of the youth. The Principal acted as any Class One idiomat should at being confronted with disharmonious information. He paused, startled, then like an actor when a fellow cast member speaks a line out of sequence, he ignored the interruption and went on with the scene.

His face regained a mood of introspection. The boy, who had been equally startled at what had come from his own mouth, also returned to the flow of the Situation. "What are we going to do, Pa?" he said.

The Principal crossed to a water barrel and dipped up a mouthful, his eyes squinting into the westering sun as he drank. "I need to think about that, Mark," he said.

And I need to think about what's going on here, Guth Bandar thought to himself. Because when he had glimpsed the resemblance to his uncle in the Principal's expression and blurted out his relative's name, he had seen more than a jolt of surprise appear in the older idiomat's eyes. For a moment, the face that had looked back at Bandar was deeply familiar. Just as Bandar had been inserted into the Helper's virtual flesh, his Uncle Fley was trapped within the Hero's.

Repetition is reality was one of the maxims drummed into undergraduates' minds in their first years at the Institute. By definition, nothing that happened in the Commons happened only once. The constantly recycling Events and Situations were distillations of events and situations in the waking world that had happened so many times, in all their varieties and permutations, that their essences had become part of humanity's psychic machinery. Anything that had occurred no more than once or twice was not retained.

Bandar considered this hoary truth as he struggled to maintain his composure. The worst mistake he could make was to let himself be caught up in the drama of the situation. If he allowed himself to be consumed by worry for his uncle, he would be drawn more deeply into the dynamics of this Situation. He might become lost in its movements, and thus unable to help Fley.

Repetition, he repeated. *It's not only how the Commons works, but how it teaches*. The Multifacet wanted him to learn something, and this was its method of instruction. The last time it had plunged him into a Situation he had been made the mute Helper to a Hero he had scarcely had time to know before events moved rapidly to the crisis. Now he was cast in the same role, but the intensity had been raised by the infusion into the Hero's persona of someone he cared for deeply.

Raise the stakes was another rule in the Commons: these kinds of Events and Situations always proceeded on an upward gradient of tension and conflict, culminating in a cathartic climax and an emotion–drenched denouement. The oxymoron that was the conscious unconscious was working to its own inbuilt rules, as if it were itself governed by unconscious drives. For a moment Bandar stopped to consider that the phenomenon of a conscious unconsciousness's unconscious would make a truly interesting paper, then decided now was surely not the time.

Very well, he told himself, *there is no way out but to see this through to the end.* He would play out the dynamic of the Situation, abiding by the rules. Uncle Fley ought to take no hurt from being attached to a Reluctant Hero. Unused to the ways of the Commons, he would tell Bandar in the morning about a particularly vivid dream—if any memory of these events even clung to his waking mind.

While Bandar had been thinking, events had moved on in the Situation. The father was now carrying a rifle similar to the one the Henchman had pointed at the boy. He had led a horse from the corral and was tightening the broad leather strap—"girth"—that looped under its belly. He slipped the weapon into a scabbard attached to the saddle then swung up onto the horse. The boy did likewise with his own mount. They wheeled the animals and rode toward the horizon. Moments later, in the way that time often compressed in the Commons, they were out on the prairie and within sight of a cluster of wooden buildings that soon resolved into a rough and ready settlement.

Riding into town, Bandar took a look through the idiomat's eyes and judged that little of import to the Situation would happen here. The idiomats walking the wooden sidewalks or crossing the single unpaved street lacked intensity. Most of the buildings were of the Essential/Representational type, with far less detail than the dwelling where he had encountered Pa. Only the ones with signs that read "General Store," "Sheriff" and "Saloon" looked to be fully realized. The two idiomats pulled their mounts to a halt outside the first, where a man attired in clothes similar to the Hero's, but with only a Sincere/Approximate level of detail, was asleep on a tilted back wooden chair, his booted ankles crossed on a railing and a broad–brimmed hat over his eyes. A five–pointed metal star was pinned to his chest.

"Mooney, where's the sheriff?" said the Principal.

The man did not move, not even to raise his hat. "This time of day, I expect he'll be over in the Nugget," he said.

The Hero and Helper turned their mounts and walked them over to the other Earnest/Realistic building. They both stepped down from the saddle then up onto the wooden porch of the saloon, but the Principal said, "Mark, you wait outside."

"But Pa– " Bandar's idiomat began, only to have his protest cut off.

"I said wait."

The Hero lifted his weapon from its scabbard and went into the building, pushing through a pair of swinging half–doors made of slatted wood. The boy obeyed but positioned himself close to the entrance so that he could see and hear what went on within.

Bandar gave the conversation between the Hero and the sheriff only a portion of his attention. This would be part of the process by which the Reluctant Hero is isolated from all hope of help and comes to know that, like it or not, he must solve his problem through his own efforts. There might be one or even two other potential supporters who would be appealed to in vain, then the Hero would resign himself to the necessity of a confrontation with the opposing Principal, Strayhorn. Bandar sketched out in his mind the likely sequence of events, half listening as he heard the elderly sheriff explaining, in a tone tinged with self–disgust, that anything outside the town limits was beyond his jurisdiction.

Soon the Hero would come out of the saloon and get on with it. Probably he would ride out to Strayhorn's center of power for the Confrontation Minor that, far from resolving the conflict, would instead intensify it. The Hero would be abused and something beyond him would be threatened—perhaps the boy or maybe a female Loved One who, if she was to play a role in the dynamic, ought to be factored into the Situation just about now. Bandar had the boy look around for a female idiomat. He was fairly sure that the tavern would not be the place to find her and so cast his eye back to the street outside.

A high–pitched, oscillating whine impinged upon his concentration and caused him to look up. A circular shape had appeared in the air above the dusty street. Bandar's initial impression of the object was colored by his having to perceive it through the idiomat boy's sensorium, so he first took it for a hat or a pie plate that someone had flung into the air. Then, as the thing descended Bandar realized that it was not a small object at a low height, but was instead something immense that was plummeting swiftly toward the town from the upper reaches of the Location's sky.

That can't be right, the noönaut thought. As a Situation, Resisting the Despot could play itself out against a background in which the cruel Tyrant was the head of an invading species from another world, but in such a Location the tyranny would have been established before the Situation began its cycle. Besides, the Initiating Incident would be completely different from the theft of cattle that had sparked the dynamic in which Bandar and Fley were trapped.

The object had by now come down to hover above the town, revealing itself to be an gigantic disc of dull gray metal. Around its rim a string of flashing lights chased themselves at high speed. As Bandar watched, four tapering and telescoping legs extended themselves from its ventral hub. One struck hard into the earth of the street, while the others plunged straight down through the roofs of the Essential/Representational buildings, with a crash of splintering wood and shattering glass. A rectangular hatch opened in the belly of what Bandar now recognized must be a fully realized assault ship from an entirely different Location, probably a variant of The Incursion of the Other, Class Two or Three..

It's a straddle, he thought. *I'm actually seeing a straddle.* Straddles were Locations that, according to some theories, had come into existence far back in the development of the collective unconscious, when new variants on archetypical events and situations were still being created by a combination of human ingenuity and the unfolding of actual events in the waking world. Elements from two substantially different but superficially similar Locations would temporarily cohere in an Event or Situation that straddled both. But their internal dynamics would quickly pull them apart.

As he pursued this line of introspection, a segmented ramp extruded from the oblong hatch. Even before it touched the ground the opening filled with armored and multi–limbed creatures that would have stood about waist high to Bandar's idiomat. But these invaders were clearly motivated to do more running than standing; they swarmed down the ramp, each skittering on some of its limbs while others discharged energy weapons at any target they spotted with their stalked eyes.

A yellow hound had been sleeping in the shade of a slab–sided wagon. Now it rose up and issued a tentative bark, then began a mournful howl—probably its only response to any stimulus, Bandar thought. A coruscating bolt of energy *whuzzed* through the air, catching the dog in mid ululation and causing the animal to glow brightly for a moment then vanish, leaving a shadowy smudge on the ground.

The invaders were firing indiscriminately. Bandar saw Mooney, the man who had been sleeping beneath a hat, stir himself. His booted heels hit the wooden sidewalk. He stood up shakily, but the hat still adhered to his brow, and Bandar surmised that the idiomat probably had no face beneath, none being needed for the minor role he was meant to play. Now his virtual existence came to an incandescent end as one of the metal–clad spiders scuttled down onto the street and opened fire.

Another leaped from the ramp onto the second–story balcony of a building whose front bore the legend "Rosie's Club for Gentlemen" and aimed its weapon down and across the street at a well realized female idiomat, mature though still youthful and dressed in high–necked blouse and full skirt topped by a gray gingham apron, who had just come out of the General Store. *The Hero's Loved One, I'd wager,* Bandar thought, a·moment before the invader's blast incinerated her.

The boy in which he was housed had reacted much as Bandar had: he stared, open–mouthed, at a spectacle of violence all the more horrific for being completely unexpected. Now it struck home to the noönaut that the straddle must soon throw the idiomat into disharmony, putting his behavior well beyond Bandar's influence.

Along with that realization came a belated awareness that he was not viewing these events from a noönaut's normal vantage—hidden from the invaders' view by the power of a chanted thran—but from deep within the frame of the action. And the next bolt of energy might be directed his way.

As that thought came, the horse he had ridden in on lit up like a sunburst then dimmed to leave a smudged horse–shadow on the saloon porch. The Hero's mount had just enough time to rear up in terror before it received the same illumination. Careful to keep his actions within his host's range of acceptable reactions, Bandar now took control and pushed through the saloon's swinging doors, ducking low as he did so.

The Principal and the sheriff were still going through their dynamic, unaware that, out in the street, their Situation had been so convincingly straddled. Bandar crossed the sawdust strewn floor to where the Hero stood frustrated above the sheriff, who shook his gray–haired head in shame and chagrin. Pa's face hardened with anger as he swung toward Bandar and said, "I told you to stay outside, boy!"

I must be careful, Bandar told himself. *This could fly off in every direction.* He could not announce that spiders with incomprehensible weaponry were incinerating the town. Instead he willed the young idiomat to call out a danger that would fit within the Situation's paradigm, then let the boy control his own vocal apparatus.

"Apaches!" the Helper cried. "They're killing everyone!"

Screams and random shouts now came from outside, along with the repeated *whuzz* of energy weapons. The invaders were indeed killing everything that moved in the street, and would soon enter the buildings to continue their work. The sheriff now stood up and moved toward the noise, confusion clouding his face. A stocky man with pomaded hair and gaitered sleeves who had been polishing a glass behind a long wooden counter set it down and came out from behind the barrier to peer over the top of the doors. A moment later, the top quarter of him incandesced and evaporated, the rest of him tumbling to the floor.

A second bolt entered through the door and cremated the sheriff. The Hero blinked, looked with puzzlement at the smear on the floor, then recovered enough to turn toward the portal. He worked a lever on the underside of his weapon, the clicking of the mechanism sounding a note of resolution. In a moment, Bandar knew, Pa would reluctantly advance to do what he could to resolve the situation, carrying Uncle Fley within him. The noönaut did not want to see his own relative go the way of the hat–faced man, but he knew that to move a Principal from his proper track he must offer a motive that was within the idiomat's frame of reference.

He took control of the boy to make him lay his hand on the Hero's arm and say, "Pa, I'm scared."

The Principal turned, as Bandar had expected, to deal with his Helper's fear. The noönaut now followed up with a plausible suggestion. "They're too many to fight. We oughta go warn the others," he said.

He did not know what others he referred to, but was confident that in a Class Two Situation, a Reluctant Hero would surely have "others" to be concerned about. He did not think it wise to mention the fate of the Loved One.

"You're right, Mark," the Hero said. "We'll go out the back and circle around, see what we can do."

They went through a door behind the bar, finding a storeroom with barred windows and a door in its outer wall. The Principal crossed the intervening space and pulled open the door then paused in the opening to peer outside. He took a half step back then seemed to freeze. Bandar heard the clatter of many metal shod feet from the saloon's main room behind him, then the sound of the invaders' weapons. There was no time to delay. He shoved Pa out through the doorway and leapt after him.

He saw immediately why the Principal had hesitated in the doorway: instead of an Essential/Representational back alley, they were confined in a corridor formed by two parallel walls of well dressed gray stone, Fully Realized. Higher above them than they could reach was a ceiling made of tightly fitted slabs of the same material. The light was dim, provided only by flickering torches ensconced in the walls before and behind them at distant intervals. The chill that came from the floor of packed earth told Bandar they were beneath the earth. Of the doorway through which they had entered, there was now no sign.

This is definitely not right, he thought. He looked to the Principal and saw signs of tension and rising disorientation. Unless Pa could be focused, he would soon fall into disharmony. Bandar had no doubt that the long barreled weapon was intrinsic to the idiomat's motif of action. If the dislocated Hero snapped, the weapon would be put to use, and Bandar's host was the only available target.

He cast about for some means of consolidating the idiomat and saw a hopeful sign in the dirt. "Look, Pa," he said, "our cattle must be up ahead."

The Principal looked where Bandar pointed. Clear in the firelit floor of the tunnel, split hoofed tracks led onward into the darkness. A pile of dung moldered nearby. There seemed to be only one set of prints, and something about their arrangement struck Bandar as odd, but he could not afford to stand around thinking about it. Idiomats were characterized by their actions; to keep an armed Hero from devolving into wholesale violence, he needed to put the Principal to the work he was meant to do.

"Come on, Pa," the noönaut said, setting off in the direction the tracks led.

The Hero paused only a moment before saying, "Wait up, boy." He caught up with Bandar and, eyes flicking between the tracks and the dimness ahead, pushed past him to lead the way. Bandar was content to follow behind. It gave him time to think.

They had entered an entirely different Location, and the noönaut had a strong hunch about what lay at the heart of all this darkness. It would be The Baiting of the Monster in Its Lair, and a very old version of the ancient trope, judging by the primitive setting and the type of ogrous being that was indicated by the tracks and dung.

But it can't be a straddle, Bandar reasoned. Scholars had argued that two Locations might temporarily cohere, but three was beyond all speculation. He wished he could deploy his globular map of the Commons. It would confirm his suspicions if he peered into the color coded globe and found no flashing indicator to specify his location. But he could not display such an out–of–context object in the presence of the Hero or the Helper without pushing the idiomatic entities toward disharmony.

I need no external confirmation, Bandar told himself. *I came into this through a dream, and even if events are being manipulated by the Multifacet, there is only one venue where all of this can be happening—in my own head, my personal unconscious.* It worried him, though, that the powers he should have commanded in a lucid dream were somehow being blocked. Then an even more worrisome thought intruded: the Commons could manipulate his dreams—the noösphere was where dreams came from, after all—but how could Uncle Fley have been transported into Bandar's personal unconscious? He did not believe his sensing of Fley's presence in the Principal, however passive that presence might be, was an illusion; an experienced noönaut was equipped to tell real from false. But these events meant that some of the most time-honored rules of how the Commons functioned could be radically overturned. For a moment Bandar imagined trying to make that case to the Grand Colloquium, then broke off the revery to concentrate on his immediate problem.

The tunnel ended at a Y–junction. Bandar saw tracks leading into both directions, but those that went into the left–hand tunnel looked fresher. "This way, Pa," he said. The Principal's chiseled features still wore a look of underlying apprehension, but he nodded and said, "Stay close to me, Mark," and followed the trail.

Soon after the Y–junction they came to a wide circular chamber from which six other passageways led. Tracks littered the dirt floor, but the Principal now had his well developed faculties focused on following the freshest trail, and he quickly chose an exit and led Bandar on. They moved at a brisk walk, the young idiomat's shorter legs striving to keep pace, turning here to the left and there to the right, occasionally climbing or descending ramps of fitted stone slabs.

They stopped at a T–intersection, the Hero's nostrils flaring as he looked from one side to the other. "I can smell 'em," he said, gesturing with his prominent chin to the right. He eased back the hammer on the rifle until it gave a faint click and crept forward.

Bandar was familiar with the motif of The Baiting of the Monster in Its Lair. The encounter of the Hero and the Monster represented the archetypical struggle for dominance between the conscious and unconscious elements of the psyche. Usually, the Hero was physically outclassed, but still managed to triumph over the stronger opponent through guile or preknowledge of some inherent weakness in the enemy. Pa could not know what he was about to face, but his weapon, being out of place in this milieu, might affect the outcome.

An odor similar to that which had wafted off the stolen cattle grew ranker as they made their way down the tunnel. Ahead was an archway limned in brighter torchlight than shone behind them, a chill breeze carrying the beast–smell to them. The Hero inched his way to the opening and eased down onto one knee before peering into the open space beyond. Bandar crept close behind and looked over the idiomat's shoulder.

We have returned to the original Location, was Bandar's first thought. Beyond the tunnel lay a stretch of twilit prairie, short grass sweeping down a slope into a broad valley. Not far from the base of the slope sprawled a massive house made of squared logs above a fieldstone foundation, with a porch shaded by a shingle roof running along its wide front. Bandar saw a barn and smithy, some low–built structures—"bunkhouses"—and a spacious corral in which stood Pa's stolen cattle.

The Principal's eyes narrowed to slits. "Stay here, Mark," he said.

Bandar could not allow the Hero to carry Fley into whatever waited down there. The idiomat had seen only what he needed to see and had ignored the anomalies that surrounded the scene: that the sky's darkness was too deep to be an effect of clouds or even night, that beyond the big house and to either side the prairie disappeared into thickening shadow, that no wind stirred the grass nor did even a Sincere/Approximate bird or beast ornament the view.

They had not returned to Resisting the Despot. They were not in any true Location of the Commons, and there was no guarantee that the Situation would play itself out by the rules. Bandar urged the boy to defy his father. "No, Pa. You'll need help with the cattle."

The Principal looked thoughtful for a moment then said, "All right, but you stay behind me. And if anything happens, you hit the ground." He checked his weapon again and, holding it loosely in one hand, set off down the slope.

The air remained unnaturally still and the silence was immense. Not even the cattle stirred in their enclosure. The darkness that surrounded the visible elements of the scene seemed to move in as they neared the house and when Bandar looked back he saw blank nothingness crowding their heels.

As they entered the wide dusty yard his eye caught motion in the shadows beneath the porch. From a wide open door filled with a stygian blackness the three Henchmen emerged into the twilight, their hands resting on the butts of their holstered weapons. Their postures argued for their being in synch with the normal dynamics of the Situation, but when Bandar examined their expressions he did not see the mocking sneers that should have animated their features at this point in their cycle. A sharp tic drew up one corner of the Chief Henchman's mouth, the heavyset one displayed a slack jaw and unfocused eyes while the thin one with the mustache alternated between flashes of stark terror punctuated by an idiot grin.

The Hero noticed none of this, of course, being intent on fulfilling his role in the conflict. When Heroes neared the cusp of a Situation's essential action, they tended to drive forward with increasing momentum, encompassing outrageous violence and destruction as if they were the stuff of day–to–day life.

"I've come for my cattle," Pa was telling the men on the porch.

The Chief Henchman was shaking now, the tic wildly distorting his features, his bootheels beating a rapid staccato rhythm on the boards as his relatively simple faculties cracked under the strain of the anomalies. He's supposed to defy the Hero, Bandar thought, *but he's becoming disharmonious.* The other two should have backed up their chief but without his lead they were falling even faster into disharmony: the chunky one toppled backwards onto the porch's wooden floor, shouting wordless sounds, his arms and legs kicking in convulsive spasms, while his mustached compadre turned weeping toward the stone wall, striking it over and over with his bony fists until flesh and blood flew.

The Hero was disregarding the breakdown of the Henchmen, an Bandar sensed that this was the point, in the normal dynamic of the Location, when the Principal Antagonist would be summoned to the Final Confrontation. His supposition was confirmed when Pa stepped onto the porch and shouted into the black hole of the front door, "Strayhorn! Come out here! Or I'm coming in!"

A cold wind, freighted with the rank stench that had hung in the air of the tunnels, gusted from the doorway. The Hero held his rifle at hip height, its muzzle aimed into the darkness. Bandar saw his square jaw twitch and his shoulders set themselves.

"Wait!" Bandar stepped onto the porch and took hold of the idiomat's arm. "Don't go in there."

"It's all right, son," said the Hero. "You wait here."

"No!" Bandar held on. "Uncle Fley! Don't go in!"

The Hero's stern face blinked. And then Fley was bemusedly

looking out through the pale eyes. "It's all right, Guth"—now the voice was unmistakably Bandar's uncle's—"it's only a dream."

"No, it's. . . " The noönaut broke off as a golden glow filled the doorway. A mist wafted toward him and from within it appeared the shifting form of the Multifacet.

"You must not interfere with the essential dynamic," said an apple–cheeked old woman.

"He will be harmed."

"He is the Hero, you the Helper. He will do as he must, you as you must."

"No, we are real. Not like them." Bandar indicated the Henchmen, who now stood or lay inert, all movement having ceased when the Multifacet appeared. "We do not recycle and begin anew."

"We see no difference," said a dog with eyes as large as dinner plates. "You come, you go, only your stories endure."

"No," Bandar said. "I will not do it."

"If you help him, he may survive," said a hulking creature made of animated stone. "If you do not, he surely will not."

"This is not fair."

A young man with checked trousers and red hair answered him with a shrug.

"Nor is it according to the rules."

He was answered by a gentle–faced deity who wept crystal tears. "You must learn or die. Accept it. And now it comes."

The glow faded and with it the tear–stained face. Bandar saw that Fley had slipped back behind the Hero's eyes and determination reclaimed its place in the Principal's face. Pa turned again to the doorway.

Bandar thought fast. "No, Pa," he said. "He'll jump you in the darkness. Make him come out."

The Principal checked himself. The Hero was always disposed to accept aid from the Helper. "You're right, son," he said. He stepped back, his weapon covering the doorway, and Bandar backed with him into the yard. A silence settled on them, but it was soon broken by a crashing of footsteps from within the house, the sound of hard, sharp hooves on a plank floor. The stench reached an overpowering intensity then the doorway filled with a creature too tall and too wide to fit easily through it: an amalgam of man and bull, spewing foam from its muzzle, shaking its needle–pointed horns, pawing with hoofed hind feet at the doorstep while its out-sized hands reflexively grasped at the air.

The thing roared, revealing teeth that were neither human nor bovine, but daggers meant to tear flesh. It ducked its head to clear the lintel, lowered one shoulder to squeeze through the doorway then stepped clear onto the porch.

The Hero fired his weapon without raising it from his hip, levering its action with speed and precision. A tight grouping of holes appeared in the center of the beast–headed thing's leathery chest and the impact of the projectiles drove it back against the sides of the doorway. But it did not fall. It brushed at the wounds with black–nailed fingers, bared its pointed teeth and roared again. Then it crossed the porch in two clattering strides and stepped down into the yard, its great hands reaching for Pa.

"Run!" Bandar shouted, but the Hero was now beyond his reach, locked into the Final Confrontation even though this version could not be anything like the Situation this Principal was intend-ed for. As the beast–man reached for him, the Hero dropped his weapon and leaped forward to seize its horns. He anchored his heels in the dust then rotated his body and pulled sideways and down as if to throw the roaring creature over his hip.

But the impulses Pa could draw upon were out of synch with this struggle. The beast–man swept one brawny arm in an arc that caught the Hero across the midriff, folding him up and breaking his grip, lifting him from the ground and throwing him across the yard. He landed hard, the breath whooshing out of him. The brute watched as he struggled to rise, but instead of charging and finishing the attack it swung its monstrous head toward Bandar.

Its eyes were an expressionless black, unrimmed by white or iris, without intelligence or self–awareness, full only of a mindless intent to do harm. Bandar had seen the creature's like before, though always while chanting a thran that kept him from being noticed. Now he felt the full impact of archetypical malevolence directed at his own being, and he gasped as if struck by a blast of icy water.

From the corner of his eye he saw the Hero trying to rise and return to the fight. That was, after all, what Heroes did, however unequal the combat. *And help is what the Helper does*, he thought, *though how can I help against this?*

The bull–man pawed the dust, its baleful glare still locked on the noönaut. Then the intensity of its gaze diminished and, for a moment, another persona inspected Bandar through its black orbs, with a gaze full of cruel and disdainful amusement.

Gabbris! Even in the face of a beast–thing, the sneer of Didrick Gabbris was unmistakable. *But it cannot be!* The thought flashed through Bandar's mind. Dreamers could meet while passing through the outer arrondisement of the Commons, though it took exceptional powers of noönaut technique for them to do so. But actual dreams took place in an individual's own unconscious, and no other person could share that psychic space. The barriers were impermeable.

And yet. . . Here was Uncle Fley inserted into a dream of Bandar's, and now Didrick Gabbris had undoubtedly appeared— not a dream–imagining by Bandar, but the actual entity that was his enemy's own psyche.

Which was impossible. Which violated all of the rules discovered and delineated over the millennia by countless explorers of the Commons, so many of whom had given their lives as the price of hard–won knowledge. And now, as the monster turned its gaze back toward the Hero who had risen to one knee, a hand to his diaphragm as he struggled to control his disrupted breathing, Bandar knew what this mad business was all about.

You must learn, the Multifacet had said. He was being taught an unprecedented lesson, but the learning was being delivered in the indirect manner by which the noösphere always transmitted its wisdom.

"I understand," he said aloud. "You are showing me that rules that I have always been taught are sacrosanct now no longer apply. Very well, I accept the lesson. I will be the Helper, and willingly. But now you must help me."

He saw no golden glow, no swirling mist or protean figure, but he knew he had been heard. Now he would see if his terms had been accepted.

He focused upon the setting. *I dream a lucid dream,* he thought, putting behind the assertion all the strength of will available to a mature noönaut. *The dream is mine. All here is mine. I take control.*

The beast–man's hind legs, human from hip through thigh, bovine from knee to hoof, quivered as it crouched and set itself to leap upon the Hero. Bandar closed the fingers of one hand as if turning the appendage into a cutting blade then swept his arm down in a chopping gesture. As the edge of his hand clove the air, the ground beneath it trembled then split open. A crack raced zigzag across the yard, dividing the monster from Bandar and the Hero. Now the noönaut flung wide his arms and the earth groaned and snapped as the crevice gaped and deepened.

The beast–man roared its rage, its hooves stamping the ground. It gnashed murderous teeth and glared at Bandar with a primal hatred in which he could still see the spiteful malice of Didrick Gabbris. Then it raced forward and flung itself headlong across the still widening gap.

For a long moment it seemed to float motionless in the air, then its chest crashed into the lip of the ruptured ground, and its huge hands clawed at the dust while its dangling hoofed feet scratched and scrabbled for purchase.

Bandar watched with satisfaction. *It will not succeed*, he thought. The thing was losing its struggle and would slip inevitably into the chasm. He saw panic appear in the fathomless depths of its eyes that still contained Gabbris. "We have beaten you," Bandar told him.

Then he saw its eyes look beyond him, saw triumph flare in their blackness. Bandar turned, a shout of "No!" forming in his mouth. But he was too late. The Principal moved past him on shaky but determined legs and raised a foot to plant one boot heel square between the horns of the enemy.

The great head snapped back and the creature lost all hope of climbing out of the riven earth. But as it slid backward into the abyss it reached and seized. Its giant fingers encircled Pa's calf and pulled him over the edge.

Bandar flung himself down, his head and shoulders over the lip of the precipice. Below him he could see the two of them falling slowly into the bottomless darkness, the monster's grip unyielding on the Hero. There was no time to control the event. Pa looked up and Bandar could see his uncle staring at him in true fear from behind Principal's widened eyes.

"Fley!" the noönaut shouted. "Wake up, Fley! It's only a dream! Wake up!"

And then they were gone.

This time, the Multifacet left Guth Bandar with a full memory of his experiences. Thus it was with both urgency and trepidation that, the following morning, the young man climbed the angled stairway that led to the apartment above the housewares store. He passed through the silent lounge and entered the hallway that led to the master sleeping chamber. No sound came from behind the closed door.

He engaged the device that caused the panel to open and poked his head around the jamb. His uncle lay face down on the sleeping pallet. Bandar listened but heard no breathing. He wished he could go back downstairs and avoid this moment, but instead he summoned up his noönautic discipline and crossed the room. He put his hand on Fley's shoulder and gently shook.

A sharp intake of breath told Bandar that the man still lived. But death, though not impossible, was not the outcome he feared. "Uncle," he said, "time to awaken."

The older man made incoherent sounds, and Bandar's heart fell within him. "Uncle," he said again and pulled at the thin shoulder to roll the man over. Fley came easily and a moment later was sprawled on his back, mouth slack and eyes staring without focus.

Oh, no, Bandar said within the confines of his skull. *He has not come back.*

Then the man on the bed blinked and smacked his lips, and the eyes that regarded Bandar filled with intelligence and affection. "Guth," he said, "I had the strangest dream."

A few days later, Bandar passed by Barr–Chevry's and cast a knowing eye over its outer display. The goods offered looked no different from those that had been sold in the establishment since time out of mind. Nor were there any signs of the allegedly intended competition with Bandar's Mercantile Emporium.

Bandar stepped inside and when he was approached by the shopkeeper, he inquired as to whether there were any insipitators on the premises.

The fellow seemed somewhat distracted but said, "Odd that you would ask. We were to have dealt in such goods, but instead we are undergoing another change of orientation. All is in limbo until the new ownership is settled in."

"I thought the new owner was operating at a remove."

The man's face expressed fatalism in the face of unavoidable difficulties. "That was the previous new owner," he said. "He is no longer part of the environment."

"I don't understand," said Bandar.

"Nor do I. Apparently he has lost all interest." He dropped his voice to a whisper. "Indeed, I have heard he has gone mad."

Bandar expressed surprise, at which the man confided that it should have been expected: the stricken owner, he had heard, was one of those odd fellows who inhabit the Institute for Historical Inquiry. "I believe they're all canted well off the vertical," he said.

"You may be right," said Bandar.

"In any case, when the new owners take charge, they will have no need of me. I've heard that Fley Bandar may require some assistance and will seek employment there."

"I wouldn't bother," Bandar said. "He has all the help he needs.

The Helper and His Hero

Guth Bandar was adrift in a formless, limitless, gray nothing. Above him was nothing, ahead and to all sides was nothing, and below was nothing. But no, far down (an arbitrary direction—it was simply the view between his feet), something moved. Something tiny that, as he watched, grew larger as it came toward him.

Now Bandar felt a shiver of fear. For this no–place could be only one place. He was adrift in the Old Sea of pre–consciousness, the inert and timeless realm that underlay the collective unconscious of humanity. Only one thing moved in the Old Sea: the great blind Worm that endlessly swam its "waters" in search of its own tail. And only one thing could divert the Worm from its eternal, futile quest. As early noönauts had discovered when they had hacked their way through the floor of the Commons and dipped into the pearl–gray nothingness beneath, the Worm sensed any consciousness that entered the Old Sea—and inerrantly swam to devour it.

It is a dream, of course, Bandar told himself. He applied the noönaut techniques that would allow him to take charge of the dream, to change its dynamic, or to wake from it.

But nothing happened. He floated in nothingness, and the Worm came on. Now it seemed as long as his hand. In moments it looked to be the length of his forearm, its undulating motion hypnotically compelling his gaze. Bandar looked away, sought to concentrate on the techniques of lucid dreaming, but when he looked again, the Worm was as long as his leg. Its great dark circle of a mouth, rimmed with triangular teeth, grew larger as he watched.

A wave of panic swept through him. He flailed against the nothingness, as if he could swim away. But there was nothing to push against, nowhere to go even if he could somehow achieve motion.

And still the Worm rose beneath him, its gaping maw now as wide as a housefront and still relentlessly enlarging.

"What do you want?" Bandar called into the void. There could be only one agent behind this: the Multifacet, the entity that was the collective unconscious paradoxically become conscious of itself, that for its own obscure ends had ruined Bandar's career only to abandon him. Was it now back, with some new demand? Or had it, as he had often feared, simply gone mad and tossed him into the Old Sea, for no other reason than it had the awful power to do so?

The mouth of the Worm loomed beneath him now like a black moon, still rising. "Tell me what you want!" Bandar screamed, while a part of his mind offered him the obvious answer: *maybe it just wants you eaten.*

"I did everything you asked!" he cried. "What do you want now?"

And as the Worm rose to swallow him a voice from the nothingness said, "More."

Bandar awoke in his comfortable seat in the well–appointed gondola of the mid–afternoon balloon–tram, the dream–fear fading along with all memory of the Worm. He discovered that, while he had been dozing, two late arrivals must have boarded just before the conveyance lifted off from the terminal in the heart of Olkney.

One of the two would have drawn attention wherever he went, for he was quite possibly the fattest person Bandar had ever seen, although he was light enough on his feet as he made his way among the scattered armchairs in which passengers disposed themselves for the trip to Farflung, at the edge of the Swept, the great, unnaturally flat sea of grass that Bandar had always longed to travel.

The fat one's companion was a young man in nondescript garb wearing a slightly soiled cravat that identified him as a third–tier graduate of the Archon's Institute for Instructive Improvement, where the great and the titled had sent their children from time immemorial; its history faculty was tangentially connected to Bandar's alma mater, the Institute for Historical Inquiry.

But it was not the possibility of academic connection that gave the noönaut a start; rather, it was a fixity of expression and a fierceness about the eyes that gave Bandar the impression that the young man's features might never have arranged themselves into the full complement of expressions that a normal human visage displays over a lifetime, even a short one. Bandar allowed this initial impression to linger in his mind while he sought to see what associations it might conjure up from his unconscious. Moments later, a series of images floated onto his inner screen, and he was surprised to note than all of them were faces he had encountered in the Commons; he realized that the stranger, who was now seating himself across the gondola's wide aisle and engaging in low–voiced argument with the fat man, showed the same simplicity of character as that of an idiomatic entity.

When the steward brought round a tray of wine and delicacies, the noönaut used the distraction to sneak another glance at the two men. He now saw a definite contrast between them. Across the plump one's multi–chinned face a succession of micro–expressions chased each other: mild irritation, bemusement, curiosity, and the indulgence shown toward a child whose behavior straddles the narrow line between amusing and aggravating. But the young man's face showed nothing but righteous anger, unalloyed by doubt or even self–consciousness, and with an intensity that Bandar found unnerving.

Fortunately, whatever concerns motivated the strange young man were none of Bandar's. He turned away and looked out the gondola's wide window. The spires and terraces of Olkney were dropping below him as the balloon from which the gondola hung was allowed to rise to its cruising height. Soon he felt the slight tug of the umbilicus that connected the balloon to its dolly, now far below. The gondola rocked gently then settled as the operator engaged the system that brought the materials of which the dolly was formed into contact with the track into which it was slotted. A collaboration of energies moved the dolly forward, at first slowly then with increasing speed, towing the tapered cylinder of the balloon and its underslung gondola in a smooth and silent passage.

Bandar's ambition to travel the Swept had long been frustrated. It was a vast, wild land, almost entirely unpopulated except for some brillion miners. The great flatness, with its shoulder–high grass, was prowled by dangerous wildlife: omnivorous garm, both the lesser and greater species; sinewy fand, with needle teeth and ravenous appetite; and the huge but cunning woollyclaw, its well concealed burrows often full of hungry whelps.

The Swept had never been repopulated after its artificial creation eons before, during a desperate effort to repel the last aggressive invasion of Old Earth by a vicious predatory hive species known as the Dree. A gravitational aggregator, normally used to assemble asteroids into convenient conglomerations, was brought down to crush the invaders and their legions of hapless human mind–slaves in their warren of tunnels. But the immense gravitational waves had created resonances deep in the planet's core; even today cysts and bubbles of various sizes and intensities rose to the surface, though no one could predict where or when. A building that happened to be in the path of a rising anomaly could find the weight of its components drastically and suddenly reordered, leading to a collapse. Persons traveling on foot faced the same peril, and flying was advisable only in emergencies.

There were two safe ways to travel the Swept. One was to take passage on a landship, a great–wheeled wind–driven vessel built with enough flexibility to withstand minor anomalies and capable of steering clear of major ones. But landships catered to the truly affluent; Bandar had never been able to afford a cruise lasting weeks and the landships did not offer day trips. The less costly option was to hire a Rover to take him out onto the Swept in a two–wheeled cart drawn by shuggra. The Rovers were a fabricated species, developed from canines during a past age when trifling with life's elementary constituents was approved of. They lived as hunters and guides on the Swept, served by their innate ability to sense gravitational fluxions.

That ability would have made the Rovers ideal for Bandar's purposes—he wished to study the effects of gravity on the formulation of noöspheric corpuscles, and the anomalies offered unique experimental conditions—but Rovers disliked gravitational fluctuations. They used their senses to avoid the very phenomena Bandar sought.

He had taken the balloon–tram to Farflung twice before, during rare vacations from the housewares emporium, and each time he had tried to engage Rover guides. For his second trip, he had even learned the odd, gobbling sounds of their speech. But the moment he made his request, any Rover he approached looked down and away and professed to know nothing of anomalies, or declared himself already engaged, or under some nebulous obligation that prevented him from accommodating Bandar.

The balloon–tram was now passing the Institute for Historical Inquiry, and Bandar looked down upon the cloisters in which he had never again been allowed to set foot after the Institute's dons judged him responsible for plunging Didrick Gabbris into permanent psychosis. That was now decades ago, and Bandar no longer let his powerful memory take him to that painful time. But the noönaut's heart still harbored a desire to return to the Institute in triumph. He would present the Grand Colloquium with irrefutable new facts. If that meant overturning dogmas grown dusty over millennia, then so be it. And now that he was able at last to travel the Swept, Bandar saw victory as a glimmering prospect.

It bothered him only slightly that he had connived, and indeed had probably broken a statute or two, in order to gain passage on the landship *Orgulon*. The cruise was offered free to persons suffering from the lassitude, the first new disease to strike the human population of Old Earth. Bandar did not have the lassitude; indeed, he knew no one who did. Astonishing himself by his own boldness, he had invented an afflicted brother and offered forged documents to the organizers. A few days later, a pair of tickets had arrived. Bandar threw one away. The other was in an inner pocket of his traveling mantle.

He turned back from the window to take another glass of wine from the steward and found that the fat man had fallen asleep in his chair while the young one was staring at Bandar with an almost palpable intensity. Again, the noönaut was startled, but it soon became apparent that the fellow hardly noticed him, that his stare was merely the outer sign of a deep introspection. Again, too, he was struck by the quality of otherness in the young man's eyes: they would not have looked out of place in the skull of some mad prophet.

Now the strange eyes blinked and focused on Bandar. The noönaut made the gestures appropriate between travelers whose ranks were unknown to each other and said, "By your scarf, may I take you for a graduate of the Archon's Institute?"

The young man fingered his neck cloth. "Yes," he said.

"May I ask if you studied history?"

"No. Criminology." He had a brusque manner of speech, but

167

Bandar sensed that it was not intended to offend. He began to speak his name, then seemed to catch himself before declaring himself one Phlevas Wasselthorpe, of the minor aristocracy. The man snoring beside him was his mentor, Erenti Abbas.

Bandar introduced himself and said, "It would have been a convenient coincidence if you had studied history. I, myself, have spent most of my life dealing in housewares. I am now retired and taking a full–time interest in my longstanding avocation: the study of history, specifically the history of the Swept."

Bandar turned the conversation toward a discussion of what was on his mind: the Dree invasion. Wasselthorpe, surprising for an Institute graduate, even third–tier, had never heard of it. He asked questions, and Bandar sketched the outline of events and mentioned his intent to study the gravitational residues.

It was clear from the young man's face that the Dree did not interest him. He abruptly turned to another issue for which the Swept was famous, asking what Bandar knew about brillion mining. Bandar knew what everyone knew: brillion was a catch–all name for substances formed in the depths of the earth from waste products deposited by the dawn–time's wastrel civilizations. Old Earth's orig-inal inhabitants, scarcely out of the caves, had fashioned many ma-terials, natural and artificial, to use but once then throw away. This ancient detritus was dumped into depressions, plowed under and capped by layers of earth. Most was eventually dug up to become fodder for mass–conversion systems; however, some of the societies that had created these deposits being later destroyed or relocated, the whereabouts of many dumps were forgotten. Over geological time, the shallow deposits were gradually buried beneath accumu-lated rock. Some were drawn even deeper into the planet by tectonic motions, and then the same forces that make diamond from coal worked upon the rich variety of substances that paleohumans had promiscuously mixed together. The result was brillion, and it came in several varieties: blue, red, white were the main types, though they could be found in some interesting blends. Each had its proper-ties and uses.

And then there was the rarest of all: black brillion, a substance so rare and precious that those who found it never advertised the news. Or so it was said. It was also said the stuff could work wonders. Bandar reserved his opinion, though Wasselthorpe pressed for a definitive answer.

Their voices awoke the fat man, Abbas. He joined the conversation and his contributions made it less an interrogation and more the kind of amiable chat engaged in by travelers with persons they were unlikely to encounter again. At some point, Bandar revealed his true vocation. Abbas said, "Ah," in a manner that implied both knowledge and interest, but his companion had never heard of the Commons and thus began a new interrogation.

Bandar was always happy to talk about the noösphere. But as he did so now he saw the young man seize upon the subject with an intensity that Bandar found unsettling. He sought to redirect the conversation back to the Swept.

"It has long been known that the existence of the Commons is in some way connected to gravity," he said. "It is difficult to access in space, for example, and some have said that human experiences that have taken place beyond gravity wells do not register strongly and are lost to the common memory."

Abbas responded to the diversion, wondering if the gravitational anomalies might enhance Bandar's abilities as a noönaut. It was a pertinent question and Bandar now noticed that attached to the lapel of his robe were the pin and pendant of a runner–up for the Fezzani Prize, a notable academic achievement. He responded as if he were addressing a colleague. "Indeed," he said. "I am hopeful of conducting some remarkable research. Out of it may come the seed of a small institute."

"The Bandar Institute," Abbas said, and the words voiced an idea Bandar had never put so bluntly. But now the other one was boring in with a question about how the Commons might figure in the field of criminal investigation. It struck Bandar that criminology was an odd pursuit for a member of the aristocracy, even a rustic. He did not want to go off on a monomaniac's tangent and answered lightly, then followed with a brief dissertation on the formation and activities of engrammatic cells, corpuscles and archetypical entities, knowing from experience that technical language would swiftly chase away casual interest. But Wasselthorpe eyes failed to glaze and he continued to regard Bandar with an unsettling intensity.

"But where is this noösphere?" he said. "Where do your engrams and archetypes do their work?"

Bandar tapped the back of the Wasselthorpe's skull, then his own head and Abbas's. "In all of us."

He saw comprehension dawn in the young man's face, then puzzlement. Wasselthorpe said he thought the collective unconscious was mere myth.

To Bandar, myth was never "mere." Myth was always an expression of fundamental truth. He would have led the discussion along other paths but again the young fellow demonstrated his unnerving literal mindedness. He quoted Bandar from a few moments ago, when the noönaut had told him that a traveler of the Commons needed a good memory and a knack for detail. He declared that he had both.

Bandar decided it was time to ease this peculiar young man out of an apparent enthusiasm that might lead to obsession. To test Wasselthorpe's memory, he said, "How many doors were in the waiting room at the balloon–tram station, in which walls were they set, and what was written on each?"

Wasselthorpe paused only a moment before saying, "Four doors, two in the west wall, one each in the north and south. The two in the west wall advertised ablutories for males and females, the one in the north wall was for a closet holding supplies and the southern door led to the station master's office." He added, "That door had a scratch in the paint above the handle."

Bandar was as impressed by the power of Wasselthorpe's eidetic memory as he was concerned by the intensity with which he had answered the challenge. But it was a violation of his noönaut's oath not to respond to a potential candidate for training. With some trepidation, he offered to test the young fellow's aptitude.

Wasselthorpe declared himself keen. Bandar threw a querying glance Abbas's way, but receiving only the facial equivalent of a shrug, he explained the different mental images that a traveler might envision as the initial portal to the Commons.

"I will see a door," Wasselthorpe said, with complete certainty. Then he wanted to know what would be behind it.

"Let us not skip before we can hop," said Bandar, and was amused to hear in his own voice the dry tone of Preceptor Huffley, who had said the same words to him, long years ago. The Commons was dangerous for anyone; for some, it was indescribably perilous.

The warning did nothing to blunt the young man's interest. The gleam in the eyes that were now locked upon his made Bandar uncomfortable. The noönaut lowered his gaze to his hands as he briefly sketched the arrangement of the psyche.

"For now, I think we should go no farther than up to the first door," Bandar said. "If you can hold it in your mind's eye for a few moments, that will show an aptitude."

Wasselthorpe was eager to make the attempt.

Bandar bade the young man close his eyes and still his limbs, then instructed him on the regulation of his breathing. The noönaut was surprised that, within moments, Wasselthorpe appeared well settled.

"Are you ready?" he asked.

"I am," said Wasselthorpe, and Bandar heard in the undertones of his voice nothing that bespoke unwillingness among any of the less obvious components of the fellow's psyche. It was yet another unusual response from a complete beginner.

"I will teach you the introductory thran," he said. He sounded a sequence of tones and asked Wasselthorpe to copy him. The thran came back note–perfect and again Bandar heard no microquavers to indicate that some element of the young man's psyche opposed what they were about to do. *How rare*, he thought.

They continued to intone the thran for a few moments, then Bandar broke off to say, "When you see anything that might be a door, raise one finger."

He resumed the chant, expecting some time to go by before he saw a response. Instead, scarcely had he sounded the first few notes before Wasselthorpe was holding a digit almost beneath Bandar's nose. The deep conviction in the young man's chanting voice strengthened even further.

It came to Bandar that he might be in the presence of a seriously unbalanced mind. The young stranger's intensity of focus could be the mark of a natural. If so, to plunge his consciousness into the Commons would have immediate and disastrous results: he would be sharing the confined space of a balloon–tram gondola with a full–blown psychotic.

Even as he followed his thought to its frightening conclusion, Bandar saw Wasselthorpe's still elevated hand move forward, fingers curling as if to grasp. *He not only sees the portal but reaches to open it*, Bandar thought. He immediately ceased chanting and called in a peremptory voice: ""Enough! Come back!"

Wasselthorpe gave a start. The hand that had been reaching out now subsided to the arm of the young man's chair. Bandar rose to stand over him and shook his shoulder. Abbas sat forward in his chair, concern on his many–chinned face.

The young man's eyes opened, blinking, and Bandar was relieved to see them fill with awareness. He let out a pent breath and said, "You were too fast! I almost lost you."

Wasselthorpe seemed unfazed. "I saw a light shining from behind the door," he said. "And my own hand was reaching to open it."

A shock went through Bandar. "You saw light and made a hand, though you had never heard of any of this before?"

Wasselthorpe said that he was not inclined to tease. Abbas vouched for the truth of the statement, describing his companion as "no bubbling fount of mirth."

Bandar passed a hand across his brow, felt cold moisture. He had never seen nor heard of such aptitude. Bandar had been talented, but it had taken weeks of instruction and practise before he could call up his own portal and discern the light beyond it, and weeks more before he could open the way for more than a twinkling.

Wasselthorpe said it had seemed only natural, a term that caused Bandar to shudder. He explained its technical meaning among Institute scholars and found that his voice was trembling. He asked to be allowed a few moments to reflect upon what had happened. But Wasselthorpe was undeterred and wanted to know more.

So did his mentor. "If my young charge is no more than a skip and a jump from a serious bout of the hoo–hahs, I would appreciate knowing the warning signs."

"He is in no danger if he does not call up the vision of the door." Bandar looked sternly at Wasselthorpe and strongly urged him not to attempt the exercise again. Once into the Commons, he might never find a way out.

But still the young man said, "I would know more."

Again Bandar found the hard fixity of Wasselthorpe's gaze difficult to bear. He wondered that such an unnaturally concentrated mind had achieved only a third–tier degree, or that he should have come from an aristocracy that frequently showed the less fortunate effects of inbreeding.

"Then let it be later," said the noönaut. "I must think on the matter."

By "later," he meant, "never." But from what the two men said to each other after Bandar returned to his seat, it appeared that they were also bound for the *Orgulon*. He turned and gazed out at the landscape unrolling far beneath them as the old orange sun eased itself down to the horizon. He had been looking forward to the vast openness of the Swept. Now a cloud of foreboding seemed to have risen before him.

At Farflung, Bandar disembarked from the balloon–tram without speaking again to the two other passengers. He hurried through the terminal to find a ground car he could hire to take him to where the *Orgulon* docked. Frugality would ordinarily have inspired him to suggest that the three of them share transportation, but he wanted to put distance between himself and Wasselthorpe. The young man's unusual facility for entering the Commons disturbed him.

As the sun slipped behind the hills at whose feet stood Farflung, the car brought him to a stretch of docks. Beyond lay the Swept. The long grass that covered the flatlands to the far horizon rippled under a constant breeze like waves on a straw–colored sea. Bandar paused to look out at the immensity and the unsettled emotions that his encounter with Wasselthorpe had evoked now gave way to a feeling that he was where he was supposed to be. It was not a sense of contentment, rather it was a sentiment of being in the right place, doing the right thing. He drew in then released a deep breath and strode toward the landship.

Close up, the *Orgulon* was enormous. The side that lay by the dock was a wall of lustrous wood, pierced by windows large and small, each bordered by polished metal. The vessel's body was a great oblong with rounded ends, resting on a network of shock–absorbing cylinders that connected it to an eight–axled chassis from which extended a score of huge rubber wheels. Bandar presented his invitation to a security officer who stood at the base of the gangplank that sloped up to an upper deck. She consulted a list and found his name then gave him a searching look.

"The passengers are all traveling in pairs," she said, "one suffering from the lassitude and one to help the afflicted. Why are you alone?"

Bandar had prepared a story. "My brother has the disease but is too ill to travel. I came to evaluate the alleged cure."

She made a noncommittal noise and named a deck and cabin number. He went aboard and followed signs to his appointed quarters. There he stowed his bag before reposing upon the sleeping pallet and allowing its systems to restore his energies. After a while, he felt motion as the *Orgulon* left the dock and slowly moved out onto the Swept. A little later a steward tapped on his door and announced that the passengers were summoned to dinner.

The easiest route to the dining salon took Bandar across a spacious promenade deck that covered most of the landship's upper surface, except for raised platforms fore and aft on which stood the great vertical pylons whose rotating vanes stole from the ever–blowing wind the ship's motive power. He would have stopped to watch their operation and to look out across the prairie to where great cloud formations moved in the far distance like mobile mountains, but he noticed Abbas and Wasselthorpe near the railing to one side. The older man's appearance had altered—his face had taken on a different shape and his skin had noticeably darkened. Unconventionality was not uncommon among the aristocracy, Bandar knew. He wondered if the pair were competing in one of those odd contests that members of the upper strata indulged in as recreation, questing after some list of unlikely objects which might include a landship captain's cap. He decided that the two were, at least, strange, and resolved to stay clear of them.

Immediately below the promenade deck, the *Orgulon*'s dining area echoed the Swept in giving an impression of vast openness. It stretched from one side of the vessel to the other, its paneled walls broken by great round windows that looked out on the now night–shaded grasslands and its glistening wooden floor covered by large circular tables draped in snowy cloth and aglitter with crystal and cutlery. Bandar found that he was assigned to a certain seat and was relieved to discover that it was a good distance from Abbas and Wasselthorpe.

Others were already seated at his table and Bandar made appropriate gestures of head and hands to acknowledge them.

They seemed a heterogeneous mix, varied in ages, social ranks and genders, their only commonality that they came in pairs and one member of each couple was in some stage of the lassitude.

Across from Bandar a large woman exercised unchallenged control of whatever conversation had preceded his arrival. She wore swathes of some frilled material, with a braided necklace of precious metal around her wattled neck and a thick scattering of blue–fire gems in her upswept white hair. Her tone bespoke a habit of being listened to. Her apparent spouse, a stocky fellow with neck and cheeks discolored by a dark birthmark, sat dull–eyed to her left. His face was frozen by the lassitude's paralysis but Bandar suspected that even in his prime he would seldom have dared to interrupt the ceaseless torrent of her opinions.

"We will see wonders," she declared as Bandar took his seat. "I am sure of it." She fixed the noönaut with a bellicose glare and continued, "You have the look of a skeptic. Don't trouble to deny it. I never err in my assessments of character. It is a gift."

"A gift you are clearly happy to share," Bandar said, "even with complete strangers who have demonstrated no desire to receive it."

"An aptitude for seeing the truth, obliges one to speak it." the woman said. "I am Brond Halorn," she said. "This is my spouse, Bleban."

Bandar named himself.

"Why are you unaccompanied?"

He told her the tale of a brother.

"So there it is," she said, looking around the table. "He is indeed a skeptic, else he would have brought his poor brother along to receive Father Olwyn's blessing." She concluded her remark with a wave of a beringed hand that signified that all had turned out precisely as she had predicted. Bandar recognized a habitual gesture.

He defended himself. "I am no more skeptical than most," he said. "I can be convinced of the unlikely, even the seemingly impossible, though the proof need be unequivocal."

A motion of her hand indicated that his arguments were too vapid to merit an answer. This movement Bandar also took as part of her characteristic repertoire.

"You will see," she said, then resumed her address to the table in general. Bandar offered a gesture of his own, though he did so beneath the lip of the table, out of her line of sight. A few moments later, stewards began to bring in the first course: a jellied salad studded with morsels of fungus that had a unique flavor, like aromatic smoke. Bandar enjoyed the dish but the several more that followed were all built around the same unusual ingredient, and the taste began to cloy. A steward informed him that it was a delicacy called "truffles of the Swept."

When the last course was eaten and the servers were clearing away, Brond Halorn favored the table with more of her opinions. Bandar chose not to listen and instead ruminated on his plans to measure gravitational fluxes. But her voice and his thoughts were both soon interrupted by the sound of a gong that drew all attention to a dais at one end of the salon where a cone of light now shone down from the ceiling. A moment of expectation passed, then the beam of illumination filled with swirls of moving color that resolved into a projection of a slight man with a beatific expression.

The simulacrum introduced himself as Father Olwyn and welcomed the passengers. He announced a program that recommended study and action as the *Orgulon* traveled the Swept, preparing the travelers for a "ceremony of inculcation" leading to "a wondrous transformation."

Bandar sighed and lowered his eyes, placing the fingertips of one hand to the center of his brow. The fellow's discourse rang of a fraudster's patter. He looked away from the projected image, to find himself the object of a glare from Brond Halorn that would doubtless have wondrously transformed him into some species of small, squeaking vermin, had she but the power. He blinked and turned his gaze back to the simulacrum.

Father Olwyn's unseeing eyes were now raised to the ceiling and he was assuring the passengers that he knew what it was to suffer the lassitude; he had borne the affliction himself. After a suitably dramatic pause, he then announced, "But I was healed."

A great hush, that of an expectant crowd that dares not even breathe, filled the salon. Then the image said, "As *you* will be healed," and Bandar heard a mass sigh of released breath, and a low moan from Brond Halorn.

Olwyn finished by instructing the passengers in a four–syllable mantra—*fah, sey, opah*—that he assured them would "open the first door" in the process of healing. Bandar knew more than most about the effects of chants and mantras, and was confident that this one would do no more than exercise the jaws of those passengers, unaffected by the lassitude, who could still move theirs.

The room took up the chant. The white–haired woman's voice rose above the rest and her loud conviction drew her table mates—though not Bandar—into the sound. Their volume encouraged others and soon the mantra filled the room, accompanied by hands slapping tables and heels thudding against the floor.

Bandar looked about him and saw a wide range of emotions—hope, resignation, embarrassment, cynicism, fervor—as the passengers responded to the dynamics of their own psyches. He saw Phlevas Wasselthorpe regarding him with interest, then the young man's eyes moved away.

The chanting went on and on, and Bandar saw many whose eyes glazed and lost focus, though when he looked to Halorn he saw that she had been waiting for his gaze to come her way. She continued to chant "*fah, sey, opah!*" in an emphatic voice, while her hand made peremptory motions, palm up and fingers tight against each other, that summoned Bandar to join the chorus. He frowned, just as the projected Olwyn lifted his hands and cried, "Enough!"

Silence fell, broken only by Brond Halorn's throaty voice, edging on the hysterical, chanting the mantra twice more before a man seated to her right nudged her. Olwyn declared that he expected some of them to feel already the effect of the mantra, which he claimed would generate in them a numinous attribute he called "chuffe."

"Yes!" said Brond Halorn, eyes afire. She could indeed feel chuffe rising within her.

Olwyn made some final remarks about the gravitational peculiarities of the Swept being conducive to the generating of chuffe and recommended more chanting and meditation. Then his image disappeared.

A hubbub of voices rose, the passengers responding as their natures dictated to the message and its bearer. At Bandar's table, Brond Halorn again took up the chant and a few others around the room did likewise. Bandar avoided her accusatory gaze by turning in his seat to survey the salon. Then someone shouted, "Look!" and he glanced about until he saw that all eyes in the room had been drawn to the table where Erenti Abbas and Phlevas Wasselthorpe sat.

But it was not the pair from the balloon–tram who were the object of the crowd's attention. Instead it was a slim young woman whose rigidity of expression argued that she was in the grip of the lassitude. She had risen to her feet, while her apparent companion, a ruddy–faced man with dark hair in a complex coiffure, looked up at her, astonished.

Her face was stiff with early–stage lassitude, but her slight body was quivering. She leaned forward, both hands on the table cloth, looking down at the dark haired man, then Bandar saw her mouth open as if to yawn. Her shivering stopped as she raised both hands to her cheeks and kneaded the muscles of her jaw.

"I can talk," she said.

Her companion rose and took her in his arms, his eyes glistening. They sat down together and held each other as the room filled with a rising tide of voices, one current of which was the chant of *fah, sey, opah!*

Bandar lost his view of the objects of all this attention as people rose to their feet, some standing on their chairs, to see what would happen next. Moments later, he heard the booming voice of a ship's officer restoring order. Stewards urged passengers to retake their seats, then produced a selection of liqueurs and essences.

Bandar chose a tincture of Red Abandon, a fiery liquor that had been a favorite in his long–ago days as an Institute undergraduate. He sipped it and avoided eye contact with anyone as the room settled. The circumstances were too pat, the timing highly suspect: the afflicted and those who cared for them had been presented with a meaningless mantra, then moments after it was chanted someone was visited by a miraculous cure. As a noönaut, he had seen at first hand the power of myth and supposition, and he had no doubt that he had just witnessed a contrived performance.

Now the dark haired man was making some kind of speech that Bandar couldn't have heard, even if he'd cared to listen, because the white–haired virago across the table was chanting *fah, sey, opah* in a guttural undertone. Then the young woman's companion escorted her out of the salon through a passageway that led to the promenade deck.

Some of the passengers were enthused by what they had seen. Others expressed doubts. Bandar sipped his liqueur then ordered another. He took no part in the debates that now broke out around him, though to himself he thought, *The sick should not be subjected to such hard–hearted shenanigans.* He did not know how Father Olwyn would gain from flim–flammery, but Bandar would have bet a month's emporium receipts that this entire expedition was aimed at transferring the contents of someone's coffers to someone else's.

"Well, skeptic," said the white–haired woman, "what do you make of that?"

Bandar's only answer was a slight lift and subsidence of one shoulder, which earned him a single syllable delivered in a harsh tone followed by Brond Halorn's observations, addressed to no one in particular, concerning rock–headedness and narrow–mindedness among those whose cerebral equipment was obviously not well connected to their visual apparatus. "They cannot see what they will not understand," she concluded.

Bandar was irked, and two Red Abandons had now done their work. "I saw and I understood all too well," he said. "Indeed, better than those who see only what they hope to see."

His show of resistance provoked a tirade of invective. When Bandar tried to correct her, his efforts were met with a renewed chant of *fah, sey, opah,* accompanied by rhythmic hand clapping. His glass empty, he turned away to seek a steward and while his third installment of Red Abandon was being poured, he saw Phlevas Wasselthorpe making his way among the tables. Bandar downed the liqueur in one gulp, and when his eyes stopped watering he noticed that the fellow was now quite near. Relieved of any trepidation by the effects of the drink, he rose and greeted him, but instead of answering the young man gestured to his lips and jaw and made wordless sounds.

"You have the lassitude?" Bandar said and felt an inchoate urge to help the odd young fellow.

Wasselthorpe spread his hands in a fatalistic gesture. His mentor, Abbas, now joined them, and told Bandar that the disease was in its early stage. "It comes and goes."

Bandar offered his sympathy.

The young man grunted something that his older companion apparently understood. Abbas relayed the information to Bandar.

"My young friend wonders if you would tell him more about the Commons. It has piqued his interest."

Bandar saw no reason not to. If Wasselthorpe was destined to be imprisoned in his own paralyzed flesh until released by an early death, it would be a kindness to show him the Commons, providing Bandar guided him only to its gentler Locations. He offered to meet them out on deck after he had changed his garments; Brond Halorn's manner of countering opposition had left his shirt front dampened by her saliva.

A short time later he joined them on the lighted promenade deck and they strolled toward the forecastle where the windvanes rotated. Abbas asked him what he thought of Father Olwyn's promises.

Bandar was blunt. "Even if I suffered from the lassitude, I would be deeply skeptical of any who claimed a mystic cure."

The conversation turned to the Commons. Now that the immediate effects of Red Abandon were fading, Bandar found himself divided about taking Wasselthorpe into the collective unconscious. Either the young man possessed an uncanny ability to focus his mind or he was a latent psychotic. Bandar expressed his concerns in candid language. Erenti Abbas vouched for the young man's sanity and declared him to be a prodigy when it came to intensity of concentration.

Bandar acceded to the request. In his first years at the Institute, he had been counted a rare talent. Perhaps he was about to assist one who would become a renowned noönaut—if the lassitude didn't kill him. He led the pair to where the promenade deck met the raised forecastle. He had Wasselthorpe sit cross–legged, back against the bulkhead, hands folded in his lap. Bandar sat opposite him, knee to knee, the traditional teaching posture.

The lassitude had stilled Wasselthorpe's lips and tongue but he could make pure notes. Bandar bade him close his eyes and voice the tones with him. "When the portal appears, tell me. I will talk you through it."

They began with the thran they had used on the balloon–tram. Scarcely more than a moment passed before Wasselthorpe grunted to show that he had achieved a vision of the door behind which shone a golden light. Bandar spoke softly, guiding him through the tones that opened the door, warning him to wait beyond the threshold.

Wasselthorpe sang the tones, pitch perfect, then grunted again. Bandar had to exert his maximum effort to form his own portal and open it. "Wait," he said, "for the light to fade. More important, allow me to catch up."

The young man had gone through like a fourth–level adept. Bandar sought for him in the glow and soon had a sense of his nearness. Here the lassitude did not affect Wasselthorpe's speech, and his voice came to the noönaut clearly. "Where am I?"

"Nowhere yet," said Bandar. "Just wait."

After a while, he asked Wasselthorpe, "Now where are you?"

The young man said he was in his boyhood home, looking out a window. Something about the scene outside disturbed him, so Bandar told him to think instead of the place where he had been most secure and happy. Wasselthorpe immediately announced that the scene had shifted to the room where he had spent much of his youth. When Bandar had him describe the setting, they soon found the anomaly: a dark mirror that should not have been in the back of the wardrobe. In its depths was a reflection that troubled the young man.

Bandar urged him not to fear his Shadow and to step boldly through it. Here was the moment when their expedition might easily have ended; it took discipline acquired through rigorous practice before most apprentice noönauts could face their own rejected attributes; some never could manage it and left the Institute for other pursuits. Yet it did not surprise Bandar that, moments later, Wasselthorpe announced he was through the mirror and descending a hillside path that led to a tarn of dark water.

"Go down the path," Bandar said, and when he reached the water, the noönaut told him to dive in. Then he hurried to descend his own staircase down to the road that led into the outer arrondisement of the Commons. He found an almost transparent, two–dimensional version of Wasselthorpe standing between the walls, looking about with wonder.

He wanted to know where he had come to. Bandar explained, then he touched Wasselthorpe's arm, performing a noönaut mentalism, and the young man's image solidified into three dimensions. Now they were linked for the duration of their stay in the Commons, so Bandar did not have to worry about losing him among the thousands of dreamers that invisibly surrounded them. He was shocked when the young man said that he was aware of others passing by, seeing them as motes of light in the corners of his vision. That was an ability that noönauts worked years to acquire.

Bandar thought it wise to remove themselves from the bare threshold of the Commons, so close to the prime arrondisement where the characteristic entities were to be found in their purest form. He was about to suggest that they visit one or two of the more benign Locations, but Wasselthorpe was now peering down the road, his virtual body slightly leaning in that direction as if pulled by magnetism. He said, "I wish to explore."

"A little, no more," Bandar said. "I grow concerned."

"But I am fine."

Bandar explained that before they had come here he had been willing to take Wasselthorpe for one of those rarities with unusually biddable memories who find it easy to enter the Commons. But now he did not know what to think. Wasselthorpe was apparently not a natural, yet he could effortlessly detect the presence of the dreamers around them when even Bandar must work to catch a glimmer.

Wasselthorpe said, "I feel no fear. I am where I should be."

The phrase troubled Bandar. "As if you were called here?" he said.

"Yes," Wasselthorpe said.

"We should go back," Bandar said.

The young man looked around. "Are we in danger?"

"Not I," said Bandar, "but you may be in great danger."

But Wasselthorpe perceived no threat. "Why should we return?"

"To see if you can," Bandar said. To be called into the Commons presupposed an entity that did the calling, a powerful archetype that Wasselthorpe, lacking an arsenal of thrans and mentalist techniques, could not withstand.

"I sense no ill intent here," Wasselthorpe said. He begged to be allowed at least to look about and promised that at the first sign of danger, Bandar could lead him back.

Perhaps it was the lingering confidence of Red Abandon, but Bandar acceded, at which point Wasselthorpe said, "I have an inclination to go down the road,' adding, when Bandar let his anxiety show, "It is only a mild inclination."

"In the Commons, nothing is 'only' anything," Bandar said.

"What could happen?"

"I cannot name any of the particular menaces because to name is to summon."

Wasselthorpe found the concept hard to encompass.

"It is not a laughing matter," said Bandar. Naturals who found their way into the Commons almost never found their way out. The unprotected consciousness was soon absorbed by a pure archetype.

Apprentice noönauts, hearing of these things, always showed some degree of fear. Yet Wasselthorpe displayed no concern and Bandar felt a rising curiosity about this odd young man.

He offered a bargain: they would go down the road together, but Bandar's commands must be instantly heeded. Wasselthorpe agreed and made to set off, but Bandar delayed their going to teach the young man the strongest of the thrans: the three, three and seven, whose tones would hide them from the characteristic entities. He bade the young man sing it loudly and without cease, then linked his arm in Wasselthorpe's and led him down the road.

They soon reached the divide that separated the threshold from the first level of the Commons. Because Bandar was conducting the journey, it presented as an old stone bridge across a black river. On the other side was an open space in which the "usual suspects" sat or stood or milled about.

Bandar was surprised to note that near the far end of the bridge sat the Hero. His Helper, as always, was nearby. That the Hero appeared in such proximity meant that that archetype must be the entity whose influence was most dominant in Wasselthorpe's personality. *Odd,* he thought, *I would have predicted the Fool for naiveté and the Seeker for his exaggerated interest in unraveling mysteries.* The Fool was indeed nearby, but although the Seeker was Bandar's own dominant archetype, it was wandering far back in the crowd.

They had meanwhile reached the middle of the bridge. Bandar, his arm still linked with Wasselthorpe's, sought to restrain his further progress. The young man continued to chant the thran but his face was taut. He pulled against Bandar's grip.

Now a curious thing happened: the Hero's head came up as if something had attracted its attention. The Helper, too, showed increased alertness. Bandar saw that many of the other archetypes had stopped their characteristic activities and had turned toward the bridge.

That shouldn't happen, was his first thought. To Wasselthorpe, he said, "Louder."

The young man increased his volume but still his body seemed to yearn toward the archetypes.

"This is wrong," Bandar said, "as if they sense us."

The Hero had turned to face them, even though the insulating thran should have denied it any perception of their presence. Now it took a step toward them. The Helper followed, as did some of the other entities, including the Wise Man. The Father left the Mother and Child and moved toward the bridge.

Wasselthorpe was still chanting, but his volume had decreased. Bandar hauled on his arm, trying to pull him back. But he felt the young man's virtual flesh resisting with unexpected strength.

Bandar now added his voice to the thran. The Hero stopped and stood still, its head turning this way and that as if listening for an elusive sound. The other entities also paused.

The noönaut had, with difficulty, returned Wasselthorpe to the top of the arched span. Now the young man exerted himself and would go no farther back. Worse, he stopped chanting the thran to half turn toward Bandar and say, "Wait!"

Bandar recognized the look on Wasselthorpe's face; it was the "wild surmise" that gripped apprentice noönauts when they first felt a resonance between their own psyches and the pure entities that blended within them to make them who they were. It was not a look he wanted to see on the face of an uninstructed beginner.

"Listen," the young man said.

Listening was the last thing Bandar intended. He chanted more loudly, almost straining the throat of his virtual body. He dragged at Wasselthorpe's arm with both hands but could not budge the resisting young man.

A frisson of horror went through the noönaut as he saw the Hero step forward again. It set the heel of one boot onto the stones of the bridge. *Impossible!* thought Bandar. *It can't do that!*

The stones of the bridge moved beneath his feet, grating against each other. Wasselthorpe stood as if entranced. The Hero raised its foot to take another step. Bandar had no doubt that the entity was somehow aware of them, despite the thran, that it was drawn to them by an attraction so powerful that it could suppress the elemental forces that separated Locations in the Commons.

He yanked on Wasselthorpe's arm, spinning the young man around to face him. He could not speak while intoning the thran, but he let his terror show in his face and raised one hand in a gesture that said, *What are you waiting for?*

To his great relief, he saw understanding dawn. Wasselthorpe rejoined him in chanting the thran. The Hero's second foot did not step onto the bridge.

Bandar signaled Wasselthorpe to sing louder and when the young man did as he was bid, Bandar pulled him back to the road that was the threshold of the noösphere. Without delay, he sang the tones that opened an emergency gate and thrust Wasselthorpe through the rift the moment it appeared. Moments later, Bandar came back to the deck of the *Orgulon*. He leaped to his feet and leaned over the still seated form of the young man, shaking his shoulders until the eyes opened and focused on him.

Wasselthorpe mumbled something and Bandar sat down again. "I believe he is all right."

"He has also regained the power of speech," said a female voice. The security officer was standing over them.

Abbas explained about Wasselthorpe's intermittent bouts of rigor. The woman showed a professional's unwillingness to accept second–hand testimony. She squatted before Wasselthorpe and said, "What happened?"

The young man was still dazed. Bandar stepped in. "We encountered an archetype," he said. "More significant, it encountered us."

"A man with a sword. His helmet had wings," said Wasselthorpe, his gaze turned inward.

Bandar found the detail interesting. "That's one of its earliest forms."

Wasselthorpe added more specifics of his view of the entity. He had seen a dawn–time barbarian wearing chain mail and the skin of an extinct canine predator. Then he lapsed back into introspection.

The security officer glowered. "What have you done to him?"

"Nothing," said Bandar. He gave a short explanation of what had happened on the lip of the prime arrondisement. "But he is fine."

The security officer expressed surprise and distaste that anyone would venture into such a hell for a pastime. Bandar assured her he had no intention of accompanying Wasselthorpe into the Commons again.

She seemed to want to take the discussion further and Bandar was conscious of not having made a good impression. But her next words were never uttered because there came a panicked scream from the darkness that shrouded the foredeck.

The ensuing few minutes were full of shouts and action. It appeared that a passenger—indeed it was the dark–haired man whose female companion had been miraculously cured of the lassitude—had fallen from the foredeck. The landship's great wheels had crushed him. The captain, a small, precise man, came on deck and ordered the vessel stopped then dispatched a flying gig to retrieve the corpse. The security officer held a whispered consultation with the captain, who then announced that the passenger's death might have involved a criminal offense. The slim young woman became hysterical. Protesting that it had been an accident, she was led below by the security officer.

The passengers had crowded around in the way that bystanders at horrific events often do. Bandar sought solitude by the landship's rail and reflected on what had transpired in the Commons. He was deeply troubled by the Hero's seeming awareness of them despite the thran, and especially its determination to come for them directly across the bridge. That should have been impossible.

When he refocused his powerful memory on the events, he was struck by a detail that had eluded him at the time. While the Hero had blindly sought Wasselthorpe, Bandar now realized that the Helper had not just been following its master. Its eyes had not lacked focus, nor were they directed at Wasselthorpe. They had been aimed straight at Guth Bandar. *It sensed me*, he thought. *Thran or no thran, it knew I was there.*

It was a worrisome thought. Bandar did not care to be absorbed and tipped into permanent psychosis. But even if he were willing to go mad, his choice would not have been the Helper, insanely serving some blustering hero. He shuddered and knew that he was not just responding to the chill breeze off the night prairie.

Abbas and Wasselthorpe joined him after the body had been removed and the crowd cleared. They speculated on how the poor fellow might have come to fall overboard. Bandar offered the opinion that the landship might have encountered a transient gravitational cyst, causing the man to unbalance and tumble over the rail. The conversation reminded him that it was just such anomalies he had come to investigate, and he excused himself then hurried below to fetch his measuring equipment. But when he came back on deck and activated his device, he detected nothing out of the ordinary.

The security officer approached him as he adjusted settings and calibrated norms. "Now what are you up to?" she wanted to know.

Bandar told her. His explanation earned him a look that let him know that he was becoming one of her least favorite passengers. Deciding it would be best to retire, he pocketed his equipment and went to his cabin.

It had been a tiring day, so Bandar decided to combine his concern about Wasselthorpe and the Hero with his need for rest. He fell asleep, allowed himself to slip into a dream then took control. He transported himself to the threshold and set off for the prime arrondisement with the intention of examining the bridge and the archetypes—especially the Hero and Helper—beyond the barrier.

He had scarcely taken three strides, however, before he felt a grip on his shoulder that sent a cold shock through his virtual torso. Startled, he turned to see what had accosted him and found himself looking up into the pleased face of Phlevas Wasselthorpe.

"What are you doing?" Bandar said.

"I am dreaming."

"This is very wrong," said the noönaut. "You should not be here."

The young man counseled him to be unconcerned. "It is only a dream."

"Yes," said Bandar, "but it is *my* dream."

"No, it is mine," said the other. "You are a figment."

"Tell me," Bandar said, "when you look at me do I seem to change in any way? Or is my form constant?"

The other looked him up and down. "It is peculiar, but you do seem to remain unchanged whereas the woods behind you have been several different kinds of forest."

"What does that tell you?"

"What should it tell me?"

"A hundred things, none of them good. I will open us a gate." Bandar sounded the first few notes of the emergency exit thran. He was astonished to find himself silenced. Wasselthorpe had placed a hand over Bandar's mouth. The hand felt very real.

This time the shock of contact was strongly colored by a bolt of fear. Bandar struggled and with a great effort managed to wrench himself free. He backed away, saying, "Oh, this is much worse than not good. I should appear to you as at best a shifting image. Instead you not only see me but can lay hands on me and prevent my following my own will."

"I am sorry," said Wasselthorpe. "I do not want to depart."

"I want nothing but," said Bandar. "Do you not understand that you frighten me?"

"I do not wish to." The young man looked around at the shifting landscape. "Do you not sense that somehow all of this is as it is meant to be?"

That was precisely what frightened Bandar. "Neither of us is experiencing an ordinary dream," he said. "Some force is shaping us to its own ends. In the Commons, the only such force is an archetype intent on absorbing a consciousness. That way lies madness."

"I do not feel irrational," said Wasselthorpe. "My mind seems unusually clear, considering that I am dreaming."

"Again, a worrying sign," said Bandar. "My sense of things tells me that you are being drawn into the role of Hero and that I am being pressed into the part of the Helper."

"I want from you only advice," Wasselthorpe said.

"Let us be exact," said Bandar. "You feel compelled to enter more deeply into the Commons and you want me be your guide."

"I suppose."

"I refuse."

"Why?"

"Because the end of this is your absorption into the entity that summons you, followed by insanity and certain death. And poor Bandar, towed along helpless in your train, suffers a comparable doom."

Wasselthorpe found the warning hard to believe. "All will be well," he said. "I am certain of it."

Bandar informed him that that was always the Hero's sure belief, right up until the moment the dragon's teeth closed upon his tender parts.

Now Wasselthorpe disputed the contention that he was ruled by the Hero. "Why can I not be a blend of several archetypical entities, like you and anyone else?"

Bandar told him to look at himself.

The young man looked down and Bandar saw mild surprise take possession of his face. Wasselthorpe was clad in chain mail, scuffed boots and rough trousers bound up by criss–crossing straps. A shaggy gray pelt covered his shoulders, its paws tied across his chest. In one hand was a sword of iron. Bandar gestured and Wasselthorpe raised a hand and touched the wings that sprouted from the helmet on his head.

"Does that seem familiar?"

The young man had to admit that it did. Yet, he was as thoroughly unconcerned as a Hero would be.

Bandar suggested that he ought to open a gate so they could discuss the situation in the waking world, where it was easier to resist an inclination to madness. He was chagrined to see the other's face fill with heroic resolve.

"No," Wasselthorpe said. He was here to do something, and felt that he must do it.

Bandar had backed a little farther away; Wasselthorpe was accompanying his declaration with sweeping gestures, and only now noticed that he was doing so with the hand that held a sword. Considerately, he laid the weapon down on the road. Instantly, it disappeared from there and reappeared in his grasp.

"What do you think the 'something' you are here to do might be?" Bandar said.

The other spoke without reflection. "I must search."

"Search for what? Something nice, like treasure? Or something with fangs and an insatiable appetite?"

A blank look came over Wasselthorpe. He did not know, he

said, but he would know it when he saw it.

"Oh, my." Bandar put his hands over his eyes and shook his head. "All right," he said. It did no good to argue with a Hero. But he begged to be allowed to shape the adventure. That way they stood some chance of surviving it.

The young man agreed to follow his advice.

The noönaut said, "Look around and tell me if there is anything that draws your attention."

Wasselthorpe immediately found that something about the woods beyond the field interested him.

"Very well," said Bandar, "let us approach them. But I must lead."

Wasselthorpe agreed.

"All right," said the noönaut, though the situation was far from it, and asked the young man to indicate the direction in which he wanted to travel. Wasselthorpe closed his eyes and let his sword hand rise to point the way. When the noönaut asked how far he thought they should go, the answer was, "Not far."

Bandar turned the globe and regarded the proposed line of travel. A short distance away was the entrance to a Class Three Event. "Curious," he said. He put away the globe. He would have liked to call an end to the expedition here and now so that he could mull the coincidence: here they were traveling the Swept, a legacy of the War Against the Dree, and now a strange young man who was powerfully influenced by the Hero had a strong urge to enter the Event that the war had carved out in the Commons.

"Just a coincidence?" Wasselthorpe suggested.

Of course it was a coincidence, Bandar said, and that worried him even more. In the waking world a coincidence was just a random, juxtaposition of events, devoid of meaning. But in the Commons, coincidence was the most meaningful circumstance of all, the immensely potent force that tied one thing to another. "Indeed," he said, "it is coincidence that connects everything to everything else."

Wasselthorpe's reaction troubled him further. The young man ought to be afraid, yet he was not. He pointed the sword once more. "I must go there," he said. "Does it mean I will die?"

Bandar did not think so. The choice of that particular Event was less worrisome than many another he might have chosen. But he warned again that Wasselthorpe must let him be their guide.

"I will."

The noönaut took a firm grip on the young man's sword arm. He taught Wasselthorpe a thran and when the rendition was perfect Bandar cautioned him to continue the chant. It would keep the Location's idiomats from detecting their presence and reacting to them as if they were part of the Event.

"How bad would that be?"

"The Dree were appalling," Bandar said, "and the war to resist them was particularly horrid." The invaders had been a hive species, each hive telepathically and pheromonically connected among all its members into one entity. They used their concentrated mental powers to enslave other species and force them to work and fight for the hive—especially the latter, because ritual combat was the basis of what passed for culture among the Dree. Status among the competing hives was everything, and status was gained and held by a hive's success on the battlefield.

Dree fighting style was mainly devoted to capturing prisoners that could be carried back to the captor's hive and tortured. The telepathic Dree relished the anguish, fear and despair of their victims, just as humans savored the flavors and textures of foods and essences. Fortunately, this strategic imperative meant that all their battle tactics centered on surrounding small groups of enemies for capture. Faced with an well organized army determined to massacre them, the Dree were heavily outclassed.

After the initial surprise of the invasion, the Dree were soon rolled up and confined to the territory now known as the Swept. No one wanted to dig them out of their warren of tunnels, so the gravitational aggregator was brought down from space to crush and bury the invaders, along with their unfortunate mind–slaves, beneath the flattened landscape.

Wasselthorpe appeared to be affected by the tale. "Are you sure you want to go on with this?" Bandar asked.

"I am somehow called to go this way," the young man said. "I must see what there is to see."

Bandar was still weighing his curiosity against his apprehension, though it could do no harm to visit the Event. But he reminded Wasselthorpe not to break off the chant. If either needed to speak, he would use hand signals to warn the other to increase the volume of the thran to keep them both covered.

He led them to the node, opened the gate and led them through. They stepped into open land beneath a sky splashed with stars. A wind whispered through tall trees and a stream chuckled not far away. Bandar took quick stock of the scene: they were near the base of a long slope leading out onto flat land where armored war vehicles and assault infantry were converging on the range of hills behind them where the Dree had consolidated their forces. He could hear the clicking and creaking of Dree warriors.

The sound must have piqued Wasselthorpe's interest because he abruptly ceased chanting. At once, a concentrated beam of energy lit up the area with green light and the ground at their feet bubbled and smoked. Bandar raised his voice and yanked at the young man's arm, bringing him back to an appreciation of where they were.

They waited briefly until the armored assault had passed them by, then moved downslope and across the stream into a pasture. The hemming was almost complete, and Bandar saw the massive aggregator above the horizon, blotting out the stars.

Bandar motioned Wasselthorpe to increase his volume again and asked: did he feel any impulse to go this way or that? The fellow looked about him and his attention was caught by something a little way off and he moved toward it. Bandar followed and found a shallow trench that contained the melted remains of some heavy weapon and four carbonized Dree.

Wasselthorpe stepped down into the declivity and pried the corpses apart with his sword, revealing the intact upper half of one of the invaders. The young man stared at the dead thing until Bandar gestured for him to increase his volume again so the noönaut could speak.

"No eyes," he said, looking down at the rounded oblong of brown chitin that was something like a head. It had feathery antennae that, in life, stood upright to detect odor with fine precision. Nerve–rich regions on the torso and head detected vibration and rendered it as sound. At close range it could also detect bio–electrical fields.

Wasselthorpe regarded the dead Dree without reaction. Bandar questioned him and learned that the young man felt no more urges. Apparently they had done whatever Wasselthorpe's motivating entity wanted done. The noönaut examined the other man closely and was interested to see the trappings of the Hero fade, leaving the young man clad in unremarkable attire.

He considered summoning an emergency exit again, but departing from the Commons by that route twice in one day could cause disorientation even to the experienced traveler. Instead, he brought out his map and navigated a path through series of innocuous Locations where they would not even need to hide behind thrans. A short while later, he was able to ease Wasselthorpe through a conduit that would lead him back into normal sleep.

But Bandar did not then wake himself. Nor did he return to the mission Wasselthorpe's arrival had interrupted. There was no point going to the bridge to study the usual suspects. He had had a good close–up look at the pure archetype that was governing the strange young man. The noönaut wanted to think about what he had seen and so he made his way to a quiet Landscape that consisted of little more than a tiny patch of sand–colored rock, set in an endless ocean and shaded by a single Sincere/Approximate palm tree. No idiomat ever came there, and Bandar had often wondered what role the simple setting could have played in human history.

But he did not pursue that idle chain of thought now. He wanted to reflect on the unprecedented sequence of events that had occurred since he had introduced Phlevas Wasselthorpe to the Commons. First, the young man had demonstrated an unheard–of ability to enter the noösphere. Bandar had studied naturals who could slip easily into the noösphere, but they did so at the sacrifice of their own identities. They became the archetypes that summoned them, disappearing into them so utterly that they no longer had any individual consciousness: there was only an archetype psychotically stalking the waking world, usually dealing out misery and horror until the authorities intervened.

But Wasselthorpe had gone in and come out unaffected, as if he merely stepped from one room to another. More shocking still, he had been able to enter Guth Bandar's dream and physically dominate the noönaut's virtual flesh. Most disturbing of all, the young man's consciousness had clearly made a connection with the Hero, yet he had not been absorbed by it. Wasselthorpe's accomplishments represented two highly unlikely results, and one that was simply impossible. There had never been, to Bandar's expert knowledge, anyone remotely like him.

Another worrisome thought occurred as Bandar sat beneath the palm tree. The Hero never went anywhere without the Helper. Bandar had played that role, indeed had slipped into it so readily that it was as if he had himself been suborned by that characteristic entity. Yet here was Bandar, thinking rational thoughts, when he should have been drowned in the soup of psychosis.

A half–fashioned memory nudged at the edge of his awareness. He reached for it with a noönaut's casual skill but was disturbed to feel it somehow slip away. He sought for it in earnest, focusing a great deal of his trained power, yet still it eluded him. Another attempted grasp, and then it was gone.

The experience left Bandar troubled. It was bad enough that something impossible was going on inside Phlevas Wasselthorpe. But for a life–long adept of the noösphere to find that elements of his own psyche could deftly avoid his grip brought the strangeness far too close to the essential core of Guth Bandar. Something was going on within him that he was unable to bring to the surface of his mind. To a noönaut, such a state of affairs must be deeply troubling.

He awakened himself and made his way to the cabin Wasselthorpe shared with Erenti Abbas. He knocked and was admitted by the young man. Bandar inspected him and was satisfied he had sustained no harm from his experiences of the night.

Wasselthorpe apologized for having overborne Bandar's objections to the mission he had felt compelled to fulfill and for forcing Bandar to guide him.

Bandar waved away the sentiment. The events were over and he had no intention of repeating them.

Now Wasselthorpe was wondering if he might someday take up the exploration of the noösphere. He even asked if he might study under Bandar.

The noönaut felt the skin of his face cool and knew he must have gone pale. He informed Wasselthorpe that it would be kinder if he simply killed Bandar on the spot. "Be assured, I will never again go willingly with you into the Commons."

Indeed, he meant to ask the *Orgulon*'s captain for the use of his gig to take him away forthwith so that he could never be pressed into the Hero's service again.

"But what of your research?" Wasselthorpe asked.

Bandar told him that he could take scant pleasure in it while constantly at risk of being dragooned to his death.

The danger seemed remote to Wasselthorpe.

"To me," said Bandar, "it is inescapable. I am in grave peril if I remain within range of you, and since I do not know what that range is, I shall set the greatest possible distance between us."

He ended with a mollifying gesture and assured Wasselthorpe that he meant no offense.

The young man said none had been taken. The matter mystified him.

Bandar looked up into the young fellow's mildly troubled face and again felt an urge to be of assistance to him. He fought it down and went in search of the captain. That interview was not a success: the captain called in the security officer, whose name Bandar now learned was Raina Haj, and she refused to let anyone leave the ship until the questions regarding the death of the passenger were cleared up.

"It was no accident," she said.

"But how can I be a suspect?" he protested. "I had just emerged from a trance and was under your direct view when it happened."

"Perhaps you were there to distract me," Haj said.

Breakfast had been served and eaten by the time Bandar entered the dining salon. Apparently, Father Olwyn had also come and gone again, leaving the lassitude sufferers and their companions with a new mantra—*bom, bom, ala, bom*—that would further elevate their chuffe. Brond Halorn, her hair still asparkle with blue–fire gems, was leading the most fervent group of chanters. When she saw Bandar enter and make his way to the remains of the buffet, she threw a challenging stare his way.

Bandar declined to return her gaze and looked for an empty seat away from her devoted chorus. The only available spaces were within too close a range to Abbas and Wasselthorpe; it would be rude to sit near them without speaking to them. He filled a plate with items from the chafing dishes—all, it turned out, featured variant renderings of the truffles of the swept—and took it along with a steaming pot of punge back to his cabin.

He slept for a while, allowing himself an ordinary dream cycle, and awoke feeling refreshed and more cheerful. He went on deck where he found the security officer. Again he offered reasoned arguments, again they were rebuffed.

"It is not some mere whim that prompts me to seek to depart," he said. "My psyche is in danger as long as I am in proximity to that young man." He unobtrusively indicated Abbas and Wasselthorpe who were standing by the rail.

An even deeper suspicion crept into Haj's already dubious expression. "What exactly is your relationship to those two?" she said.

"I have no relationship. I encountered them on the balloon–tram on the way here."

"Do you often encounter strangers who threaten your sanity?"

"No, but there is something odd about Wasselthorpe. He is able to do things he should not be capable of."

The security officer tilted her head to regard Bandar. "Both you and they stand out from the rest of the passengers," she said. "You arrived claiming a lassitude affected brother. His illness comes and goes."

"I am in danger. Last night Wasselthorpe invaded my dream."

Haj's skepticism visibly intensified. "Uh huh," she said.

Bandar concluded there was no point in further argument. He went below and sat in his cabin until boredom made him take up his measurement equipment and go back on deck. If he could not escape, he might as well do something useful.

He was taking readings from various points of the compass when Wasselthorpe approached him.

"I have been thinking about what happened last night," the young man said.

"I do not wish to be impolite," said Bandar, squinting at a read–out, "but I must refuse to discuss the matter with you. I would not still be here but Raina Haj will not let me depart."

"I am sorry you are troubled," the other said. "For myself, I feel as if a door has opened on a world whose existence I'd never heard of. Yet I grow increasingly sure that there is something for me there."

"A destiny, perhaps?" said Bandar.

Wasselthorpe's normally serious expression broke under a sudden surge of excitement. "Yes, exactly! A destiny!"

"You cannot imagine how frightening that is," said Bandar. "I do not know what you are or how you can do what you do. But such abilities, yoked to a sense of destiny, then coupled to the power to draw me, of all people, helplessly into your wake, are enough to give me the abdabs."

"I sense no harm in my fascination."

Bandar sighed. "Of course you don't. But the Commons is full of surprises, many of them hideously final." He begged the young man to let him be and told him that he resolved to sleep at odd times so that his dreams might be unviolated, and asked Wasselthorpe not to meddle with any other dreamers he might encounter in his sleep.

The day wore on. Bandar would again have taken dinner in his cabin, but when he summoned a steward the fellow told him that Raina Haj had decreed that all passengers must dine together. Apparently the security officer had installed surveillance systems in the salon that could read and assess subliminal reactions among the passengers. She hoped some investigatory leads would develop from throwing them all together.

Bandar decided he would demonstrate that he had no ties to Abbas and Wasselthorpe by dining at their table and making no attempt to hide his face. Two seats had been left empty—the dead man's and his companion's, who was confined to her quarters under guard. The ship's first officer, who had sat there the previous night, was also missing, so that Bandar, Wasselthorpe and Abbas were joined only by a retired couple from the Isle of Cyc, who were introduced as Ule Gazz and her spouse, Olleg Ebersol. He was paralyzed by the lassitude, while her face showed enough animation for both of them. They were enthusiasts of the Lho–tso school of practical enlightenment and she spoke glowingly of mantras and rising chuffe and the cure she expected. Ebersol's opinions on these matters were impossible to determine but Bandar saw genuine suffering in the man's eyes.

The cuisine was again entirely built around truffles—Bandar wondered if the cruise might be some ploy to market the fungus, though how the lassitude and truffles might commercially intersect was beyond him. After the meal, Father Olwyn again appeared in simulacrum and offered a sermon that Bandar found all too vague, along with an exhortation for all to chant *bom, bom, ala, bom.*

The chant rose throughout the room as Olwyn disappeared. Bandar dismissed the sermon as, "A pile of piety and platitudes," at which Ule Gazz took offense. The couple went to the other side of the salon, where Brond Halorn was vigorously conducting more than half the passengers in a mass chant. The slap of dozens of hands on tables and feet on floorboards shook the room.

Phlevas Wasselthorpe once more tried to draw Bandar into a discussion of their mutual experience in the Commons. Bandar again had to fight down an initial urge to help the young man, but he transformed the impulse into a brief lecture: "For your own good, don't go there. And if you find yourself wandering the Commons, please do not seek my company."

He extracted a promise that Wasselthorpe would not sleep until later in the evening, then retired to his cabin to snatch as much rest as he could before their dreams might again overlap. He dreamt lucidly and the moment his noönaut's senses detected the presence of Wasselthorpe in the Commons, he promptly woke himself and spent the rest of the night in meditation.

With the tired old sun barely creeping above the horizon, the passengers were summoned to breakfast. Bandar had had enough of the truffles of the Swept—the flavor, though rich, soon cloyed. He took plain cakes and punge and carried them again to the table where Abbas and Wasselthorpe sat, tendered the basic formalities then ate without offering conversation.

As he was finishing his second mug of punge Bandar noted that the landship was slowing. The other two men did likewise and turned in their seats to peer out of one of the great round windows. Something attracted their attention and Bandar rose to look over their shoulders. For the first time since he had boarded the *Orgulon* he experienced a thrill of pleasure.

"Those are Rover carts," he said.

The landship came to a halt near a place where a wide circle of the long grass had been trampled flat. Gangplanks extended themselves and the passengers debarked, the lassitude sufferers in whom the disease was most advanced being transported on come–alongs, small platforms fitted with gravity obviators and normally used to tow heavy baggage.

Bandar came down onto the Swept, looking about avidly. The projector that allowed Father Olwyn to address the passengers was deployed and he heard some more blather about chuffe and mantras. But the noönaut's attention was drawn to the Rovers and their vehicles. Seven of the lightweight, high–wheeled carts were spread around the rim of the flattened area. Made of plaited bamboo withes, each rode on two tall metal–and–rubber wheels, thin–spoked and fat tired. Bamboo ribs curved from one side to the other, surmounted by a canopy of tightly woven grass to shade passengers from sun and rain.

Each cart was drawn by a team of eight shuggras, round–eared, sharp–incisored, oversized rodents bred up long ago from vermin. Their legs were long and powerful, ending in splayed hairless feet with spoon–shaped leathery digits. At the moment they crouched, resting but keeping up a constant muttering.

Wasselthorpe also seemed to lack interest in Olwyn's sermonizing. He was clearly curious about the Rovers and drifted in the direction of the nearest team. Bandar felt a strong impulse to warn him away. Shuggras were intensely social, but only amongst themselves; any creature outside their own clan or their Rover master's family might suffer an unprovoked attack.

The Rovers had been lying beneath the carts until the passengers came down from the *Orgulon*. Now they emerged and each went to his vehicle and pulled down a tailboard that unfolded into steps.

Wasselthorpe was clearly surprised by the Rovers' nonhuman appearance. He asked Bandar if they were of ultraterrene origin. Now it was Bandar's turn to be surprised: even a provincial lordling ought to have heard of Rovers. They had been sharing the planet with humans for eons. The noönaut wondered about the young man's education. Much commonplace knowledge seemed to have eluded him.

His plump mentor made a remark that revealed his unhappiness about exchanging the landship's comforts for the more austere conditions of a Rover cart. Still, Abbas assumed a look of resignation and steered Wasselthorpe toward one of the vehicles. The young man was staring at the nearest Rover, a mature male who was showing his species's usual discomfort at direct eye contact. Bandar stepped up beside Wasselthorpe and advised him to try a less direct inspection. He also briefly summarized the creatures' origins.

"They are dogs?" Wasselthorpe said.

"That is not a word they like to hear," Abbas said. They climbed into the cart, making its leather springs creak. On each side of the interior, four seats of woven wicker faced forward. Erenti Abbas expressed some relief that the seats were cushioned by pads of woven grass. He and Wasselthorpe took the foremost pair and Bandar sat behind the young man. The cart squeaked and bounced again as Ule Gazz and Olleg Ebersol boarded, the former helping her spouse into a seat behind Bandar. Despite the efforts they had made to elevate their chuffe, Bandar thought that Ebersol showed signs of sinking deeper into the lassitude.

Two more passengers climbed in, a pair of sturdy young women who had the look of students. Bandar had seen them on the *Orgulon* but had not met them. The new arrivals named themselves as Corje Sooke and Pollus Ermatage, though in fact Ermatage did all the speaking, Sooke having been rendered mute by the disease. They identified themselves as cohorts, a lifelong relationship of intense closeness practiced by citizens of the county of Fasfallia.

The remaining seat was soon filled by the slim young woman whose companion had been crushed beneath the landship. She was escorted to the cart by Raina Haj, demanding all the way to be allowed to leave and return home. Haj said something to her that Bandar didn't catch but which clearly did not please its hearer. She flung herself onto the seat cushion, crossed her arms and glowered at all of them before turning to glare at the Swept.

Bandar overheard Abbas and Wasselthorpe discussing the new arrival—he learned that her name was Flix—but their low-voiced conversation was interrupted by their Rover's securing of the cart's tailboard, accompanied by a yelp that Bandar knew meant "Important information follows."

"Yaffak I am called," the Rover said in his species's odd way of speaking, that always sounded to Bandar like a modified howl. Seeing incomprehension on the faces of the other passengers, the noönaut translated the statement for them.

Yaffak went around to the front of the cart and leaped into the driver's uncovered seat. He seized the reins and flourished a whip, and in a moment eight whining shuggras pressed powerful shoulders against the padded harness. The cart jerked forward but settled into a smooth passage across the unnaturally level ground. They picked up speed, racing straight into the sunrise, leaving a cart–wide track through the long grass.

Bandar watched the other carts with interest. He had learned from his studies that Rovers were intensely competitive, with a strong instinct for hierarchy. A pack of Rovers driving their carts across the Swept should be, he thought, a kind of race, each driver struggling to be the leader. He was disappointed, therefore, to see the carts take up a line–abreast formation.

"I don't understand," he said.

"Don't understand what?" said Erenti Abbas.

Bandar explained about the Rovers' supposed competitive spirit. That brought a dismissal of the usefulness of competition from Ule Gazz. She extolled the Lho–tso philosophy of fatalism.

Erenti Abbas engaged her from an epicurean's point of view, using his enjoyment of food as a metaphor for seizing pleasure from the passing transience of life. Then Pollus Ermatage weighed in with an observation that, from the perspective of manure, the whole cycle of fertilization, growth, harvest, processing and consumption was just a complex way of producing fresh manure.

It was the kind of discussion Bandar remembered from his early years at the Institute, when undergraduates would sit around a tavern table and regale each other with beery perspectives on the meaning of life. Now he offered the view that some things were effectively eternal, and cited the noösphere as an example of permanence, whereas individual human lives tended to be repetitions of generic themes, with minor embellishments.

Wasselthorpe protested that his life was not a trivium. No one had ever been him, doing what he was doing, in the way he was doing it, and for the reasons that moved him.

Viewed from within that life, Bandar replied, all that was indubitably correct. But from a wider scope, whatever the shape of Wasselthorpe's life might be, it differed only marginally from those of the billions upon billions of young men who had come before him.

"What is your quest: power, passion, riches, spiritual insight? Each has been looked for and found—or not found—countless times. At best you might add some slight variation to the grand scheme. But the effort is ultimately no more important than to have shifted one grain of a desert's sand."

Bandar saw forlorn sadness wash across the young man's face. There was pain somewhere in his history, pain and loss. And Bandar's glib words had somehow evoked a memory of it. Now something else stirred in the back of the noönaut's mind: a vague sense that what he had said to Phlevas Wasselthorpe was completely untrue; that this young man's quest might be more than a minor variation on a theme.

It is fatigue, Bandar told himself. *I have not slept well. And perhaps a disappointment brought on by the failure of the Rovers to live up to my romantic expectations.*

While he was immersed in his own thoughts, the discussion had moved on, but only to spread a glum mood over the other passengers. Conversation dwindled then stopped. After a lengthening silence, Pollus Ermatage suggested singing the new chuffe–raising chant that Father Olwyn had taught the believers while Bandar had been inspecting the Rover carts. More nonsense, Bandar thought, but this one's rhythm—*ta–tumpa, ta–tey,* repeated endlessly— matched the rocking of the cart as they drove across the grass.

He joined in for a while, out of politeness, but soon the chanting and the growing heat of the advancing day made him sleepy. He broke off to enjoy a capacious yawn. Wasselthorpe also ceased to chant and wanted again to ply him with questions about the Commons.

"The Commons is not for you," the noönaut said. "Find another interest."

"But I am called there," Wasselthorpe said.

"All the more reason not to go. Now I mean to make good some of the sleep I did not get last night." He folded his arms across his small chest and leaned one shoulder against the upcurving rib that supported the cart's plaited roof. He elicited a promise from Abbas to ensure that Wasselthorpe remained awake while Bandar slept.

Bandar slipped into dream. His first impulse was to exert his noönaut ability to control its direction, but some other part of him counseled letting it unroll under its own dynamic.

He was in a garden, with neatly ordered lawn and well tended but unremarkable flower beds. Wasselthorpe appeared and Bandar felt a frisson of fear before he realized that this was not an incursion of the other's consciousness but merely a rendering of the young man created by Bandar's own mind.

He was in the Hero's guise and, as Bandar regarded him, now memory filtered up from somewhere. He vaguely recalled the variant that wore mail, winged helmet and wolf pelt. It was a Hero who slew a foul monster that had preyed upon ordinary men, tearing its arm off so that it ran away and died. But then a worse threat loomed, though he couldn't remember exactly what it was; the information dated from his undergraduate years, before he had fully developed his memory. Besides, noönauts worked to remember categories, not individual incidents—the totality of the Commons was far more than any mind could encompass.

Bandar observed Wasselthorpe–as–Hero cross the garden, sword held low and positioned for a coming thrust. Then the man shimmered and became just a sad–faced boy at play. He held a wooden sword and wore a toy helmet, but the way he thrust at empty air with the rough weapon showed a man's determination. And the young face showed the same serious cast of expression that governed the mature man.

Bandar sensed an unbearable poignancy in the scene and turned away. But now his gaze fell upon the Rover Yaffak. The creature stood disconsolate, ears drooping and black lips drawn downward. The noönaut took control of the dream and addressed the Rover. "What is wrong? Why do you grieve?"

Yaffak opened his mouth to answer but the only sound that emerged was an odd creaking.

Bandar awoke to the creaking of the carts. They had slowed and the Rovers were driving them in a circle to create another broad area of trampled grass. Erenti Abbas rubbed his substantial stomach, expressing optimism that lunch was imminent. Bandar informed him that it was too soon for the passengers to be fed. They would be stopping to rest the shuggras, which were not built for the long haul and required frequent pauses.

When the grass was flattened the Rovers positioned the carts in a small circle at the center of the larger one, with the teams of shuggras facing outward. They lowered the tailboards that the passengers might dismount. Yaffak indicated the tall grass and said, "Empty your bodies."

Bandar translated the words into a more seemly phrase then asked, "How long will we stay?"

"Small time," Yaffak answered. "Rest shuggras. Also Rovers rest, eat little before big heat comes."

Bandar relayed the sense of this to his fellow passengers, then watched with interest as Yaffak went to join the other Rovers in the center of the circled carts where one of them had piled up jerked meat and some kind of hard biscuits. He would have liked to see a display of Rover dominance–and–submission behavior, with the junior members of the pack shouldering each other aside to eat a larger share. Instead, the Rovers took their rations without ceremony and squatted down to chew. None looked at the others or demonstrated any of the displays Bandar's studies had told him should be natural to them.

After a while, Bandar shook his head and turned away. Wasselthorpe had wandered over and now asked if something disturbed him. Bandar revealed his puzzlement at the Rovers's uncharacteristic behavior. Wasselthorpe proposed that the Rovers might have changed their ways, but Bandar dismissed the idea as not possible. Rover consciousness was a thin layer over a deep–set mass of instinct.

"They do not change," he said.

"Disease, perhaps?" the other suggested. "Perhaps this is how the lassitude affects them."

No," Bandar said. He explained the Rovers' reaction to illness, which was for the sick one to go away and either return cured or die alone. It was an instinct that protected the pack.

They walked back to where Abbas sat in the shade of one of the carts. "You know a great deal about Rovers," Wasselthorpe said.

"Not much more than what is common knowledge."

The young man showed a puzzled countenance. "Not

common to me," he said.

Bandar wondered aloud about what other commonplaces were unknown to Wasselthorpe. Abbas pointed out that the question was a tautology; the young man could not be expected to know what else he didn't know.

Bandar conceded the point. Provincial gentleman were not required to know much beyond the folderols of fashion and the intricacies of social rank that separated one from one's neighbors. "Yet he wears the scarf of an Institute graduate."

He saw a look pass between Abbas and Wasselthorpe. "Though only third–tier," said the fat man.

Bandar shrugged. Third–tier matriculates from country aristocracy could not be expected to shine. Still, his ignorance was sometimes startling. "What was your field of study again?" he asked.

"Criminology."

"A curious pursuit for an aristocrat," Bandar said.

Abbas chimed in with a fresh note: Wasselthorpe could quote lengthy passages from Bureau of Scrutiny manuals.

Bandar thought this peculiar distinction. "I am sure the ability would be useful to a Bureau employee, but even the most dedicated scroot needs to encompass a wider field of knowledge than official manuals and standing orders."

Bandar saw Abbas give his student an odd look. "Perhaps the most dedicated scroot might not be aware of the need."

"A troubling thought," said Bandar, "for it would mean the man was narrow and strange, like those too tightly wound types who know everything about some limited pursuit but cannot manage a conversation about the weather."

Wasselthorpe seemed stung. "What is wrong with feeling that one has a calling?" he said.

The term gave Bandar a slight shiver. A call from the Commons was a summons that offered no return. "I remember a tale about a man who pursued a bright star. His eyes on its brilliance, he did not notice that his feet were leading him over a cliff."

Wasselthorpe said that he was not familiar with that story. Bandar was not surprised, since it was unlikely to be found in a scroot manual.

They had walked back to their cart. "I believe I must sleep," Wasselthorpe said. Indeed, he seemed to Bandar to be almost weaving on his feet. The noönaut felt a upwelling of concern: an sudden, unaccountable need for sleep could indicate that the unconscious was exerting its influence.

"I will be sure to remain awake until you are done," he told the young man. Indeed, he meant to keep an eye on Wasselthorpe and rouse him back to consciousness if he showed signs of distressed dreaming.

The young man thanked him and laid himself down in the shade of the cart. After a moment he rolled onto his stomach and regarded the Rovers who, their meal finished, were now lying asleep. He drew Bandar's attention to Yaffak, whose legs were twitching as if he dreamed of running, and wondered if there was any danger of his intruding into the Rover's dream, as he had into Bandar's.

Bandar complimented him on his ambition, but assured him of the impenetrable Wall between Commonses of different species—though even as he said the words he thought about the Bololo and the Hydromants of Gamza. There had been attempts to educate Rovers enough to have them explore their own Commons, but though some of the creatures had managed to get to the entry level of the Rover noösphere and even to view the archetypes in the prime arrondisement, they were too easily captured by the characteristic entities, and none made more than a few visits to the Rover Commons before being absorbed and lost.

"Their psyches are too much closed around by instinct," Bandar said, "nor are their upper and lower brains well separated. Not far beneath Rover consciousness lies the Old Sea of pre–sapience, where the great blind Worm swims eternally in pursuit of its own tail."

Abbas opined that the young man might be a visionary. His offhand tone annoyed Bandar who snapped back that Wasselthorpe might also be a full–tilt loon, the terms being all too often interchangeable.

While they argued, Wasselthorpe slipped into slumber, his cheek pressed against the trampled grass. Bandar sat with his back against the cartwheel and engaged in a desultory conversation with Erenti Abbas. But he found the fat man's cynicism difficult to take in sustained doses, and after a while their conversation lapsed and Abbas reposed himself to sleep, as had many of the passengers. A group of others, including the two couples from Bandar's cart, had gathered to chant *ta–tumpa, ta–tey*, Brond Halorn's voice rising above the common chorus. The handful of stewards who were accompanying the passengers on this leg of the journey sat in a ring, engaged in some game of chance that brought occasional shouts and hoots of celebration or schadenfreude.

Time went by. Suddenly, Bandar saw the sleeping Yaffak give a mighty kick of one leg. The Rover's eyes flew open, so wide that Bandar could see a rim of white around each great brown iris. Yaffak sprang into a crouch, growling something Bandar could not make out. The sound awoke the other Rovers, who gazed at their enraged fellow without visible emotion.

The behavior went against everything Bandar knew about the Rovers. Yaffak's display should have earned him either growls and bristling manes or lowered heads and turned away eyes. The one reaction it shouldn't have brought was no reaction. But the rest still looked back at the snarling Rover with cold indifference, even as Yaffak stood erect, his ruff standing straight up and his teeth bared. He barked something that Bandar thought was, "Wrong!" before he suddenly turned and raced toward his team of shuggras. He leapt onto the back of one, yanked a strap that freed the eight from the wagon and dug his heels into his mount and raced the whole team out into the long grass.

The other Rovers had risen and for a moment Bandar thought they might go in pursuit. Then, as one, they visibly lost interest in the incident. They yelped at the stewards, who left their game and began to rouse the passengers to reboard the carts.

"What of these?" the chief steward called to the Rovers in their own language, indicating Bandar's cart.

"No seats," said the largest of the Rovers, the one who ought to have been pack leader, by Bandar's lights, but who showed none of the traits of a dominant male. Still, when the chief steward sought to argue with him about stranding eight passengers, the Rover showed his teeth. The crewman backed away, his hands offering placatory gestures, and came to Bandar's cart.

"I am sorry," he said. "There is nothing to be done."

Abbas had risen. "We cannot stay here," he said. "Right now, a ravenous fand might be slavering over the prospect of tender human flesh. Or a woollyclaw might amble by, bundle us all into a ball of crushed limbs and torsos, then roll us off to gratify its whelps."

"The air hangs heavy with the scent of angry Rover," said the chief steward. "That will deter predators. But here is an energy pistol." He produced the weapon from a pouch at his waist. "I advise you to remain in the cart until the *Orgulon*'s gig arrives."

"How long will that be?" Bandar asked.

"It will rendezvous with the Rover carts at a place east of here, bringing a luncheon. I will summon it on my communicator, and instruct it to come and pick you up as soon as supplies have been unloaded. You will not be here long."

Abbas said, "Can you leave a communicator with us?"

"I have but the one," the man said. Waving away further protestations and trailing assurances that all would soon be well, he went to where the impatient Rover leader waited, mounted the cart and was gone.

The stranded passengers reacted as their individual natures dictated: Ule Gazz was fatalistic, Pollus Ermatage cheerful, Abbas affecting a breezy unconcern beneath which Bandar thought to see a cool mind calculating risks and options. Flix's black mood darkened to become stygian. The lassitude sufferers were as inert as ever. It was only after cataloging these impressions that Bandar thought to take notice of the still sleeping Phlevas Wasselthorpe.

"With all the fuss, he should have awakened," he said to Abbas.

The fat man knelt and shook the sleeper, turned him over on his back and lightly slapped one cheek. He thumbed up one eyelid and saw nothing but white, the eyeball rolled up into the head. Abbas slapped him again, harder. There was no response.

"He has lapsed beyond sleep," he said. "I think he may be comatose."

"Try to rouse him," Bandar said. "I will see what I can do."

He closed his eyes and summoned the portal, went through at record speed and was soon descending the staircase to the first level. The road was empty, except for scintillating flashes made by passing dreamers. Bandar knew he would not find Wasselthorpe among them.

He summoned up a noönaut mentalism that he had not used in all the years since he had been an undergraduate learning his portfolio of techniques. But before he exercised the procedure, he paused and took thought for a moment. *In the Commons, it is always best to be quite clear as to what one is about,* he reminded himself. *If this brings me to Wasselthorpe, then it means that he and I are linked at some level below the obvious. And I must deal with that reality, whatever it portends.*

He focused his mind, chanted five rising tones then two descenders, holding the last note. A ripple appeared in the air before him and he stepped through into a terrifying scene: the young man, clad again in his ancient Hero's garb, sword in hand, stood beside the great white Wall that marked the limit of the human commons. At his feet was a scar in the virtual earth, a scar that must have been a large gash shortly before, because even as Bandar took note of it the wound was healing.

But none of those sights were what frightened Bandar. Grouped around Wasselthorpe, close enough to touch, were several pure archetypes—the Hero, the Wise Man, the Father, Mother and Child, the Destroyer, the Fool, and more—a jostling crowd of characteristic entities, any one of which, at this range, should have drawn the young man's consciousness into permanent, psychotic thralldom.

Yet Wasselthorpe stood there, talking with them, uninsulated by thran, untouched by raw psychic power. Bandar immediately chanted the three, three and seven, seized Wasselthorpe by the arm, and pulled him through the gate. They arrived back in the first level of the Commons, where Bandar opened an emergency gate and brought them directly back to the waking world.

Bandar felt a wave of dizziness come over him, but he fought it down and opened his eyes. Abbas was still kneeling over his student, methodically slapping his cheeks and calling upon him to come forth from whatever corner of his psyche he had tumbled into.

Bandar reached down and restrained the fat man's hand. "It's all right," he said, "I have brought him back."

Wasselthorpe was sitting up, putting a hand to his reddened cheek.

When Abbas told him that he had been deep in coma, the young man said, "I was in the Commons of the Rovers. I entered Yaffak's dream."

"That cannot be so," Bandar said. "They would have attacked you." But even as he said it, he felt his innards chill and turn over.

"I believe they perceived me as the Good Man, just as we sometimes encounter a friendly beast when we dream."

"Nonsense!" Bandar said, though he knew it was not. "How could you get through the Wall? It cannot be breached."

"I went by way of the Old Sea."

Bandar vehemently denied Wasselthorpe's assertion. "Only death awaits the consciousness that enters the utoposphere. It hangs there, incapable of motion, until the Worm comes to devour it."

But Wasselthorpe insisted. He said terrible things: that the archetypes had approached and had helped him, that they had given him power to cut through the floor of the Commons, swim through the gray nothingness then cut his way up into the Rover Commons. He had found Yaffak suffering, bound by some leash that went up into the sky. He had cut the tether with his Hero's sword and the Rover had raced off, free and joyous. Then he had swum back through the sea, had even seen the Worm coming, but had made it back through the opening before it could take him.

"You are lying!" Bandar muttered through clenched teeth, even as a part of him said, *He speaks the truth.*

Wasselthorpe casually mentioned that, from the Rover's side, the Wall appeared to be a hedge of black thorn bushes. Bandar wanted to clap his hands over his ears. That was a prime secret of the Institute, which no one outside its cloisters could know.

Wasselthorpe burbled on: the Wise Man had shown the way; he had used the Hero's sword to cut a gash in the earth. Bandar knew it must be true; he had seen the healing wound.

The noönaut felt as if his head might burst. The Commons was governed by rules. Thousands of noönauts had died, and tens of thousands had suffered, to delineate those rules. Then along came Wasselthorpe to pull the foundation stones from beneath a hundred millennia of established procedure. And yet, some part of Bandar said, *This is how it must be.*

The events of the morning had left him no choice but to face the grim facts: Guth Bandar was bound to Phlevas Wasselthorpe, and together their fates were entwined with the history of the Dree. What any of this meant, he did not yet know, but when he had encountered the young man at the Wall, he had seen in his face the unmistakable expression of a Hero. And if the two of them were linked, Bandar must play the Helper. Yet Helpers frequently failed to survive the Hero's catharsis.

"I have more to tell," Wasselthorpe said.

"Well, you would, wouldn't you?" Bandar snapped. "Spare me."

"I believe we must hear him," Abbas said. "It might illuminate the events that happened while he was wandering in dreams."

"What happened?" Wasselthorpe said.

Abbas drew his attention to the absence of the Rover carts and their passengers and stewards. He briefly recounted Yaffak's flight and the abandonment of their party. "The steward left us a weapon to defend ourselves against wild beasts.

"Or against Yaffak," said Bandar, "who seems to have gone insane."

"Yaffak will not do us harm," Wasselthorpe said, rising to his feet. "I freed him from a hateful bondage."

He told again the tale of how he had sawed through the leash that tied the dreaming Rover and wanted Bandar to tell him its meaning. But Bandar was beyond answering questions. He wished he had never heard of Phlevas Wasselthorpe and his catalog of impossibilities, so innocently recounted.

Bandar turned his back and looked away. But his outward composure belied his inner turmoil. Somewhere inside him a voice was speaking softly, telling him to be of help. He sought to close his mind against it.

Abbas took charge. "We must pull the cart into the center of the clearing and get aboard. Right now we are an easy meal for any passing fand." He summoned the chanters and Flix, now glowering ever more deeply, and they did as he directed.

Once aboard, the fat man flourished the energy pistol and asked if anyone was competent in its use. Bandar was surprised when Wasselthorpe took the weapon, expertly stripped and reassembled it, then placed it under the seat for safety's sake. The noönaut would not have thought that a provincial lordling, for all his interest in criminology, could have handled a weapon with such aplomb.

In the close confines of the stationary cart, the passengers fell to squabbling. Ule Gazz wished all to chant; she felt her chuffe swelling. Wasselthorpe rejected the concept of chuffe and sought to explore his alleged meeting with Yaffak in the Rover Commons, but Bandar refused to be drawn. Nor would he chant. His rebuff to Gazz caused her to disparage the relevance of the noösphere compared to the Lho–tso enlightenment. That caused Bandar to snap at her. Tempers were heating when Wasselthorpe suddenly made a startling announcement.

"Chuffe is entirely an illusion," he said. "Father Olwyn is in reality the notorious confidence trickster Horslan Gebbling, who will be taken into custody the moment my partner and I encounter him."

Ule Gazz greeted this assertion with disdain, at which Wasselthorpe declared that he and Abbas were not what they appeared to be. Instead, they were undercover agents of the Bureau of Scrutiny, sent on the cruise to apprehend Gebbling.

The others demanded proof. Wasselthorpe and Abbas dug within their clothing and produced official scroot plaques. Bandar squinted at each and learned that Wasselthorpe's true name was Baro Harkless, while Abbas was named Luff Imbry. Both held the rank of agent–ordinary.

Hence the fascination with criminal investigation, thought Bandar. Several more thoughts flitted rapidly through his mind, but the one he seized in passing was: "Your plaques allow you to call for assistance."

"We are ordered to remain incommunicado until we secure an arrest," said Harkless/Wasselthorpe.

His answer set off a new round of altercation that ended only when Flix spoke up from her corner seat to alert them to the imminent arrival of the *Orgulon*'s gig, flying in from the east.

The sight of their rescue should have brought Bandar relief. Instead he dismounted from the cart with a glum sense of foreboding. His noönaut's sensibilities were aroused and he felt as if he were not in the waking world but in a high–classification Event. Worse, it was that part of an Event's cycle when the action begins to flow rapidly toward the climax.

The gig dropped down, piloted by the landship's first officer, whose name Bandar had not acquired. Beside him was Raina Haj. The vehicle settled at the edge of the clearing and the passengers rushed from the cart to greet it, the lassitude sufferers towed on their come–alongs. Flix came last, her hands clasped behind her back.

Haj dismounted and lowered the aircraft's rear gate while the first officer remained at the controls. Bandar saw Harkless (he supposed he might as well adjust to the fellow's name) go to confer with the security officer, who seemed to be unimpressed with whatever the agent–ordinary told her.

Haj waved the stranded party to board the gig. Something was moving out in the grass, she said. The passengers lined up, with Flix at the tail of the queue.

"Are we going back to the *Orgulon*? she asked.

Haj said they were not. They would be taken to a temporary camp just beyond the immense stone plateau known as the Monument, where tents and tables were laid on for a luncheon. Father Olwyn was expected to appear and offer something called "the inculcation." The *Orgulon* had been delivering equipment to the brillion mines at nearby Victor and would rendezvous with the passengers by nightfall.

Flix now advanced another agenda. She demanded to bypass the ceremony and be flown to Victor so she could arrange passage home.

"That is not a matter for you to decide," Haj told her.

Again Flix differed, but instead of offering a fresh argument, she produced the energy pistol Harkless had left in the cart. She pointed it in an unsteady two–handed grip at Raina Haj.

Now Flix looked to the first officer, who had remained in the gig's operator's seat. She addressed him by his given name and said, "Get her weapon."

The man did as he was ordered, the smirk on his face telling Bandar that there was more of a relationship between him and the young woman than they had hitherto revealed. The officer came at Haj from the rear and relieved her of her sidearm. Then he circled around the passengers to stand beside Flix, his pistol leveled at all and sundry.

"Move away from the aircraft," he told them.

Raina Haj spoke up, addressing Flix. "This is not necessary," she said.

The first officer told her to shut up, but Haj spoke on, telling Flix "I know you didn't kill him."

"I told you it was an accident," Flix said.

"No, not an accident," Haj said.

"Shut up," the first officer repeated, aiming his weapon at

Haj. Bandar saw his thumb extend toward the discharge stud, but Flix laid a hand on his arm and pushed it down.

"What are you trying to say?" she asked Haj.

"Lies," the man with the weapon said.

But Flix wanted to hear what the security officer had to say. She moved off a couple of steps and now her energy weapon swung halfway from Haj to the other officer.

The man did not delay a moment. A bright flash dazzled Bandar's eyes and when his vision cleared Flix was face down on the grass, a smoking hole burned through her torso.

Someone screamed and Bandar stared with both fascination and fright at the young woman's corpse. It took him a long moment to recover his equilibrium. But the murderer had remained calm; the energy pistol did not waver in his hand as he stepped back to give himself room should they try to rush him. Bandar was bemused to think that he had seen just such a look on the faces of villains many times in the Commons, though he had always done so from within the protection of a thran.

"So you know," the officer said, addressing Haj.

"Yes."

The pistol swung toward her. "Well, then."

Now Harkless spoke up. "How are you going to explain it?"

Bandar could have predicted it. The Hero would always seek to engage the villain in talk, delaying the killing stroke while he worked out some tactic to save the day. But the man with the weapon barely glanced at Harkless, and instead spoke to Haj: he would blame the killings on the unstable Flix's having gone berserk when the gig landed, even wounding him before he was able to seize Haj's pistol and dispatch her.

Bandar watched Harkless as the killer spoke. Some silent signal passed between the young agent and his plump partner. The undercover scroots were going to try something. Bandar felt a rising urge to help. He wanted to fight it, but found that his will to do so was fading. He gauged the distance between him and the man with the gun, wondering how fast his old legs would allow him to close the distance.

Now the young agent was saying something about a forgotten witness. The officer was still keeping his eye on Haj, the known danger. Bandar realized that the killer must see Harkless as only a feckless young lordling, afflicted by the lassitude. *This might work*, he thought, then realized with an inner start that the opinion had come not from his usual inner critic, but from a new source: the Helper was rising in him.

Bandar was struck by a sense of irreality, as if he were observing an Event or Situation in the noösphere. He saw again the Hero in the young agent's stark expression and now there came to him the particular details of the myth that featured a Hero in a wolf pelt and winged helmet: it told of a dawn–time Hero who, after defeating a man–devouring monster, dove deep into a frigid lake to confront the troll's even more powerful mother. And in that lake, the Hero died.

He is not the Hero Triumphant, Bandar thought. *He is the Hero Sacrificial. His dynamic ends with his dying to save those he protects.*

Harkless was telling the man that Yaffak had not gone far, that the Rover was what they had seen moving in the grass as they brought the gig down, and was hearing and seeing all.

Not bad, Bandar thought. *Simple, believable. Enough to make the man stop and think.*

But when Harkless pointed to draw the officer's attention, the man did not fall for the ruse. Bandar sighed. *In real life, I suppose these things don't work as well*, he thought. He saw Harkless's muscles tense for whatever he was going to try and readied himself to join in the rush.

Harkless was at least partially in thrall to the Hero Sacrificial, but Bandar did not see in his aspect the look of one who expects to die. His face wore the assurance of one who intends to defeat an enemy then march on to fresh challenges.

The murderer showed the same confidence. But his conviction was fortified by his possession of an energy pistol and a demonstrated capacity to use it.

As his thumb slid toward the firing stud, the grass behind him opened and the missing Rover burst into the clearing, running at a four–legged gallop low to the ground. He rose to his hind legs and leapt to smash bodily into the officer's back, sending him sprawling. Then Yaffak rolled clear and came smoothly to his hind feet, ready to strike again.

Harkless and Imbry sprang forward. So did Haj. But the villain had the almost admirable concentration Bandar had seen before in persons with psyches dominated by darker elements. He was already levering himself to his knees and aiming the energy pistol. It discharged just as Harkless struck him with a flying tackle, and its concentrated beam of force sliced the air like a long thin blade.

Then it was over. The man was face down on the ground, his wrists pinioned by a restraint, and Haj had secured both pistols. Yaffak took a brief look at the defeated prisoner then, Rover–like, walked unconcernedly away to summon his team of shuggras from where they crouched in the long grass. He quickly rehitched their harness to the cart.

They pulled the killer to his feet. He gave them a look that expressed no apology. They prepared to board the gig but the fat agent had discovered that the long discharge of the energy pistol had disabled its controls. They would have to press on by Rover cart.

Haj enlisted Bandar to translate as she asked the Rover to take them east to where the day camp was set up.

"No," said Yaffak.

Now Imbry had a question. He pointed to the bound man and wanted to know why Yaffak had attacked him.

"For the Good Man," Yaffak said, his eyes going to Harkless.

Harkless said, "Why for me?"

Yaffak struggled to express his thoughts. "In the other place, the bad thing, the bad rope. Good Man come, cut rope, make me free."

Bandar asked, "How did you know he was the Good Man?"

Yaffak sniffed loudly and described Harkless's odor in terms that only a Rover truly understood. Bandar translated for the others.

The young agent wanted to know what Yaffak thought had restrained him in the dream. The Rover did not want to talk about it. The loose skin on his shoulders shook and his ruff rose in agitation.

"He lacks the words," Bandar said. "To him it was just a bad dream."

Harkless asked if the Rover would take him where the other Rovers had carried the other passengers.

Yaffak looked down and to the side. Bandar translated the posture as one of the Rovers' ways of saying no. Then Yaffak said to Harkless, "Come west, hunt skippit. Big food. Good fun."

"I must go to the others," Harkless said.

Bandar was amazed to see the Rover's face take on a look of

unwilling resolution. "For you, Yaffak goes east. Take people not sick. Leave wrong, leave dead." He looked at the bound prisoner. "Leave killer, let eaters find."

Bandar translated.

Ule Gazz began to protest but Harkless cut her off. Bandar saw the Hero's determination glowing in the young man's eyes as he told Yaffak that the sick must go with them.

"Not sick," Yaffak said. "Sick is belly pain, food comes up. These not sick. Smell *wrong*."

Harkless asked the others if Rovers got the lassitude. No one knew. He spoke again to Yaffak. "Did your pack smell like these?"

Yaffak struggled to express himself. "Rovers smell like Rovers, not *do* like Rovers. Yaffak see them wrong but not feel them wrong. Then Yaffak in bad place, Good Man come, free Yaffak. Then see and feel Rovers wrong. Yaffak angry–scared, run to grass."

Bandar translated as best he could, then added his view that Yaffak had had a traumatic experience and did not want to meet the "wrong" Rovers again.

Harkless suggested a compromise: if the Rover would take them to within sight of the mining town of Victor, he would not ask him to go near his packmates.

Yaffak said, "For Good Man, will do."

And he must take the sick, the young agent insisted.

"Not sick, wrong," Yaffak insisted, but then lowered his head.

"He agrees to take them, too," Bandar said.

Flix's body went into the gig, secure from predators under a locked canopy. The rest reboarded the cart, laying the first officer face down in the aisle between the seats. Bandar sat in his former seat near the front so that he could translate if required. The two agents sat nearby and soon fell into a discussion with Raina Haj regarding their pursuit of the confidence trickster posing as Father Olwyn. The conversation led nowhere, since none could envision how the fraudster stood to gain from mounting an expensive cruise for lassitude sufferers who were, for the most part, not wealthy. They thought it might have something to do with black brillion.

Bandar also learned that Haj was herself an undercover agent of the Bureau of Scrutiny who had been in pursuit of the man lying on the floor. The *Orgulon*'s first officer—his name was Kosmir—had been involved in some complex scheme to murder Flix's companion, a once–celebrated artist whose reputation had faded, in order to drive up the value of the man's works. Flix, it seemed, had been his unwitting dupe.

None of this meant much to Bandar. He focused not on the back–and–forth between the officers, nor on Ule Gazz's futile attempts to defend Olwyn, but on Baro Harkless. Earlier, he had called him narrow and strange, and had formed the impression that the young man had grown up peculiar. He seemed to be missing not only common knowledge, but certain elements of a normal personality. His being a Bureau agent explained nothing.

He is too simple, the noönaut thought. *His psyche is not the subtle blend of tints and shades that emerge from the interaction of a varied mix of elements. It is as if he has been painted only in primary colors.*

Bandar had studied naturals in his undergraduate years at the Institute. This Harkless was not quite like those loons, even though it was obvious to a noönaut's eye that the Hero archetype was growing increasingly dominant within him. It was there to be seen in the gleam of the eye and the set of the jaw.

No, not a natural. But not quite a fully rendered human, either. He was hypothesizing rare neuronic disorders caused by accidents in the womb, when the picture suddenly fell into focus. He played back in his memory the young man's interaction with the other agents and the passengers, and particularly how he had behaved with Bandar himself.

Now he remembered his first impression of Harkless, when he and Imbry had come aboard the balloon–tram: he had reminded Bandar of the idiomatic entities that populated the Locations of the Commons. If that were so it meant that, where normal human beings had complex structures, Baro Harkless had empty spaces, where humans had personalities, he had only a selection of interconnected characteristics. It was debatable whether the young man was a person at all, or just a facsimile of one.

Bandar had never felt empathy for idiomats he had encountered in the Commons. But for an idiomat loose in the waking world, Bandar had to feel sympathy. What a strange growing up it must have been, like being able to see only black and white while navigating a world whose directional signs were all color coded.

After a while, the cart left the Swept and drove up a sloping ramp of stone onto the Monument. This was a vast assemblage of close fitted blocks of gray rock that formed the image of a man's helmeted head and neck, so large that it was easily visible from near orbit. It was said to be the likeness of the commander whose strategy had defeated the Dree. The mining town of Victor, near the Monument's southeast extremity, was also believed to have been named for him.

The immense platform of stone was ten times a man's height. Travelers who ascended to its upper surface found a great plain of featureless rock, with here and there a growth of hardy grass or thorny brush sprouting from cracks and fissures opened by the alternation over eons of winter cold and summer heat.

They were crossing at the Monument's narrowest stretch, the neck, and Yaffak was whipping his shuggras along. Soon they would reach the down–ramp that sloped back onto the prairie, and shortly thereafter they should come to the day camp where the *Orgulon* would meet them. The mystery of the murder being concluded, Bandar intended to make strong representations to be allowed to leave immediately.

Harkless touched his shoulder and he turned. "I offended you and I am sorry," the young agent said. "I am surprised that I have attracted the Hero, since I have surely spent my life playing the Fool."

Bandar felt a upsurge of feeling for the unhappy youth. "You did nothing that was ill–meant," he said. "Perhaps I have been too proud of my learning."

Harkless then made an unexpected proposal. "When this business is done, might you consider taking me as a student noönaut? The Commons does draw me."

"You would leave the Bureau of Scrutiny?"

Harkless referred to a conversation he had had with his partner, Imbry. "He believes that, in life, some are called, and some are driven. Until now, it appears that I have been one of the driven. Now I have found something that calls me."

Again, Bandar felt an urge to help the young man and his first instinct was to fight it. But when he looked into the unhappy face he saw no glint of the Hero, just a lost and lonely child. And then a thought occurred: a noönaut with the power to move between Commonses would be an unparalleled innovation. Whole new schools might open. Bandar imagined returning to the Institute like a thunderclap.

His attention was drawn to a faint sound from the rear of the cart. Ule Gazz's hands were palpating her throat. Open mouthed, she struggled to chant the *ta–tumpa, ta–tey*, but could produce only a dry croaking. Across the aisle from her, Pollus Ermatage had also fallen silent. She reached to touch Gazz's jaw then felt her own throat. When she spoke, her voice was weak: "Ule Gazz has the lassitude. As do I."

Bandar raised his fingers to his own neck and jaw. Nothing seemed amiss, but his determination to leave grew stronger.

They reached the far side of the Monument's neck and saw the town of Victor out on the Swept. It was a small, unpretentious mining town, with a scattering of buildings linked by a few paved roads beneath the elevated structures that marked where the shafts of two almost played out brillion mines descended into the earth. Beyond the town, at a flattened berm of tailings that served as a landship wharf, stood the *Orgulon*. Just south of the wharf Rovertown began, a sprawl of unpretentious habitations where the Rovers lived in close proximity to their shuggras.

A wave of relief went through Bandar, and even the newly stricken lassitude sufferers seemed to show hope. But from his seat at the front of the cart, Yaffak snuffled the air and pointed with his nose. "Dead eaters," he said.

Bandar told the others that the Rover had spotted a flock of stingwhiffles between them and Victor. A congregation of the leathery winged carrion eaters meant something lay dead on the prairie.

They found a ramp leading down onto the Swept and descended. The stingwhiffles were contending over something in the grass not far off the cart trail that went toward Victor.

Haj's voice took on a worried note. "The tents and tables were set up there. Olwyn was about to go into his act when I left to find you people."

They came to a place where the grass was flattened. Upturned folding tables and shreds of fabric lay scattered about, the buffet table and its heaps of truffle cuisine tipped over. Yaffak pulled up and the three agents dismounted.

Bandar followed them but paused to ask Yaffak, "Do you smell fand or woollyclaw?"

The Rover's nose winnowed the air and he turned to scan in every direction. The muscles of his neck twitched and his ruff stood erect, but he said, "No.".

Haj set her pistol for wide dispersal and swept a beam of yellow energy through the circling stingwhiffles. The gaggle that had been squabbling over whatever was on the ground, burst into the air in a squawking cloud of leather.

Bandar hung back and said, "What is there?"

"It is that white–haired woman from the landship," Harkless said.

He kneeled to examine the remains. Bandar came up behind him. Brand Halorn's flesh was torn by long, deep wounds and her head was half severed from her neck. "That is not the work of sting–whiffles," he said.

Haj thought it might have been a woollyclaw, but if so the people of nearby Victor would be out in force.

"And what of this?" said Imbry. He had found nearby what looked to be a discarded garment of cloth and leather. He held it up then almost retched as he realized what it was: a human skin, split open along the spine and with ribbons of flesh where the hands and feet should have been.

Bandar recognized its owner. "The birthmark," he said. "It is her husband."

"This is not a woollyclaw's doing," said Haj. She searched the grass. "His clothes are here, torn to pieces, and his skin. But where is the body? Where is the blood?"

Harkless said, "We should go into town. This place is not safe." But Imbry counseled against it. The town was silent when its inhabitants should have been astir.

Haj exerted her seniority. She had one of the landships' short–range communicators and now sought to contact the *Orgulon*. But the signal could not get through. She tried her Bureau of Scrutiny plaque, a more sophisticated instrument, but again it was as if the frequency was blocked.

She then gave her second pistol to Harkless and declared that she would walk to the *Orgulon*, circling around the town. The captain was a capable man and would be able to tell her the situation.

Someone was shouting, back where Yaffak had remained with his cart. Bandar and the agents hurried there to find that the noise came from the prisoner Kosmir. The Rover was hauling him from the vehicle. The two couples who had succumbed to the lassitude were lying in a row in the grass. Ule Gazz was struggling to get her feet under her, but the disease was rapidly stealing her mobility; the other three lay motionless, and Bandar saw that Ebersol and Sooke, who had caught the disease first, had reached the stage of stark rigidity and polished skin, as if they had been waxed. Their eyes were as stone.

Yaffak set Kosmir upright then turned back to the cart to bring out the two come–alongs. He closed and locked the tailboard.

Raina Haj confronted the Rover and demanded to know his intent. Yaffak dropped his eyes and said, "No more. Wrong smell, all over. Town, these." He gestured at the lassitude victims. "Yaffak goes."

Bandar translated. Haj told the Rover they would skirt the town and go to the landship.

Yaffak said, "Yaffak goes."

Haj looked grim and drew her energy pistol.

Yaffak did not flinch. "Shooting bad. Some things more bad. Yaffak goes."

Haj reholstered the weapon. The Rover made to climb into the driver's seat, but instead he turned toward Harkless. "Good Man come with Yaffak. Safe."

Bandar translated and saw in the agent's eyes a response to the Rover's obvious affection. But then the noönaut saw the Hero harden Harkless's young face.

"I cannot," Harkless said. "Something else calls me."

Yaffak mounted the cart, turned the team back toward the Monument, and with one regretful rearward glance, he was gone.

The three agents now fell into a procedural argument about who had authority to decide what to do next. Harkless quoted from manuals while Haj looked uncomfortable and made remarks about risking her career. Bandar paid no attention. He studied the four lassitude victims. All the chanting and chuffe raising had done nothing to address the conditions of those who boarded the *Orgulon* already in the clutch of the disease; if anything, it seemed to have hurried them to the crisis; worse, those who had not had the disease to begin with had developed galloping cases.

He wondered if that result, rather than a cure, had been the intent of the cruise. Was Father Olwyn, or Horslan Gebbling, actively promoting the spread of the disease, possibly out of some apocalyptic motive? Bandar had seen many versions of the Mad Messiah preserved in the Locations of the Commons. Could Olwyn be psychically captive to such a dangerous archetype? Might a cult have sprung up around his charismatic presence, a millennial sect out to bring on the end of the world through pestilence?

If so, the chanting would not have had any effect. But perhaps bringing many sufferers together in close quarters amplified the disease's onslaught, as if they transferred spores back and forth to each other and. . . And then it struck him: the other common factor had been the truffles of the Swept; they had been the main ingredient in almost every dish that had come out of the landship's galley, even the gruel fed to the ill.

Bandar had not cared for the taste and had eaten little of it. He was, as much as he could tell, unvisited by the lassitude. He was pursuing this line of inquiry when he heard Harkless speak his name.

"Bandar and I will tend to the sick," the agent had said. The noönaut regarded the earnest young face and saw more than mere traces of the Hero in his expression of stern resolve. And the cavalier way he had included Bandar in his plan was exactly the manner in which a Hero assumed decisions for his Helper.

Still, Bandar would be of no use in an expedition to the town or the landship. If a death cult had sprung up—*Might the Rovers have succumbed?* he thought; he knew little of whatever piety they might practice—Bandar would rather stay on the Monument.

That was where they carried the paralyzed, Harkless and Haj slinging the still bendable Gazz and Ermatage over their shoulders while Imbry and Bandar towed Ebersol and Sooke on their come-alongs. Kosmir walked ahead of the party, with Harkless's energy pistol trained on him.

Back atop the Monument, they laid the four paralytics on the sun-warmed stone. The three agents used their plaques to inspect the deserted streets of Victor and Rovertown. They saw evidence of violence and the discharge of energy weapons, conferring about these matters in low voices. But Bandar could hear enough; he would stay out of the town.

Haj left to make her way to the landship. Harkless ordered the prisoner to sit apart from the sick. "If you try to stand I will shoot you in the leg," he said, then turned to Bandar. "Shout if he moves."

Bandar said he would, but once again the order was clearly from the Hero to the Helper.

Harkless and Imbry went to look at the four lassitude victims. Imbry thought the crisis would soon be upon them. Harkless knelt beside Ule Gazz then expressed surprise that apparently she continued to try to chant Olwyn's last mantra. He took off his Institute scarf and folded it to make a pad under Pollus Ermatage's head.

The two agents left the sick and returned to where Bandar watched Kosmir.

"If whatever attacked that loud woman comes for us," the prisoner said, "I would be more use without this restraint."

Harkless would not hear of it. "You will take your chances as you are," he said, reminding the prisoner that he had seen him kill Flix after murdering her companion for financial gain.

Kosmir quoted an unflattering saying about the likelihood of securing mercy from a scroot.

Harkless sighted along his pistol and said, "In an emergency, you would be even more hampered by the loss of some toes."

"You wouldn't," said Kosmir.

"I'm increasingly sure that I will if you do not stop talking."

Bandar heard the tone even stronger now. The young man was slipping ever more firmly into the grip of the Hero.

They sat without talking, Harkless watching the town while Bandar watched Harkless. After a while, the noönaut sought to probe the extent to which the agent was affected.

He chose an indirect line of inquiry. "The call you said you felt, might it be a vocation to explore the Commons?"

Harkless mulled the question then said that something about the noösphere called to him. A moment later, he clarified his answer: something *in* the noösphere was calling him, though he knew not what called nor what he was called to do.

Bandar admitted to being conflicted. It delighted him that Harkless's strange facility for the Commons might open up new avenues of research. But he did not like to think that he had been an instrument to put the young man in peril of being absorbed.

Harkless told him not to worry. "The instrument is never responsible, only the hand that employs it." Besides, if it was his fate to be where he was, then perhaps it was also Bandar's.

The calm with which he accepted the possibility of imminent doom was quintessentially that of the Hero Sacrificial, Bandar saw. Moment by moment, there was less and less of Baro Harkless, and more and more of the archetype.

Bandar said, "It would pain me to think that my life–long love of the noösphere has been not truly of my own will but just a part of some grand plot."

Harkless paid no attention. The noönaut watched as an intense stillness came over the young man's face. He sat staring at nothing for a long while and Bandar saw the grim certitude of the Hero gain a stronger hold.

Suddenly the young man's eyes went wide and he said, "What?" and looked at Kosmir as if he thought the prisoner had spoken, though Bandar knew that whatever voice Harkless had heard had come from deep within.

The agent now turned to Bandar and said, "Did you speak to me?"

"No." Bandar kept his voice even, but it worried him that the young fellow was now hearing a voice. That was a long step beyond merely being influenced by an archetype. He sought to plant an antidote to the growing poisoning of the young man's psyche by the Hero by offering another archetype as a focus for Harkless's thoughts. Because to name was to summon, Bandar deliberately chose the most effective counter to the Hero, saying, "The voice probably came from the Wise Man."

Bandar saw speculation in the agent's eyes. *Good*, he thought, *Heroes do not speculate.* He was searching for a way to keep the process rolling when Kosmir announced that he had something important to say. Immediately, Bandar saw the Hero resurge within the young man.

Harkless pointed the pistol at Kosmir's foot and said, "I do not care to be interrupted when I am thinking."

The prisoner squirmed but pressed on. "It is something the scroots need to know."

The Hero looked out through Harkless's eyes with character-istic disdain for a villain. He heard the Hero's voice tell Kosmir he had other concerns.

The prisoner said he had information about a serious crime.

The Hero's mouth set in a skeptical sneer. "More serious than a double murder?"

"Yes."

Bandar saw Harkless dismiss the subject. The Hero was now back in control and had larger issues to occupy him. Bandar was growing increasingly frightened. They were stranded up here on the bare rock with an armed man who was visibly sinking into the clutches of an archetype. And who was certain to look upon the noönaut as his fated Helper.

"You are Haj's prisoner," the agent told Kosmir. "Reveal all to her when she comes back."

Kosmir had a villain's cunning and knew the right thing to say to the Hero. "She may not be coming back. She has likely walked into peril."

Bandar saw a jolt pass through Harkless at the mention of a damsel in distress. Harkless leapt to his feet and brought out his plaque, trying to reach Haj through the short–range emergency fre-quency. A few undecipherable squawks overlaid by static was all the answer he received.

The agent turned back to Kosmir and Bandar saw the Hero's single–mindedness plain in his young face and heard the Hero's un-compromising voice say, "Tell me."

Kosmir made the mistake of trying to bargain. He wanted the charges dropped and to keep his ill–gotten gains.

But a Hero did not haggle and the prisoner now compounded his error by assuming that he was dealing with a sane scroot. He made demands. The Hero simply discharged the energy pistol into the rock immediately in front of Kosmir's crossed legs. Instantly, the prisoner's calves were splattered with white hot molten rock. The man shrieked and fell back onto his pinioned arms, frantically rubbing his legs against each other, trying to remove the lava from his smoldering flesh.

Harkless calmly aimed the pistol at Kosmir's feet and asked if he found the terms satisfactory.

Bandar said, "That was unnecessarily cruel."

Typical of a Hero approaching the crisis, Harkless paid the Helper no heed. He put his thumb on the weapon's activation stud and said, "Well?"

Kosmir announced that he would tell all. Harkless gestured with the pistol to suggest that he do so quickly.

Kosmir began to talk, telling an involved tale about having overheard one side of a conversation involving Gebbling. He had not been able to hear the other communicant's voice, but he had heard enough to make out the elements of a plot to spread the lassitude, which was apparently somehow caused by eating truffles of the Swept. Bandar did not pay close attention; he was more concerned with the obvious transformation that was overcoming young Baro Harkless. There was less and less of Harkless left to see in the face that confronted Kosmir, and the hand that held the pistol did not waver.

Bandar said, "Ask the Wise Man to evaluate this information."

The Hero pressed on with his interrogation. Bandar repeated his words, but now he was sure that no one was there to hear them.

Kosmir tried to hold back some crucial element of what he knew, to keep something he might trade to his advantage. The Hero aimed the pistol and offered to burn off his feet.

Kosmir talked on. Finally the Hero that had filled Harkless was satisfied. It had Harkless take out his Bureau of Scrutiny plaque and again try to contact Haj. This time, there was a reply, but not from the missing sergeant. Instead, a new voice spoke from the air, announcing that this was a restricted frequency and demanding to know who was using it.

"Baro Harkless, agent ordinary." The words came from the agent's mouth, but Bandar could hear the Hero speaking them.

The voice from the air identified itself as that of Directing Agent Ardmander Arboghast of the Bureau of Scrutiny. Harkless reported to him that he believed Raina Haj was in danger. He also told his superior that he had discovered the source of the lassitude.

Arboghast told him that everything was now secure and asked for his location. Harkless told him where he and the others were and that they had four people critically ill with the disease. Arboghast ordered him to remain where he was; help was on the way.

Harkless looked down at Kosmir with the uncompromising stare of the Hero. "The Bureau knows everything," he said. "You have nothing to bargain with."

A sly look had crept over Kosmir. He said, "I have something now."

Harkless said he could try it on the senior scroot when he got there.

The prisoner said, "This is something you need to know, and before he arrives."

Baro took out the pistol again. "Shall I burn off a toe?"

Kosmir affected an air of unconcern and told Harkless he could shoot if he wished. The pain would not last long.

Bandar saw puzzlement in the Hero's face. "What makes you say that?" Harkless said.

Kosmir mocked him with a simpering expression. "I say it because none of us here has long to live, not me, not you, nor those sick lumps, unless you listen to what I can tell you."

Harkless looked over at where the lassitude sufferers lay inert. Olleg Ebersol was having trouble breathing. Imbry struggled up from where he was sitting and went over to him.

Bandar saw Harkless's face reflect the pity that the Hero reflexively showed toward helpless victims. Then he saw it harden back into a grim mask as the Hero turned back to Kosmir. The pistol did not waver as it came to bear on the prisoner's feet.

"Tell me, or die one piece at a time."

Bandar tried to reason with the archetype. "It is evil to torture a prisoner."

The Hero turned toward the noönaut and in the glitter of his eyes Bandar saw only the faintest trace of the young man Harkless, and heard almost nothing but pure archetype in the voice that answered him. "It is he who is evil. I do what is necessary."

Some of Harkless was still there, but what little was left of him was sinking rapidly. Bandar made an attempt to reach him. "You are allowing yourself to be absorbed by an archetype, to be made into a simple–minded monster. Fight it."

The noönaut saw a gleam of a response deep in the unblinking eyes, but then the Hero's voice said, "I do not wish to fight it." He looked back at Kosmir with casual coldness and aimed the weapon.

Bandar stood up and sang eight notes. It was a subthran that interfered with the perceptions of a specific subset of the Hero archetype that included the Hero Sacrificial—interfered with them in the Commons, that is. He had no idea if the sequence would have any affect in the waking world, but he could think of nothing else to do.

He continued to sing the eight notes, over and over again. The Hero looked at him curiously, then the hardness in the eyes softened and Bandar saw Baro Harkless re–emerge. The young man blinked and said, "I have broken through. Thank you."

"You must continue to fight its influence," said Bandar.

Harkless said he would try. He bent and helped Kosmir sit upright. "Whatever you were holding back, tell me now," he said.

"I will if you first free me," Kosmir said, his eyes searching the sky to the east over Victor and the Rovers' town. "But there is no time to waste."

"If the information is truly important, I promise to free you."

But Kosmir was not a man to trust a scroot, especially one who had moments before given him a convincing display of madness.

Nor did Harkless have cause to trust the prisoner.

"We have reached an impasse," Harkless said.

"An impasse that will not last," said Kosmir. He pointed with his chin to the vehicle that had risen above the town. "Free me before that aircar gets here. After will be too late."

Bandar looked and saw an official scroot volante. Harkless saw it too.

Now Kosmir was pleading, scootching around on his buttocks to present his restrained arms to Harkless.

"You are trying to trick me," Harkless said.

"I think he is not," Bandar said. "His fear seems genuine."

"He has reason to be afraid. That aircar will take him on a journey that ends in the contemplarium."

Kosmir was frantic. "No, the aircar brings death to all of us!"

The thrum of the aircar's gravity obviators grew louder. Harkless chewed his lip as he regarded the prisoner, then Bandar saw that the scroot had made his decision. The agent reset the weapon's controls. He aimed it at the holdtight.

The gargling noise from Ebersol was growing louder. It drew Harkless's attention to where the four inert sufferers lay, tended by Luff Imbry.

"They are coming to the catharsis," Bandar said. "Death will soon end their suffering."

"Ignore them!" Kosmir said. "Release me!"

Harkless directed a pulse of energy into the restraint's control center. The holdtight broke open and clattered onto the rock. Kosmir leapt to his feet, swinging his arms to bring the blood back into his hands. "Set your pistol on maximum!" he said. "When the aircar tries to land, shoot it down!"

Harkless gave him a skeptical look and made no move to adjust the weapon's setting. Kosmir spoke frantically—"No time!" and sought to seize the pistol.

Harkless pushed him back, and the man stumbled and fell. "Now who is mad?" the young man said. "It is a Bureau of Scrutiny aircar and its operator is Ardmander Arboghast, my section chief!"

Kosmir put his hands together in the posture of the Reformed Penitent. Bandar had seen the archetype in many a Class Two Situation and believed the man's emotion to be genuine.

"I lied when I said I'd told you everything!" Kosmir said. "I was holding back something to bargain with—that I did hear the voice of the man who was the mastermind behind the lassitude. I did not know his name but I know that his voice was the same as that of the man you spoke with on your commuicator. Whoever he is, he is responsible for scores of deaths, and he will surely kill us all!"

"No!" Harkless said, "you are trying to trick us!"

Bandar was only half aware of what was going on between the scroot and the pleading prisoner. His eyes were on the four lassitude sufferers. He tugged on the young agent's sleeve. "Baro!" he cried.

The young man swung around and looked to the sky behind them, where the noise of the aircar grew louder.

"No," said Bandar, "look there!" A cold wave of horror crept up his back and he pointed at where the four bodies lay.

Olleg Ebersol was sitting up. Corje Sooke's torso was also rising from the rock. But it was all wrong. *Human beings don't move that way,* Bandar thought. *Nor do they bend that way.*

Neither the man nor the woman had bent at the waist, but their upper torsos had levered themselves upright at the point where ribs met diaphragm, the small of the back staying flat on the ground. It shouldn't have happened without bones snapping, but the only sound was a sighing intake and release of breath, remarkably calm.

Now Olleg Ebersol's head turned left then right, rotating almost until his chin went past each shoulder. His arms rose and extended straight out, as if he were reaching for something in the air before him. The man's hands seemed to elongate, the fingers stretching to an impossible length. Then the skin at the fingertips burst, falling back in strips like ribbons, and from them emerged a bundle of dark green sticks, jointed in several places, that unrolled and flexed themselves.

Now the arms with their spiky appendages reached up toward Ebersol's head. Bandar saw the man's skin slide down his arms like loose cuffs, but where bones and flesh should have been exposed was a thick length of the same dark green material, shiny and hard–surfaced as an arthropod's limb. The stick–like digits dug into the flesh at the back of the neck and with a sound like the tearing of coarse cloth the skin of the head was torn away. Where Ebersol's face had been was a featureless rounded oblong of the same dark green, glistening like a beetle's wingcase. Two fern–like antennae unrolled themselves and began to turn as if sampling the air.

Now the claws went again to the skin at the back of the neck and the jointed arms exerted a great strength. Ebersol's clothing split down the back, and with it the skin along his spine also parted. A hard shelled thorax emerged, then a segmented abdomen, long and cylindrical, finally a pair of lower limbs from which thorn–like spikes sprouted.

Bandar's first thought was, *I have seen that before*. Aloud, he said, "That is a Dree."

The sound of his voice caused the eyeless head to rotate toward him. The tendrils quivered and leaned in his direction. The thing's multi–digited hands and feet underwent a transformation, the spiky appendages suddenly clicking together, each fitting tightly into its neighbors to form solid, curved claws. Bandar looked at those wicked edges and remembered the wounds on Brond Halorn's body.

This is a coincidence, he thought, and the word brought with it all of its terrifying import to a noönaut. All of this—the lassitude, the Dree, the strange young man called to the Commons—they were all part of one great story, a story being acted out not in the theater of the noösphere, but in the waking world. And, for this story, Guth Bandar could not be a detached observer; he must be an active participant.

A second Dree had already torn its way out of what had been Corje Sooke. It stood, its clawed feet rasping on the rock, kicking its legs to free their spikes of the woman's hampering skin. Its antennae questioned the air. Between it and the creature that had come out of Olleg Ebersol, Luff Imbry still knelt where he had been ministering to what they had thought were the dying. Now, as the creatures loomed over him, he scrambled to his feet but stumbled as he tried to put distance between himself and the Dree.

Harkless shouted to him to stand clear and aimed the energy pistol at the one that was already on its feet. but now the first Dree also sprang up, its tendrils quivering toward the sound of the young man's voice. Its hind legs flexed and it flung itself at Harkless. The *zivv* of the energy pistol was accompanied by a beam of focused force that caught the Dree in the air, burning a hole the size of a fist through its thorax. The thing fell clattering to the rock, its momentum carrying it skidding almost to Harkless's feet.

The second Dree was still seeking to disengage itself from Sooke's skin, but its clawed forelimb had already reached out to snag Imbry's robe, jerking him back as he tried to flee. The fat man twisted around, frantically pulling at the fasteners, trying to free himself from the garment. The cloth enveloped his head.

Bandar looked to Harkless and saw that the Hero had come back into the young man's face. *Well, if there ever was a time for a Hero. . .*, the noönaut thought. The young agent calmly aimed the pistol at the Dree that was attacking his partner. But as his thumb moved to the discharge control, Bandar heard him gasp in agony and looked down to see that the first Dree, though dying, had sunk a talon into the flesh of the young man's calf and was raising a second clawed limb to open his belly.

Harkless's pierced leg collapsed under him, but even as he fell he placed the weapon against the Dree's faceless head and fired. The green smoothness blackened then exploded. Harkless yanked its claw from his flesh and aimed at the one that had seized Imbry.

The fat agent had not been able to pull free of his garment before the Dree had disentangled itself from Corje Sooke's shed skin. The man had fallen heavily onto his face, and now the creature was upon him, its powerful hind legs ready to rip him apart.

Harkless fired the pistol into the Dree in a sustained discharge that obliterated its head and upper body. But Imbry did not stir.

"I will tend to him," Bandar said. "You must deal with the other two." The lumps that had been Ule Gazz and Pollus Ermatage were twitching the way the first two had just before the emergence.

The Hero looked at him through Harkless's eyes. "You opposed me," it said.

A chill went through Bandar, but he thought fast. "I am your Helper. It is my duty to oppose you when I see you go the wrong way."

The eyes held on him for a long moment, then the Hero nodded. It rose and limped on Harkless's injured leg to where Imbry lay, pulled back the cloth from the head. Bandar came with him. "See, he lives," the noönaut said. "Now kill the other Dree before they emerge."

The Hero knelt, adjusting the weapon to maximum discharge and aimed at the jerking chrysalises that had been Gazz and Ermatage.

The thrumming of a powerful aircar was suddenly loud all round them, and the wind of its bowfront wave swept over the scene. Bandar turned to see a Bureau of Scrutiny volante alighting almost upon them. A man of mature years stepped from the vehicle. He wore the green and black uniform of a Bureau officer and a face that made Bandar's heart sink. *This one, too, is fully in the grip of an archetype,* he thought. And it looked to be one of the worst: the Tyrant.

The Hero glanced back at the new arrival as the scroot officer took from a belt holster the standard Bureau sidearm: a shocker. The Hero turned back to the Dree and said, "I do not think your weapon will do more than subdue them temporarily. They are a deadly offworld species."

"I know," said the Tyrant in black and green. Then it raised the shocker and shot the young man.

The Hero fell senseless to the ground and the Tyrant stepped nimbly forward and seized the energy pistol. It aimed the weapon at Bandar and said, "If you want to live, do as I say."

Bandar indicated that he would accept the suggestion, but first indicated the prone Luff Imbry. "I think this man is only stunned," he said.

"Leave him, but bring the young one." Bandar knew better than to argue and went to where Harkless lay.

The Tyrant turned to where Kosmir had stood, frozen with

fear, during the violence. "You, help him."

But the landship officer was in the grip of terror. He said something unintelligible then turned and ran, heading west out onto the expanse of the Monument. The Tyrant in the Bureau uniform raised the pistol, then lowered it. It turned a cruel face toward Bandar and said, "Hurry, they will soon emerge," then helped the noönaut drag Harkless's unconscious form to the aircar. They manhandled him into the prisoner's compartment then the Tyrant ordered Bandar in after him. "There are bandages and restorative in the first–aid kit," it said, before climbing into the operator's position and lifting the volante into the air. They hovered at a low height in silent mode.

Bandar watched through the transparent canopy as the last two Dree ripped themselves free. They stood, digits opening and closing into claws, their tendrils straining toward the two charred corpses. Then a distant sound caught their attention and, as one, their faceless heads and questing antennae turned west.

Far out on the Monument the tiny figure of the landship officer ran. Kosmir's legs pumped with fear–fueled energy, his arms pistoning tight against his sides.

Bandar saw the Dree tense and crouch. Then each sprang forward in a prodigious leap that carried them at least twice their body length. They landed on limbs like springs and the second leap carried them even farther than their first. They bounded across the flat rock, hardly seeming to touch the surface before they were in the air again.

Kosmir might as well have been standing still for all the good that running did him. The Tyrant eased the volante forward, cruising above and behind the leaping Dree, so that Bandar was an eye-witness to what happened when they caught the man.

One sprang onto the officer's back, sinking the claws of its forelimbs into the muscles of his shoulders while its heavy hind legs, with their great curved claws, shredded the flesh from Kosmir's legs.

The second Dree had leaped neatly over its sibling and its prize, turning in the air so that it landed on its back right in front of Kosmir, its claws raised to receive him. Sandwiched between the two of them, he screamed for a long time before they tore something vital.

"Instinctive behavior," said the Tyrant. "First they hunt, then they feed."

Bandar thought it was talking to itself, then remembered that this archetype always enjoyed seeing its self–worth reflected in the awe of another. "You're right," he said.

Bandar looked down and saw that a ventral slit had opened in the abdomen of each Dree. Their claws were ripping free pieces of Kosmir and cramming them into the openings. Something like teeth flashed as they shredded the raw meat.

"Now they rest," said the Tyrant when the feeding was done. It landed the volante near the Dree, unlocked the prisoners' compartment and beckoned Bandar out. The noönaut was frightened but the creatures seemed to have become dormant.

The Tyrant adjusted the shocker's setting and turned it on the Dree. They toppled over and lay on their backs like dead insects.

"We'll put them in the cargo bay," the Tyrant said.

They overflew Victor at rooftop height. Bodies lay in the streets—mostly human, though Bandar saw one Rover. The noönaut was piecing together a picture of what must have happened: the Rovers, with their less complex minds, would have been the first to be mentally enslaved. The Dree would have made them get their hunting weapons and come up from Rovertown at night in a coordinated strike. Victor had no Bureau of Scrutiny detachment; it would have been quickly overrun, its population captured and put under guard.

But how could there be a Dree to enslave anyone? They had been wiped out eons before, traced back to their home world and brutally expunged. Bandar believed he knew how: the Swept was home to extreme gravitational anomalies; gravity was necessary for the formation of noöspheres; was it possible that the Dree equivalent of a collective unconscious had been captured by the aggregator that had crushed the invaders, had been carried intact down to the core of Old Earth and been reflected back in a process that occurred over geological time?

Bandar had to assume it was possible because that was the only way it could have happened. And now the anomaly and its noöspheric cargo had reached the surface and come within range of humans and Rovers.

But how had the lassitude sufferers been transformed into Dree? It appeared that the original invaders had had a secret: they had not bred, as had been assumed, by laying eggs to be tended by enslaved species. So powerful was the Dree hive mind that it could alter the very gene plasm of its captives, with a chemical assist from a particular fungus grown in the hives. The Dree fed its captives truffles of the Swept then exerted its immense psychic powers against the most intimate constituents of their cells, transforming them into replicas of itself.

Those who did not eat the fungus but came under the spell of the Dree fell into the lassitude. When the transformative crisis arrived, they died. Those who met the crisis with the truffles in their systems became Dree.

But what of Arboghast, the scroot officer? He was neither Dree in the making nor a mind–slave. But he was unquestionably psychotic, a mind absorbed completely by the Tyrant archetype. That opened an interesting avenue of speculation: would Harkless's possession by the Hero (or Bandar's by the Helper if he gave in to it), protect him from mind–slavery, or even from the lassitude? The noönaut automatically began examining the question as if he might begin drafting a paper. Then it struck him that, if the Dree were truly resurgent on an Old Earth that no longer possessed substantial military forces, there would be no one to publish his thoughts, nor any to read them.

The Bureau volante slid down toward the south end of Victor, passed over Rovertown, and alighted on the open promenade deck of the *Orgulon*. A forward hatch gaped, guarded by two Rovers with pulse rifles. Arboghast summoned them to haul Harkless's still unconscious body from the vehicle. The guards responded immediately, and Bandar deduced that the psychotic scroot must be a willing ally of the Dree.

The relationship was not too far–fetched. Typically, all the Tyrant ever wanted was to stand atop a heap of humanity. The greater the heap, the greater the archetype's satisfaction. To Arboghast, the nonhuman Dree would be just another natural force to be worked with to produce the desired end.

The renegade gestured for Bandar to precede them as the Rovers dragged the inert young agent to the hatch. Below the deck began a stairway guarded by two more armed Rovers. Bandar was directed downward to a great open space, one of the landship's cargo holds, where a number of people sat or lay upon the floor. Some wore the uniforms of the *Orgulon*'s crew, others were in sleeping attire and must have been brought here from their homes in Victor.

The guards laid Harkless on his back on a pile of rough sacking on the floor of the hold. Bandar sat beside the young man and examined him, finding his breathing regular and his pulse steady and strong. Physically, the agent was fine, although too strong a dose from a shocker could permanently disrupt neural processes essential to personality and memory.

A man sitting nearby rose and came to take a look at the unconscious young man as Bandar tried gently tapping Harkless's cheek. The noönaut looked up, thought the man's face was familiar, then realized that he had been seeing that saintly visage regularly projected to the passengers on the cruise: Father Olwyn, more commonly known as Horslan Gebbling, fraudster.

"How is he?" the man said.

Harkless's eyes fluttered and opened. "We'll know in a moment," Bandar said.

"He'll be fine," said another voice, and Bandar turned to see that Raina Haj was seated not far away, a grim look in her eyes and a dark bruise on her jaw. "Arboghast was eager to take him alive and aware. It seems they have a history."

The young man was swimming back up into consciousness now. "He's coming to," Gebbling said. "That futterer didn't turn his brain to jelly."

Grunting with pain, Harkless sat up and his hands went first to his bandaged leg. Then he looked about him, registering faces before asking, "Where is Imbry?"

Bandar told him his partner was still up on the Monument. The noönaut watched the young man's eyes as he delivered the news and was sure he saw no evidence there of the Hero. That was not unexpected—shockers grievously overstimulated the body's own electrochemistry, generating a powerful internal surge of electrical current that had the same mind–clearing effect as a shock delivered from an external source. But now, after all his efforts to deliver the young man from the archetype's grasp, Bandar was coming to believe that a Hero was precisely what the situation called for.

"Imbry will die out there," the young man was saying.

"We will all die, in one manner or another," Bandar said. Nothing summoned a Hero like an expression of despair, and the noönaut looked to see if the provocative comment had raised a glimmer behind the agent's eyes, but saw nothing.

"And Kosmir?" the scroot said.

Bandar described the gory end of the prisoner and again sought for the Hero, but again saw no sign of his return.

Harkless's voice was a croak. He asked for water. Bandar had seen people dipping from a barrel not far away. He pointed it out to the young man, leaving him to rise and get his own drink. Pain could help bring up the Hero. Before Harkless took his first limping step toward the barrel, the noönaut warned him that the Rover guards would shoot without warning. *An imminent threat can also summon the Hero*, he thought.

But when Harkless came to sit with them again, his face remained his own. He watched as two Rovers descended the steps from the deck above, carrying between them a man in a landship uniform whose legs would not support him. They laid the crewman moaning on the deck.

The young agent watched as the Rovers chose a plump female in the attire of a steward and led her away. He stared at the armed guards at the top of the stairs. "Those are not hunting weapons," he said. "They are pulse rifles."

"They came in the 'mining machinery' that the *Orgulon* delivered," Gebbling said. He had also seen heavy weapons and some kind of armor that would convert the gig and Arboghast's volante into fighting vehicles.

"Where do they take the people?" Harkless asked.

"To be tested," Gebbling said. "Only the ones who fail are returned here. Most pass the test and are consigned to the creches."

"Test? Creches?" Harkless's face hardened and Bandar saw the first spark of the archetype in his eyes. He fanned it into flame, offering a lurid account of how the Dree transformed their captives into copies of themselves. The threat of losing a sense of identity could always outrage a pure archetype. He watched as the madness rose steadily in the young scroot. Eventually the power of the psychosis would overcome the residual effects of the shocker, and Harkless would become a potent weapon to use against their captors—deter-

238

mined, superbly coordinated in the arts of violence, and completely ruthless.

When he was finished, there was an almost luminous glow to the young man's face. Its youthful features now looked as if carved from old wood. "So some become Dree," Harkless said, "and the rest are slaves?"

"Except for the tiny few who go mad," Bandar told him.

"I would rather die fighting the guards," the Hero said. The transition had been made.

The conversation turned to Arboghast and how, as the scroot pursued Gebbling into a played–out brillion mine the fraudster was salting with high–grade ore samples, they had both encountered the Dree entity imprisoned within a gravitational cyst. The Dree had easily enslaved Gebbling, but Arboghast's psychosis had armored his mind against its power. Instead, they had struck a bargain to spread the lassitude and create a new Dree hive. The forgotten enemy would secretly burrow beneath the population centers of Old Earth, capturing humans and converting them into legions of hive–mates, until they burst onto a defenseless world.

Having sketched this dark vision of despair, Bandar now offered that most powerful stimulus to the Hero: a small ray of hope. He speculated that the only missing step between the Dree and its victory was that the Dree archetype had not yet been able to create enough actual Dree for the hive mind to coalesce.

Harkless had been staring at his feet. His head jerked up and he looked sharply at the noönaut. "It has not coalesced?"

Bandar recalled the feral manner in which the new–made Dree had savaged Kosmir. He said he believed that there was prob-ably a need for a critical mass of Dree brains before their behavior rose above the instinctual and a unified consciousness emerged.

Bandar could see the Hero was strong in Harkless, though the young agent's body remained weak from the effect of the shocker. Still, would soon be fully restored. The noönaut looked around the cargo hold, counting guards and noting their dispositions. Not too long and the moment would be right for the Helper to outline a desperate plan that the Hero would soon come to think of as its own.

But as he regarded the young man, sitting with his knees drawn up, absently rubbing the spot on his calf where the Dree had punctured the muscle, Bandar felt a pang of misgiving. The young scroot would almost certainly die in the coming violence, and Bandar would be complicit in his death.

Yet, if nothing is done, Bandar thought, *we will all die, one way or another: transmogrified into Dree, worked to death by Dree, or excruciatingly tormented to death for the delectation of Dree. Besides, to die for the good of all is what the Hero Sacrificial is for.* But somehow the voice did not sound like his own. Bandar wondered how much he, himself, was under the spell of the Helper archetype. *Or is that what I am for?* he wondered.

But he put aside these qualms and concentrated on the elements of the immediate situation, while keeping a close eye on the Hero.

The pair of Rovers who had taken away the plump steward now came back without her. She had either been sent to the creches or to toil in the fungus beds, Raina Haj said.

Bandar saw the Hero's resolve deepen further. "When they are taken, how are they tested?" the young man said, and the noönaut could hear a deeper note in his voice.

Gebbling explained that each captive was brought near to the gravitational anomaly where the Dree entity was encapsulated. In moments its mental powers ransacked the mind and decided the prisoner's fate.

"I will fight its power," said the Hero.

Soon, Bandar thought. *Very soon.* He watched as the Rovers reached the bottom of the stairs. The ones who came for the testees carried no weapons that could be seized. But if a strong, highly coordinated Hero were to attack them, they might be battered unconscious—Rovers had thin skulls—then that powerful Hero might pick up one of their inert forms and, using him as a shield against the pulse rifles, rush up the stairs and disarm one of the guards before they could seal the hold.

And once the Hero had a pulse rifle, the balance of power in the confined space would soon shift in his favor.

Bandar looked at the young man, saw residual tremors in his legs and arms. *Very well,* he thought. *A little while longer for him to recover. Then we'll see.*

But the pair of Rovers did not take one of the landship's crew. Their strong fingers, set with thick, dark nails, closed upon the still trembling arms of Baro Harkless. They pulled him to his feet and hauled him to the stairs. The Hero struggled, but the strength was not there. In a few moments, Harkless was dragged protesting through the hatch.

And the Helper was left helpless.

Guth Bandar made his way to where the great white Wall loomed. He approached it, searching with the corners of his eyes until he found the discoloration that marked where the Dree had broken through eons before. It tended to slip from the gaze when he looked at it directly so he employed an Institute mentalism that let him hold it in focus.

Gingerly, he raised a hand and touched a finger to the faint mark. It was solid, no different from any other stretch of the wall. Bandar lowered his hand and considered what he had learned. The Dree of old had broken through into the human Commons, just as humans on Gamza had broken into the Bololo noösphere. Yet the surviving Dree entity had not done so this time. Or at least, not yet. Bandar could only assume that the entity itself, though it had the strength to enslave individual humans and even to break into the Rover Commons and seize them all, was not yet powerful enough to smash its way through the wall. On Gamza, it had taken a mass of humans concentrating on the same archetypical material to make the Bololos cavort and dance. It must require a critical mass of Dree, unified into a hive–mind, to crash through the Wall. But soon that hive–mind would cohere, and when it did, the Dree would spread with the same virulence that had allowed the original invaders to overrun vast territories, even whole worlds down The Spray.

How this information could help, however, was an answer that eluded him. He was convinced that the situation was now beyond hope. The Rovers had taken away the Hero. Bandar presumed that Arboghast, at his leisure, had had the young scroot brought before him and had simply killed him, probably painfully and with maximum humiliation. It was what Tyrants invariably did with failed Heroes.

Not long after, the Rovers had come for Bandar. They had taken him from the landship, walked him to a nearby mine entrance, then down a series of interconnecting tunnels until a strong gravitational anomaly had pulled him to his knees.

He felt the Dree archetype touch his mind, and sought to defend himself with the three, three, seven thran. But the tones meant nothing to the alien entity. He felt it winnow the contents of his psyche with cold precision, brushing aside his individuality and disdaining the Institute mentalisms he tried to summon against it. He might as well have been the most ignorant loblolly on First Day.

In a moment it was over. The Dree did not tell him what fate had been assigned to him, but the Rovers soon made it clear by their actions. He was taken to a deeper part of the mine where row upon row of coffin–sized holes had been bored into the rock. Here he was handed over to humans from Victor, dull–eyed mind slaves in the garb of miners, who efficiently swaddled Bandar from head to toe in a shroud of semitransparent material that tightly bound his limbs to his body. One of them tore a hole in the stuff where it covered the noönaut's nose and mouth, allowing him to take a relieved breath, but the relief was shortlived: two of them tilted him back on his heels, then lifted him and shoved him feet first into a waist–high hole. A moment later, calloused fingers pressed against his teeth, forced his mouth open so that a feeding tube could be inserted roughly into his gullet. Almost immediately, he felt a pulse of coldness pass down the tube and into his body. *Truffles of the Swept*, he thought, *to speed the transformation.*

Now Bandar's body lay in its crypt–like creche, alien fungus insinuating its substance into his tissues, while his consciousness wandered the Commons seeking a last desperate hope. But there was nothing he could do at the Wall and he turned away. As he did so, his eye noticed on the ground the long pale scar he had seen before. He remembered what Harkless has said about swimming through the Old Sea to the Rover Commons, how he had freed the dreaming Yaffak.

But Bandar had no means to cut through the floor of the Commons. He deployed his globular map and looked for a route to a Location where magical weapons were an important element of the dynamic. *Might as well get the best*, he thought. Then he dismissed the notion. He knew all too well what happened to noönauts who entered the Old Sea: they lost all volition, hanging helpless and inert in the pearly waters until the great Worm inerrantly came to swallow them.

A profound sadness washed over him, a true despair, for there was nothing he could do. This was work for a Hero, but even the Hero had been murdered before it could lift its sword.

A spot in the globe was blinking, yellow alternating with red. The map remembered the last Location its owner had been. It was reminding Bandar of his recent visit with Harkless to the Event that memorialized the hemming of the Dree. There was a quick route to it from where he now stood at the Wall, and Bandar made his way there. Perhaps whatever coincidence had brought him and the young scroot there would give Bandar an idea. If not, he could pass from the Event to one of the nicer Class One Heavens, walk without a thran and let himself be absorbed into paradise—before the Dree robbed him of his essence.

He arrived in the Location when it was reaching just about the same point in its cycle as when he had left it. The armored assault had passed by and the aggregator was descending from space, blotting out the stars. Singing the insulating thran, Bandar went down onto the plain and sought the ditch where the Dree weapons crew had died. It was to this spot that the Commons had called Harkless. Perhaps there was something here that would make itself known to Bandar, now that he knew what the young man's strangeness had been all about.

But when he bent, chanting, over the charred Dree corpses, he found no revelation. He pulled at the carbonized chitin, looking for some object that would provide a clue. But there was nothing.

Something hard and cold touched his shoulder. Bandar leapt up, an unintentional shriek taking the place of the thran. He landed crookedly and fell back upon the dead Dree. Above him, against the splash of stars and near–space orbitals, limned by green and orange flashes of weapons fire in the hills above the plain, he saw the outline of a man wearing a winged helmet. The cold, hard thing that had touched his shoulder was a sword of iron.

The Hero bent over him, chanting in Baro Harkless's voice the thran that hid them from the battle.

"What are you doing?" Bandar said.

The Hero gestured at him and Bandar realized he must take over the thran while the other answered: "I have come for you. You are the Helper."

"There is nothing to be done. I am sealed in a creche being transmogrified into a Dree. They are all taken: Gebbling, Haj, the last of the landship crew. It is too late."

"Yet here you are prodding the Dree dead."

"I had a faint hope there would be something here that would serve us," Bandar said. "I found nothing."

By the light of an explosion out on the plain he saw the expression on the Hero's face: assured, almost amused. *Typical*, he thought.

Harkless was suggesting they go somewhere where they could talk without having to switch the thran back and forth. Bandar consulted his map and sang the tones that opened a nearby gate. They went through into an Earnest/Realistic blizzard. Two steps in the direction his noönaut sense provided and he opened another gate that admitted them to the searing heat of a desert.

The sun above them was yellow, almost white, an early rendering. Sweat sprouted all over Bandar's body. Harkless, though in mail armor and animal pelt showed no sign of discomfort. Indeed, he wore that characteristic look of excited anticipation that was so essentially the Hero's.

And yet there was something else there. It was impossible for a psychotic to be possessed by two archetypes—they would inevitably clash—yet there was a complexity to the Hero's aspect that Bandar couldn't account for. He even believed he still saw remnants of the strange young man.

"I thought you'd be dead," he said.

"Arboghast taunted me then sent me to be made into a Dree," the other said, and it seemed to be Harkless who was speaking. "Now I am in a creche, awaiting transformation."

The noönaut led them to a slope of sand ornamented by wind–scoured bones. "You said you had an idea?" he said.

"Out on the Swept, I entered the Rover Commons and freed Yaffak from his bonds," Harkless said.

"I have come to accept that," Bandar said. "I have even seen the scar in the floor beside the Wall."

"I believe I could return by the same route and free the others. I would enter their dreams, cut the tethers, one by one. They would turn on the Dree and slaughter them before the hive mind consolidates. They could then free those who have been placed in the creches, including you and me."

It did not seem practical to Bandar. He pointed out that when Yaffak had been freed the Rover had been physically far from where the Dree entity lay imprisoned in its gravitational anomaly. Here, the bonds were surely stronger. "And what of the Rovers that are not asleep and dreaming?"

As he spoke, the noönaut watched for a reaction. This late in its dynamic, a fully engaged Hero would show impatience, even anger, at any attempt by the Helper to divert it from the catharsis. But the figure in front of him maintained a cheerful equanimity.

"I hoped you would show more enthusiasm," the Hero said. "It seems a good plan to me. I got it from the Wise Man, after all."

"The Wise Man?" Bandar said, carefully keeping an even tone.

"Yes. The one with the long white beard and the staff."

"And where did you encounter him?"

"At the Wall. Now he speaks within me." The Hero's face turned uncharacteristically thoughtful, and Bandar was fairly sure he was hearing Baro Harkless. The shifting of faces and voices reminded him of something, but when he sought for it it faded away.

Harkless was saying, "It works best if I don't try to get a direct answer, but his thoughts come into my mind."

"Oh, really?" Bandar said. "And have you heard from any others?"

Harkless pulled at his chin. "The Father, I think. He doesn't speak directly to me, but I sense that he takes an interest. The others just watch."

Bandar rested his forehead on his spread fingertips and addressed the Sincere/Approximate grains of sand on the slope before him. "You have come into close contact with several pure characteristic entities?"

"All of them, I believe. Though some kept their distance."

"And none of them absorbed you?"

"I think the Hero has taken an interest."

Bandar lifted his head and looked at the leather–belted leggings, the helmet and the shaggy paw–crossed pelt. "Taken an interest," he said, as if talking to himself.

"Hmm," said Harkless. "That's how it seems."

Bandar stared out across the lone and level sands. "All of this is, of course, quite impossible," he said after a moment. "Anyone approached by a characteristic entity is absorbed. The archetypi-cal energy is immense, overpowering—a great wind encountering a tiny flame. Poof! And that is that."

"I have not found it so," said Harkless. "Perhaps it has some-thing to do with the presence of the Dree entity, right next door, so to speak."

"Well, of course it has something to do with the Dree!" Bandar snapped. "It has *everything* to do with the Dree! But that's not an ex-planation for the impossible."

"Nonetheless, the Wise Man is very confident."

"Archetypes," Bandar said, "are always sure of their plans. That is why it is dangerous to listen solely to one of them. Even two can be mutually reinforcing in their madness. A prudent fellow samples a wide range of opinions and creates a consensus."

"A prudent fellow would not end up wrapped snugly in a hole in a rock wall, awaiting transformation into a Dree."

"I fail to see your point," Bandar said.

"My point is that even if the Hero and the Wise Man are wrong, their plan is at least an attempt to resist. And even if its chances of success are minimal, they are still greater than if we lie passive in our creches waiting to be extinguished."

Bandar looked off into the heat haze. "I had formed my own plan. The Dree may inherit my empty shell. I will have fled to Para-dise."

He saw a wistful look appear on the young man's face, but it was almost immediately supplanted by the Hero. "I would rather die doing all that I could to defeat the enemy."

"I believe it to be a lost cause," Bandar said.

The Hero Sacrificial solidified in Harkless's eyes. "That is the best kind of cause," he said.

Bandar made it clear that he was not convinced, then grew concerned at the flash of anger that he saw in the Hero's face. An angry Hero within sword's length was an uncomfortable compan-ion, even for a Helper. He decided to evoke the Wise Man. "Perhaps the one with the long beard could convince me," he said.

He saw the shift take place behind the young man's eyes. A cool and level gaze now looked back at him. The voice that came out of Harkless's mouth had a different timbre. "I know what will move you."

"Indeed? What would that be?"

The hand that did not hold a sword gestured to the emptiness around them and the eyes twinkled.

"What? The desert?" Bandar said.

"The Commons."

Well played, thought Bandar, though he said nothing.

The Wise Man said, "You have devoted your life to the noö-sphere. Though there be only the slightest hope of saving this great and ancient work of humanity, would you not clutch at that hope even over the certainty of Paradise?"

Bandar sighed and rose to his feet. He called up his map and plotted a route back to the Wall. He swore softly under his breath then chanted the thran that opened a gate.

The scar in the ground had faded to a faint scratch. The Hero had dimmed a little in Harkless's face and Bandar saw a trace of fear. He could understand the young man's trepidation. To swim once in the Old Sea and see the Worm coming would be hard enough. To do it twice was more than the noönaut cared to contemplate.

"If we had a rope to tie around one leg, you could pull me back. It would be faster than swimming."

"But we have no rope."

"Can you not bring one from some other part of the Commons?"

Bandar was not sure that an object purloined from a Location could survive in the Old Sea. He now found himself facing a Hero's impatience. "Why don't we find out?"

Bandar examined his map and sang a thran. He passed into a stone chamber where a white–bearded king sat upon a throne and watched as his young queen threw smoldering glances at a muscular young bravo in tunic and sandals, then entered a wasteland of shat-tered brick and broken glass, where the ground trembled to a violent aftershock. He slid down a pile of masonry, opened another gate, and stepped onto the planked deck of a ship powered by serried banks of oars. The vessel was tilted sharply to one side and Bandar heard the sound of inrushing water. Another galley was backing away, its bronze beak fouled with wreckage. Around him, cursing men in figured breastplates and shining grieves struggled to strip off their armor before sliding and tumbling into the sea. From below decks came screams.

Chanting a thran, Bandar traversed the slanting deck and scooped up a coiled rope. He examined it closely, finding it to be a densely fibered Earnest/Realistic type, as suited such a Class One Event as a Decisive Sea Battle. He slid the coil up his arm and over his shoulder, then made his way back, via a shortcut through a night forest, to where Harkless waited at the Wall.

The Hero was still ascendant. It took the cord and knotted it around one ankle, leaving the rest coiled upon the ground. Then it rose and pressed the sword's point into one end of the scar made by his earlier passage. The ground dimpled then the sword went through, and the Hero's muscles bunched as it forced the edge along the thin line and then well beyond.

"I've made a bigger gap," it said, "since I will surely be longer freeing many than I was freeing one. Try to keep the gap open. It will immediately begin to heal over."

"I will," Bandar said. "I am the Helper."

"Then I go." Bandar saw that the Hero was full in Harkless as it parted the lips of the wound and made a shallow dive into the Old Sea. The slit swallowed the mail–clad body like a lipless mouth. Immediately its edges pressed themselves back together around the rope, but Bandar was relieved to see the cord steadily sliding into the incision; the Hero was willing itself through nothingness toward the Rover Commons.

True to his promise, Bandar knelt and slipped his fingers into the gash to pull it apart and keep it from healing. The effort strained his virtual muscles and he used an Institute mentalism to pour more of his being into his reified hands and arms. The gap appeared again and he found himself looking into the ancient realm of pre–sapience.

No noönaut had gazed upon the Old Sea in time out of mind. Bandar looked down into its seeming waters, suffused by a source-less glow of pearly light, and marveled at its luminous mystery. Some early explorers had recorded a common reaction to the sight of the Unknowingness, as it was originally known: a strange yearning to sink into its depths, to be shed of the burden of self–awareness and become, as our prehuman ancestors were, one with the nothingness of pure being. Bandar stared into the endless depths and waited to see if there arose in him a desire not to be. After a while, he decided it was a quality he lacked. *Being Bandar these many years has not been an unalloyed joy*, he mused, *but, all taken in all, I would rather have been Bandar than not have been anything.*

His thoughts were interrupted by a flicker of motion at the edge of his vision. He angled his head to look down through the gap at a slant. A tiny creature appeared to undulate slowly toward him. But Bandar knew that it was neither tiny nor slow; it was the great Worm, and it was coming to devour Harkless and return the Old Sea to a population of one.

He watched in mingled fascination and dread as the mindless entity swam toward him. Gradually, it grew in apparent size from the length of the smallest segment on the smallest of Bandar's fingers to the length of the entire digit. From that change, Bandar tried to estimate how long it would take the Worm to reach the gap. But he abandoned the calculation; he had no idea how long it would take for the Hero to reach the Rover Commons, find and free a dreaming Rover, then repeat the process. And, besides, time was not time in the Commons nor in the Old Sea.

But even if the scheme worked, what use would be a few free Rovers against all their enslaved fellows and all the humans who were by now mind–thralls of the Dree? Bandar sighed and looked again at the Worm. It was the size of his longest finger and growing steadily. He could make out the circular orifice that was its face, opening and closing as it swam, revealing a rim of triangular teeth, flashing white against the blackness of its maw.

The rope had ceased to slide into the gap. Either Harkless had made it to the other side or he hung helpless in the grip of the gray void, as emptied of all volition as had been its first explorers. After a moment, another length of the cord was jerked through and Bandar decided that the young man had yanked it from the other side of the Wall, creating some slack so that he could hang it coiled on the thorn hedge against his return.

The Worm was closer now, appearing as long as Bandar's hand from wrist to fingertip. Bandar looked up and away from it and was startled, then terrified, to find that he was not alone.

A crowd had gathered in the seeming field that led to the Wall, forming a demilune around a narrow crescent of space at the center of which was Bandar and the gap in the Common floor.

The noönaut knew them all: there stood the Magus, behind him the Thing–in–the–Dark, and over there was the Bully and the trio of Maiden, Matron and Crone, and beyond them the Seer and the Believer, and scores more, the entire throng of usual suspects from the prime arrondisement. Prominent in the center front of the crowd were the Father and the Fool, the Wise Man and the Hero and Helper. This last figure looked at Bandar, cocked its head and winked.

Trembling, Bandar rose to his feet and sought an avenue of escape, but they surrounded him on every side except the unpassable Wall. Stark fear shook him; he fought to subdue it. But all of his training, since the day Preceptor Huffley had first led him to stand on the bridge and see the characteristic entities, had assured him that to be in the presence of a pure archetype without the protection of a thran meant certain absorption. Now it was as if he had crossed the bridge to gambol amongst them.

And yet. . . nothing happened. He remained Bandar, and the thran that had wanted to spring to his lips got no further than the opening of his mouth.

The Wise Man made a small gesture of its gnarled hand and said, "You are in no more danger than we are."

Bandar conquered his fear. "How can this be?" he said.

The answer came suddenly, in a burst of released memory. He remembered all of it, the smith and the mute, being laughed out of the Institute, his uncle's battle with the bull–headed monstrosity, the encounters with the Multifacet, the manipulation that had denied him everything that he had wished his life to be. He saw how they had used him, had even coerced him into reluctantly agreeing to be used. He wondered how much of his life had been bizarrely twisted, that he might fulfill this role he now played. Anger flooded him.

"It had to be a noönaut," the Wise Man said.

"Did it have to be me? Why not Didrick Gabbris?"

"It required an exceptional mind, one that could accept innovation. The Helper must be able to help."

And now they showed him more: the shape of Baro Harkless's life, the death of the boy's father by the conniving of Ardmander Arboghast, the years of obsession with becoming an agent of the Bureau of Scrutiny—a devotion that separated young Harkless from the ordinary run of humankind, walling him off, time and again, from the simple human experiences that ought to have been part of his growing up.

A welter of emotions surged and clashed in Bandar—anger, resentment, pity, even wonder. He looked into the eyes of the Wise Man, then into those of the Hero and Helper, the Father and the others, seeing their terrible simplicity that was at once both essentially human and inhuman, just the raw, rough bricks out of which real people were built.

They had shaped Baro Harkless into a kind of replica of themselves: a simplified facsimile of a human being; an instrument; a tool to do a job. They had shaped Guth Bandar as well, twisting and chopping the substance of his life so that he would answer to the purpose they would put him to. Still, the Helper could not be as simple as the Hero; he would have a subtler part to play, so they had left Bandar enough of a life for him to realize what had been done to him.

And enough to know what they intended for Baro Harkless. "You have sent him to die for you," he said. "That is why you fashioned him to be the Hero Sacrificial—not the Conqueror, not the Reluctant Champion, not the Commoner Who Rises. There is no chance that he can free dreaming Rovers and set them on the Dree."

The Wise Man returned his angry stare with equanimity. "He will do as he must, as we did what we must."

"But he is not one of you! He is a real human being, for all that you have edited him into a cripple! He can no more survive in the waking world than a glove can function without a hand."

"This is about survival," said the archetype. "We could not defeat the Dree. We could not do it the first time, we cannot do it now that it returns. It is one where we are many, a fist against fingers."

"But how can Harkless defeat that thing?"

The Wise Man's eyes showed no emotion, had none to show, Bandar realized. "He cannot defeat it," the entity said. "There is only one force that can." The archetype turned its affectless eyes toward the gap in the Commons floor.

Bandar understood. "The Dree entity is like the newly made Dree. If Harkless runs, it will pursue him. And you will have made sure that stratagem will occur to him."

251

"It will," said the Wise Man, "for I am part of him."

"So he will lead the Dree back to the gash in the ground on the Rovers' side, and it will follow him into the Old Sea."

"And there the Worm will take it."

"And him," said Bandar.

The Wise Man's gaze was unperturbed. "Perhaps."

The Hero spoke. "Sometimes the one must die to save the many."

And the Father said, "I believe he will not die."

"And if he doesn't," said Bandar, "then what?"

"Then he will live," said the Wise Man.

"Yes, but live as what? He is not fit for this world. He is like one of you, a rough draft who strides about in his simplicity, constantly colliding with the disorderliness of real life, always bumping his nose against nuances and contradictions the rest of us easily avoid."

The archetypes regarded him without comprehension, as if he were speaking a language they did not understand. Only the Father looked troubled.

There was nothing to do but wait, and hope. Bandar seated himself on the ground at the base of the slit and took the rope in his hands. The gash was still trying to close, and he put his heels to it, straining with his legs, forcing it open. He looked down and saw the Worm again, larger now, nearer. And swimming mindlessly toward the gap.

A tug on the rope drew a length of it through Bandar's hands and into the Old Sea. Bandar's fists closed on the rough Earnest/ Realistic fibers. He leapt to his feet and pulled hard, felt weight.

"He is coming!" he called to the archetypes. "He has made it!"

"Unless," said the Wise Man, "it is the Dree. Do not pull."

Bandar addressed the archetype as no noönaut had ever done, using a phrase he had scarcely ever uttered since his student days. The Wise Man's bushy white eyebrows rose slightly, but it said nothing.

Bandar saw a shadow darken the lip of the incision, then a hand appeared pulling at the rope. Baro Harkless, mailed and helmeted, his sword in its scabbard, hauled himself from the Old Sea. Not a drop of its "waters" clung to him.

Harkless stood on legs that were none too steady. There was a blankness in his gaze, as if the Old Sea had leached some of the life from him. But he drew his sword and took a two–handed grip, raising it above his head, positioning himself over the closing hole.

He did not notice the crowd around them, Bandar saw. Pure archetypes were not aware of each other, and Harkless was now pure Hero.

"Stand clear," it said. "It came after me. I doubt I can kill it, but if I can stop it from coming through the gap, the Worm will take it."

Bandar backed away, giving him room to swing the weapon. "I doubt it, too," he said. "But I would have had the same doubts about your being able to cross from one Commons to another by the Old Sea, yet twice have you done it."

"Take the rope and pull," the Hero said. "Draw it to me."

Bandar did as he was asked, but gave the rope only the slightest tug. It came freely. He felt no weight, no Dree. Still, again he gave it only the smallest pull.

"Do it again." Bandar heard the Hero rising high, and it called up the Helper in his own being. He did not resist. He gave the rope a strong yank, still felt no resistance. He drew it, hand over hand, and it came freely through the incision, until the end appeared.

He called to the Hero, standing with sword raised above the shrinking gap. "Can you see anything?"

"No. Perhaps the Worm has it."

Or the Old Sea has stolen its will, Bandar thought. *Either way, we are saved*.

Aloud, he said, "Then, right now, the Rovers are turning on your renegade scroot officer. They will hunt him and likely kill him. The miners will be rescuing the captives from the creches."

The gap in the ground was closing rapidly now. The crowd of archetypes stood silent but made no move to withdraw to their proper place. Bandar wanted to be away from them as swiftly as he could. He took out his globular map and said, "I will plot us a route to one of the Heavens. We can rest there until they come to free us from our niches."

Harkless lowered his sword. The gap in the ground was now almost completely healed. Bandar saw that a node only a few steps away would take them to a benign Landscape from which there were several exits. He opened his mouth to sing the tones that would open the gate.

An astonishing pain tore through the back of his right knee, followed almost instantly by a chill of frigid cold, as if a claw of ice had been thrust into his virtual flesh. Bandar looked down and saw between his legs a gash in the floor of the Commons, wider than the one Harkless had made, ripped by the weapons at the ends of the Dree's forelimbs. Its hooked claw was sunk deep into Bandar.

Now the Dree tore the rent wider, forcing its thorax through from below. It reached up and sank a second talon into Bandar's thigh muscle and this time the noönaut screamed as it hooked itself into him to haul itself free of the Old Sea. It dug its scimitar–clawed feet into the floor of the human noösphere and lifted Bandar clear of the ground, then flung him at the Wall.

He struck with an impact that shook his virtual body, and fell to the ground, stunned. His globular map, shaken from his grip at the first stab of pain, had rolled free. He saw the Dree notice the motion, its tendrils questing, then it scooped up the object, raised it to the eyeless face, and Bandar sensed an emotion radiating from the entity, a wave of cruel satisfaction.

He attempted to rise, but his torn legs would not respond. He looked toward the throng of archetypes and saw that they were all looking to the Dree. Then, as one, their eyes turned toward Harkless.

The young man was thoroughly in the grip of the Hero. He shouted defiance at the invader, rushing forward and swinging the iron sword in a lateral arc that knocked the map from its grip. The Dree reared back, its thoracic orifice opening and closing to emit a sound like fire in dry tinder. Then it joined the digits of one forelimb into a dirk–like talon, straight and pointed, and shot it toward Harkless's belly in a blur of speed.

The man back–swung the blade, striking the claw and diverting it from his virtual flesh. But just barely, and Bandar could see that the clash of metal against chitin had sent a shock through Harkless. Still, the Hero blazed in the young man's eyes as he shifted his weight to his back foot then lunged with the weapon's point against the Dree's eyeless head.

The invader batted the thrust away with an ease that bespoke contempt.

Harkless spoke aloud, in his own voice. "How do I defeat this?"

Bandar thought he was being asked, but then he realized that the answer had come from within Harkless's being, where the Hero and the Fool and the Wise Man had made spaces for themselves. A shifting array of emotions crossed the man's face and Bandar knew that Harkless was seeing the shape of his life, the forces that had molded him to bring him to this moment.

Now all was clear to him, and Harkless said, "So I am not the Hero. Rather, I am the Fool."

He stood, listening to an answer that only he could hear, then said, "Why have you brought me to my destruction?"

The Dree had cocked its head and was regarding him. Bandar wondered if it eavesdropped on whatever conversation was going on between Harkless and the Multifacet. The noönaut had no doubt that all of the archetypes had cohered again for this moment, though to his eyes they remained a crowd. *They're not talking to me this time,* he thought. *I've played my part.*

The Dree was growing larger, was now half again the size it had been when it came through the floor of the noösphere. *There must be enough new Dree for the hive mind to emerge,* Bandar thought. *We are defeated.*

Harkless seemed lost in thought, but Bandar could imagine the colloquy that was going on between him and the Multifacet. The chosen one was being shown the true and final shape of things.

The Dree entity shook itself. Its digits clicked into curved claws and it moved toward Harkless.

"It will kill me," Harkless said. He looked at the sword that had done no harm to the enemy, but there was no fear in his face. The Hero had him now.

Again, the noönaut struggled to rise. He knew it was because the Helper was reaching into him, willing him to aid the Hero in this last sacrifice. But he did not resist.

The Dree came at Harkless, jabbing a claw at his face. He warded it off with the sword, but Bandar saw again that contact with the thing's icy power sent a shock though him. The arm that held the sword drooped, the weapon perilously loose in his failing grip.

"I cannot kill it," he said.

Bandar saw him receive the message, knew that the voice in Harkless's mind was telling him that this had never been about his killing the Dree—though it was surely about dying.

And it was about choosing.

"It is about sacrifice," Harkless said. "And willingness."

The Dree was fashioning a thrusting claw again, a poniard to pierce the Hero's chest. Harkless watched it, but his attention was focused within. Bandar saw him make the decision, offer the final acceptance.

"So it appears I am to be the Hero," Harkless said. "Just not the kind of Hero I thought I was." He turned his eyes for a moment to Bandar. "Look after my Helper," he said. "He did not ask for this."

He said something else, but Bandar could not hear it over the clicking of the Dree's claws against the ground as it set itself and sprang.

But the Hero did not raise his sword. Instead, Harkless thrust out his chest and stepped forward. The Dree's claw tore into his side to lance up and inward. Bandar saw pain blossom in the young man's face, followed by a shiver as the agony turned to an icy chill. For a moment he saw despair.

Then, with a shout, Harkless clamped his free arm around the Dree's neck, lifting his feet from the ground so that his full weight hung from its upper body. Now he wrapped his legs around it and the Dree was forced to bend toward the ground. Harkless swung with his sword hand, slashing again and again at the earth where the Dree had broken through. The light of the Old Sea glowed on the iron blade.

The Dree reacted, attempting to straighten. One forelimb was stuck in Harkless's virtual flesh, but it reached now to sink the other's claw into his back and rip him free. It gave off a rank odor that Bandar realized was the reek of fear.

Bandar saw the shape of the plan, and knew that the Helper must help. His legs still would not function but he dragged himself forward until he was beneath the Dree's feet. He sank his hands into the gap that the Hero's sword had torn and stretched it wider.

He looked up and saw the tip of the thing's claw touch Harkless's spine but at that moment the sword that had torn the ground sliced into the lowermost joint of one of the Dree's hind legs. The chitin was thinnest there. The green armor parted, spilling a yellow ichor, and the Dree emitted a hiss. Its stench became overpowering.

Harkless cut again, into the other leg. The Dree twisted, trying to throw him clear, but he held on. The thing's legs buckled and it pitched forward. Together, invader and Hero tumbled through the rent in the ground and into the Old Sea.

Bandar saw them sink. But the endless eerie gray luminescence of the realm below no longer dominated his view: instead, he saw the mindless Worm, its great lightless circle of a mouth as vast as a dark planet. Harkless and the Dree, the Hero still embracing the monster, were falling into the blackness that rose to engulf them.

Then the Dree gave a mighty spasm of its entire form, yanking its imprisoned claw free of Harkless's body. It kicked its hind legs and pushed with its forelimbs against the substance of the Old Sea, struggling to rise again to the gap where Bandar watched.

But as it pulled free of Harkless, the young man reached up after it. He grasped its legs. The cruel spikes that protruded from its limbs pierced his palms, but he held on, and Bandar saw the immense will in him not to let the creature win free and return to the Commons.

Then the Worm took them both. Bandar watched them sink into its cavernous mouth, the Dree still struggling to pull free of Harkless's grasp. The huge triangular teeth closed upon the Dree where abdomen met thorax and sliced it into two pieces. The mouth opened again to let the dead thing fall into its maw. Bandar saw Harkless free his hands of the creature's remnants then, its task completed, he saw the Hero leave the young man's face. Now there was only Baro Harkless, sinking forever into oblivion, wearing a look of hope mingled with apprehension.

"No!" The cry came from somewhere deep in Bandar. He looked up at the crowd of archetypes. Their faces were filling again with the monomanias that formed their intrinsic natures. They were drifting away. One of them—the Healer, he realized—had paused near him. The figure absently waved a hand and at once the pain in Bandar's legs was gone.

"That is not enough!" Bandar rose to his knees and called to the Wise Man who, with the Father, the Fool and the Hero and his Helper, were among the last to turn away. The graybeard turned toward him and for a moment Bandar quailed at what he saw in those wrinkle–framed eyes, but he rallied and said, "It is not right to leave him there! Not after he did all that you required of him!"

"It was what he was for," said the Wise Man. "Now it is done."

"You know it is not right!"

The Wise Man turned away. Yet the other three hesitated. But there was no time to argue and convince. Bandar seized the rope, and tossed one end of it to the Helper, saying, "You're the Helper. So help."

Then he tied the other end to his ankle, and without looking to see what the archetype had done, and before his fear could stop him, he dove through the gap and went down into the Old Sea.

And into the mouth of the Worm.

It had risen almost to the roof of its world and now was sinking back down, its huge mouth still open but beginning to close. Bandar plunged straight into the darkness, then began to stroke with his arms like a diver in a pool. He passed the pieces of the Dree, saw that they were already half dissolved, then kept his eyes fixed on the grayish outline of Baro Harkless far down in the dimness of the Worm's gullet. The light was fading as the Worm's mouth slowly closed.

Bandar doubted that moving his arms could help; indeed, he was surprised he could move at all. *It is an expression of will*, he concluded. *I do not accept this outcome and will make it different.* It occurred to him that he had the seeds of a seminal paper for the Institute. Then he countered that thought with the consideration that his chances of preparing and presenting any paper, ever again, were highly dubious.

Harkless was closer now. Bandar could make out the young man's face. The Hero had left him. Instead, Bandar saw behind the young man's features the face of Baro as a young boy, full of innocence and simplicity. Then the man sank farther into the darkness.

Bandar dug with his hands and arms against the substance of what was supposed to be nothingness. *Within the Worm, there is more than the void of the Old Sea*, he thought, feeling something resisting his motions and thus letting them propel himself deeper. *There's another great paper*, he thought. He stretched out his arms for another double stroke and his palms smacked into something solid. A moment later, two strong hands seized his wrists.

I have him! he thought. *Now, does anyone have me?*

Then the rope jerked his ankle and together they rose toward the rent in the floor of the noösphere. The Worm was assisting by sinking back into the Old Sea. But when Bandar looked over his shoulder he saw the huge wedges of its teeth approaching each other, like gears about to mesh. He closed his eyes and willed that he and Harkless should rise faster, then opened them to see the serrated edge of one great pale triangle pass by him with barely a handsbreadth to spare. Then he was out of the mouth, with Harkless coming after him. Bandar gripped the animal pelt that the young man still wore and yanked Harkless toward him, pulling him free of the mouth just as the teeth came together. Moments later they were hauled through the rip and back into the Commons.

The red lips of the gash closed rapidly. Bandar and Harkless lay for a moment on the warm fleshy floor of the noösphere. Then the noönaut rolled over and sat up to untie the rope from his ankle. Not far away he saw the Father, the Fool, the Hero and Helper, lined up one behind the next, the cord still in their hands. They regarded him with understanding, but already he could see the blankness creeping back into their eyes.

He threw off the rope and shook Harkless. The young man turned to him a face that was still suffused with the acceptance of his own death. Bandar shook him again and said, "We must depart. They are reverting to their true natures."

The noönaut sang the three, three and seven thran and was gratified to hear Harkless chime in. The archetypes lost their perception of them and turned away, letting fall the rope, which immediately began to dissolve into the ground. Last to go was the Helper, who cast a look back over his shoulder in the direction of Bandar and dropped one eyelid.

Bandar shuddered. Then he looked about and saw his map lying against the wall. He used a mentalism to summon it back to his hand then sang open a gate.

But Harkless held back, gesturing to the departing archetypes. Now that the Hero was fled from him, he could see them. "How did you get them to aid you?" he said.

"I called on them and they helped."

"Were you not afraid one of them would absorb you?"

"They were not here for me," Bandar said. "They were here for you."

They passed through a series of Locations until they came back to the Landscape of the Prairie. Bandar had not been back here since the episode with the pigs. He was glad to see that no trace of those events remained. He led Harkless over a roll of ground that sheltered them from the constant wind and they sat together.

"We should go back to our bodies," the young man said. "I will arrest Ardmander Arboghast, if he lives."

Bandar peered at him. "Is that a vestige of the Hero I hear?"

But the eyes that looked back at him held none of the archetype's elementary madness. "No," Harkless said, "all that died in the Worm. You are hearing a man who wishes to bring to justice the killer of his father."

"We will not lose much time here," Bandar said. "And first I have to tell you a story."

"I have had enough of stories. I wonder if I have had only stories, all these years, and never a real life."

"That is what this story is about," the noönaut said. "It began a long, long time ago, when I was a student. . . "

Bandar reentered waking life to find that he was in a ward of the Victor infirmary and that Baro Harkless was engaged in an argument with Raina Haj. The young agent had risen from his bed and was determined to go after Arboghast, who had escaped when the Rovers had begun killing the Dree. She insisted that he must remain in Victor to testify at a Bureau of Scrutiny inquiry that was soon to convene. A bandaged Luff Imbry, rescued from the Monument, reposed on one of the beds, eating fruit and taking his partner's side.

The argument had reached the point where Harkless had resigned from the scroots and Haj had drawn her shocker to prevent his leaving. Now Bandar intervened.

"Let me offer a proposal," he said.

Not long after, he and Harkless stood on the road that led into the Commons, watching the motes of light that were dreamers flitting past them. Bandar was gratified to see that the young man now manifested in his own guise, without the trappings of a dawn–time Hero.

"So you will not be a scroot," Bandar said. "What will you do?"

"Study under you and become a noönaut," the young man said. "Or be," he said, smiling, "your helper."

Bandar had been considering the same prospect. In some way his life was still bound to that of Baro Harkless, but he was not sure he wholly welcomed the connection. The young man remained almost as dangerously simple as an archetype, and when seized by determination he was no less terrifying than he had been when they had stood on the bridge overlooking the prime arrondisement. At the same time, Harkless had opened doors that led to great shining territories of new research.

I am a trained noönaut with an unparalleled experience of the Commons, he told himself. *He is a young man with unheard of abilities. I could spend years just delineating his capacities. It is not unthinkable that the two of us could found a new Institute that would soon rival. . .*

He realized that Harkless was expecting an answer. "We may be able to work something out," Bandar told him.

The young man started to speak but then something caught his attention and he pointed back down the road. "He is here," he said.

Bandar approached the mote of light Harkless was following with his finger. He exerted a mentalism while chanting a complicated thran. A faint image of Ardmander Arboghast wavered before them, snatched from his dream, puzzlement vying in his face with fear. Bandar had the young man lay tight hold of the renegade scroot, while he employed the technique that drew more of the prisoner's being into the Commons, leaving only enough of him in the waking world to sustain minimal existence. It was a tense struggle—the Tyrant was strong in Arboghast—but Harkless's will was also unnaturally powerful and the issue was soon decided.

Bandar led them to a nearby gate. They stepped through into a Heaven that was familiar to the noönaut. He wondered if its cycle had renewed itself since last he was here, or whether one Principal was still laughing over the look of surprise on the Other's face.

Bandar sang the insulating thran loudly so that Harkless could conduct a conversation with his prisoner. He did not hear what was said, but gathered from Arboghast's increasing look of terror and dismay that the discussion was not going well from the Tyrant's point of view.

They marched across the lush grass, the prisoner squirming in Harkless's adamantine grasp, then descended a short slope that ended at the Abyss. Bandar, still singing, looked down and saw the great flat–topped tower just below and to one side, with black–armored demons swarming up ladders to battle a formation of angelic defenders. He motioned to Harkless to move along the edge away from the assault point and they came to a quiet sector. The only movement was that of a giant leather–winged demon, wheeling and gliding back and forth below them in intersecting double loops.

Harkless said something to Arboghast and now the Tyrant struggled in earnest. But the dynamic of this moment had been established long ago. The young man flung his father's killer out into the emptiness. The demon saw the plummeting man and indolently flapped its wings to bring itself under his descent.

It caught Arboghast with talons that pierced his virtual flesh then turned and dropped toward the smoking black pit below. Bandar heard its captive's screams dwindle to the faintest whine.

Harkless stood and watched until the thing was out of sight. Then Bandar put a hand on his shoulder. The man turned and Bandar saw on the young face an expression that had no name. "Now what do I do?" he said.

"Wait here," Bandar said. "You may play with the three maidens if you wish, but you should know that they are not equipped for anything but the most innocent of sport."

The blonde, brunette and redheaded girls were splashing in the shallow surf, casting coquettish glances their way. Harkless stared at them in a manner that caused Bandar to think that his companion was as inexperienced as the three idiomats.

"Are you leaving me here?" Harkless asked.

"Only for a short time." Bandar approached the Sincere/Approximate jungle beneath the palm trees that fringed the tropical beach. He used his Institute–trained memory to lead him to a spot then stopped. He was reasonably sure that he had come the correct distance in the right direction. Now he exercised the noönaut's sense that could detect the presence of an inter–Locational node, and felt a tingle on his left side. He turned that way, inching forward until the sensation became so strong as to be unmistakable.

He opened his mouth and sang the most common gate–opening thran. No fissure appeared in the air, nor did he feel the quality that noönauts called "resonancy." He chanted the next most common sequence of tones and again nothing happened. He continued to work his way down the thran ladder, chanting more than two score sequences, before he established that none of the gate–openers worked. But two of them had returned a resonancy: the five, eight and two had produced a weak response, while the five, four and six had won him a strong return.

From there it was a matter of trying all the possible combinations, which would have been a mathematically immense number except that Bandar was guided by the resonancy that increased the closer he came to the right sequence. In less than an hour, he chanted five ascending tones, followed by three descenders and completed by the same two notes an octave apart. The air rippled.

Bandar paused a moment to mark the occasion. For the first time in millennia upon millennia, an explorer of the Commons had found a new gate. To demonstrate this achievement to the scholars of the Institute for Historical Inquiry would be like. . . but his mind could not achieve an appropriate equivalent. He put the thought aside and stepped through.

He found no mist, and hadn't expected to. The fog that had shrouded the Multifacet would have been merely for effect. He stood in a lighted space that seemed to have no limit, though there would be walls somewhere, probably of the same colorless substance as the floor beneath Bandar's feet. The place was neither hot nor cold, but warm enough for comfort, the light neither too bright nor too dim. The air was wholesome but carried no draft or breeze.

Bandar deployed his globular map. *And now we'll see*, he thought. He directed at the display the mentalism that would cause his present Location to show itself. A moment later, a new spot came into being within the matrix of lines and colored shapes: a white circle, connected only to the beach where the three nymphets frolicked.

Bandar put away the globe and surveyed the emptiness around him. This place had no dynamic. Nothing he did here could cause disharmony. He decided to try an experiment. He removed a garment and laid it on the floor, one finger still touching it to retain a connection. Then he concentrated and exerted a mentalism, holding in his mind an image of the red–cushioned, ornately carved seat of black wood on which the First Overdean sat during formal dinners in the Institute's refectory. After a moment, the air before him wavered, the garment faded and the chair appeared. Bandar sat upon it, finding it less comfortable than he had expected.

It will take time to build it all, he told himself, then came another thought: *unless Harkless's exceptional talents extend in that direction too.*

He reopened the gate and returned to the beach. The young man was high–stepping through the surf, giving the redhead a piggyback ride while the blonde and brunette chased them both. They were all laughing.

"Baro!" Bandar called. "Come away. I want to show you something."

The young man let the girl slide from his back. "I'll be right back," he said when she pouted. He followed Bandar off the beach and into the jungle.

Bandar called up the node and they passed through. "You wanted to show me a chair?" Harkless said.

"No," said Bandar, "I wanted to show you the Bandar–Harkless Institute for Noöspheric Innovation."

"Where is it?"

"Well," Bandar said, "I'd like you to sit in the chair. Now close your eyes and think about a very large, well appointed building, with spacious rooms, quiet cloisters, a good library. Oh, and an excellent wine cellar."

Harkless sat and closed his eyes. "All right," he said, "I'm thinking of it. Now what?"

Bandar looked about him. "Oh, my," he said.

About the Author

I write space opera science fiction and fantasy mostly set in my extrapolation of Jack Vance's Dying Earth. I make no bones about being heavily influenced by Vance, whose work I first encountered as a thirteen-year-old in the early 1960s.

Booklist has called me Vance's "heir apparent" and George R.R. Martin says I "do Jack Vance better than anyone except Jack himself." I am very proud to have been authorized by the Vance estate to write Barbarians of the Beyond, a companion novel to The Demon Princes series

I'm Canadian, a university drop-out from a working-poor background. I've sold twenty-four novels to publishers large and small in the UK, US, and Canada, as well as nearly 100 works of short fiction to professional markets.

I've won the Crime Writers of Canada's Arthur Ellis Award and the Endeavour, and have been shortlisted for the Aurora, Locus, Nebula, Philip K. Dick, Endeavour (twice), A.E. Van Vogt, Neffy, and Derringer Awards.

My web page is www.matthewhughes.org.

I also have a Patreon page: https://www.patreon.com/user?u=4687520

www.ingramcontent.com/pod-product-compliance
Lightning Source LLC
Chambersburg PA
CBHW060906250626
47159CB00008B/2883